Stranger and Alone

Other titles in the Northeastern Library of Black Literature

STRANGER
AND
ALONE

A NOVEL BY

J. Saunders Redding

Northeastern University Press
BOSTON

Northeastern University Press edition 1989

Library of Congress Cataloging-in-Publication Data

Redding, J. Saunders (Jay Saunders), 1906–
    Stranger and alone : a novel / by J. Saunders Redding
       p.   cm.—(The Northeastern library of Black literature)
    Originally published by Harcourt, Brace & World, 1950.
    ISBN 1-55553-055-9 (alk. paper)
    ISBN 1-55553-053-2 (pbk. : alk. paper)
       I. Title.   II. Series.
    PS 3535. E2233J64   1989   89-32447
    813'.54—dc 20   CIP

Printed and bound by McNaughton & Gunn, Saline, Michigan.
The paper is Glatfelter Offset, an acid-free sheet.

MANUFACTURED IN THE UNITED STATES OF AMERICA
93 92 91 90 89   5 4 3 2 1

for
GWENDOLYN, LILLIAN *and* LOUIS

I N THE EARLY YEARS of the twentieth century, much of the discourse in the African-American community was centered on the debate between Booker T. Washington and W. E. B. Du Bois. Two of the major topics of that debate were the function of higher education for blacks and the relationship between education and the social-political world at large. In his Atlanta Exposition Address of 1895, Washington called for manual education over mental education, suggesting that whites in the South should be trusted to control the fate of those whom they had so recently enslaved, that "the agitation of questions of social equality [was] the extremest folly," and that "in all things that are purely social we can be as separate as the fingers, yet one as the hand in all things essential to mutual progress." Eight years later, in 1903, Du Bois attacked Washington's position in *The Souls of Black Folk* and pointed out that "Mr. Washington's programme practically accepts the alleged inferiority of the Negro races." In his fifth and sixth chapters, "Of the Wings of Atalanta" and "Of the Training of Black Men," Du Bois asserted:

> The function of the university is not simply to teach bread-winning, or to furnish teachers for the public schools or to be a centre of polite society; it is, above all, to be the organ of that fine adjustment between real life and the growing knowledge of life, an adjustment which forms the secret of civilization. . . . The function of the Negro college, then, is clear: it must maintain the standards of popular education, it must seek the social regeneration of the Negro, and it must help in the solution of problems of race contact and cooperation. And finally, beyond all this, it must develop men.

Washington, however, became the chief spokesperson for African-Americans in the South—to whites. And in that position, he controlled and influenced many aspects of black public life. As

vii

J. Saunders Redding (1906–88) notes in *They Came in Chains: Americans from Africa* (1950), Washington was the "umpire in all important appointments of Negroes, the channel through which philanthropy flowed, or did not flow, to Negro institutions; the creator and destroyer of careers; the maker and breaker of men." Redding also points out that "practically nothing by Negroes touching upon Negroes was brought out in books and magazines without Washington's sanction." Washington's power was, thus, enormous, particularly in education, as he was also the president of Tuskegee Institute, which he had founded in Alabama in 1881 and which he led for thirty-four years until his death in 1915. Thus, black colleges were for the most part producing not potential leaders who would help African-Americans move into the future, but traditionalists who would continue the past and maintain the status quo. While it is true that Du Bois earned a B.A. at Fisk, it is also true that he went to Harvard and got a second B.A., and that both William Monroe Trotter and Alain Locke also received B.A.s from Harvard. Du Bois was the exception rather than the rule for graduates from black colleges.

Twenty-five years after Washington's death, this situation, as J. Saunders Redding discovered, had not substantially changed. In 1940, Redding was awarded a Rockefeller Foundation grant to "go out into Negro life in the South" and report on his findings. Redding was awarded the grant on the basis of the publication in the previous year of *To Make a Poet Black*. In this, his first book, he became one of the first scholars to establish critical principles by which African-American literature could be judged. Moreover, he asserted that the folk–vernacular tradition—as exemplified in the works of James Weldon Johnson, Jean Toomer, Sterling Brown, and Zora Neale Hurston—was the basis of all significant African-American literature. As contemporary African-American literary theorist Henry Louis Gates succinctly puts it in the introduction to the Cornell University Press reprint of *To Make a Poet Black* (1988), Redding "establishes . . . a canon built upon a black vernacular foundation." Thus, it is possible to argue that despite his relative obscurity (compared to Du Bois), Saunders Redding's achievements in the field of literary criticism are as important as those of Du Bois in history and sociology.

On his journey through the South in 1940, which resulted in *No Day of Triumph* (1942), Redding was looking for enduring values in African-American life. One of the places he hoped to find them was in the black college system. He encountered instead something very different:

> Negro schoolmen are terrific snobs, the true bourgeoisie. Grasping eagerly for straws of recognition, a great many of them proclaim loudly their race-faith and avow social radicalism. Some let it be known discreetly that they are Communists. But theirs is a puerile profession of faith, a smart-alecky, show-off kind of radicalism. In reality they look to the upper-middle-class whites for their social philosophy and in actual practice ape that class's indifference to social and political matters and reforms. They are a bulwark against positive action, liberal or even independent thought, and spiritual and economic freedom. . . . There was a shocking indecency in their intellectual pretensions. . . . Too many of them were mere manipulators of knowledge. . . . Few of them seemed to realize that there were great issues abroad in the world, or even that there was a war being fought to settle them. . . . They seemed to take the attitude that passive pessimism was the smart thing, a really brilliant and saving grace for them. And yet they were angered by the passivism of others.

The black college president whom Redding visits is even worse, since he believes that "the plight of the Negro was altogether due to certain traits in the racial character," that African-Americans are by nature "improvident, immoral, and generally no good." He has even gone so far as to fire a faculty member for trying to vote. He announces to Redding, "My job is to train these black boys and girls to do their prescribed work with a singleness of purpose. That's my job. To train men, you've got to tough out of 'em certain crazy notions. That's different from educating them."

This was not an isolated incident. In 1931, Redding himself had been fired by Morehouse College in Atlanta after teaching there for three years and being labeled "radical." His radicalism had consisted of his refusal, unlike his fellow faculty members, to cut himself off from his history, and his refusal to acknowledge that there was nothing more to life than "spiritual decay" and "material values."

These two experiences convinced Redding to attempt his third book and only published novel, *Stranger and Alone* (1950), which centers on the relationship of African-Americans to higher education. As Robert Stepto has demonstrated in *From Behind the Veil* (1979), the quest for education—and especially for literacy—is one of the most dominant themes in African-American literature, from the slave narratives to the present. At the other extreme from quests for and achievement of literacy are narratives of victimization, such as Richard Wright's *Native Son* (1940) and Ann Petry's *The Street* (1946). Here, although they are defeated, the protagonists are victims of forces outside themselves, most notably racism. *Stranger and Alone* is unique because it falls into neither of these categories. In Shelton Howden, Redding has created an intelligent, articulate, realistic, African-American college professor who is willing to betray anyone in order to stay in the good graces of the white power structure in the South. On the one hand, although we despise Howden, we are fascinated by his story. On the other hand, the fact that this novel has been out of print for so many years suggests that the issue it grapples with is one most people do not want to consider: Are we willing to sell our souls and the collective soul of our communities in order to gain personal advancement and power?

Redding gets us hooked by changing the meaning of the novel's title as the story unfolds. When the novel opens, Howden is a freshman at New Hope College in Louisiana in 1923. He is a stranger and alone through no fault of his own: he is older than most of his fellows; he has no money; both his parents are dead; his father was white; he was raised in an orphanage; and he has been admitted to college conditionally. Finally, unlike most of the students, he has to work a significant number of hours during the school year and during the summer, and consequently it will take five years to graduate instead of the usual four. Thus, it is easy to feel sympathetic when, early on, we read:

> But someday he'd be somebody. The thought of what he'd be someday gave him dreamy satisfaction. He'd be a doctor or a lawyer or—something. He had no doubt of it. His ambition began to burn steadily again. You couldn't keep a good man down, and someday he was going to prove himself a better man than any of them. (11–12)

The first questions begin to arise when, after hearing a series of lectures on the "scientific truth" of black inferiority, Howden seeks advice from New Hope's lone black faculty member, who assures Howden that it is possible to "ignore" the question of race, that it is a "nuisance" to discuss it, and that Howden must promise never to raise the issue again. "Anger," Professor Clarkson tells Howden, is "futile" (52–53). Questions are again raised when, after graduation, Howden feels alienated from his fellow railroad workers who often talk about the racial situation (Howden has taken the job to save money for medical school); but Redding subtly cloaks this in class issues. Howden's alienation appears greatest because he is a "college man" going somewhere and the others are not. In fact, Howden is equally alienated by the fact that his coworkers constantly talk about America's racial situation. He is concerned with his own individual success, and the controversy of race is best avoided.

After an accident forces Howden to give up the idea of being a doctor, he attends graduate school and then secures a teaching job at Arcadia State College for Negroes. By now, we have read one-third of the novel and Howden is, at worst, an ambiguous figure. Once at Arcadia, however, Howden's values, or lack thereof, become clear. The faculty is filled with "race men," and Howden wants no part:

> He had heard all about race too. No topic, Howden discovered, was ever more than one remove from that. All topics led to it. Howden found that his colleagues were all members of one progressive race group

or another and that they held regular meetings in each other's homes and rooms, but he never went. . . . When his colleagues talked about race, it was like being surrounded by squawking parrots pretending to be screaming eagles. And Howden told himself besides that it was as futile as it was passionate. He did not want to become a party to their futility. What he wanted was peace. He did not want to think about the race problem nor live on two levels nor make life more difficult by trying to analyze everything. All he wanted was to get what he could out of life. He didn't want to spatter his brains against stone walls. (119–20)

It is this philosophy that endears Howden to the college's black president, Perkins Thomas Wimbush. Wimbush takes Howden under his wing, and Howden is soon giving speeches for him in which African-Americans are accused of "sloth and ignorance" (126) and held to be responsible for all their problems. Howden adopts Wimbush's habit of referring to African-Americans as "darkies"; and within a short time, "his own personality seemed purely derivative when he was with the Old Man" (132). For Wimbush, and therefore for Howden, race men like W. E. B. Du Bois, Walter White, and William Monroe Trotter are filled with madness. What is needed is "reality." And Wimbush describes reality this way: "[In] the truest sense, my boy, we're the white man's niggers. . . . There's nothing wrong with being the white man's nigger. We can't help it, can we? And we're conditioned to it, aren't we?" (136). After making Howden director of summer school at Arcadia, Wimbush sees that his young protégé is appointed "the first full-time supervisor of Niggra schools in the state" (210), as the first step on the road to ultimately succeeding him as president of Arcadia. In this position, Howden's real job is to keep tabs on radicals who want such unreasonable things as equal pay for black teachers and new textbooks for black children. He joins the NAACP and the League for Interracial Comity in order to spy and report back to Wimbush and Judge Jefferson A. Reed, who is white and therefore the real power in the area.

As the novel closes, Howden has learned of a secret plan to attempt to get African-Americans registered to vote, and he hurries dutifully to Judge Reed's office, hat in hand, to report what he has learned. While Judge Reed will, no doubt, prevent this voter registration and reward his "boy" Shelton Howden for the information, it is also the mid-1940s. As the title of the last section of the novel makes clear, "the time on the clock of the world" is getting late. As a teacher of history, Shelton Howden should have realized the inevitability of change and the necessity of being involved in helping that change happen. He fails to learn this lesson, and history—and a new generation in the South—will soon pass him by.

As the fortieth anniversary of its publication approaches, we still need to hear the message of *Stranger and Alone*. Many things have changed since 1950. African-Americans have gained voting rights and have succeeded in desegregating schools. (Redding's brother Louis was one of the lawyers who successfully argued *Brown v. The Board of Education* before the U.S. Supreme Court in 1954.) African-American students are attending universities in the North in large numbers. African-American professors, following in Saunders Redding's footsteps, are teaching at Ivy League universities. (When Redding became a visiting professor at his alma mater, Brown, in 1949, he was the first African-American to teach at an Ivy League school. And as late as 1970, when he took up his final teaching post at Cornell, he became the first African-American professor in Cornell's College of Arts and Sciences.)

But that isn't enough. When he reviewed *Stranger and Alone* positively for the *New York Times Book Review* in February of 1950, Ralph Ellison perfectly summed up Shelton Howden in his title, "Collaborator with His Own Enemy." It isn't enough, as Shelton Howden is ample proof, merely to be in the university. The university must be changed so that it is no longer fostering inhumanness. As Saunders Redding's career as both teacher and writer makes clear, the university must be a place that fosters education for social change, not education for social stagnation.

PANCHO SAVERY

A J. SAUNDERS REDDING BIBLIOGRAPHY

BOOKS

To Make a Poet Black. Chapel Hill: University of North Carolina Press, 1939.

No Day of Triumph. New York: Harper, 1942.

Stranger and Alone. New York: Harcourt, Brace, 1950.

They Came in Chains: Americans from Africa. Philadelphia: Lippincott, 1950.

On Being Negro in America. Indianapolis: Bobbs-Merrill, 1951.

An American in India: A Personal Report on the Indian Dilemma and the Nature of Her Conflicts. Indianapolis: Bobbs-Merrill, 1954.

The Lonesome Road: The Story of the Negro's Part in America. Garden City, N.Y.: Doubleday, 1958.

The Negro. Washington, D.C.: Potomac Books, 1967.

EDITED BOOKS

Reading for Writing (with Ivan E. Taylor). New York: Ronald Press, 1952.

Cavalcade: Negro American Writing from 1760 to the Present (with Arthur P. Davis). Boston: Houghton Mifflin, 1971.

SELECTED PERIODICAL PUBLICATIONS

"Playing the Numbers." *North American Review* 238 (December 1934): 533–42.

"First Appendix." *Carolina Review* 1 (1939): 1–6.

"A Negro Looks at This War." *American Mercury* 55 (November 1942): 585–92.

"A Negro Speaks for His People." *Atlantic Monthly* 171 (March 1943): 58–63.

"The Black Man's Burden." *Antioch Review* 3 (December 1943): 587–95.

"Here's a New Thing Altogether." *Survey Graphic* 33 (August 1944): 358–59, 366–67.

"My Most Humiliating Jim Crow Experience." *Negro Digest* 3 (December 1944): 43–44.

"The Negro Author: His Publisher, His Public, and His Purse." *Publishers' Weekly* 147 (1945): 1284–88.

"Portrait: W. E. Burghardt Du Bois." *American Scholar* 18 (January 1949): 93–96.

"American Negro Literature." *American Scholar* 18 (April 1949): 137–48. Rept. in *Afro-American Literature: An Introduction.* Ed. Robert Hayden, David J. Burrows, and Frederick R. Lapides. New York: Harcourt, Brace, Jovanovich, 1971, pp. 273–82.

"The Negro Writer—Shadow and Substance." In "The Negro in Literature: The Current Scene," *Phylon* 2 (1950): 371–73.

"The Wonder and the Fear." *American Scholar* 22 (1953): 137–39.

"Report from India." *American Scholar* 22 (1953): 441–49.

"No Envy, No Handicap." *Saturday Review* 37 (February 13, 1954): 23, 40.

"Up from Reconstruction." *Nation* 179 (September 4, 1954): 196–97.

"The Meaning of Bandung." *American Scholar* 25 (1956): 411–20.

"Tonight for Freedom." *American Heritage* 9 (June 1958): 52–55, 90.

"Contradiction de la littérature negro-américaine." *Présence Africaine*, nos. 27–28 (August–November 1959): 11–15.

"The Negro Writer and His Relationship to His Roots." In *The American Negro Writer and His Roots.* New York: American Society of African Culture, 1960, pp. 1–8.

"Negro Writing in America." *New Leader* 42 (May 16, 1960): 8–10.

"In the Vanguard of Civil Rights," *Saturday Review* 44 (August 12, 1961): 34.

"Introduction and Preface to *Souls of Black Folk*" (with W. E. B. Du Bois). *Freedomways* 2 (1962): 161–66.

"The Alien Land of Richard Wright." In *Soon, One Morning: New Writing by American Negroes, 1940–1962.* Ed. Herbert Hill. New York: Alfred A. Knopf, 1963, pp. 48–59.

"J. S. Redding Talks about African Literature." *AMSAC Newsletter* 5 (September 1962): 1, 4–6.

"Home to Africa." *American Scholar* 32 (Spring 1963): 183–91.

"Sound of Their Masters' Voices." *Saturday Review* 46 (June 29, 1963): 26.

"Modern African Literature." *CLA Journal* 7 (March 1964): 191–201.

"Man against Myth and Malice." *Saturday Review* 47 (May 9, 1964): 48–49.

"The Problems of the Negro Writer." *Massachusetts Review* 6 (Autumn–Winter 1964/5): 57–70.

"The Task of the Negro Writer as Artist: A Symposium." *Negro Digest* 14 (April 1965): 66, 74.

"Escape into Pride and Dignity." Introduction to *Laughing on the Outside:*

The Intelligent Reader's Guide to Negro Tales and Humor. Ed. Philip Sterling. New York: Grosset & Dunlap, 1965, pp. 17–19.

"The Negro Writer and American Literature." In *Anger, and Beyond: The Negro Writer in the United States.* Ed. Herbert Hill. New York: Harper & Row, 1966, pp. 1–19.

"Reflections on Richard Wright: A Symposium on an Exiled Native Son" (with Herbert Hill, Horace Cayton, and Arna Bontemps). In *Anger and Beyond*, pp. 196–212.

"Since Richard Wright." *African Forum* 1 (Spring 1966): 21–31.

"A Survey: Black Writers' Views on Literary Lions and Values." *Negro Digest* 17 (January 1968): 12.

"Literature and the Negro." *Contemporary Literature* 9 (Winter 1968); 130–35.

"Equality and Excellence: The Eternal Dilemma." *William and Mary Review* 6 (Spring 1968): 5–11.

"Of Men and the Writing of Books." Lincoln, Pa.: Vail Memorial Library, Lincoln University, 1969.

"The Negro Writer: The Road Where?" *Boston University Journal* 17 (Winter 1969): 6–10.

"The Black Youth Movement." *American Scholar* 38 (Autumn 1969): 584–87.

"Ends and Means in the Struggle for Equality." In *Prejudice U.S.A.* Ed. Charles Y. Glock and Ellen Siegelman. New York: Praeger, 1969, pp. 3–16.

"Negro Writing and the Political Climate." Lincoln, Pa.: Vail Memorial Library, Lincoln University, 1970.

"*The Souls of Black Folk:* Du Bois' Masterpiece Lives On." In *Black Titan: W. E. B. Du Bois, An Anthology by the Editors of "Freedomways."* Ed. John Henrik Clarke, Esther Jackson, Ernest Kaiser, and J. H. O'Dell. Boston: Beacon Press, 1970, pp. 47–51.

"The Black Revolution in American Studies." *American Studies: An International Newsletter* 9 (Autumn 1970): 3–9.

"Foreword" to Langston Hughes, *Good Morning Revolution.* Ed. Faith Berry. New York: Lawrence Hill, 1973, pp. ix–x.

"The Black Arts Movement in Negro Poetry." *American Scholar* 42 (1973): 330–36.

"Portrait against Background." In *A Singer in the Dawn: Reinterpretations of*

Paul Laurence Dunbar. Ed. Jay Martin. New York: Dodd, Mead, 1975,
pp. 39–44.
"Interview with Gloria Oden." *Weid: The Sensibility Review* 14 (March 1978):
7–28.

WORKS ABOUT J. SAUNDERS REDDING

"J. Saunders Redding." *Twentieth Century Authors* (First Supplement, 1955).
"J. Saunders Redding." *Contemporary Authors*, vol. IV (1963).
"J. Saunders Redding." *Who's Who in America, 1968–69.*
"(Jay) Saunders Redding." *Current Biography, 1969*, pp. 356–57.

FINALLY, brethren, whatsoever things are true, whatsoever things are honest, whatsoever things are just, whatsoever things are pure, whatsoever things are lovely, whatsoever things are of good report; if there be any virtue, and if there be any praise, think on these things.

—PAUL'S EPISTLE TO THE PHILIPPIANS

PART ONE

"NEW HOPE"

CHAPTER ONE

ALL AROUND him voices called out in happy recognition, but no voice called to him. He felt alone and lost. He wished that the line shuffling slowly toward the grilled window would get a move on. Groups of young men, their registration completed, stood about in the wide hall, making it hum and gurgle with their easy talk, their bursts of laughter. He resented the young men. The indifferent appraisal of their casual glances embarrassed him, made him feel out of place. He wished that by a wave of the hand he could wipe them out. Yet he wished also that he were like them, had their assurance, their manner, their clothes. In his tight-fitting, soapy-shiny blue suit, cut to the jazzbo pattern, he felt like a fool. Being here at all made him feel like a fool. It wasn't worth it, he told himself miserably. It wasn't worth the long years of working and saving to come here if this was the way it was.

He closed his eyes, and a sharp sense of vague longing, ambition, and pride overwhelmed him. It renewed his resolution. In the grip of the compounded emotion, he felt strong, almost exultant. All others were puny and weak. When he opened his eyes again, he stared defiantly at a dark young man dressed in sack coat and plus-four knickers and wondered scornfully who he thought he was. Or that muddy yellow one—the one with his hands in his pockets and his head thrown back—did he think he was better than anyone else? He'd show them, Shelton Howden told himself. Goddamn it, he thought, he'd show the world!

The line straggled a few steps nearer the window. In the sudden spasm of a new concern, Shelton Howden looked down at the papers grasped in his reddish yellow hand. The papers were all there and in order but smudged with sweat, and he shifted them to his other hand. The action somehow bringing back his

3

acute self-consciousness, he kept his head lowered. He tried not to listen to the talk and the laughter. He tried to assume an air of indifference, but his facial muscles ached with tightness and his throat was dry. He wanted to look up and around him boldly, with shriveling contempt. He wished he were of giant size, of infinite power—or of compelling charm. He wished that one of the young men lounging on the broad staircase midway the hall would throw up his hand at him and call him by his name. If only he could tap the shoulder of the fellow ahead and say, "Hey, Bunk, how did your summer go?" But the fellow ahead of him was busy talking to the one next in line.

"For crying out loud, Phil," Shelton Howden heard him say, "that's stuff! That's bushwa!"

"I'm telling you," Phil said. "Didn't you come down here with her all the way from Memphis?"

"If she gets on the same train I'm on, can I help it? I don't own the doggone train, for crying out loud."

"I'm only telling you," Phil, an olive yellow youth with slick hair, said indifferently. "And you know what's going to happen when you-know-who finds out? Boy, she's going to drop you like a hot potato. She's going to put you right on out of her sweet young life."

"Bushwa. Stuff!"

The speech was mannered. The coarse locutions sounded oddly polished, ultra-refined.

"All right, Rudolph Valentino. All right, Sheik of Araby," Phil said with elaborate sarcasm. "I'm just telling you. A pretty pink and yellow broad like her, you ought to play her straight. You ought to star her in your show."

"Is she the only pink?" the other demanded. "For crying out loud, there're plenty of pinks here, and you know it as well as I do."

Howden saw the one called Phil shrug.

The line moved up again. In the hall the groups had begun to dissolve and drift through the double doors onto the wide veranda. The late afternoon light, the whole atmosphere was soft, limpid, evoking in Howden a feeling of vague sadness which had no memory content. He just felt lonely and alone. As he gazed through the door, his mind drifting wistfully, a bevy of girls appeared beyond the railing of the porch. They looked golden and beautiful to Howden. Some of the young men left the porch to join them and stroll out of sight, and Howden was stung with envy. He wished he were one of them. He wanted to belong. He wanted to have clothes and friends and perhaps a pretty pink and yellow girl.

"All right, young man," a quiet, precise voice said.

Howden looked through the grill into a pair of gray, weak-looking eyes. His hand felt moist as he lifted his papers to the ledge. He managed a weak and diffident smile.

"Hmmmmm," the registrar murmured, studying the papers. There was a blank, impersonalized expression on his face. His wispy hair had receded from his forehead, leaving a great expanse of pallid brow. Beneath his thin lower lip he wore a tiny triangle of graying goatee, and, as Howden watched, he curled his lip absently into his mouth and scratched the hair with his teeth. A small gold cross glittered on his watch chain.

"Hmmmmm," the registrar murmured again. "Shelton Howden."

"Yes, sir," Howden said, and the registrar looked briefly, blankly out at him, then back at the papers again.

"Twenty—" the registrar said and paused. "And a conditional freshman—" He paused again. It was clear that he was puzzled and interested in a detached kind of way. He went through the papers again: the transcript, which he studied for several minutes; the admission slip; the form letter from the dean.

Howden wondered whether the dean or the registrar had the final sayso. He had got by the dean, who had scarcely glanced at his papers. Was this old goat going to hold him up? At the corners of Howden's mouth the tiny muscles quivered with anxiety. Although the man behind the grill was not looking at him,

Howden freshened his diffident smile. He could never tell what white people were thinking. He could never tell what anyone was thinking.

"And a work student too. Hmmmmm," the registrar said softly.

"Yes, sir," Howden said hesitantly. He started to go on. "I—I—"

Again the registrar looked out at him, for a second locking him in the complete disinterest of his gaze. Then a surprising thing happened: the registrar smiled. The smile seemed friendly but impersonal, and it came so unexpectedly that Howden could only stare.

"All right, young man," the registrar said, his face empty again. "I think Thompson must be out there somewhere." He pushed a small, worn Bible and a schedule of classes through the wicket. "I think you had better wait over there," he said, nodding vaguely. "Thompson will be along to show you where to go."

[2]

Howden stepped away from the window. He felt relieved. He felt almost happy. But in a moment new doubts assailed him. He could never be like those fellows he had been seeing all day. He could never be like that fellow Phil. And who was Thompson? Was he one of those who had ignored him? He did not like to think of himself as one who could be ignored. He was as good as any of them and better than some. That dark fellow he had seen earlier, for instance—he'd show them.

Shelton Howden's mind was a mass of details and confused impressions, his feelings contradictory. Beneath the brittle, watchful expression on his face there were lines that might mean anything in time to come. It was neither a good face nor a bad one. It gave an impression of premature hardness but not of strength. Yellow as a summer squash growing in the shade, there was too much of something about it. The jaw was box-like, the mouth a trifle thick, and above these the well-set hazel eyes had an habitual masked look of suspicion. Relaxed, the face was some-what inclined to grossness. But it was seldom relaxed.

Standing opposite the wicket but well back, head lowered, Howden clutched the worn Bible in one hand, his cheap plaid cap in the other. He was suddenly tired, and his body sagged a little. Such thoughts as he had moved sluggishly, never quite achieving completion but being absorbed by other thoughts that rose like thick vapor from the depths of his turbid mind. Lifting his gaze, he looked slowly about him. The hall was empty now, quiet, and hazy blue with evening. There was a light burning behind the wicket, but Howden did not see the registrar. What had he done—forgotten all about him? Left him there like a— like a—? He felt deserted, cast off. Then he heard footsteps and saw the registrar coming from the back of the hall. There was a young man with him.

"This is Thompson," the registrar said. "I think he will orient you all right. Thompson, this is Shelton—" He paused, and a frown of embarrassment crossed his mild-looking face. "Snow-den?"

"Howden," Howden said, a trifle surlily.

Thompson held out his hand. He was a stalky, bony, slope-shouldered fellow whose uneven features, though big, had a shrunken, ashen look about them. His coat, of a brown stuff skimpily cut, hung loosely on him and did not match his trousers. He smiled warmly, but Howden felt an immediate sense of re-sentment and kept his eyes averted. He could tell that Thompson was no great shakes at New Hope College; he could tell that Thompson was a nobody.

"You take care of him, Thompson," the registrar said; then, looking past Howden's shoulder, "I think you have a worthy ambition. I hope you do well. I hope you like it here," he went away back down the hall.

"Just get on it and stay on it, you'll like it," Thompson said, grinning widely. His voice was husky-light, his speech slightly burred and elisive, unlike the careful speech Howden had been hearing all day. Hair, eyes, and skin were all of the same cinnamon brown color.

"I think I will," Howden said.

"Sure you will," Thompson said. "Just stick with me. Get on it and stay on it."

Howden did not say anything.

"All right, let's go," Thompson said. "Where's your stuff?"

"Stuff?"

"Got no suitcase or nothing?"

"Oh," Howden said. "Out there. Out on the gallery."

"Everything around here is stuff, and I mean everything," Thompson said with a sudden laugh. "Courses are stuff, food's stuff, women are stuff. Where do you come from?"

Howden was slow to answer, and Thompson looked at him speculatively.

"Up around Rayville," Howden said.

"What you mean, 'up around Rayville'?"

"Well—" Howden said, and then he stopped. He did not like to have his business pried into. "That's what I said," he answered shortly. "Up around Rayville." As he picked up his flimsy cardboard suitcase, he could feel Thompson looking at him. All the things he wanted to get away from and forget seemed to be right there with him. There was a pointed, uneasy silence until Thompson spoke again, as heartily as ever.

"Country boy, hunh?" Thompson grinned. "I'm kind of a country boy too. For crying out loud, nothing wrong with being a country boy."

"Where do you come from?"

"Oh, lots of places. My old man's a jackleg preacher."

Howden could think of nothing to say as they walked across the campus. A smoky, lavender evening was falling. Along the row of seven large white houses, which formed one boundary of the campus, all was shadowy, bemused, remote. Mimosa, magnolia, and ragged cedar trees, planted in no orderly design, plopped thick shadows on the ground. As they approached the center of the campus, Howden began to see groups of girls and fellows standing in front of buildings, strolling the gravel paths. The sweet decay of the soft October evening gave a sad sort of beauty to everything.

They left the main walk and skirted the end of one of the women's buildings. When they turned the corner and started down the narrow path, a couple moved suddenly in the shadow. Howden could see the girl's wide eyes, frightened to defiance, staring at him in the gloam.

"Hunh," Thompson sniffed disdainfully. "You wait till tomorrow when these broads register, they'll think they're in jail."

"How do you mean?" Howden asked.

"You'll see," said Thompson. "They won't get away with that kind of stuff. These Yankee matrons are tough titty. Tomorrow it'll be different. These matrons really set on them."

"Are they white too?"

"Matrons? Sure. Everybody on the faculty's white except Prof Clarkson—you know, the registrar. That's him."

"You mean he's colored?"

Thompson laughed. "He ain't white."

Howden thought of the gray eyes, the wispy hair, the pale, thin-lipped face. He told himself that if he had looked more closely, he would have known. Then he remembered the manner, the voice. All of his life he had been on the outside looking in at white people who had position and authority. He had thought how lucky they were, how privileged, and how smart. He had thought how good it must be to be white. Now he was vaguely resentful that a colored man, no better than he himself, should lord it over him. But the registrar was *almost* white, and that made it somewhat different, he told himself.

Somewhere a group of male voices had struck up a song and were sending it floating across the campus. Howden knew the melody, but the words, drifting through the purple dusk, were strange to him and full of sweet, sad meaning, like a kept promise.

—these sacred walls, this old haven.
And the great love of New Hope, keeping us strong,
Shall e'er on our hearts be engraven—

They were approaching a building that stood a good way off from the others, at the far bare end of the campus. Topped by a wooden bell tower, it was a high and rather narrow three-story structure with a low one-story wing on one end. A line of overflowing trash barrels stood against the wall of the wing, and the ground was littered with rubbish. From the main building came the sound of boisterous shouts, of feet echoing hollowly on bare floors, of heavy objects being shoved about with great abandon. Someone was practicing "It Ain't Gon'na Rain No More" on a horn.

"This is us," Thompson said, but instead of going up the high steps to the open front door, he led Howden around to the side of the building where a door opened at ground level into the low wing. "Look," Thompson said. He stopped momentarily and gestured toward the fields that stretched darkly away behind the building. "That's where we'll work."

But Howden could see nothing. He wanted to think about something else. He was still hearing that song, still savoring the sweetness of its promise. "And the great love of New Hope—" He was thinking of getting inside, of getting quickly to be a part of that love and of the life he imagined. He wanted to sing that song too.

As they entered the short narrow passageway, the lights were switched on from somewhere, and the cry "Lights on! Lights on!" rang merrily through the building. There was a door in each side of the passage, and at the end of it a short flight of steps led up to a wide corridor. They saw no one, but they heard the horn braying raucously and several voices singing madly out of key. "Oh, it ain't goin'a rain no mo', no mo' . . ."

"Crazy greenies. Damn cake-eaters," Thompson snorted. Then he opened the door in the right of the narrow hall.

[3]

The room seemed to leap out at him. Jammed against the wall on each side of the door, a double-decker bunk reared to within a foot and a half of the low, damp-stained ceiling. The bunks were agonizingly familiar. He tried to shut out the memories that squeezed into his mind until it bulged, but he could not. The present was wiped out. The past three years, when he had been physically removed from all he wanted to forget, had never been. He could smell the close, fetid odor of stale sweat, of unclean clothes. He felt that he had been tricked; by some dark magic Thompson had contrived it all. His eyes filled with disappointment, revulsion, anger as he looked at Thompson.

"What's the matter?" asked Thompson apprehensively, his face showing his bewilderment.

Howden veiled his eyes. Setting down his suitcase, he walked toward the single window. At the foot of each bunk stood a cheap four-drawer dresser. Thompson was watching him anxiously. Howden laid the Bible on the scarred table under the window.

"Are—are all the rooms like this?" He kept his voice from quavering.

"Why, what's the matter?" Thompson asked solicitously.

"Matter—?" The stupidity of the question angered him. Then all at once he felt only gloomy disappointment, a deep melancholy. "Nothing," he said and sat down wearily.

The asthmatic horn had gone into another tune, the voices following it stridently. Whoever they were up there, they were having fun banging things about, stamping their feet. Howden was thinking that there'd be no fun for him, no carefree hours. He'd have to work and study. He'd have to get on it and stay on it, as Thompson had said. But someday he'd be somebody. The thought of what he'd be someday gave him dreamy satisfaction. He'd be a doctor or a lawyer or—something. He had no doubt of it. His ambition began to burn steadily again. You couldn't keep a good man down, and someday he was going to prove himself a better man than any of them.

All through supper, which he ate with Thompson in the barnlike, nearly empty dining hall, he felt a warm glow of self-confidence. A sense of basic melancholy lent it piquancy. It did not matter that they ate at the work students' table close to the kitchen and that they ate alone. It did not matter that in one end of the big room the greenies were having a good time. It was a sort of party for the greenies. A thin-chested, white-haired matron in a black velvet choker had them stand up one at a time and tell their names, where they came from, and why they had chosen New Hope College. They came from a lot of places: Chicago, St. Louis, Memphis, Tulsa, Cleveland, Savannah, New York. By Howden's count there were ninety freshmen—excluding himself, he thought with melancholy irony—fifty-five of them girls, and no two of them came from the same place. There was a girl from Salt Lake City, and there was a black boy—the only really black freshman—who stood up proudly and said that he was Prince Yakona Mukasa or something like that. He had a strange accent, and everyone looked at him intently, and there were a few titters. He was one of the very small number who had not chosen New Hope because his parents were alumni.

Then, led by the matron, whose voice was beginning to crack, the greenies sang songs, college songs, haltingly at first, but with great certainty and sincerity and verve as they learned the words and lost their shyness. The songs sounded sweet and melancholy to Howden. When they were done, the matron, whose back was to the rest of the dining room, where only Howden and Thompson were anyway, made a little speech and invited the greenies to a "get-acquainted" sociable in the parlors of one of the women's dormitories. The matron didn't include Howden. She didn't know that he was a freshman or even that he was there; and it didn't matter. Someday they would all know that he was there.

Later Howden wondered idly where all the students were he had seen at registration, and when Thompson told him that they were probably having a party or something in New Orleans, which was only seven miles away, it didn't matter. Nor did it when Thompson went on to say that their roommates, Inky Spillman and Dallas George, were off somewhere too—probably catting around, Thompson said, with some biffers in the village.

That he and Thompson were out of things seemed to draw them together. As they walked back toward the dormitory through the velvet dark, Howden experienced a faint flush of warmth for Thompson. Thompson said that he had worked at New Hope all summer with Spillman and George, and those guys just had to mess around. Last year, when they were freshmen, those guys never cracked a book. Nobody should waste his time like that, Thompson said—nor his money either, if he had any money.

Feeling friendly and indulgent, Howden listened while Thompson, with pensive gravity, warned him about the pitfalls, gave him maxims and precepts. Lights burned lonesomely over the entrances of the silent buildings. Off to the left across the stubble field, a string of a dozen lights marked the village. The tall weeds bordering the back path whispered against their legs as they walked. The damp wind of the tidelands blew in their faces. Thompson's voice came softly.

"You think your kin people'll help you out a little, send you a little change now and then?"

Howden tightened uneasily. Annoyance took stitches in his chest. "No," he said.

Thompson sighed. "Neither will mine."

They kept a little silence.

"What about your old man?" Thompson asked.

"What do you mean, what about him?"

"Ain't he no good to you at all?" He turned his head to look at Howden in the dark.

"He's dead."

"Oh."

Howden stayed guarded, his resentment near the surface. He didn't like these questions. Partly it was because they violated his sense of self, his reserve. Partly it was something else. He had no father. At the orphan home and school where he was raised, the inmates drew a belligerent distinction between those who had and those who hadn't fathers. Half-white bastard—Howden could still hear the treble-noted jeer. The boys resented him, called him a rhiny woods colt. With his bright skin, he stood out among them. "Half-white nigger bastard—" As he grew older and came to know about things, he took a kind of pride in his distinction. But somehow he could not openly defend his pride, so it was close and secret. Whoever his father was, he had been white.

The dormitory was as still and silent as an empty church. All the students were off somewhere. The room in the low wing seemed lonelier and more isolated. Thompson tilted his chair back against the wall next to the window. He did not speak for a while. His long face, ashen and moist-looking, wore an absent look. Moodily worrying a splinter on the table, Shelton Howden kept his eyes down.

"It's my mother who's dead," Thompson volunteered after a time. "If she was living, she'd make my old man fork over a little something once in a while. What was your old man like, Old Lady?"

"Don't remember him." It was a short, irritable reply, but Thompson must not have noticed.

"Been dead that long?"

"I told you I don't remember him," Howden mumbled.

"Well, my old man—he's all right in his way, you understand. Sends me a box sometimes when he thinks of it. Travels around preaching. Didn't do that when my mother was living. Once he had a church in El Dorado, Arkansas, and once he had one in Marked Tree. That's where my mother died." He paused, looking across the table at Howden. "Your mother living?"

Howden pulled at the splinter, and it came away with a sharp ripping sound. "No."

"Oh?" The way he said it this time made it a question, gently sympathetic and inviting. But Howden did not respond to it. He wanted Thompson to stay out of his business. In his mind he cursed Thompson. The muscles at the corners of his tight-held, down-drawn mouth quivered with resentment.

"Then who raised you, Old Lady, your grandmother?"

"Let me alone, for Christ sake!" Howden said, slamming up. He saw the blank look of shock give way to hurt in Thompson's face. "Mind your own frigging business," Howden said. Then, giving the chair an angry shove, he went to his bunk and began to undress. He undressed very quickly, climbed into his bunk, and turned his face to the wall.

[4]

Shelton Howden was awakened by a horny hand roughly shaking his shoulder. He did not know where he was for a moment. Through the top of the shadeless, curtainless window, he could see the morning sun, thin and watery, slanting across a patch of blackened, burned-out field. The hand shook his shoulder again, making his whole body rock from side to side. He turned his head and looked straight into a pair of gummy, bloodshot eyes.

"Get the lead out," a thick voice growled. "Got to hit it sooner'n this tomorrow morning. Haul it, nigger!"

As he got his bearings, the hand shaking him violently once more and then withdrawing, Howden heard the voice again.

"All right, Fred Thompson, let's go back," Howden heard it say. "I'm doing you a favor, waking you up for breakfast. Let's go back, man!"

Howden swung his feet up and over the side and let himself down to the gritty floor. Standing squat and solid at the foot of the bunk and grinning evilly was the fellow who had roused him. His dark, elongated head sat on a short length of thick neck, and his dark features ran together like something liquid. His face looked smashed in, his body hammered down.

"Thomp," he said, keeping his eyes fixed on Howden, "where in the hell did you find this red-rhiny nigger at?"

Thompson, in the bunk under Howden's, coughed, sat up, sighed. He put his face in his hands to smother another cough.

"Old Lady," he said in his light-husky voice, "that's Inky Spillman."

CHAPTER TWO

THERE were several things about New Hope College that many outsiders, either perversely spiteful or woefully ignorant, would not or could not get straight.

New Hope was a "Christian" college, established in 1873 and run by Northern-born Congregationalist missionaries, most of whom had spent a goodly portion of their lives in the mission fields of Africa, China, and Seringapatam. In the early days they had been much discouraged by their work among the freedmen, but they had persisted in it, and at the end of the first ten years the founding president, the Reverend Jubal Hooker, reported to the board of trustees:

> . . . Their natural laziness is being dispelled under a system of duty work. Their irresponsibility and a profligate tendency to sit late at night are disappearing under the benign influence of a noble and self-sacrificing faculty. It is nothing short of remarkable. Just as our Christian efforts in Seringapatam were more successful in proportion to the number of Anglo-Indians to whom we carried our message, so our work here, these ten years past

has taught us, will be successful in proportion to the number of mulatto students we attract. For with these our arduous labors have often been gratifyingly repaid. If it be the will of the Almighty, then what happier eventuality than that New Hope College devote itself to the education of mulattoes who in turn, embued with the true Christian spirit, will go out and serve the degraded blacks to whom they are brothers in Christ and half-brothers in blood?

When Shelton Howden was admitted to New Hope in 1923, the Reverend Jubal Hooker had been long gone to his reward, but the college was the attenuated shadow of the man. For the most part, the teachers were still missionaries or their descendants, New England- and Midwestern-accented men and women (the latter predominating), some of whom let it be known that it was a great sacrifice to teach at New Hope. The Bible was still in the curriculum, but also there were some very "meaty" courses in the sciences and the humanities, in education, argumentation, and comparative religion. Every day in the week and twice on Sunday there were chapel exercises, but these did not interfere with the dances, the parties, and the elegant, formal quarterly balls. The student body generally shaded out from tea-leaf brown to white, but if this circumstance was in the tradition of the college—and, indeed, probably because it was in the tradition—few at New Hope gave it thought.

However, it had a curious effect outside—as the college song put it—those "sacred walls." People outside thought of New Hope as a "prestige" school (as did also its students and alumni, though too well-mannered to admit it), some interpreting it to mean color snobbish, venal, and, as the expression went, dickty. But venal it was not. It is true that most of the parents who sent their children there were professional folk of comfortable income, and some were really wealthy; but the state of one's purse was not an overbearing consideration for admission. Shelton Howden could not have got in at all, for he had less than ten dollars over and above his entrance fees. As a matter of fact, the catalog of the

college specifically set it forth that every student had to participate "in the democracy of work." Solvent students worked six
hours a week at such tasks as waiting table in the faculty dining
room, checking chapel attendance, and distributing student mail.
Poor students, a small and somewhat seedy lot, worked thirty
hours a week, and it took them a minimum of five years to complete their courses.

They were up before dawn and at work by four-thirty. From
eight-thirty until noon they went to classes, and after midday
chapel they went back to their work at three and stayed until
five. Supper came at six, followed by a general social hour for
underclassmen, during which the young men and women could
promenade the long walk between Christian Hall and the college
gates or sit in whispering pairs in the stuffy, frilly parlors of the
women's dormitories.

But social hour meant nothing to the eight or ten work students. Work and eat and classes, study and sleep—there was no
time for anything else. Day scurried by, night fell, and morning
came. Morning always came too quickly.

[2]

"Aw right," Howden would hear Inky Spillman call in a furry
whisper. "Let's go, big boy. Let's go." He did not like to feel
that hand tugging at his shoulder with such diabolic satisfaction.
Every night he resolved to get up ahead of Spillman, but in two
months he had not done so.

"Aw right," Spillman would say again. "Let's go. White man
call you, it's all right; nigger call you, you want'a fight. Let's go
back, big boy." A pause, the hand again, and then, more maddening and insistent than ever, "Come on, Red, haul it!"

Howden could feel Fred Thompson stirring in the bunk below,
and then came the waking cough that never seemed to dislodge
the phlegm in Thompson's throat. The master switch had been
thrown the night before, and there was no light except in the

hall. But before dawn of winter mornings the hall was like a corridor of ice. The still, cold, rancid air of the room was better. They stumbled and fumbled at dressing in the dark. At the touch of his sodden clothes, Howden's flesh went goose-pimply with shock. He took a long breath and held it.

"Dallas, how you coming?" he heard Inky say.

Their trousers made a ripping sound as they hauled into them. When they got to their feet, their rubber boots squished.

"If I just didn't have to see no more hogs," Dallas George moaned. "I'd give up pork chops the rest of my life not to see no more goddamn hogs. How about you, Red?"

Howden did not answer. George and Spillman were always trying to bait him. At first they had invited him to join them on Saturday-night forays to the village; then they had asked him to play pinochle in the room across the hall. But he would have no truck with them. Even their presumption that he would irritated him. They kidded his refusals at first. Then, dully injured by his rebuffs, their kidding began to get vicious, ugly. Howden was impervious to it. He ignored the kidders. When the easygoing Dallas George occasionally forgot himself and made friendly overtures, Howden was deaf to them.

But he got along with Fred Thompson all right. After Howden's outburst of the first night, Thompson had been a little distant and reserved, but this had gradually broken down. They were in the room alone together a great deal, and Howden found that he needed Thompson to help him with his studies, to teach him the ropes. So he suppressed the resentment he often felt at Thompson's pious attitudes and opinions and, indeed, at Thompson himself just for being himself—for admitting his poverty and his insecure background, for making them a source of pride so that he did not even envy the students who had them. For his part, Thompson was friendly and solicitous, though sometimes his puzzled eyes looked at Howden covertly.

"You heard what the man said," Spillman muttered provocatively to George. "The man ain't said nothing. Ain't he made you small!" He laughed unpleasantly.

"He's made his mammy small," George said.

"O-whee! Somebody's been slipped," Spillman said. "Man, why'n you quit talking about the boy's momma like that!"

Reaching for the heavy sweater, which he also used to supplement his bed covering, Howden pulled it on. He said nothing.

"Maybe he ain't got no mammy," George said, taking Inky's bait.

"Man, I told you, quit messing with the boy's momma. He's goin'a hit you so hard one time, he'll knock your asshole clean loose."

"I wish he'd try it," Dallas George said. "I wish to hell he'd try it."

"Cut it, you guys." Thompson spoke sharply in the dark. "For crying out loud."

"Aw right, let's go. Work ain't hard and the boss ain't mean. You guys ain't dressed yet?"

"You go on," Thompson said.

But Spillman did not go. He stamped heavily around in his rubber boots, stirring up the clammy air.

"What you come here for?" his surly voice demanded of no one in particular. "If you can't pee, get off the pot. Nobody asked you to come, and ain't nobody begging you to stay. Now come on, hit the chillies!" Suddenly he flung open the door, making an icy draft, and stood there for a moment massively framed by the dim light behind him. Then he stamped off down the hall.

Howden buttoned his sweater, tucked the ragged tail of it down into his trousers, and fastened his belt. Dressed now, he waited for Fred Thompson. He could hear Spillman somewhere outside talking with a work student from across the hall. Howden felt nothing but scorn for Spillman and George. They didn't count. Living in this room, rising at this forbidding pre-dawn hour, working on the farm, eating in the dining hall at the table nearest the kitchen gave him nothing in common with them, he thought. And yet it was these very things that blocked his association with all those others—those who stayed abed until the first bell rang at six forty-five, who had decent clothes to wear, money to spend, and parents to go home to. He had nothing in common with them either. He felt wretchedly alone.

And this aloneness rode him like an incubus when he stumbled through the door into the frost-hardened path that led behind the building to the fields.

There were always five or six of them. Their breath made little clouds in the tart winter air. Behind them the college buildings, each with a pale light over the door, fell sharply away to shadow and looked like sets on a dim, unpeopled stage. Their boots thudded against the loose stones; their sweat- and dirt-stiffened clothes creaked; the stubble whistled dryly against their legs. All else was still. The darkness was like something physical, a viscid, jellied mass. Off in the distance, a lantern swinging and casting broken circles of light increased Howden's sense of theatrical unreality, of playing a part. The cows were standing at the fence when they reached the gate. The hogs heard them coming and started grunting and snuffling and milling around the empty feed troughs, and someone said, "Shut up, you bastards!" with surly quiet to the hogs. Then they were all slogging through the acrid muck of the piglot.

Years later when he remembered, Howden still experienced a feeling of unreality about these mornings. Later, hearing people talk about college days, glamorizing them with adventure, imbuing them with happiness, Howden always told himself that his college days were like that too: they were full of fun and romance and devil-may-care. Some people he came to know later were all midnight revelers in college, and he pretended to have been one too, staggering home to his souvenir-pennant-picture-hung room under a load of needled beer.

But even later that familiar feeling of aloneness would come over him, and then he would remember truthfully how he had always expected it to be gone when full morning came. But it

never was. The mist-shrouded fields would turn smoky blue, and
the reluctant dawn, trailing slack streamers of uncertain light,
would break. Soon after he would hear the plangent jangle of the
rising bell coming from the distance. When he looked up, the
others would be in a jogging, strung-out line loping over the red-
earthed fields toward the college buildings. Fred Thompson
would be waiting for him at the fence; but even with Thompson
there, Howden would feel alone.

[3]

As the first year flowed imperceptibly into the second, it seemed
to Shelton Howden that he was making no real progress toward
his goal. He was gnawed by a hunger he could find no food to
feed. He had no love of knowledge for itself, but books, he'd
thought, held secrets that would satisfy his confused desires. Books
disappointed him. The learning of such knowledge as books held
seemed at times a useless, heartbreaking chore. His memory
tricked him. He had to review, review, review. In elementary
physics basic principles gave him trouble. History he could get,
but he could not find the beauty and sublimity he was supposed
to find in *Paradise Lost*. Abstract thought was not at all his line.
Thompson said consolingly that he had trouble with certain sub-
jects too, but the admission only annoyed Howden.

"The hell with it," he said, pushing his book aside.

Thompson looked up. His long face had grown more angular
the past year. His eyes were worried.

"What's the matter, Old Lady?"

"Oh, nothing," Howden said peevishly. But there was something the matter—with him, with Thompson, with everything.
Other students seemed to get their stuff. Shuttling between
classes or standing self-consciously apart near the dining hall before meals, Howden would see them in excited little groups. They
were always in high spirits, always alive in a way that he was
not, and bound together by interests beyond his imagining. He

viewed them from a great social distance. He wished that he had their assurance, their sense of belonging, but he did not, and neither, he thought disdainfully, for all his stupid acceptance of who and what he was, neither did Fred Thompson. He and Thompson were just a couple of damn fool pokes.

"Just hold your C average, Old Lady," Thompson said quietly. "You'll be all right."

That C average had disappointed Howden. He thought he had done better and deserved more. But Professor Clarkson had congratulated him and invited him to his house. Howden had gone because it was a good thing to stay on the right side of the registrar. Afterwards he went because the professor's sister and his wife gave him things to eat.

Moses Hall was full of after-supper sounds, and Howden listened to them. He could hear talking outside on the landing and fellows coming in and going upstairs to their high-ceilinged, painted-walled rooms. Someone was shouting for a game of pinochle, and someone else was practicing on a violin, patiently repeating a difficult chord. After supper Howden was always more conscious of the ebb and flow of campus life. There were student meetings and play rehearsals, and the forensic society had gone away to Washington, D.C., for a debate with Howard, and there were fellows calling on girls in the dormitory parlors—but he was not one of them. These things were entirely out of the range of his experience. Listening, no longer idly now, he nursed each sound until it bloomed in his imagination like a poisonous flower. A new wave of feeling engulfed him.

"There's something else, something besides a lot of damned facts and figures and dead men's names!" he burst out, striking his open book with the back of his hand and glaring challengingly at Thompson.

"All right, I grant you," Thompson said. The calm concession angered Howden. He resented Thompson's steadiness, his placidity. "All right," Thompson said again, "but what, Old Lady?"

Howden did not answer; he looked away. To hell with Fred

Thompson, who didn't know what anything was about, who didn't know enough to know what he was missing. After a while his face, topped by the coarse, almost yellow hair, relaxed, became a trifle gross. He was not really thinking. His mind was frequently a snare for all sorts of dreams and wishes, and trifles hung in it like baubles on a Christmas tree.

But if Shelton Howden's mind was no more discriminating than it had been, it was considerably more aware. He had had some good teachers these several months. One, a woman from the Middle West who, rumor had it, smoked on occasion, had made her classes conscious of what was happening in the world.

Miss Braswell blew through New Hope College like a fresh and fractious wind, created a minor tempest, and whisked out within a term. In her lectures on current history, she made scathing comments on people like Reed Smoot and Andrew Mellon and Calvin Coolidge and Peggy Hopkins, who were all in the news. There were the war debts, which England and France reneged on. Every now and then—"like an exclamation mark," Miss Braswell said, "in the puling prose of prosperity"—appeared an item about a couple of men named Sacco and Vanzetti. There was talk too about the "Red Peril" and the "Yellow Peril," but Miss Braswell said that the yellow peril was the streak up some men's backs and the red peril was just an old-fashioned case of pox. (She was asked to leave New Hope on the evening of the day she made this remark.) There were rum runners, and Hollywood scandals and the refurbished details of an infamous divorce case involving the wife of a millionaire and a Canadian Indian guide, all illustrated in the color-printed magazine pages of the Sunday *Orleans American*. There were half-page cartoons too, depicting "flappers" and "jazz babies" and college boys with whisky flasks; and the heavy black type of Arthur Brisbane's editorials shouted: ARE WE GOING TO THE DOGS?

Unrealized by Shelton Howden, there were forces of knowledge and acceptance and compromise, of wonder and speculation and doubt, of wish and dream and ambition, of envy and resentment and pride, shaping noiselessly, scoring indelibly the still flexible contours of his mind. There were teachers and students, attitudes and opinions. There were books that he heard about and which he planned to read someday: *This Side of Paradise, Flaming Youth, Birthright, Mother India*. And there were the words and music of songs floating across the campus in the tremulant spring night air, floating from student dances in the dining hall, floating from the throats of boys serenading girls on the porches of dormitories. ". . . We've danced the whole night through. . . ." "All alone, I'm so all alone. There's no one else but you. . . ."

"Fred—" Howden looked up suddenly, and then he paused. He wanted to say it casually. "Did you ever think about calling on a girl here?"

Thompson gave him a penetrating glance. "What girl, for instance?"

"Any girl," Howden answered brusquely, irritably. "Just calling on any girl."

"I used to think about it, but I got over it," Thompson said.

"Got over it?"

"That's right."

"Oh, go to hell, Fred," Howden said. Thompson disgusted him with his sacrifices, his self-denial.

"If you got no money, you can't mess around with these broads," Thompson said gravely. "They're gold-diggers. They'd take the sweat off your you-know-what."

Howden didn't listen. He was thinking of some of the girls he had seen. He was thinking of the firm, clean, sweet look of their legs. In classes, in the dining hall, in chapel, through half-averted eyes he had seen the ivory pink, golden sweet-fleshed girls, and he was remembering the alert tilt of their heads, the indescribable fragrance of their brisk young bodies. His thoughts thickened in his throat.

"Let somebody else go for them," Thompson said, lowering his eyes to his book and then raising them again at once. He smiled a little. "We got no time, Old Lady."

And, indeed, though the separate days and weeks dragged heavily, there was no time. Work and classes and study—a laborious, crabbed round. There was not enough time, although the end of it seemed far away. There were other courses under other teachers, and new student faces and new situations and sometimes new and vaguely disturbing ideas, but there was never enough time.

[4]

The dormitory lights went out at ten o'clock. One night when they blinked their warning at five minutes of the hour, Howden looked up in resentful surprise. Where had the time gone? The dormitory came instantly alive. Spillman and George drifted in from the room across the hall. Upstairs someone yelled, "Pee-time! Pee-time!" and the cry was taken up by a dozen strident voices on each floor. Then there followed yells and catcalls and Indian war whoops and the joist-shaking stumble and clatter of feet from all over the building rushing to the toilets in the basement.

Fred Thompson sighed wearily and gathered his books.

"Say, Fred, let's get us some kind of lamp," Howden said eagerly. The idea had just occurred to him.

"Lamp?"

"Then we can study after lights-out."

"That's an idea, Old Lady," said Thompson listlessly, "but what are we going to use for money?"

Howden did not know whether he was annoyed by the fact that money was a consideration or by Thompson's intrusion of the thought. Thompson was a wet blanket; he was a joy killer. Howden could hear doors banging and voices yelling and feet clattering furiously down the stairs. Spillman and George were undressing.

"What about the farm? Can't we get a lantern from the farm?"

"Say, now that is an idea." His long face brightened. "That's all right."

"And oil too," Howden said. "For crying out loud, they keep it around down there in ten-gallon drums."

The lantern which they got from the farm the next day provided even better light to study by than the electric bulb. Set up in the center of the table, the lantern cast a light of soft intensity over their books, washed their blurred, monstrous shadows against walls and ceiling. But Spillman made objections. Hiking up on his elbows in his bunk, he said he couldn't sleep with a light on. He was sullen and ugly. He was goddamned, he said, if he was going to have his sleep messed up because somebody wanted to study all night. He said it was his room too, and goddamn if he wasn't going to have some say about it. The lights were supposed to go out at ten o'clock, weren't they? Well, that's when they'd go out too, or his mother was a whore. Howden wasn't Mr. Jesus sure enough, and Fred Thompson didn't look like a pope to him.

But three or four nights later Howden thought of an expedient. He and Thompson pinned their blankets together and rigged them up from one wall to the other across the narrow room. Though Spillman eyed this arrangement menacingly, he said nothing, for the joined blankets did shut off the light from the bunks. Howden liked the feeling of having built a wall behind which he could retire. It became a regular thing for him and Thompson to study late, to get along on five hours' sleep. Indeed, Howden took pride in it. But as the weeks passed, Fred Thompson grew haggard.

"Look, Old Lady, I just got to turn in," he said late one night. "And you ought to turn in too."

"Not yet," Howden said. He did not look up.

Sitting hunched against the chilly damp of the spring night, Thompson said nothing for several minutes. Then softly, anxiously: "Old Lady, I—"

Howden looked up, suddenly exasperated. He was trying to concentrate. "What's the matter?" he demanded shortly.

"I got to hit the hay, Old Lady. Look, we can—if we shove the table back—"

"All right. All right."

One blanket just reached across the corner from the wall to a nail in the top of the window frame. Light streaked thinly into the rest of the room, but it was late, and Spillman was snoring raspingly. Disturbed by Thompson's coughing once or twice, Howden raised his head to listen, but all was still. He gave himself up to his plodding effort. He felt exhilarated, proud, superior. He exulted that he was the only student at New Hope studying at this hour.

He was working on a paper in general sociology. The course was given by a professor who was a member of the faculty of Tulane University but who, principally in the interest of observation and research, taught six hours a week at New Hope. Dr. Posey had written several articles on the Negro. The subject was a hobby which he rode very hard. For him New Hope was a kind of laboratory in which he could study the Negro at close range and so document his articles with the telling phrase, "As I observed . . ." He had quite a reputation among scholars; his articles on race were always being quoted somewhere.

Until he went into Dr. Posey's course, Howden had thought the Negro outside the scheme of things, a paragraph in the geography books, a line in history, a cipher in the white man's thoughts, left alone by all save a small handful of Yankees like those on the faculty at New Hope. Now he was beginning to learn that actually it was not like this. There were theses and theories. Books had been written, experiments made, data recorded on race. Whole systems of arguments, with their corresponding practices, had developed over the years. Dr. Posey pointed out that if one took all aspects of the race problem, he would have to be versed in anthropology, biology, history, philosophy, economics, bionomics, and a lot of other ologies and onomies of which Shelton Howden had never heard. "And then," Dr. Posey had said with waggish, pointed amusement, "there is that factor in the blood, or in the heart if you wish—that X which no one knows." The race problem was very complicated. In moments of unusual perception, Howden could find clear traces of this thinking—that the race problem was very complicated—in other faculty members too and in other courses. There was more than a trace of it in the textbook entitled *Southern History Since the War Between the States*. What seemed to make much of Southern social history so bloody was the fact that now and then some ill-advised, impatient, and ofttimes corrupted schemer tried to change the equations in the problem. Changing the equations, Dr. Posey once told his class, did not change the thing itself. And anyway, who was qualified to change it? Who understood it well enough and sympathetically enough? Why, only the Southern white man. All anyone else could do was watch and wait—and there was nothing to be gained by watching.

Once in class there had been a short-lived argument between Dr. Posey and a student on this very point. The student (who had a non-boarding status, which was no better than a work-student status) had maintained that there was something more to do than wait. He broke right into the middle of the lecture to say it, and Dr. Posey had looked archly down at him from the heights of his superior knowledge.

"Such as what?" Dr. Posey had questioned roguishly.

"Suppose all the Negroes got together and demanded their rights," the student had said, not making it a question but a challenge. His voice was high, edgy, and the class looked at him uneasily. Howden stirred in his seat in the back of the room and fiddled with his notebook.

"What rights?" Dr. Posey asked. He was smiling; his eyebrows slanted up into his forehead like carets.

"What ri—!" Howden heard the student exclaim and saw him sit up straighter in his chair.

"Yes. What rights? Is it an unfair question?" Then his voice changed, dropped sweetly, coyly. "Has that little censor in your blood, or in your heart, come up to whisper a warning to you?" He moved elastically across the front of the room and turned abruptly to face the class. There was an amused expression on his sallow, thin-lipped face and a stagy simper in his voice when he spoke again. The room was absolutely quiet.

"There's an old saying about the Niggra's rights: he has none which anyone is bound to respect."

The student half rose, fumbling for his books on the writing arm of his chair. He looked around at his classmates with a look of angry shock, desperate entreaty, pain. Howden could feel himself tightening, holding his breath. He experienced a sense of black anger at the student for taking the discussion out of the realm of the academic, for making it something real.

"Do you mean to say—?" the student began with high-pitched emphasis.

Dr. Posey, blanched now, broke in. "I don't mean to say anything," he snapped icily, "and don't use that tone of voice with me, you—!" But then he recovered himself. He raised one eyebrow waggishly, smirked indulgently. "I asked a question. In fact, I asked two questions."

But the student did not answer. Flinging a taut look of something that may have been contempt first at his classmates and then at Dr. Posey, he gathered his books and slammed abruptly from the room. Smiling urbanely, Dr. Posey went on with his lecture.

Howden thought of this now as he sat bent over his lecture notes and the digests of all Dr. Posey's recent articles. He was reading through a digest, trying to find a springboard from which to leap into the concluding section of his paper. The room was airless, damp and chill, but Howden was unaware of it.

He had just touched his pen to paper when suddenly the suspended blanket fell with a swoosh from its anchorage on the wall. Its own weight had loosened it, he thought. As he got up to replace it, easing his chair quietly back from the table, he gave an involuntary start, heard his own sharp intake of breath. Fronting him, his face twisted with hate, stood Inky Spillman in long gray underwear, baggy at the knees.

"Goddamn it, I told you I couldn't sleep with no light on!"

"I thought—" Howden began.

"You thought hell! I told you I couldn't sleep with no light on!" His voice came like a growl, vibrating through the mucus in his throat. In one hand he clutched the fallen end of the blanket. The lantern light, the grotesque shadows on walls and ceiling, the noise of Spillman's stepped-up, shallow breathing, the surrounding inert hush made the scene unreal to Howden. He had the queer sensation of struggling to awaken from a dream. Spillman gave a tug on the blanket, and the end that was fastened to the window frame whipped down.

"Keep your shirt on," Howden mumbled, surprised that his voice was barely audible, that his throat was tight. He did not think that Spillman would do more than shoot off his mouth, yet he felt himself tense, brittle. His biceps and the muscles of his calves twitched; his stomach knotted. He tried to reinvoke the contempt he had always felt for Inky Spillman, but what he experienced now was fear. Spillman flung the blanket to the floor.

"Watch yourself," Howden forced himself to say.

"Watch myself for what, you yellow bastard!"

"Keep your shirt on." The scorn was there, but the fear was there also. He was superior, he thought, to Inky Spillman, and he should not be afraid.

"Shut your goddamn mouth, or I bust you in it!"

It was all crazy and unreal. Beyond Spillman's shoulder he could see Dallas George grinning over the edge of his bunk. When he brought his eyes back to Spillman, he saw the knife. He must have known about the knife all the time, for he was not surprised. His only thought was that the knife was an entirely unnecessary exaggeration. Spillman was holding the knife at waist level, and his forefinger was extended along the back edge of the glittering blade.

"You think you better'n me, don't you? You rusty sonofabitch, you think you got my water on." His lips quivered tautly, skinned back over his white teeth. "You think your ass weighs a ton. You think you the only bastard in this goddamn room!"

Howden wanted to walk past Spillman into the other part of the room, but he was blocked in. He wished for a power that he did not have. He wished that by a disdainful flick of his finger he could freeze Spillman to the floor. He wished that he could go up to Spillman, command him to drop the knife, and then spit in his black face. He could see Dallas George now sitting forward in the bunk, the bedclothes bunched around his shoulders. He heard Fred Thompson stir restlessly in his sleep.

"You ain't no better'n nobody else. You ain't as good as nobody else. Some drunk white man got you on a nickel whore. I got a good mind to slice you down just on general principles. I ain't got nothing to lose. I'm leaving on out soon anyway. I got a good mind to carve my name all over your yellow ass."

Howden said nothing for a moment, and then he forced himself to say: "Keep your shirt—"

"Shut up!" Spillman commanded, lifting the knife a little. Thus they held for several seconds, until Spillman seemed satisfied, until he seemed to relax a bit. He took a half step back. Then into the silence Dallas George dropped a taunt.

"Aw, man, you bluffing. Why don't you do something? If you goin'a fight, fight. He ain't no kin to you."

Spillman feinted at Howden, making him flinch; drew back; feinted again with the same result. He laughed scornfully and, turning to glance over his shoulder at George, tripped in the blanket. At that instant, suddenly, without knowing he would do it, in hatred as well as fear, Howden leaped upon him and bore him to the floor. The knife skittered from Spillman's grasp. In a blind rage, Howden's fists beat down into the shocked face. Spillman managed to turn over. Feeling the muscles straining under him, the body heaving and twisting to throw him off, Howden's fear came back. Spillman struggled to his hands and knees, but Howden clung to him. He was no longer striking blows, just clinging.

"Turn me a-loose! Turn me a-loose!" Spillman shouted breathlessly. "Where's my goddamn knife!"

George had jumped down from his bunk, and Fred Thompson was up too, but Howden saw them only through a blurred haze of motion. His life was filled with one great urgency. He wanted to cry out for help, but the words would not come through his constricted throat. He felt himself lifted off his feet, his grip torn away. Then, as if it came from someone else, he heard a cry escape him. A sharp zigzag of pain screamed upward from his groin, paralyzing him, making him feel hollowed out. For a moment he clung to one of the uprights of the bunk, but his arms turned to water, his thighs to rubber; his knees collapsed. A terrifying cramp seized his entrails.

When he came to, he was lying on Spillman's bunk, and Thompson was bent over him. The electric light was on. His trousers were loosened, and his shirt was pulled up over his stomach. Thompson was gently massaging him. Howden tried to sit up.

"How does it feel now?" Thompson asked.

"I'm all right," Howden said, pushing Thompson's hands away. Thompson straightened up. "What happened?" Howden asked.

"He kneed you, Old Lady. Looks like the whole dormitory was down here, and then the night watchman came. When he dropped the knife, I picked it up," Thompson said. "Can you make it now?"

"I'm all right," Howden said. He sat up gingerly, and an icy ache stabbed up from his groin into his bowels. "What happened to Inky?"

"Night watchman took him, him and Dallas. They were flunking out anyway," Thompson said. He went across the room in his bare feet and picked up the blanket and threw it on Howden's bunk. "Come on, Old Lady. Better get your clothes off."

After he had climbed painfully to his bunk and Thompson had put out the light, Howden's nerves seemed to snap and jangle and to come unwound very fast. He lay trembling for a long time, staring into the dark, and remembering and remembering things he wanted to forget.

CHAPTER THREE

AT THE close of his third year at New Hope, the routine of Shelton Howden's life changed. There was nothing remarkable in this; it was simply that in the normal course of things he was given a new job. Though he welcomed the change, it made no great difference in his relations to anything, for his habits of thought and the pattern of his emotions underwent no telling alteration. His confused desires were still unsatisfied. The same often trivial thoughts raced in his mind; the same emotions churned in him. He brooded still (if it could be called brooding that brought forth nothing new) over his lot and on the present and the future. But never on the past. Behind him there was nothing he wanted to look back on, no smallest flag of pride a-flutter in the winds of memory.

Both Howden and Fred Thompson were taken off the college farm and assigned to the small maintenance staff that kept up the buildings through the summer. It was an easy job, after the farm. Except for an occasional inspection by the woman who supervised them, they were not interfered with. The departure of the students for the summer vacation was a great relief to Howden. He did not have to duck and scurry out of their sight. Now that they were gone, he did not feel envious and resentful. It was pleasant working in the cool, deserted buildings, waxing floors, washing windows, cleaning paints. No condescending eyes fell on him; no sound of careless laughter mocked him.

But Fred Thompson was ill, and his illness would have been noticeable to anyone but Howden. In the morning he always seemed all right, but later in the day his feet would begin to drag and his frame to droop like a stripped corn stalk withering in the sun. Always by mid-afternoon his eyes burned feverishly. One day he collapsed. He tried to make a joke of it. He said it must have been something he ate. The next morning he was too weak to get out of bed.

During nearly all of July, Thompson lay helpless in the stifling room, and Howden was forced to take such care of him as he could. Thompson said that he didn't want a doctor. And anyway, what could he pay him with? Besides, he said, he'd be all right. Later his mood changed for a while, and he said that the thing that was the matter with him no doctor could do anything about. Howden brought him his meals, kept fresh water there for him, and tried to suppress his impatience with Thompson's illness. Gradually Thompson seemed to grow stronger, although he looked thin and pale and dryly wasted. One evening near the end of the month, he declared that he was feeling fine.

"Old Lady," he said, "I'll be able to work tomorrow."

Howden didn't say anything. He simply looked at Thompson.

"All I needed was a rest," Thompson said. He sounded much stronger.

"And you feel all right?"

"I'm telling you," Thompson said. His lips skinned back in a sudden grin over teeth that now seemed monstrous. "I've got an iron constitution, Old Lady."

Howden felt genial all at once. "You've got an iron head," he joked. "Old Iron-head Fred."

Thompson responded to Howden's mood. "Boy, I sure put it over on you," he said. "I was fooling the whole time. I just didn't want to work. I wanted a vacation, and I got it. I made a sucker out of you."

"Old Iron-head," Howden said. "From now on, you're just old Iron-head."

"I had you buffaloed," Thompson said, still grinning. He threw the sheet back and sat up. Howden watched him narrowly.

"What are you going to do?"

"I'm doing it. I'm getting up. We're going to take a walk down to the gate," Thompson said. "Old Iron Constitution wants to try out his pins." Swinging his legs out slowly, he put his feet on the floor. His grin brightened confidently. His ankles looked like brittle sticks, brown and parched, such as one would gather for kindling wood. The soles of his feet were very pink and soft-looking.

"Look at that campus out there," Thompson said. "Ain't it pretty?"

The limpid, old-gold light of the summer evening lay soft on the campus, giving a kind of glowing, picture-like definition to everything. The cows that had gone dry and would be slaughtered for meat had been brought up from the farm to pasture on the lawns through the summer, and a dozen of them, lazily swinging their tails, stood bunched under the trees near the dining hall.

"Hand me my pants, Old Lady. We're going out and sit on old Hooker."

"You know I can't sit on old Hooker. Iron-head's trying to rub it in because he can sit on old Hooker. Iron-head's razzing me because I'm not a senior."

"You can watch me sit," Thompson said. "No. My good pants, my Sunday pants, Old Lady. This is my coming-out party, for crying out loud."

Suddenly, sitting there on the edge of the bunk, he made a gasping sound. An expression of shocked wonder overspread his emaciated face. He fastened on Howden a quick, alarmed, wild-eyed look and started to get up—indeed, half rose like one in a spell. Then he sat slowly down again, coughed, and a gush of bright blood spilled from his mouth. He did not look at it. Instead, his incredulous, blank stare fixed on Howden while the blood trickled from chin to chest and streaked the front of his long-sleeved undershirt. His eyes went slowly dead.

"Old Lady," he said weakly, "did you ever see iron bleed?" The grotesque levity of the remark disgusted and angered Howden. The impatience he had felt with Thompson's illness nearly burst out of him, but he contained it. In this new emergency he did not know what to do. He looked dumbly around, trying to think of something, trying not to look at his roommate, further angered because he knew Thompson was looking to him, waiting for him, depending on him. Snatching a towel from the rack, he rushed from the room.

On his way to the lavatory and back, he wished that he did not have to go into that room again. He hated Fred Thompson for bringing this on, for involving him in his suffering. He'd carried Thompson's work, brought him his meals. He'd done enough. It wasn't fair. And then to joke about it! It was no joke to be so poor that you couldn't have a doctor. There was nothing funny about imposing your suffering on someone else.

Thompson had not changed his position when Howden returned. "Here," Howden said gruffly, handing him the dampened towel. Thompson wiped the blood from his mouth and chin and dabbed at the front of his undershirt. "Go on and lie down," Howden said, his voice edged with impatience. Standing with one shoulder against the window frame, his back half turned to Thompson, he stared stonily out of the window.

"What about that walk, Old Lady? What about sitting on old Hooker?" Thompson asked. "I've still got you buffaloed, Old Lady. It's just a part of the joke. You know what that is? That's iron rust. Old Iron Constitu—"

Howden swung around from the window. "For Christ sake, stop it! And lie down!"

They stared at each other for a moment.

"Yes. Guess I better lie back down, Old Lady," Thompson said apathetically, weakly. He lay down on his back and pulled the gray, rumpled sheet up over him and closed his eyes. "My God," he said in a kind of weary whisper. And a moment or two later, "My God."

Shelton Howden abruptly left the room.

[2]

That was a restless, jumpy night for Howden. He fell asleep only to be snatched violently awake by the spastic clutch of foreboding. It seemed to him that Thompson's raspy breathing filled the room, the building, the hot night. Tomorrow, Howden thought, he'd report to someone. He wouldn't be responsible any longer. He would move to another room. No one could make him stay with Thompson's sickness. There were plenty of vacant rooms.

In the morning Thompson seemed much better. Besides, there was no one for Howden to report to except the woman on the maintenance staff, who had nothing to do with it. The faculty houses were all closed and empty. The superintendent of grounds and buildings could not be found.

For several days Thompson continued to improve. He grew strong enough to sit up on the edge of his bunk and then to walk around the room. He wrote a letter to his father, addressed General Delivery, Pinkett, Arkansas, and after that he seemed to have his hope renewed, to become cheerful.

Howden's feeling of long-suffering patience was just beginning to relax when Thompson had another hemorrhage. Howden discovered it one noon. Supine in the bunk, his eyes two bottomless pools of despair and the blood crusting around the mouth and the slack line of the jaw, Thompson was too weak to move. His skin was drawn drum tight over his skull, revealing the skeleton structure. Mute gloom pervaded the atmosphere. Howden put the plate of food on the chair by the bunk and left quickly. In the evening he lingered until dark to return. He did not put on the light. Tense and silent, he sat by the window. He hated the wretched atmosphere of failure and defeat.

"Old Lady, I'm sorry if I've been trouble," Thompson said apologetically in the dark. His voice was low but clear.

Howden said nothing.

"You mailed that letter to my old man, didn't you?"

"Yes," Howden said. "Sure."

Thompson sighed. "I'm asking him to do me a favor. I haven't asked my old man to do a thing for me since I was twelve. He'll jump out of his skin when he reads that letter." He made a sound that might have been wry laughter.

Howden didn't answer. There was nothing to answer to. A hot, damp breeze came up and blew into the room, working at the clothes hanging on the wall at the end of the bunk.

"Old Lady, I wonder what it's like," Thompson said a little later.

"What?"

"Dying," Thompson said.

Howden's whole body clenched. He did not speak. He felt that to speak would be to scream out curses. He felt that to move would be to act with violence. He sat frozen.

"I imagine it's like taking ether or something," Thompson said. "Pretty soon you realize that while you're fighting it, you're breathing it in. It's been buffaloing you all the time. Then you don't fight any more. You just relax." He sounded quite calm, almost matter-of-fact.

"It's a funny thing how you relax, Old Lady," Thompson went on. "I saw my mother do it. There we were, not wanting her to die, my old man praying and carrying on, and some neighbors taking turns fanning her, and she was all relaxed. She died of T.B. too."

Howden flung himself so violently out of his chair that it tipped over, making a loud clatter in the room. He thought he could see Thompson's eyes burning up at him in the dark. For a moment he stood there, feeling he knew not what, fearing he

knew not what, hating he knew not what. He started to speak
but checked himself and fled from the room.

When he returned at dawn, Fred Thompson had drowned in
his own blood.

[3]

That fall Shelton Howden got the choicest job of all: he was
made the college bellringer. He lived alone in the turret room
a short flight of steps above the third floor of Moses Hall. It
was a much better room than the other. The previous bellringer
had left an ancient Morris chair, a raveled scrap of rug, and a
hanging bookshelf. The bell rope dangled through a hole in the
center of the ceiling. Pasted on the wall above the iron cot
were magazine cartoons by John Held, Jr., and there were faded
curtains at both windows.

Howden was lonely, but sometimes he exulted in his loneliness.
Up there in his room he was Shelton Howden, and he fancied
himself striding the earth like a giant. "What care I for those who
hate my name—?" He had read the words somewhere, and they
thrilled him. He was above man's malice, beyond envy, topping
the stars!

But the exultancy never lasted. From this he would sink into
a pit of despond, think of failure, think of death, and pity himself beyond words to express.

Because he had time for it now, he was carrying his first full
schedule. He had begun his laboratory courses in anatomy and
inorganic chemistry, and he was finishing up his minor in history and social science. His classes seemed to be full of clever
students who knew all the answers and who seemed to look upon
his stumbling responses with impersonal, amused curiosity. They
made him conscious that he was older than they, that he was
mentally slower than they. He felt resentful and abashed in their
presence.

He studied doggedly. In the anatomy lab he could see what he had heard in lectures, and this helped. Peering and memorizing and drawing his way through the simpler species, genera, and families, he began gradually to see a logic in the physical structure and the bionomics of the lower animal world. It made sense, like two and two, like a column of figures without fractions that added up to something exactly. But this adding up vaguely disturbed him. The relation of muscle to organ, organ to function, and function to environment had no counterpart in rational life. Man's mind was not the predictably functioning machine man's body was. Thought, emotion, will—these were the great unknowns, and these were man. Howden, who imagined that he had hit upon something original, felt uneasy in the presence of this notion. You could learn all about man's body, but you couldn't foresee his reactions, you couldn't peer into his mind. For all he knew, his teachers and his fellow-students might be secretly laughing at him. He could not ever tell what they were thinking and feeling.

There was no one with whom he could talk. His relations with his classmates were cold and polite; with instructors, formal, academic, and constrained. Three or four times in the preceding year he had accepted invitations to Professor Clarkson's, but he got no real pleasure from going there. The Clarksons were kind to him—perhaps too kind—and he felt socially inept. Striking up a friendship or an acquaintance on his own initiative was beyond him. He was wary and suspicious. He had not yet learned what instincts to trust, what impulses to follow. Though he grew more alert, and his slow mind somewhat more responsive, he also grew more self-held. A springy hardness of self-interest formed over him.

[4]

Dr. Hubert Posey was giving a new course in the structure of American society since 1865, and Howden was taking it because he needed it to complete his minor. Dr. Posey was a skilled and interesting lecturer. For the whole class hour, without a moment's hesitancy, without fumbling at notes, and without once losing an air of amused expectancy, words issued from his lips with an almost physical definition, like superbly accurate gunfire. "Are there superior and inferior races?" he began one day.

The thirty-five young men and women in the class stirred and then composed themselves alertly.

"Aha!" Dr. Posey said, as if some expectation had been fulfilled. It was curious about his eyes. They never really seemed to smile, though they were constantly amused. Now his glance flicked from row to row as he prowled slowly across the front of the room. Pushing the lank lock of sorrel blond hair back off his forehead, he said "Aha" again.

"Man has always thought so. From the earliest times a race or a class or a group of men has deemed itself superior to all others. The Hebrew children of Biblical times called themselves the chosen people. The Greeks considered themselves the favored of the gods. Rome was the eternal city and the Romans the sons of light. Undoubtedly your own ancestors in Africa—until the European came along and taught them different," he threw in parenthetically, smirking—"thought that no magic was as strong as their black magic and no spirit as potent as their Obeah."

In the back of the room, Howden kept his head down and listened intently. The whole class listened.

"So the idea of race superiority is very old," Dr. Posey said, moving slowly back and forth before the class. His yellowish eyes glittered like mica. "It is very old and very important. It is as old as man himself, and it has been an agency—or shall I say *the* agency?—from which has originated a long chain of prodigious events. Indeed, it might be said that the idea of race superiority is the mother-force of man's advancement. Do I make myself clear?" He paused a moment, smiling archly.

"In what is our times, some of the most brilliant thinkers and writers, social theorists, anthropologists, and practicing sociologists are advocates of the notion of race superiority. Many of them—in fact, most of them—support their belief with the evidence of scientific investigation. What I am trying to make clear to you is that here we do not have mere emotionalism and demagoguery. These men are sober, sound, careful, and objective. Let us consider for a moment Arthur, Count de Gobineau—" He broke off abruptly and went to the blackboard. "I want you to take these names down, because I shall have reason to refer to them quite often in this unit of lectures."

The class, which had been following his every word without taking notes, now bent over their pads and scratched away.

"Gobineau left four important volumes," Dr. Posey went on. "These set forth the theories on race superiority which, in the main—in the main, mind you," he emphasized—"have been substantiated by scientific fact and which are followed today. And what are these theories?" His voice lightened, became almost sportive though no less deliberate, and his eyes skipped about unsmiling but amused.

"Gobineau says that, of all the races that people this happy globe, the white race is superior, and, of the white race, the Aryan branch is superior to all. The white race produces the thinkers, the civilization builders, the finders and the creators of the useful. Civilization was created and is continually re-created by the white race. Culture, in other words, is due to inborn racial factors. The purer the white blood, the higher the culture—and of course the converse is true. It's too bad you people can't read Gobineau in the original. There's not a really good translation."

Eyebrows raised waggishly, he stared intently at the class, then turned back to the blackboard.

"An Englishman, Houston Chamberlain, a French anthropologist, Lapouge," he went on writing rapidly, "and the German social thinkers, Fischer and Nicolai, to name only a few, are disciples of Gobineau. Chamberlain, who spent many years in Germany—he was the son-in-law of Richard Wagner; you've all heard of Wagner?—Chamberlain, going beyond Gobineau, who was satisfied merely to ascribe superiority to the whites, held

Jews and Niggras were the lowest in the scale of human families. According to his notion, Jews—who, by the way, constitute less an ethnic than a cultural group—Jews are mean-minded, avaricious, destructive, immoral, while Niggras, especially when caught in the ever-swelling flux of the white man's civilization, are amoral, parasitic, and asocial—that is, without a sense of society, without social consciousness. When a race is lacking in regard for the structure, the components, and the drift of the society, then it is asocial. Do I make myself clear?"

Dr. Posey paused again and pushed the lock of hair off his brow. His eyes jumped over the faces before him. The silence was heavy, had weight and mass, like a paper sack half full of water. Howden could feel it thudding against him. He was responding emotionally. The class sat immobile as stones.

"But, after all, we are dealing with the structure of American society, and it is more pertinent to discover what American social thinkers have concluded about these matters. You will remember that in the first unit of this course I pointed out to you a speech made by Abraham Lincoln at Peoria, Illinois, in 1854. That speech would not be important had Lincoln not summed up in it the thought that has controlled race relations in America ever since. You people must remember that Lincoln was an idealist and that it was he who, because of his idealism, which was a little distorted, shall we say?" He stopped pointedly, his mouth working at a smile of amused condescension, then went on deliberately, "It was he who made the reorganization of the American social structure necessary. But for all his altruism, in that Peoria speech Lincoln said that his own feelings would not admit of the political and social equality of the Niggra.

"What I am trying to make you see"—he was beginning to hurry now, but in a deliberate kind of way, for the hour was nearly up—"is that entirely independently of European thinking, we in America have come to some conclusions of our own, and with more reason. American social theorists have lived with the Niggra question. They have observed it at first hand. Two of these, Madison Grant and Lothrop Stoddard, are going to claim our particular attention.

"So that none of you will have any excuse for failing to do the reading, I have added personal copies of these men's works to those already in the library. You will find that from the basis provided by the general thesis of Gobineau, the more specific studies of Chamberlain, and the anthropological theories derived from Lapouge's work with cephalic indexes—or do you prefer indices?—these men have made a distinct contribution to our social thinking. And they are not just moldy thinkers. They are not remote foreigners. Only seven years ago Stoddard's *The Rising Tide of Color* was published, and only five years ago his *Revolt Against Civilization*. Madison Grant brought out the fourth revised edition of *The Passing of the Great Race* since most of you people came here as freshmen."

He was striding up and down in front of the class now, speaking quickly but without losing the inflectional nuances, the facial expressions, and the gestures that were a kind of emphatic overtone, even a kind of speaking of their own.

"I just have time to mention today the two theories of race inferiority that bear upon the Niggra problem in America. First there is that one which holds that the Niggra's status here has been produced by his innate inferiority. The segregation under which he lives, the political, economic, and social discriminations which are his lot are results, not causes. Those who hold this view adduce evidence that cannot be overlooked. They cite the Niggra's various attempts—all failures—to colonize, and his lack of organizational ability, which is requisite in the development of a political body. They mention the all-Niggra communities which have never succeeded in becoming the co-operately structured towns they set out to be. They mention Liberia. Until Niggras prove that they can govern themselves and produce at least a nominal level of culture, then, the holders of this theory say, what else is there to believe but that their condition is the result of innate inferiority?" He spread his hands; his eyebrows went up. Smiling, he held the pose for a moment.

"The second theory is that, though the Niggra is inferior, he is not innately so, and that therefore his inferiority can be overcome because it is an environmental imposition. But as Ammon, a German anthropologist, points out—what of Africa? What of Brazil, which has no racial prejudice? Why is it that in Brazil not a single Niggra holds a high place in the economic, the political, or the social life of the country? Why—?"

The electric bell tinkled feebly, and Dr. Posey cut himself off at once. The class stirred. There was a ripple of indefinite sound and then silence. Smiling with amused inquisitiveness, Dr. Posey looked at the class for a moment. The silence held until someone near the center of the room snapped his notebook shut with a sound as of the report of a pistol. Books snapped emphatically shut all over the room. The instructor's amused, sardonic glance followed the sounds until they stopped. Then, by way of dismissal, he turned crisply and walked to a window where he stood with his back on the room. Whispering sibilantly, heels clicking angrily loud against the floor, the class filed out. Howden closed his notebook quietly.

Twice a week for six weeks Dr. Hubert Posey explored the Negro's place in the structure of American society. He did it with sardonic deftness, with cynical, clinical thoroughness. No one interrupted him, no one asked a question, but he knew that he was getting a response, and the resentment and hatred he felt in the taut-eyed muteness of the class made no difference to him. When some members of the class dropped out, quite willing to take a failure, Dr. Posey's eyes simply grew more amused but harder, his voice more deliberate but colder, his waggishness more whimsical but more sharply pointed.

Though Shelton Howden sat through lecture after lecture, feeling his selfhood to be no proof against those drumming words, feeling that he was hearing the indisputable artillery of scientific truth, it was not until he got into the reading that his responses were fully aroused. Alone in his room, the light slanting across his worried, yellow face and the pages of his book, he felt that the marshaled lines of type had a direct personal application. His mind worked slowly and painfully at thought. Negroness was a fundamental condition of being which—and here he turned it into a question—nothing could overcome? He felt impotent. He tried to find a loophole through which his self, his ego could escape.

"Thus the view," he read in Madison Grant, "that the Negro slave was an unfortunate cousin of the white man, deeply tanned by the tropic sun and denied the blessings of Christianity and civilization, played no small part with the sentimentalists of the Civil War period and it has taken us fifty years to learn that speaking English, wearing good clothes and going to school and church do not transform a Negro into . . ."

Education, the acquisition of the accepted symbols of advancement, Howden reflected gropingly, the adoption of certain patterns of living, of certain attitudes, habits, and inclinations—did these mean nothing? Or were they, as Madison Grant declared, merely imitative accretions? And was there something deeper, some X quantity in the Negro mind and spirit and blood—in him himself—that could never be transmuted, that made him eternally different? In the natural crises of life, did the Negro react with a difference? In love, did he not take joy, and in death, sorrow? Didn't he hate and have ambition, and hope and despair, and exult in triumph and brood in defeat, the same as other men?

"The practically universal assumption is that the Negro cannot be made equal. . . ." Howden could hear the words. He could see the amused, expectant lift of Dr. Posey's brow. But these were words in a book, and he read on. ". . . The result of the mixture of the two races, in the long run, gives us a race reverting to the more ancient, generalized type. . . ." He moved restively and stared at the book, but he was no longer reading. He was trying to discover where it all left him. His grim struggle with abstract thought had given him a headache.

But it was all there, he told himself, set down by men who knew more than he did. They were supported by footnotes and by cross references to other authorities. If there were contradicting authorities (Dr. Posey had never mentioned any), Howden did not know them. It never occurred to him that the books he was reading and the lectures he had heard might be the scholarship of prejudice, the rationalizations of fallible men whose conclusions were questionable. Against the testimony of these scholars he had only subjective experience to offer, and subjective experience seemed to support the scholars. The whole climate and weather of the world were on their side. All Howden knew, all he had seen, felt, heard, read supported them.

Yet there were those Negroes who looked and acted white. There was Professor Clarkson. At New Hope there were many students who, seen in another place, would be altogether indistinguishable from whites. Howden wished he were as white as they. He wished— Getting up suddenly, Howden went to the cracked mirror over the washstand and examined his reflection carefully. His tawny hair had a crisp, loose curl; his lips were full almost to thickness; his skin had as much red as yellow in it. Howden stared at himself for a long time.

[5]

When he left Dr. Posey's class late one afternoon, Howden was struck by an impulse to talk to someone. He saw his classmates straggling off across the campus in all directions. There was not one of them to whom he could talk; they were almost complete strangers to him. Going down the little-used back path that he always took to his room, he thought of Professor Clarkson. He turned impulsively, giving himself no time to reconsider, and went back to the center of the campus. A moment later Professor Clarkson was greeting him with mild and friendly graciousness.

"Come in. Come in and sit down," Professor Clarkson said. His smile was always a little wan, and everything about him seemed remote, tenuous, and abstracted. But on visits to the professor's house, Howden had learned that beneath the ghostly exterior lay gentle kindness.

"Worrying about your marks?" Professor Clarkson asked.

"Well, yes, sir—a little," Howden answered. It was not for this reason that he had come, but he could think of no way to lead up to the thing that was on his mind.

"You have a good, solid record," Professor Clarkson said. His voice was soft, but he never used contractions, and his speech sounded stiff and affected. "I like good records." He smiled. "You plan to teach?"

"I'd like to study medicine," replied Howden.

"Hmmmm," Professor Clarkson murmured. "Everybody wants to study medicine, it seems. Nobody wants to teach or preach any more." The thought seemed to distract him. Biting at the patch of hair beneath his lower lip, he turned and looked absently out of the window. A dribble of watery sun came into the room, trickled across the desk, and fell with a gentle glitter on Professor Clarkson's gold cross watch charm. "No one thinks about teaching any more. Ah, Howden, a really fine profession is going to pot because the old enthusiasm is dying."

Howden tried to look interested, but he felt impatient. He hadn't come for a lecture. Professor Clarkson looked out of the window for several seconds longer.

"How old are you, Howden—twenty-four?"

Howden nodded, flushing slowly. He was ashamed of his age. He did not like being older than his classmates.

"You will have to work before you can go to medical school." It was a question without a question mark. He hesitated. His pale face looked mildly distressed, and then he went on apologetically, "I do not know any of the educational foundations that offer scholarships for medical study. If you have to work two or three years after college—" Smiling diffidently, he left it there.

Howden had not thought of the factor of his age in this way

before. He would be twenty-seven, perhaps twenty-eight before
he could enter medical school. He resented having it brought
to his attention. He felt old, suddenly discouraged.

"If you were going into teaching, it would be different," Professor Clarkson said.

Howden answered nothing. For two years now the study of
medicine had been the height of his ambition. The doctors he
had seen, themselves alumni and the fathers of students, come
back to commencement always seemed prosperous, assured. They
had the shiniest cars, the prettiest wives. He wasn't going to give
up now, Howden told himself. He'd study medicine if it took
ten years. He'd show them. He'd—

The professor's pale voice broke in on Howden's thoughts.
"But you must understand, I am not trying to dissuade you. I am
not trying—" He laughed a thin, tinkling, apologetic laugh.
"Well—? Because of course you did not come to talk with me
about that." Then his face was like a clean sheet of paper, blank,
empty.

Howden stirred. His thoughts had been sidetracked, and he
did not seem able to switch them back again. Yet to sit here saying nothing would make him look like a fool. This apprehension
made him wonder what sort of picture of him Professor Clarkson
had in his mind. Professor Clarkson, who was practically white,
who indeed could not be distinguished from a white man—did he
think like a white man too? Did he think that Negroes were inferior? Howden's thoughts churned uneasily in the silence until
the silence itself oppressed him.

"I'm taking that terminal course under Dr. Posey," he broke
out impulsively.

Professor Clarkson's pale eyes flickered alertly, and his arm,
which had been relaxed on his desk, seemed to stiffen.

"All that stuff," Howden said. "Those books by Nearing and
Grant and men like that." He stopped and tried to bring his
thoughts under some kind of control. "Is all that true? I mean—
is it true?"

Professor Clarkson's face had gone as immobile as the face of a statue. He turned his head and looked fixedly out of the window. Glancing across at him, Howden could see a pulse fluttering rapidly in the professor's pale temple.

"It is only true—" Professor Clarkson said at last in a dry voice, "it is only true if you believe it."

"But what else is there to believe? Professor Clarkson, I want to be somebody, and that stuff—" He stopped again, feeling utterly frustrated. There was no use trying to put it into words. There were a lot of things that could not be put into words. Howden looked down at his cracked shoes, his threadbare trousers ends.

"You are somebody," Professor Clarkson said, turning from the window and looking past Howden off into space.

Howden checked a fresh impulse to speak. He remembered reading in Scott Nearing that one of the characteristics of Negroes was their lack of emotional control. It was better to keep quiet. Through the window he saw a couple standing in a spot of sun. Then he saw a lone girl hurrying, and then a fellow. Scattered across the campus were the brown shrubs, the naked bushes, and the gray-green-leafed trees of winter. Nothing out there seemed to have any depth or roundness. A dimension was missing, as in shadows thrown on a screen.

Howden shook his head. He made another effort to express himself.

"Professor Clarkson, all I want— I don't know how to say it. I don't know, sir, but I came here thinking that if I could get an education— I wasn't thinking about race. I wanted to be somebody. I wanted to be somebody myself, for myself. I wanted— But now this course."

He realized that he was not saying it. He did not know whether Professor Clarkson understood him or not. He did not look at Professor Clarkson; he simply plunged on.

"Before I went into it, I guess I'd always thought— I guess I hadn't thought, not consciously anyway, you know, that colored were just naturally inferior to— I don't think I thought that. And yet, you know, maybe I did—you know, think—but I thought that if I got a chance—"

He stopped in miserable confusion, convinced that he was making a fool of himself, convinced of it the more the longer the silence lasted; and the silence seemed to last a long while indeed. Then, as if from far off, he heard Professor Clarkson's voice.

"You must not let yourself get upset." It was a gentle rebuke, and the professor's ghostly smile appeared for a second. "Anger and bitterness are not for such as you. The day you came here, the moment you registered as a freshman, you renounced the luxury of futile anger."

"But—" Howden began.

Professor Clarkson went on with a mild sort of eagerness now. "Do you remember that young man who raised an argument with Dr. Posey? Anger did him no good. He is out of college. He will have a hard time getting admission to another one. Whatever ambition, whatever hope, whatever talent he has may be destroyed by his anger."

"But, sir, it's not anger I feel," Howden said. "It's—it's something else. Have you read any of those books, sir?"

Professor Clarkson held up his thin white hands. "No, I have not read them. I never put myself in the position of being embarrassed by opinions I cannot credit," he said with surprising pomposity.

"You mean you don't believe that Nearing and Stoddard and Grant know what they're talking about?" Howden asked eagerly, hopefully.

Professor Clarkson's smile came out again, but he did not answer the question.

"You know, my boy, it has been twenty years since I have discussed the so-called race problem with anyone. It is possible to live without it, you know. There is a middle ground, a dead center, a place where the outrage and indignity cannot reach

you." He paused and smiled faintly. "I think I have found it.
I think—" He left the rest in silence.

After a moment, Howden got up. He felt calmer, better. He
did not try to appraise this feeling nor to discover where it came
from. He did not know whether it stemmed from something
Professor Clarkson had said or whether his own effort to express
himself had been a kind of purge. There was just one more question he wanted to ask.

"Do you think that it's possible to forget it, sir?"

Professor Clarkson looked far away and scratched at the triangle of hair beneath his lip. "My boy," he said, "it is possible to
ignore it."

Then his smile came really alive. It lighted up the lines and
hollows in his ascetic-looking face. He rose.

"Why not come to see us on Sunday? We are three somewhat
lonely old people."

"Thank you, sir," Howden said.

"But promise me this—" and his soft, thin laughter issued
forth nervously. "Promise me that we will not bring up the race
question. It is a nuisance."

CHAPTER FOUR

IN THE final semester of his senior year Shelton Howden made
his first acquaintance with a girl. She was assigned to the
other space at his two-space bench in the anatomy laboratory, which was at one end of the general biology lab. She came
in that first afternoon, spilled her notebooks and a case of instruments on her end of the bench, and spoke to Howden briefly,
positively. "Hello," she said. Her forehead puckering, she looked

around at the freshmen who were swarming noisily about the tables in the rest of the long room. Still frowning, she looked back at Howden.

"Prof Stone ought to have another lab assistant," she said.

Howden was not prepared for her or for anyone like her. He knew who she was—her name was Valrie Tillet—for she was one of those persons whom everyone knew. Her name was signed to notices on the women's bulletin board. Two years ago she had organized the Women's Senate. She was high on the dean's list. She was on the president's roll of honor.

"It would be better if they put up a partition," she said thoughtfully.

"Yes," Howden said, but he did not look at her. He only knew that she was tall for a girl and that her presence seemed to magnetize the air.

"Those greenies are noisy like nobody's business," she said.

Nothing else passed between them for several days. She would come into the lab, speak positively to Howden, perch herself on her stool, and go busily to work. She worked with absolute absorption, without a single disturbing thought for the circumstance that she was the only woman among seven men in anatomy.

One of the students, a pre-medic named Brown, who seemed to fancy himself a good deal, frequently left his bench to come across and talk to her. His yellow face was spotted with a mild acne, and he wore his crimpy hair too long and too glossy with oil, and Howden wondered what Valrie Tillet saw in him; but they seemed to be great friends. With his back on Howden, Brown would lean nonchalantly against the bench and talk to Valrie about vertebrate and invertebrate structure, carnivora, and all the order of mammals. He was supposed to be very clever, very funny. Howden did not see anything erudite in Brown nor anything funny nor anything the least attractive. But Brown was able to make Valrie Tillet laugh, and she always listened to him, it seemed to Howden, with as much attentiveness as to Professor Stone himself.

Howden himself could not initiate a conversation with her. Except when someone interrupted her, she gave herself so completely to her studies that sometimes she did not move during the two-hour lab period. Stealing veiled glances from time to time, Howden put her all together gradually: her color, which was like pale gold; her thick, dark hair; her lithe, long-legged body.

One day in February, when they had been working side by side for almost a month, she looked up suddenly, put down the tweezers with which she had just manipulated into place the tiny bones to complete the mounting of a bird's skeleton, and rubbed her hands slowly down the front of her green smock. The upper section of the room was murmurous with the subdued voices of students in general biology. The lights were on over all the tables, for it was a gray, rainy day with much wind. The wind blew gusts of rain against the long windows. Outside Howden could see the naked, splay-limbed mimosa trees and the ragged cedars jerking frantically in the wind.

"What a day," Valrie Tillet said, and Howden heard her sigh. She was staring out of one of the windows. Her end of the bench was messy with a glue pot, torn bits of paper, and leaves from her loose-leafed manual. Her instruments lay scattered about. Howden envied her those instruments, which were not the cheap tin kind you bought for a dollar and a quarter, but fine-edged, tempered steel scalpels and tweezers and knives that fitted into a velour-lined leather case. Valrie Tillet sighed again and straightened up on her stool and began putting things in order.

"Are you ready for the cat yet?"

There was no mistaking that she was addressing him. She was looking at him directly, a small frown of inquiry wrinkling the flesh between her eyebrows. She had a large, firm, full-lipped mouth.

"Oh!" Howden said. "The cat? I'm almost ready."

"Well, I'm ready now," Valrie Tillet said, "but I'm not going to tell Professor Stone yet a while. Do you like the rain?"

"As long as I'm inside," Howden said, regretting his smartness instantly. Then he tried to laugh. There was a silence during which Valrie Tillet looked from him to the nearest window and back again.

"What are you doing, labeling?" She had not adopted the mannered speech of most New Hope students. Howden had noticed that she did not even use the customary "sir" when she spoke to Professor Stone. She had a tendency to slur her words too. Howden decided that he liked the way she talked. He liked her voice. He liked her mouth.

"You're ahead of me, I guess." He had the fragile bones of his bird laid out on the mounting board.

"You're probably more careful than I am," Valrie Tillet said. She leaned across to look, and Howden scrambled up quickly. Her thick, dark, vital-looking hair was parted in the middle, with a coiled bun of it over each ear. Where the hair was parted, Howden could see the clean, creamy line of her scalp.

"Oh, no," Howden replied. He could see that her mounting was perfect, a work of art. "I guess I'm pretty clumsy."

"How did you do on your drawings?"

"I'm not much good with that kind of thing."

Frowning, Valrie Tillet straightened up and looked at him.

"You mustn't low-rate yourself so much," she said shortly, almost angrily.

He wanted to tell her that she did that to him, that she made him low-rate himself, made him modest.

For several minutes, making her bench tidy, she said nothing. Howden decided that she was not beautiful. There was no general term with which to describe her inverted-triangle face and her grave brown eyes and the firm, clean-lined curves of her body. But there was something about her—a bloom, a glow.

"Are you through with the labels now?" she asked after a while.

"There're still quite a few." He looked down at the little gummed slips on which he was printing the names of the bones to be pasted in the appropriate places around the skeleton.

"Here. I'll help you," Valrie Tillet said, reaching for some of the labels. She paused and looked at him. "It won't matter if there're two different scripts on them?"

"I guess not. Only—" He stopped.

"Only what?"

"I was getting them fixed in my mind as I went along."

"Oh," she said. "I see."

She sat back on her stool. Dragging her anatomy text out of the drawer, she opened it, cocked an elbow on each side of it, put her head against the heels of her hands, and started reading. In a moment she was utterly absorbed. Her fingers dug gently into her scalp as she read.

Howden told himself that his social awkwardness had rebuffed her. A little attention from a girl at New Hope was one of the things he had always wanted, and now when it had been offered him, he had refused it. He went on working at his labels, trying to forget that she was there. He could not reopen a conversation with her. Besides, she was concentrating on her book. He thought of Clarence Brown, who never seemed to care what she was doing if he wanted to come over and say something to her. Howden wondered whether he would have been like Brown had he had Brown's breaks. Would he have been as assertive and as easy in his manner had he had an opportunity to enter college at the usual age, had he had parents who could afford to give him things so that he would not lack for clothes and could belong to one of the college clubs? He could never be like Brown. He could never go up to Valrie Tillet and say, "For crying out loud, you look gorgeous today! Whose wedding, yours?" and lean against her bench and make her laugh.

He heard Valrie put her book away, and he was aware of her motions as she took off her smock. Then he heard her voice.

"I'm not too bright today," she said. "I've got the willies, and I'm going to slip off."

But she did not slip off. Howden saw her go to the clothes rack against the wall, put on her coat, take out her umbrella. Some other members of the class said something to her, and then she walked straight back to Professor Stone's office, and Howden wondered if she were saying, "I'm not too bright today—"

When she went through the swing doors into the hall, the lab seemed suddenly empty.

[2]

It was after this that Howden began to see Valrie Tillet every time he crossed the campus. Approaching or leaving the library, he would see her, or passing the college store, he would see her sitting there with all the other students who had money to spend on sandwiches and sodas and ice cream between meals. He frequently found himself close enough to touch her, though of course he never did. He could recognize her walk, which was neither a loose and careless walk nor a studied, self-conscious one, but somewhere in between—a graceful, gently swinging motion that seemed to have some connection with the pit of his stomach. He could recognize the straight set of her shoulders too, at a distance.

Even before he saw her—and he always saw her—he could sense her presence in a group. He told himself that he was simply aware of her as a person now, whereas formerly she had been just a name to him. It was the working out of one of those principles of perception which he had learned in elementary psychology. Nevertheless he began to feel that there was something fated in these chance glimpses. He told himself that he never consciously tried to see Valrie Tillet—indeed, he tried not to see her—but some inscrutable fate had taken a hand. Sensing her presence as he approached a group, if he could not turn aside altogether, then he dropped his head lower than usual and increased his pace as he hurried by. But invariably she saw him and would call out "Hello," and it seemed that everyone would stop to look at him, and he would feel acutely self-conscious of his clothes, his walk, and the way he carried his books.

One day she asked him why he always rushed by like that, and he told her that he was not aware that he rushed by, but he guessed it was just habit. She smiled her disbelief, and Howden flushed. It was near the close of the period, all through which Valrie had concentrated on drawing the abdominal cavity of the cat. She had scarcely looked up at all. Now, with her feet hooked around the forward uprights of her stool, she sat up straight and her face relaxed. Her hair had come loose from the knot at the nape of her neck, and she lifted her arms and took out the hairpins, holding them between her teeth. A heavy coil of hair dropped down her back.

"Are you always in a hurry?" she asked, her lips very mobile over the hairpins. "Are you always rushing somewhere to put out a fire?"

"No," Howden said, and he tried to laugh. Her neck was bent a little forward because she was pinning up her hair, but he could see her frank gaze upon him.

"You always seem to be. Every time I see you, you're in a tear." She took another of the thick bone pins from between her teeth.

"I guess I just have things to do," Howden said. Then one of those strange impulses seized him, and he added, "I'm a work student." He was glad that her expression did not change.

"What've you got to do now? This is the last class hour today. What are you rushing for now?"

"I didn't know I was rushing," he said.

"You just go wringing and twisting and tearing through life, don't you? What are you trying to catch up with?"

Her words made him acutely aware that she had formed an image of him in her mind, and other people must have images too. Somehow it made him want to hide himself from her.

"I guess it's just habit," he said dourly.

"Well, it seems to me it would make you miss a lot."

He did not know why she said that or what her smile meant, or whether it meant anything. The trouble was that he was always expecting double meanings and innuendoes. He looked at her with quick suspicion.

"How do you mean?"

"For instance—" She paused while she put the last pin in her hair and pressed the knot firm. "I never see you with anyone. I don't mean any particular person. But I never see you with anyone at all. Why is that? Don't you like people? Don't you like friends?"

"Miss Tillet—" Howden began, but Miss Tillet interrupted him. She threw up her hand and jerked it down impatiently. Howden had a sense of her imperiousness but of her warm friendliness too.

"Oh, for crying out loud! My name's Valrie." She looked at him steadily for a moment, and then a smile came to her eyes. Rising, she slipped off her smock and folded it, stooped, and threw it in the locker where her case of instruments and her own personal microscope were.

There was a lot of talk about college "flappers" and "jazz babies" and flaming youth, but Valrie Tillet did not fit Howden's conception of them. Though her clothes were obviously of excellent quality, Valrie never dressed to kill in high heels and spangled, frilly things. She did not have bobbed hair or bold come-hither eyes. When she stooped to put her smock away, he could see that her stockings were not rolled below her knees either.

"But what were you going to say?"

"Sometimes I go over to Professor Clarkson's," Howden answered.

She looked a little surprised and a little merry. "You do?"

The question sounded mocking, and he could not find the answer which he felt it deserved. He wanted something sharp to put Valrie Tillet in her place.

"I like him," said Howden, though the thought of liking Professor Clarkson had never crossed his mind before. He said it defensively. "I like all the Clarksons."

"I should hope so," she said. "Why else would you go?" Her brow puckered, and then she shook herself. "But suppose you wait for me now. I won't be a minute."

Howden felt ill at ease as he followed her across the laboratory. He was glad that everyone except Professor Stone had gone. Going down the stairs, Howden tried to think of something to say that would be casual and interesting. He wondered what Clarence Brown would have said. He did not want her to regret having asked him to wait. Suppose, he thought, they should run into a group of her friends. What would he do then? Would he slink off, or stand like a dummy, or would he find something to say? Bracing his shoulder against the heavy door, he let her out.

He did not know how to say good-by at the moment when it would have seemed natural and appropriate. As they started in the direction of her dormitory, Valrie said that the air was beginning to get the salty, fishy odor that always meant spring. Had he ever noticed it? But Howden scarcely heard her. He was conscious of the fixity of his stare, the ramrod rigidity of his neck and shoulders. Cursing himself for a fool, he tried to relax, telling himself that after all Valrie was just another girl. He had never been nearer to either of the women's buildings than the paths that bordered them, and now he found himself going straight toward one. Forbidding and hostile it looked to him. He imagined that there were whisperings and peerings from behind those frilly curtains. He imagined that students coming out of Christian Hall and Freedman Hall were watching with amused, mocking, quizzical eyes as he walked across the campus with Valrie Tillet. He imagined that for the general amusement she was leading him into a trap. It made him wonder how he had got there. It made him wish he were some place else. They came to a junction of paths.

"Miss— I've got to leave you here. I—"

She stopped dead still and looked at him. Then her shoulders lifted and her mouth tightened and her eyes blazed up, whether with surprise or anger he could not tell. "Oh, all right. Good-by," she said and walked swiftly away from him.

CHAPTER FIVE

FOR THE next several days Howden saw Valrie only in anatomy lab, where she seemed formal and withdrawn. He wanted to talk to her, but he found no way to do this, for her mere civility put a great distance between them. At one moment he wished he had some way to humiliate her, and at another he told himself that she was concentrating very hard, that, in fact, they both were, now that they were working on the cat.

But in other classes things were not as they had been either. His mind continually wandered from the subject and got lost in foggy dreams. Miss Bonaphon's course in European history did not interest him any more. Dr. Posey's lectures on the structure of American society grew pretty meaningless to Howden, and he did the assigned reading perfunctorily. What significance did all the hypotheses, deductions, and concepts of race have when he was face to face with a personal fact, an emotional truth that had nothing to do with race? Neither Stoddard nor Chamberlain nor anyone else could make him believe that what he was experiencing was grotesque and somewhat laughable because he was a Negro. What did it matter what Dowd said about the race in general when he was only Shelton Howden, a person, a self, representing no one but himself—and that self in love, and that self jealous!

Howden did not know when he began to realize that he was jealous of Valrie Tillet. He was jealous of her sorority sisters and of those who looked like they might be her sorority sisters. He was jealous of the deep absorption in which she probed among the formaldehyde-stinking entrails of her dead cat and of the colored inks with which she did her scientific drawings. Whenever Clarence Brown crossed the room to have a word with her, Howden filled with misery, flamed with jealous hate. What could she see in that woods colt! There were stories about instructors at New Hope—white Christian missionaries though they were—having more than professorial relations with comely female students, and all these came to Howden's mind. The groups Valrie was a member of, the activities in which she engaged seemed like so many unjustifiable interests whose sole, willful purpose was to interpose between him and her. His studies began to slip. At night, instead of being at them, he composed letters to Valrie. Some were bittersweet with melancholy, some cynical and abusive, some abjectly pleading—all were hot with love. He destroyed them as he wrote them.

In the lab he tried to conduct himself with resolute yet casual aplomb, but he knew it did not go off very well. He felt that Valrie was secretly laughing at him, and his mind raged against her. Her politeness was too polite, it seemed to him, of the kind bestowed upon a stranger. He tried to concentrate on his work as she did on hers; but this did not work either.

One day, in desperation, he addressed her.

"Miss Tillet," he said. His throat was as dry as straw. He swallowed hard.

Instantly her head came up. She had lately started wearing glasses in the lab, heavy, tortoise-shell affairs, and she snatched these off and looked at him, peering a little.

"Yes, what is it?"

"Will you walk down to the gate with me after lab?" He could not tell whether it was a smile, but a flicker of something shot up in her eyes.

"You won't embarrass me again by leaving me in the middle of the campus? Is that what you want to do?"

"No. I—I—" He shook his head dumbly, while she looked at him for a moment more.

"All right," she said. Then, putting on her glasses, she went back to drawing the kidney of the cat that was spread out on the rubber sheet before her.

It was not far to the gate. Between it and the library there was a strip of lawn facing the road to the village. At one end of the lawn a line of silver poplars separated the campus from the farmland, and across the campus walk, which divided the lawn, stood the monumental shaft above old Jubal Hooker's grave.

"Well, here we are," Valrie said when they reached the gate, and she gave him an inquiring glance.

"Yes, that's so," Howden said. He looked up and down the dusty road. He saw Professor Clarkson's house across the road and behind that a patch of woods.

"But doesn't it look kind of dumb just to stand here?" Valrie said. "We can at least walk up to those trees and back. Or are you getting the feeling that you must leave me now?"

"Oh, no," Howden said. He did not know how to follow this up, though he thought that she expected something, some explanation or apology. They were silent until they reached the line of poplars and started back toward old Hooker's grave. He could feel her looking at him, studying him.

"You're a strange person," Valrie Tillet said at last.

Perturbed and curious, he shot a glance at her. It was never possible to see oneself as others saw one, and at the same time it was never possible for others to know what you were really like. No one could know your exact thoughts and feelings, even when you made an honest effort to express them.

"I've known some strange people, but I've never known anyone like you," Valrie said. "Why are you always so silent?"

"I'm not always silent," Howden replied. "I talk."

"To whom, yourself?"

He looked at her again. She had been frowning in a puzzled way, but now her mood must have changed, for she laughed.

"Or do you save it up for someone special?"

"Someone special?"

"Yes."

"I don't know what—"

"Oh, you don't know?" Valrie said and laughed again.

He was anxious to get on with her, anxious to understand her. She must have seen that he was taking her teasing seriously.

"Never mind," she said. Then, gravely, a moment later, "But you ought to talk more."

He was thinking of Clarence Brown and Dock Traynor, who never had any trouble finding things to say, and wishing he were like them.

"Well, I'll talk to you. Maybe that will help. Do you think so?" Valrie asked quite seriously.

"I don't know." He felt inadequate. He felt a fool. Was she just teasing him, "showing out" as the expression had it? And would she later laugh and tell her friends what a poke he was?

But after a while Valrie Tillet did talk, lightly at first—though not inconsequentially—about herself and then, with increasing seriousness, about her family, her plans.

Howden forgot his suspicions. Her words caught him up and transported him to a world much larger and brighter than any he had ever known. That his imagination might be filling in the background never occurred to him. He had no idea that over the libretto of her words he was playing a romantic obligato.

She had one of those families, Valrie Tillet said, that would be a drag on her if she let it. Howden did not know what she meant by this, especially since it was obvious that her family, or someone, provided for her handsomely. Then she said that she was going to study medicine but that her father was trying to discourage her because he wanted her to go into his undertaking

business. It sounded mean, unreasonable, ridiculous of her father.
Howden could see him, a domineering, spiteful, crusty old fool,
issuing threats and denouncements. Valrie said that she didn't
want one of those signs that said "Female Attendant" on undertaking parlors to mean her.

"I want to be a physician and bring living things into this
world, instead of taking dead things out," she said, turning toward
Howden defiantly. "And of course that's what I'm going to be."

"But your father?" Howden said.

"Oh, he's all right," Valrie said, destroying the ogre in Howden's mind.

The assurance with which she faced life made Howden sad and
self-pitying. She had the stable background of parentage and
security and education which he associated with the normal advantages of being white, and it was entirely outside his experience. No threat to her were the things that harried him. She did
not have to play a wary, defensive game against want and indignity and fear. A phrase of her own came back into his mind.
She did not have "to wring and twist and tear her way through
life." She talked about her family, and about Cleveland, Ohio,
where she lived, and about a place called Idlewild, up in Michigan, where they had a summer cottage. She mentioned motor
trips into Canada, visits to friends, and people she had met in
Chicago, New York, San Francisco. To Howden it all sounded
very privileged and carefree. None of it had any point of reference to the things he had known.

"Do you have any brothers or sisters?" Valrie wanted to know.

"No," he told her, looking away. All at once he was thinking
of the orphanage, and he had not really thought of it for a long
time.

"No brothers or sisters?"

It was all back again, and he tried to shut his mind against it
because there was nothing there that he wanted to remember.

"No, I told you," he answered gruffly.

"You don't have to be so abrupt," Valrie said.

"I was thinking."

"Thinking what?"

"You wouldn't be interested," he said morosely. Suddenly he felt a kind of anger against her. As he walked beside her, he felt angry and jealous and cheated of all the things she had, of all the things she could do. "I'm not Clarence Brown. You wouldn't be interested in what I was thinking," he said.

Valrie stopped and looked at him with smoldering eyes.

"What kind of a line is that? What are you talking about?" she demanded, leaning a little toward him. "If that's a joke, or even if it isn't, I don't like it. Clarence Brown's a friend of mine, but I don't want you adding two and two about him and me." She walked on again, striding angrily a pace or two ahead.

"I wasn't adding two and two," he said, disturbed, made miserable by her anger. "It's only that Clarence Brown knows how to talk to you."

"Do you think there's some special way you have to talk to me? Do you think you have to hand me some kind of line?"

He did not know what to answer. He felt like a fool, utterly defenseless. Valrie must have seen his misery in his face because when she spoke again, her voice was softer.

"All you have to do is talk to me like you'd talk to anyone else."

"I'm not like them. I'm—" and there he checked himself.

"What *them* are you talking about, Shelton?" Valrie asked, more puzzled now than piqued.

"All your friends," Howden said. "All the people I see you with and talking to you. I'm not like them," he repeated lamely.

"You're not supposed to be like them, Shelton. You're just supposed to be yourself," Valrie said gently. She was looking at him with a frank, puzzled gaze. Then she turned her head away and said very quietly, "But you're so strange—and I'm not good at strange things."

[2]

Howden was not good at strange things either, and that's what the days were now—strange and sometimes wonderful. There were days that swelled and swelled until it seemed that the world must surely burst. There were other days when the joy, ambition, hope drained out of him like liquid out of an upturned bottle.

He was troubled by a feeling of distance between Valrie and himself. When he was with her in the presence of others, he had the uneasy sensation of being out of place, of fishing in a stream where there was one of those prohibitive signs announcing penalties against it. What was worse, he thought that others felt the same way about him and that they looked upon him with a kind of surprised tolerance and condescension. In an effort to override and defy this and to keep his ego bolstered, he did things which he afterwards realized to be foolish and in bad taste. An unaccountable compulsion would seize him, and he would reach out in some gesture of possession which gave to anyone watching an entirely false impression of the degree and the kind of relations between him and Valrie. He would reach out and take the silver-clipped pencil from the collar of her blouse, or he would sometimes tuck in the strands of fine hair that escaped from the bun at the back of her neck. He wanted people to see these gestures. In anatomy lab, when Clarence Brown or Dock Traynor or Cliff Humbles stopped to chat with Valrie, Howden would break in with some jejune remark, overanimated and overemphasized, to let them know he was right there. A shadow sometimes passed over Valrie's face, but she never evinced any anger or impatience. She would turn to him with her direct, "What? What did you say, Shelton?" and draw him into the conversation. But to him the distance never seemed to lessen.

Once suddenly emerging into the center of the campus from behind Christian Hall, he saw Valrie standing with a group of her friends. Ordinarily he would have turned away or gone by with lowered head and hurried steps, but one of those compulsions, almost psychopathic in its intensity, mastered him. He called to her peremptorily. Valrie turned, threw up her hand in greeting, and turned back to her friends. He was angry. He wanted to humble her.

"Valrie," he called again, "I said I want to speak to you."

She swung around quite suddenly and sharply, her face gone stiff. Howden saw her friends look at him and then at her, and he felt that his will was caught up in combat against theirs and against Valrie's also. Valrie separated herself from the group and strode quickly toward him.

"What's the matter with you?" she demanded through clenched teeth, tight-drawn lips. Her eyes were dark and stormy. "Are you crazy?"

"I want to speak to you," Howden said.

"How dare you embarrass me like that! How dare you!" Her eyes filled with tears of anger and outrage.

"Valrie, I—"

"If you wanted to speak to me, all you had to do was come up quietly and say so. I'm no—no woman off Rampart Street, and don't you ever, ever forget it!" Giving him no time to answer, head high, shoulders stiff, she swept around and left him.

Howden wrote her that night, begging to be forgiven. But he did not see her the next day nor the next. Obviously avoiding him, she did not come to the lab. When he saw her on the fourth day, she looked at him coldly, spoke icily.

"I got your note," she said. But all at once her eyes blazed wrathfully. "What made you do it?"

"Valrie—please— Please, can't we take a walk?" he entreated wretchedly. "I can explain."

But when they took the walk, he did not really explain because he could not. Speech stumbled drunkenly from him. Valrie listened with lowered head, and he found it hard to talk against her cold silence. He pleaded; he defended himself. He was downcast, abject. He said he couldn't say it right, couldn't make her understand. He said that there was no use trying to put it into words,

but wouldn't she try to realize how he felt? His whole body
was a wretched plea. And after a while Valrie was somewhat mol-
lified.

But it was another week before she let him feel easy with her
again, before her constraint dissolved and she talked to him in the
old free way. His happiness returned. Less guarded with Valrie
than he had ever been with anyone, he tried to match her frank-
ness, but he could not achieve it. He feared self-exposure. He
feared making a fool of himself. Nevertheless he said some things
to her that he had no idea he would say. He told her about
his first reactions to Dr. Posey's course, which she had not
taken, and she said that from all she could understand it was
sheer poison, that course. Howden said that none of it seemed
to have much to do with him any longer, and Valrie told him
not to fool himself—the very fact that he mentioned it, she
said, proved that it had a lot to do with him. They talked about
it for quite a while.

Then he started to tell her something about the orphanage and
had the reward of her quick sympathy. But he suffered vague
misgivings and abruptly changed the subject. He suffered misgivings again when he told her what his plans were, that he was
taking a job on a railroad dining car because he thought that was
the quickest way to make enough money for medical school.
Valrie wanted to know how long he thought he'd have to work,
and he told her eighteen months, maybe two years. She said
nothing for a while, and then she told him please to be careful
and not get stuck in a rut. He wanted to know what made her say
that. He wouldn't get stuck in a rut, he assured her defiantly,
but he was disturbed. He thought resentfully of the ease with
which she could go on directly to medical school.

"Don't worry," he said. "That won't happen to me." She gave
him an optimistic smile, but then her forehead crinkled thoughtfully, and Howden could tell that her next remark was just a sort
of unrelated filler.

"My father's coming for commencement," she said.

"He is?"

But, preoccupied, Valrie kept a long silence. Then she was talking all at once in a quiet, admonitory tone. She said that she had met a lot of fellows who were going to work a little while to get money to study medicine or law or something, and they had got stuck in ruts. The Illinois Central Station in Chicago and the Grand Central Station in New York, Valrie said, were full of such fellows, and some of them had been there redcapping for years. There were all those men too who used to come into Idlewild, Michigan, on their days off from summer hotels in Mackinac. They still dressed like college boys, Valrie said, and they still wore their fraternity pins, and they knew a lot of people, and they made a sort of brazen game of life, but they were stuck too, running from place to place working in hotels, and now it was all they were good for or would ever do. She said that it was not the fact that they worked in hotels for a living, which itself was come-down enough for college-educated men, but it was the horrible thing the retreat from their ambitions had done to them. It had made them very hard and brittle outside, Valrie said, and very soft inside, like two-minute eggs. If you crack the shell, she said, everything runs out. Laying her hand on Howden's arm, she told him that she just wouldn't want a friend of hers to be like that.

"Don't worry," he told her again, not wishing to go on with it. "That won't happen to me."

But he himself brought it up again a few days later. It worried him that she had said it in the first place. It worried him that she could think that he would ever be like a two-minute egg. She had an entirely false picture of him, he told himself.

"Valrie," he asked, "do you think I'll retreat from my ambitions?"

"I hope not, Shelton," she answered.

It was not the unqualified and positive reply he wanted.

"But what made you say it in the first place?" he went on insistently.

"I don't know."

"Was it because you think I might get to be like—like a two-minute egg?"

"I just don't want it to happen to you, Shelton."

It was an unusual day for May. The sky seemed very high and thin; a stiff, cool breeze blew off the Gulf. They were walking in the old place. The lawn was deserted, for practically all of the seniors were busy decorating the dining hall for the Prelim, the last informal party of the college year. Valrie was on the committee of arrangements, but she said she had done enough without having to help make crepe paper streamers and fill penny balloons with air too.

She was having trouble with her skirt, which the wind kept whipping up, exposing the warm, pale gold flesh above her knees. Pressing her skirt down with both hands, she turned her back to the wind. "Shoot! This is silly," she said. "Can't we sit down? Do we have to walk?"

They crossed the campus path and sat down on the concrete curbing around the grassy mound of old Hooker's grave. Behind them the college buildings stood out sharply against the high, thin sky. There was a winy lightness in the air. Across the road they could see the tops of the pines behind Professor Clarkson's house swaying in the wind.

"What are you thinking about, Shelton?" Valrie asked after a time.

"Nothing," Howden said, but there were a lot of things on his mind. "The kind of day it is, the senior Prelim— Valrie, who's taking you to the Prelim?"

She swung around to face him. "Why, aren't you?" she asked incredulously.

It pleased him to have her say it like that, but it also touched up the melancholy he had felt all day. "Oh, no," he said, smiling ruefully.

"But why? I thought it was understood."

He had no idea that she would think any such thing, and his heart stepped up.

"But I can't."

"But why do you say you can't?"

"I can't."

"But why?" she persisted, an edge of exasperation in her voice.

"I just can't," said Howden unhappily. He didn't have white flannel trousers; he didn't have a decent blue coat. And even if he had them, he asked himself, what would he do after he got there —sit around like a bump on a log, watching all the others having a good time? He couldn't dance.

"That's a stupid sort of answer that doesn't answer anything," Valrie said shortly. Sighing, she turned away. "Well, if I'm going, I guess I'll have to find another escort."

Though he knew that was what she would have to do, having her say it made a difference. "That ought to be easy for you," he said bitterly.

She stiffened a little but said nothing. The bread truck from the city came down the road and turned in at the college gate, and Valrie's eyes followed it up the drive until it disappeared behind the refectory.

"Do you know what's the matter with you, Shelton?" She sat up a little straighter. "You're not all of a piece somehow, are you? Or maybe you are. Maybe it's just that you're not frank with me, or with anybody else." She turned to him and smiled in a way to let him know that she had no wish to hurt him, but her eyes were resolute. "I don't mind your not taking me to the Prelim, but don't you see you should have told me at least a week ago? It was a sort of untruth, your not telling me. You're full of little untruths like that, and contradictions. And really, I mean— it's because—"

"Did you learn all that in psych two-twelve?" Howden's voice cut in sarcastically. He did not know why he said it. He did not know why he should desire to hurt her. It was not the way he wanted things to be. Yet he could hear himself going on. "You're quite a psychologist, aren't you? After one course in psychology, you turn out to be a whiz-bang, jam-up mind reader?"

The shocked hurt went slowly out of Valrie's face. Then she gave a self-deprecating little laugh and jumped up quickly.

"I was only trying to understand you," she said in a tone that was light, almost gay. "I was only trying to help—" With a toss of her head, she started away.

"Valrie—" All at once he was engulfed in regret. "Valrie," he said again, springing up. He did not want her to go. He took her hand and brought her back to the curbing around the grave. "Please, please sit down again." Her grave eyes watched him as she sat slowly down.

"Valrie, I—it's—" Howden began, and then he threw out his hand in a gesture of hopelessness. "You can't put everything into words."

"You can try," Valrie said quietly. "What are you afraid of, Shelton? I just want to know."

He stared at the ground, but he could feel her watching him. The wind rippled the hem of her skirt, and she cupped her hands over her knees.

"I'm not afraid of anything," Howden said. "It's not that. If I were like Brown—"

"There you go. You see?" Valrie interposed quietly. "I just don't understand you, Shelton. Why should you want to be like Clarence Brown, or anyone else?"

"I didn't say I wanted to be like Clarence Brown. I was simply—"

"Don't let other people's personalities just happen to you."

It was an odd way of putting it, but he knew what she meant. Only of course she was wrong. She didn't understand him at all. If he had had Brown's background— But she couldn't understand that. She had parents, she had a home; she had security, like Brown. She represented something stable and safe, but she didn't understand.

Valrie sat quietly beside him, and when he looked at her, her eyes were still and very grave. Her pale gold, inverted-triangle face was somehow mobile even in its stillness. Over her temples the wind had loosed the hair and a wisp of it blew across her cheek. All at once Howden wanted to kneel and lay his head in her lap. Indeed, feeling a compulsion to do this, he stood up and walked a step or two away. He wanted to absorb her, to take her into himself. Impulsively he turned toward her.

"Valrie, I love you," he said.

She gave a slight start, and a shadow passed over her face, breaking its stillness, and hovered in her eyes.

"Oh, Shelton!" she said and looked away.

"I love you," he repeated thickly, coming closer, stooping before her.

"Shelton—"

"You don't— You don't care for me?" he asked, trying to make her look at him.

"Sometimes I think—" She paused then and brought her eyes back to him. "Sometimes I almost think I love you too."

"Oh, Valrie!"

"Get up, dear. You must get up," Valrie said and rose.

She said it as though that finished it, as if a curtain had dropped; and he stood without speaking. Then she sighed.

"Don't you think we'd better get back now?" she asked.

"Yes," he answered, "I guess so."

CHAPTER SIX

VALRIE's father did not look like an undertaker; he did not act like one. He was a big copper-colored man with a head, Howden noted with a kind of jaundiced satisfaction, as bald as a monkey's behind. Though he beamed benevolently and clapped Howden warmly on the shoulder with a hearty, "Well,

well, well," Mr. Tillet did not seem to have much time. Howden was first abashed and then resentful.

Mr. Tillet scudded and boomed and blazed all over the place. He knew, or quickly came to know, all the prominent alumni who had come back—and there were some big names among them. Within the flash of a smile and the pressure of a handclasp, Mr. Tillet was conspicuously identified with a small, select, and highly ebullient group of doctors, dentists, insurance managers, and their wives. Employing an irresistible mixture of cajolery and paternal authority the very evening of his arrival, he took Valrie off to New Orleans for a private dinner with a very special crowd and the sons and daughters of the special crowd.

Howden hated Mr. Tillet. He had never seen anyone like him or like the prominent alumni either. The very way they talked to one another galled him. They were entirely out of his world and of a freer, happier concourse of people he had never known. Watching Valrie move among them with a sedate young-girl ease, all his misgivings came to the surface. He told himself that he could not have her. She belonged to a world of comfort and security. She belonged to awninged houses on paved streets, to summer cottages in far-off Michigan, and to hopes that never were deferred. It was a world that was white in everything but color, and nearly white in that too.

That night Shelton Howden lay sleepless, trying to recall all that Valrie had ever said to him and all that he had ever said to her. He felt lonely, lost, betrayed.

Of course Mr. Tillet was at the president's reception for alumni, the graduating class, and their parents. Everyone knew he was there because after all, as he boomed jokingly to a Mr. Benswich, "it was no funeral." Though at the height of the festivities there must have been three hundred people crowded in the small auditorium, and caterer's assistants in white monkey jackets dodged about with trays of punch and ice cream, and there was a great babble even without one of the traveling New Hope quartets which kept breaking into song, Mr. Tillet was easy to see and to hear. He was always being introduced to someone or greeting someone he had not seen for half an hour. Once or twice he called to Valrie, calling her over whatever heads happened to be in the way, to have her meet some lately arrived but important alumnus. When President McKenna made a little speech from the platform, soliciting financial pledges from old and young graduates, Mr. Tillet pledged five hundred dollars in the name of his daughter Valrie. It was the largest single amount pledged, although I. M. Muldrow, whose Firmament Life Insurance Company had a Dun and Bradstreet rating, was right there.

"Your father's a high-powered man," Howden told Valrie sarcastically. That inexplicable desire to hurt her was back.

"What do you mean by that?"

"He knows everybody, all the big shots," he sneered. "Does he always go around signing five-hundred-dollar pledges—" he snapped his fingers—"like that?"

"Oh, Shelton—" Valrie said. Then she tossed her head, and her dark eyes narrowed. "I'm not going to answer you. I don't apologize for my father."

Howden was wretched. He was experiencing the old feeling of being at a disadvantage, of not belonging. Dumb misery in his eyes, he looked over the crowd. Everyone was talking and milling around and having a good time. He was the only lost one there. He saw Professor Clarkson, and then he saw Miss Sadie Clarkson. Up on the platform, the quartet—three fat black men and a lean yellow one, who had been melodiously soliciting funds for New Hope for twenty years—broke into a rollicking song. Everyone paused to watch and listen because the quartet was very funny in this song. They grinned and rolled their eyes and shook their shoulders, exactly as they must have done before the crowned heads of Europe and before hundreds of audiences in Rochester, Springfield, Providence, and Boston.

"Put on de skillet, put on de lid, 'cause mammy's goin'a . . ."

"Valrie," Howden said.

She turned to him slowly, frowning.

"Valrie, I'm sorry. It's—"

"Never mind. It's all right." She paused a moment. "But, oh, Shelton, what makes you like you are!" It was a little cry of exasperation, of tormented indulgence.

"Valrie," Howden whispered with difficulty, taking her arm, "I love you."

She pressed his arm lightly against her side.

"Love you, love you," he whispered, the same stopped-up feeling in his throat.

". . . Shortnin', shortnin', mammy's little babies wants . . ."

"But, Shelton—"

"I love you."

Her skin glowed pale gold, ivory rose-tinted, creamy fresh; her dark hair was lustrous; her lips dewy. All at once he wanted to get her out of here, away from all these people, alone.

"Valrie—Valrie, let's go sit on old Hooker. For the last time," he pleaded.

"All right," she said after a moment. "For the last time."

[2]

The night was warm, milky-clouded. A furtive, moisture-laden wind scratched in the cedars and snickered among the leaves of the magnolias. Arms linked, Howden and Valrie strolled along the path toward the gate. They could still hear the applause from the building behind them, but then the quartet must have gone into an encore, for suddenly all was quiet. Passing Science Hall, where the shadow made the darkness absolute, Howden had a desire to draw Valrie to him, to kiss her; but he checked it and merely pressed her arm a little tighter.

"We can't stay long," Valrie said.

Just as they reached the curbing around old Hooker's grave, the moon came out, grinned momentarily on the granite shaft, and slipped behind the curdy clouds again.

There was nothing to say, now that he was here. He felt disappointed and let-down. A curious sensation of injury and loss grew and diffused through him like a mortal pain. Valrie was leaving tomorrow, he thought. He could feel the firm, cool flesh of her arm against his hand, the light stuff of her skirt brushing his knee. Face softly luminous in the darkness, she sat poised and straight beside him. She was leaving tomorrow, but already she seemed far away and lost to him. He sighed deeply.

"What's the matter, Shelton?" she asked.

"Nothing," he said, but he sighed again.

"I think we'd better go back now." She made a move to get up. Restrained by his tightened hand, she sat down again, sitting erect as before but with something waiting, perhaps faintly wondering in her attitude.

"Suppose I don't let you go back," he said. He did not know why he said such an absurd thing.

Valrie laughed quietly. "Don't be ridiculous. We'll have to. They'll miss us. Come on." Still laughing, she tugged gently to free her arm.

"Kiss me first," he said almost roughly and felt her draw back a little. Then he clasped her and pressed his mouth against hers. One moment she was passive and the next patiently struggling to loose his hands.

"Please, please," she said, imploring softly as to a willful child at first. And then, "Please!" imperiously.

Scarcely knowing what he was doing, but feeling somehow a hot wave of love topping a black trough of frustration, feeling somehow that what he worshiped he longed madly now to degrade, Howden clasped her tighter. He forced her back onto the grassy mound. Lust and love galloped in him like a team of mismatched, red-eyed horses. If he heard her low, shocked cries of surprise, outrage, pain, he gave no sign. A wild desire for dominion seethed thickly in him. When he plunged his hand under her dress, she stopped resisting, and went spastic, frozen, like a dead thing under him. Then he realized what he had been about to do. He staggered up.

"I'm going to hate you!" he heard her anguished cry. "I'm going to hate you for doing this to me!"

He was aware of her tortured sobbing and then that she was running away. He saw her dimly as she reached the path, and he heard her running, stumbling footfalls grow faint and fainter.

[3]

Howden went through the commencement exercises the next morning under a gloomy cloud of foreboding. Valrie was not in the line of march; she was not at the program. Every movement, every stir behind him made him turn to search the rows of faces stretching to the doors. The final realization that she was not coming brought him close to panic. Unable to contain himself, he made cautious inquiry of the graduates sitting on his right and left, of those in front of and behind him. No one seemed to know. No one had seen Valrie or her father either since the night before. When Valrie's name was called, President McKenna said, "Conferred in absentia," and passed on to the next name on the list.

Howden went through it all feeling restive and anxious. He did not think that it was because of the night before that she was not there. Surely she would not make so much of so little! Or would she? Suppose she had told her father he had tried— Of course it wasn't true, but suppose Valrie's mind had exaggerated it like that! Howden was suddenly afraid. He tried to shake off the feeling. He told himself that feeling afraid was itself a kind of exaggeration. All he had done, all he had wanted to do was kiss her.

When he looked back upon the night before, Howden saw himself as one whose intentions were misunderstood. Valrie had always misunderstood him, he told himself. That day when he had called her, for instance. And there were other times too, and Valrie had made too much of them also. From the very first day she had made him suffer—and she had no right. She had made him crawl and beg and—suffer. It was her doing and her fault. Last night was her fault. She had put him at odds with all his inclinations, with his very nature. She always had.

The thought gave him sorrowful comfort as, clutching his diploma, he made his way to the door. Everybody was moving out. On the lawn in front of chapel little family groups seemed to be gathering around all the fifty-seven other graduates, who were still wearing their caps and gowns. Howden pulled his off, wadding the robe under his arm. There were no relatives to be proud of him, no one to make him pose self-conscious and smiling in academic robes before the family camera. He was the one graduate, he thought with self-pity, who had nobody there to cheer as he spread sail and tacked into the winds of life. He could hear the commencement speaker's final words again: ". . . There is a strong wind blowing on the sea of life. Spread sail and tack into it. . . ."

Just as he saw an opening in the crowd and started down the steps, someone called his name. It was Professor Clarkson, wearing the purple velvet-trimmed robe of a doctor of divinity. Miss Sadie and Mrs. Clarkson were with him. Fragile-looking and blue-veined and gloved to the elbows, they looked more like sisters than sisters-in-law. They wore identically shaped but differently color-trimmed, homemade hats. Miss Sadie took a quiet pride in the clothes she made.

"Where's your cap and gown?" Miss Sadie asked. "I want to get your picture." She was carrying one of those cameras called a Brownie.

"We have to get out in the sun," Professor Clarkson said.

Going down the steps, Howden said as casually as he could, "I wonder why Valrie Tillet—"

"Oh, poor girl!" Miss Sadie interrupted, shaking her bird-like head. "To have to miss her own commencement! She had one of those nervous, blinding headaches, her father said, and simply had to miss it." Unlike her brother, who never emphasized anything, Miss Sadie emphasized nearly everything.

"Yes, it was too bad," Professor Clarkson said. "Mr. Tillet took her to a friend's in the city."

"There's a good place over there," Miss Sadie said. "Over there near that tree."

"It's a lovely day to graduate," Mrs. Clarkson said in the high, atonal voice of the deaf. She nodded and smiled and her gray eyes looked quite bright and empty in the sun.

Miss Sadie kept shifting back and forth and moving the camera up and down to get the proper focus. Howden was glad that they were away from the crowd.

"Set your cap on straight and don't frown," Miss Sadie said. "Look dignified, but don't frown."

"Look at the camera," Professor Clarkson said.

"Yes, be sure to look at the camera. Now, that's better," Miss Sadie said. "Are you ready? I'm going to snap it now. Here I go."

Howden took his cap and gown off again at once.

"You'll be over this evening?" Miss Sadie asked solicitously. "A little supper. A going-away supper, you might say."

"Yes," Professor Clarkson said, "a going-away supper," and he smiled.

Howden didn't want to go, but he promised. He had some vague idea of trying to find Valrie, but he knew it was foolish. All he wanted to do now was to get away from the campus, from all this. He wished he were reporting to the railroad commissary today instead of tomorrow. The groups on the lawn in front of chapel were beginning to break up; people were saying good-by; cars were easing gently along the driveway looking for places to turn and head back toward the gate. As he passed the women's dormitories, he saw a few people standing among the trunks and suitcases on the porches, but the buildings already had a melancholy, deserted look. For him, he thought, they would always be deserted now. Never again would they be a shelter for Valrie.

The moment he entered his room he saw the letter. The cream

yellow envelope had been smudged from sliding under the door. The beat of his heart changed and his hand shook as he picked it up. There was no salutation.

> I don't think you'll understand how I feel [the note began], and I'm not going to try to explain. What you did last night was such a terrible violation of the kind of friendship we had that there could never be anything between us now. I'm going away without ever seeing you again. I don't want any apology. I don't want anything but the luck never to see you again.

There was no signature either.

Howden was not sure that he felt anything at all. He put the note back into its envelope, tore it in half, then in quarters, and finally into bits. When he had done this, a boiling tide of memory and feeling washed over him. He flung the torn bits of paper on the floor and, in scornful irritation, scattered them with his foot.

That evening he walked across the campus past the closed and empty buildings to the Clarksons' house. After supper, when it was quite dark, he sat with Miss Sadie and Professor Clarkson on their narrow porch. They were like three uncommunicative ghosts. Once the professor gave a little sigh and said that another commencement had come and gone, but a long silence followed this before Miss Sadie also sighed and said, yes, that was right. Then there was another silence.

Howden had the feeling that each of them was thinking things which he could not share. People met and fostered all sorts of personal relationships, but there were things they could not communicate and could not share, even when they were sister and brother, man and wife, sweethearts. There were always reservations, qualifications, screens. Everyone had them. No one ever got to know another very well.

Before he left to go back across the campus, where the only lights were in two or three houses along Professors' Row, Miss Sadie gave him a package prettily done up and said it was from all of them—a little commencement gift. Opening it in his room, he saw that it was a leather billfold with an identification card under the isinglass. Later, idly, just for something to do, he filled in the identification card and in the place opposite "In Case of Illness or Accident Notify" he printed the name and address of Professor Matthew Clarkson.

PART TWO

LAY THE BURDEN DOWN

AT FIRST, because he knew it was only a stepping stone, Shelton Howden didn't mind railroading. As soon as he had saved enough money (perhaps within a year, for money was coming in faster even than he had hoped), he was going to medical school at Howard University. He had put away two hundred dollars by mid-September. He had bought practically nothing. The possession of money gave him a good feeling of security.

He liked seeing new places. Having no regular run, he did not know where he would be from one day to the next, and this gave him a feeling of recklessness and adventure. He thrilled at first to the sense of travel. Somewhere in the back of his head was an obscure notion that in movement, in journey, man fulfilled some basic need, some primal urge. Travel was a constant escape. Pulling into the smoky gloom of rumbling stations, seeing the travelers, all of them wearing the same indefinable look of expectancy, he experienced a sense of something tremendously vital and yet a little sad. There were all the people and all the multiple sounds and sights: the smoke-fogged lights high up in the purgatorial gloam of the black iron-raftered shed; the trainmen's lanterns swinging; the swaggering, blue-uniformed guards; the loaded baggage trucks rumbling by; the hurrying porters; the cries of "All aboard!"—Howden never quite lost the thrill of it.

He saw all of west Louisiana and east Texas. The drab, slaty towns of Mississippi, the flatlands of Arkansas, and the pine barrens of Florida stroked by in blurred images, like a moving picture travelogue that is run too fast. He saw Savannah, Mobile, and Louisville, Kentucky. Once his car went as far west as Cincinnati. He thought of himself as traveled; and he was, though,

87

as a matter of fact, whenever his car lay over in some strange
town or city, he never wandered more than a few blocks beyond
the station or the waiters' sleeping quarters deep in the railroad
yards. He liked to be able to say that he had seen such places,
but he did not have much curiosity about them really.

He had no curiosity about the men with whom he worked
either. He had catalogued them within three days. He thought
them an improvident, shiftless, ignorant, and, at times, an amusing lot who gambled and drank up their money, fornicated in-
satiably, and cut the fool in spite of hell. Withdrawn and condescending in a way which he did not realize they resented
(and would not have changed if he had), Howden knew nothing of their private lives. He never saw any of them anywhere
except on the dining car. Arrived in some city at the end of an
outbound run, instead of going to the railroad bunkhouse, they
prowled off into the dark purlieus of niggertown. Back in New
Orleans again, they vanished as completely as if they had never
been, and Howden, making his way to his room at the Y.M.C.A.,
not so much as wondered where they had gone.

Sometimes they outraged his concept of what he thought they
were and of the way they should look at life. It annoyed him
to catch unexpected glimpses of brooding thought and bitter
social awareness in them. It was like looking into a grinning face,
accepting it for that, and then in a moment of penetration realizing that the grin is just a mask.

The crew, for instance, were all avid readers of the weekly
Negro press. They pored over the heavy, smudged, close-packed
print with a passionate absorption that seemed to Howden completely foreign to their general characters. It did not square with
anything he had learned about common, ignorant Negroes. It
was completely contrary to their body-loosening laughter, their
cheap and vulgar clowning. They found in the papers the smallest
item that reflected credit on their race; no mention of injustice
or prejudice escaped their eager, eagle eyes. Back in the stifling
pantry, they often talked about race among themselves. A casual

remark or even a greeting was sometimes enough to set them off in venomous pursuit of the subject on which, Howden told himself scornfully, they were ignorant. All they had were their emotions, blown up by the Negro press.

"What say, man?" one of them might greet another glumly.

"White folks still on top."

"Ain't no lie about that."

"Sonabitches got the world in a jug and the stopper in they hand," a third would say.

There might follow a pause, not too long, but a working, brooding absence of speech.

"Seen where they's a colored man in Congress. Man name of DePriest."

"Is?" Suspiciously, incredulously. "Where he from?"

"Chicago. Man, colored has it better out there."

"How this colored fellow get in Congress?" Still unbelieving.

"Voted in, just like anybody else. Colored out there got together an' voted him in. It's right in the paper."

"Ain't goin'a do no good. He all alone by himself in there. What kin he do?"

"Any time a nigger with white folks, he alone."

Another silence.

"If you want to know what hell is, just wake up black some morning."

"First thing, you got two strikes 'gainst you, an' the damn umpire he blind."

"Sometime seem like we might's well be dead as to be like we is."

"No." Slowly, thoughfully. "We more trouble to white folks alive."

"Trouble!" A short, bitter laugh. "We ain't no more trouble, Chef, then it take to get a rope and a gun."

"Yeah. I seen in the *Colored Call* they done lynch one more nigger."

"Where'bouts, man? They lynches so many niggers."

"Burnt the courthouse down, burnt it clean on down to get him."

"Sonabitches. Bastards." Almost without anger, something automatic and reflexive.

"You reckon this colored fella was voted in Congress other day can—?"

"Shit!" Drawn out with scornful emphasis.

"They got us by the nuts, an' that ain't shit."

"Ain't they got nuts, goddamn it?" Shifting his feet on the swaying, clattering floor, changing his stance, supporting himself against the quivering green steel cabinet. "We ain't got to take it, is we!"

"Do a frog have to bump his ass when he jump?"

Several spurts of laughter, almost but not quite lifting the spell of brooding, almost but not quite making it all seem funny. The silence now a little easier, lighter.

Shelton Howden was as completely and as arrogantly withdrawn from these discussions as a plane in flight. He did not hide his apartness nor try to minimize his difference from the rest of the crew. As the fall deepened, he became dissatisfied. He was tired of the field runs, which now took him monotonously across Louisiana, into east Texas, and back again to Florida and Alabama. The long lay-overs in sun-baked railroad yards, the slow runs, the uncertain delays, the last-minute changes in schedules irritated him. Moreover, with colleges opening everywhere, he felt left behind, cheated. He wondered whether he was falling into a rut.

As waiter number three, Howden's extra duty was to be the steward's man. He served that official's meals, kept his shoes and the brass buttons of his uniform polished, and rendered any other service for which the steward might feel the need or the whim. Under a taciturn steward named Elwin, Howden's extra duties were not onerous through the summer, but as travel reached its seasonal peak in October, stewards for the car were shifted often. Each of them wanted things done in a different way; each was harder to please than the one before. Howden no sooner got used

to one than another took his place. He came to feel apprehensive
about these changes. New stewards put on a field run for the sake
of experience were likely to be very exacting. Old stewards transferred from a regular run to the discomforts of the field were
undergoing disciplinary action, and they were resentful. New or
old, another steward meant another adjustment for Howden,
meant trying to divine what was expected of him. It meant living
at a taut E-string pitch of consciousness in an atmosphere grown
electric with unpredictable hazard. What unlooked-for difficulty
might arise he could not tell. He was conscious of risk which,
though possibly slight, was nevertheless beyond his control. He
had a twitching, vague uneasiness that a chance situation might
suddenly and unmanageably flare into something unpleasant and
even dangerous. In dealing with these white men, and with the
patrons of the dining car too, he was doubtful of his own judgment, and he sometimes appeared stupid and halting, without
initiative and without enterprise.

[2]

When Steward Maroney came on the car in the middle of November, Howden felt that he could relax a little. The steward was
a jovial-looking Irishman with a big, fleshy, pear-shaped face
about the color of an inside slice of rare beef, and a flabby, pendu-
lous belly. He made no bones of the fact that he had been "pulled
down" from a good run. "Them bastards up front screwed me,
boys," he once said. He was always kidding the crew about
women and liquor and crap-shooting, indulgence in which he
called "having a little sport." Never obviously drunk, he generally smelled faintly puky of liquor, and he drank with bold ro-
guishness on long lay-overs and when they were standing by for
assignment, even in the New Orleans yard.

The crew took all sorts of liberties with him. When patronage
was slack during meal call, they strolled through the train at will.
They lounged and smoked anywhere. Sometimes the steward shot

craps with them in the pantry. The car began to stink of rats because the traps went unset. Medical inspection went by the board. Steward Maroney, the crew agreed, was all right. Yes, sir, he was one easygoing white man.

In this atmosphere Howden relaxed. But he did what he was supposed to do, and he kept both distance and distinction between himself and the others. He did not josh nor clown nor gamble nor talk about women nor drink. When he spoke his voice was modulated, mannered. On dead-head runs, he sat apart from the rest of the crew. Sometimes he would catch the steward's eyes fixed on him curiously, with a flinty, speculative gleam, but Howden could not tell what Steward Maroney was thinking.

One day while he was serving the steward's lunch, the old subject of women came up. The banter, exchanged constantly during periods of leisure, usually developed around this inexhaustible theme. The steward, who never actually sat with crew members but liked to be near enough to wisecrack with them, was at a table halfway down the car. The crew lounged at the tables nearest the kitchen. They were talking about "fast" women. Crump, the fifth waiter, said that the fastest women in the world came from Florida, and Geter, one of the cooks, said that that was some stuff because the fastest women came from Kentucky, just like the fastest horses. The waiter named Peet expressed the opinion that one woman was just as fast as another if you had enough money up on her; and the chef said that if they were talking about fast women, he didn't want one himself—he didn't want a woman to be fast, especially in bed. He'd take a slow, easy-riding mamma, like one he knew out on Pontchartrain Road.

"By God, you boys is holding out on me!" Steward Maroney's voice rolled out as flat as a carpet, arresting hearing, arresting gaze. All eyes were immediately upon him, guarded and suspenseful, waiting for the clue which would tell them how to respond. The steward laughed.

"How's that, Chief?"

"Why don't you boys take me out with you sometimes?" Steward Maroney said, simulating an injured whine. "Hear y'all boys talking about them pretty high-yaller broads out on Pontchartrain Road and out around Upperline Street, but I notice don't none y'all invite me to go along with you. We get back to N'Orle'ns, you boys ought to take me creeping with you. I like a little sport."

Everyone laughed, everyone except Shelton Howden.

"We ain't got no money where our mouths is, Chief," one of the waiters said. "All we does is talk. Them Upperline broads costs money."

Howden took away the steward's dirty dishes and placed the dessert.

"You ain't kidding me none," the steward said, still in that tone of injury and disbelief. He cocked his head and looked up at Howden who had just stepped back with the tray of dirty dishes. "Maybe Number Three'll take me creeping sometime. What say, boy? You take me creeping sometime?"

"Creeping?"

"Jolly-house jumping," Mr. Maroney said, his eyes narrowing as if a sudden light had struck them. "Don't come with that crap. You know what a goddamn jolly-house is."

"Chief, I don' believe he do," the cook named Geter said, with eye-rolling irony. "I swear 'fore God I don'. He ain't no rounder like us, Chief. He don' mess with no bad women."

Howden flung a scornful glance at Geter and then looked past the steward and out of the window, where the frayed and raveled landscape of Mississippi frittered by.

"Bad women!" the steward roared incredulously. "Them high yallers is the best goddamn whores in the Crescent City. Number Three's got you boys all crapped up. He gets his nuts busted, just like the rest of y'all."

"Chief, I don' believe it. Swear 'fore God I don' believe it. Ask any of the boys. They don' believe it neither. He don' go no place with us," Geter said. He paused for emphasis. "Chief, you know what? I believe that nigger jacks off."

"You reckon?" Again with mock incredulity, "Where he learn that at? Boy, where you learn that at?"

Feeling inadequate and humiliated, feeling unable to cope with this raw kidding, feeling the crew's malicious glee at his discomfiture, Howden tried a weak smile to let the steward know that he could take a joke from him, but so far as the crew was concerned— Howden felt as though he had two distinct personalities.

"He learn that in college, Chief," Geter said with soft malignance, his hard, narrow brown face grinning sarcastically. "Didn' you know he been to college, Chief?"

The gleam brightened in the steward's eyes, and a look of discovery came into his face, but the kidding tone did not leave his voice.

"Boy, you been to college sure 'nough?"

"Steward, that's old Joe College hisself," one of the waiters said.

No one seemed really amused any more. Behind the grins lurked something else. Howden could feel them all watching him. Then he heard the steward laugh, heard his flat joking voice again.

"Well, by jumping Jesus," the steward said, "we don't want him spouting none o' his education round here, do we, boys? No, sir, we don't want none of that crap. I ain't seen a education yet that done a waiter any goddamn good."

[3]

From then on there was a difference. Howden was no longer secure in his isolated world of pride. The crew he could ignore, but the steward's attitude, though often cloaked in bawdy humor, also dripped the green gall of hostility. He grew capricious. Nothing Howden did pleased him. Sensing this, the crew members too became more venomous, their hatred of Howden more open.

Late in the afternoon of the Saturday following Thanksgiving, the car was standing by in the New Orleans yard. The crew had been on the road since Wednesday, and now the car was to be made up in a special train that was leaving for Montgomery, Alabama, at six o'clock. Nobody liked the assignment. The crew had hoped to have at least Saturday night in New Orleans, and they were in a sullen mood. Steward Maroney, who had been drinking slyly all afternoon and was now somewhat less than sober, said that "the boys up front had screwed" him again. Wobbling a little as he walked restively up and down the aisle, he said that there was a jinx somewhere.

"Boys, somebody's put the goofer on us. Why, goddamn it, we li'ble be out to Christmas," the steward said in his flat, whisky-thickened voice. "An' you know what?" he went on with sudden inspiration. "I'm goin'a give you boys a drink, damn if I ain't."

"Right now, Chief? Right here?" one of the waiters asked dubiously. "We still in the yard."

"Don't give a goddamn where we are," the steward said. "I'm running this car. And ain't she ready?" He looked around at the tables gleaming with napery and silver.

"She ready, Chief," someone said.

"Kitchen ready too," one of the cooks said.

"Well, all right then," the steward said defiantly. Going to his closet, he brought out a transparent gallon jug. It was more than half full. "Y'all bring your glasses."

Laughing and joshing now, emboldened by the white man's authority and by their own lack of responsibilty since the steward was boss, they crowded around with their glasses.

No one said anything to Howden, who sat alone and kept his gaze fixed out of a window. He had made up his mind that this would be his last trip with this crew. When they returned, he would go to the commissary superintendent and ask to be transferred. The resolution brought him a feeling of relief. Let them drink, he thought scornfully. Let the stupid darkies drink with that white man. Though the inspector had already been on the car, Howden hoped that he would suddenly appear again.

It was raining steadily outside in the dusk. Workmen in glistening black raincoats and little electric trucks and engines greasy with rain went by in the yard. Rain angled blackly against the window. Howden could just make out the massy bulk of freight cars standing three sets of track away. The scored and broken macadam pavement, which separated every other double line of track, was slimily iridescent with rain over a film of oil. An engine lumbered by, stopped, backed up, and stumbled forward again. The dining car shuddered.

"Number Three!"

The voice startled Howden, rendered him suddenly immobile. At the moment he could not even turn to see where the voice had come from.

"Goddamn it, you hear me, Number Three, you—"

"Yes, sir," Howden said, scrambling up. The steward, holding the jug loosely, was standing at the front end of the car. Members of the crew had taken up stations between the tables.

"I said get a goddamn glass," the steward said.

"Boss, that's another thing," one of the waiters said. "He don't drink neither."

"Well, by jumping Jesus, he's going to drink now," the steward said. "Bring a glass on up here, Number Three."

It was a situation Howden had not foreseen. He flushed. If he went forward with a glass, he would prove himself no different and no better than the rest of the crew. If he refused— But he knew he could not refuse. Even from the distance he stood, he could see the cold enmity and the challenge in Steward Maroney's eyes. He could sense the scornful hate in the eyes of the crew. Picking up a glass from the table at which he had been sitting, he started toward the steward.

"Not that glass," the steward said. "You know better'n unset Number Two's table. Number Two'll knock hell out of you, boy. Unset your own table."

"An' don't you even down park at my table no more neither," the number two waiter said.

"What you goin'a do if he park there again, Number Two?" someone asked insinuatingly.

"He'll see what I do," Number Two said.

But Howden did not even glance at them. He was concentrating on the white man. Lifting a glass from his own station, he went up the aisle. He was trying not to think, trying not to feel. He was aware that his face ached with a weak, sickly grin and that the crew was laughing at him. Steward Maroney's eyes narrowed with cunning. When Howden held out the glass, the steward filled it nearly to the top.

"Now drink it," he said almost pleasantly.

The crew laughed.

"Drink it right on down," the steward said.

"Jesus!" someone said and exploded with laughter.

"Come on, boy, drink!" the steward said.

Howden did not know whom he hated more, the steward or the crew. His hatred for the white man was mixed with fear. He wished a miracle would happen. He was caught, trapped. If he drank it, he would get drunk, and the steward could report him for being drunk, could have him fired. If he did not drink it—

"Goddamn it, we ain't got all evening," the steward said, again pleasantly. "We want you to drink a toast, don't we, boys?"

Howden felt helpless as he raised the glass slowly to his lips. But just then a locomotive hit the car, making Howden spill half the whisky.

"Goddamn it," Steward Maroney said angrily, jumping back. "Don't you spill no more of my good whisky. Hold that glass out here." He filled it again.

The car tautened and grew solid and took on greater density as the locomotive rolled with it.

The whisky had a green, poisonous taste. Howden gagged as it went down. Tears stung his eyes. Half through, he had to exert great effort not to throw up. He pressed one hand into his stomach to stop its sickening churning. The crew laughed. Suddenly he could not swallow another drop. Sloshing the remaining whisky as he set the glass down, he bolted past the steward and through the narrow vestibule to the door. When he had opened it at last, he bent over, holding to the handgrip, and puked for dear life. Guffaws of laughter, quavering through the steely clatter of the moving train, came to him from the dining car.

He would not go back in there, he told himself. He hated them all. Such a wave of hatred for the crew overwhelmed him that he retched again and could not stop. Bending there in the open door with the rain spuming against him, he dizzily watched the macadam pavement slithering wetly away. The lighted windows of the empty train threw slanted squares of dancing light as it rumbled through the yard. When the train pulled into the station, Howden told himself, he would simply walk away.

"A sick nigger." Howden heard a laughing voice behind him. Then he was aware that the crew had followed him and were standing in the vestibule. He did not look around.

"Get him back in here, y'all," the steward's voice said.

"Come on, Joe College," someone said scornfully.

The train had slowed for the switch-in to the station.

"Get him out'a that goddamn door," the steward said, irritably now.

All at once Howden stood erect. Drawing in his breath sharply, he let go of the handgrip. The shock of the jump jarred him to his teeth. The ground wheeled crazily away under his pounding feet. But then something struck him a great blow, and a red-crested, black-troughed comber of pain rushed out through his body like an explosion.

CHAPTER EIGHT

SHELTON HOWDEN was in the hospital four weeks and a few odd days. From time to time there were a dozen other men in the basement Negro ward too, but Howden did not talk to any of them. The ward was small and constricted, and the beds were close together, and Howden could hear everything that was said, but he did not really listen. When the frail, leather-hided man in the next bed tried to make conversation in an ancient, quavering voice, Howden pretended not to hear. Somehow the century of misery in the wizened black face angered Howden, and he kept his eyes averted.

Indeed, for more than a week he was barely congenial to Professor Clarkson and Miss Sadie, who were at the hospital the first moment they permitted him to see anyone, and who, one or the other or both, visited him every day. He wished they wouldn't come so often. They brought him things to eat and books to read, but their conversation bored him, and he had the greatest difficulty trying to show an appreciation he did not feel.

He had been badly injured. The night when he had jumped, running as in an obstacle race through the quivering pattern of light and shadow that the train made, he had seen too late the heavy hand truck that someone had left on the pavement between the tracks. He had smashed into it, crushing his arm at the elbow and breaking four of his ribs, one of which punctured the visceral sac. So besides being injured, he was very ill, although he did not know it. A great deal of pus developed. Grimly half joking, the doctor said that they could never drain it all off and that Howden's system would have to absorb it. They drained off as much as they could through a tube in his side.

The doctor, who was himself young and who handled the patients in the ward with a brusque but not unkindly realism, explained to Howden about the arm. The bone in the elbow was crushed, he said, not for a moment dreaming that Howden knew the name of the bone. Looking steadily at Howden, the doctor lifted his white, strong hand and made a hook of the thumb and forefinger. "The bone is like this," the doctor had said, "and this—"

"The trochlea," Howden said.

"Yes," the doctor said, showing his surprise, lowering his hand a little. "How did you know?"

"I studi—" Howden began and stopped, a sense of fear over-
coming him. Maybe this white man too would not like the fact
that he had been to college. Maybe this one too wanted all
niggers to be alike. The doctor was waiting.

"The nurse told me," Howden lied.

"Oh," the doctor said and raised his hand again. "Well, the
bone is like this, and this—" tapping the hooked thumb—"was
crushed. That ruins articulation." He looked at Howden very
hard. "You'll not be able to use it for much ever again. You'll be
permanently but not noticeably crippled."

In the pause that followed, Howden had said nothing, and the
doctor had gone on speaking. "You'll get used to it. You'll get
used to the idea of it after a while." Then he had turned and
walked away between the double row of beds and out of the
ward.

Thus Howden had learned that he could never be a doctor,
and he thought at first that he would never get used to the idea
of that. He would have to start all over again, he told himself.
He was a cripple, he told himself, a wreck—and he felt a little
contemptuous of the wreck he was.

But this soon gave way to self-pity. Lying there in the basement ward of the hospital, it was not difficult to cast himself in
a tragic role, to play the tragic mulatto. He did not see why
whatever power that controlled such things let him get this far
only to cast him down. He did not see how he was to pick up
the pieces of his life and fit them together into some kind of
reasonable pattern.

This was what he had been thinking when Professor Clarkson
came.

"How do you feel today?" Professor Clarkson had asked,
smiling wanly, gently down at him.

Howden turned his head away. All the Clarksons' smiles, guileless as morning sunlight, embarrassed him; they somehow always
made him feel that he owed them something. Sometimes he
wanted to curse the Clarksons for making him feel that way.

"How are you, my boy?" Professor Clarkson had asked, putting his newly blocked gray hat on the bedside stand, unbuttoning his worn black overcoat, taking off his gloves.

"They put a brace on my elbow today," Howden had said. "I can't study medicine now. I'm a permanent cripple." It relieved him to say it.

Professor Clarkson had looked disturbed, flustered, painfully distressed; and then, biting at the patch of hair under his lower lip, he had sat down very quickly.

[2]

Howden left the hospital two days after Christmas. The Clarksons came for him in their Ford. He was to stay with them until he was completely recovered. Howden didn't think he could stand it, but what else was there to do? He was still very weak. The moment he was strong enough, he told himself, he would go away. But where? And to do what? He did not know. He tried not to think about it.

When the Clarksons came, Miss Sadie was brimming with something.

"We saved your Christmas," Miss Sadie whispered brightly, hands fluttering, head nodding bird-like. "I think you'll like it." Then she raised her voice above the sound of the chugging motor. "Matthew, don't you think he'll like it?"

But Professor Clarkson was more restrained. "I hope he will," he said solemnly. Mrs. Clarkson, who was sitting beside him and who heard none of this, said nothing.

"You will. You really will!" Miss Sadie said happily.

The house smelled of Christmas. There was a withering pine wreath on the door, and there were red and green electric candles in the windows. On the table in the living room stood a small tinsel-spangled tree. Lonely-looking presents and bright holiday cards were set around it. There were a tie, a shirt, and two pairs of socks for Howden, who could not help thinking that if this was the Christmas they had saved for him, Miss Sadie had made too much of it. He wanted to laugh at the ludicrousness of the whole thing.

Then while he stood there trying to think of something nice to say, Miss Sadie, with a quick, nervous motion, picked up an envelope from under the tree, handed it to him, and stepped back. They were all watching him. Mrs. Clarkson's face was brightly vacuous. The professor looked dubious and worried. Miss Sadie's smile had gone still with anxiety, expectation, hope.

Suppressing a cruel desire to laugh, Howden opened the large, Christmasy envelope. Inside was another official-looking envelope addressed to him in care of Dr. Matthew Clarkson. Opening this too, Howden took out the single sheet of letterhead. "National Congregational Board," he read, and skipped the rest of the heading.

> We are happy to inform you that upon the recommendation of Dr. Matthew Clarkson we are offering you a graduate scholarship carrying a stipend of one hundred dollars a month, for study toward the master of arts degree in the field of your choice. Though it is not usually our policy to grant scholarships at this time of the year, Dr. Clarkson urged upon us the unusual circumstances and recommended you so highly. . . .

Howden looked up and saw the Clarksons all still watching him. He smiled. Then feeling that it was not big enough, not sincere enough, he stretched it until his yellow face, pale from illness, ached with the effort to make it real. He must have succeeded, for he heard Miss Sadie exclaim happily, "Oh, you do like it! I told you, Matthew." She lifted her blue-veined hands, spiny as claws, and beat them gently together.

"Oh, yes, ma'am," Howden said, "I like it."

"It is not medicine," Professor Clarkson said, smiling apologetically, "but I thought—" and his voice trailed off.

"I certainly want to thank you," Howden said. But he had not asked them for anything. He didn't owe them anything. And if they thought he owed them something, he had nothing to give.

CHAPTER NINE

From the early spring of 1929 until the autumn of 1931, Shelton Howden attended the University in New York. His contacts there were extremely limited. One or two of his white fellow students tried at first to be friendly, but Howden, abashed and suspicious, instinctively retreated. He sat in lectures and slipped almost furtively about the halls of the University, wearing a strained look of acute self-consciousness that was at once a confession and an apology.

Yet he was glad that he was the only Negro in his classes. The fact stimulated his pride in a strange, inexplicable way. It made him feel particularly privileged, the one out of many, an exception to the generality of Negroes. By the beginning of his second year, when the grip of the economic depression became most paralyzing, Howden seldom saw another Negro on the Heights. He did not have to worry about being racially linked to some ignorant burr-head out of nowhere, some poke who would surely have disgraced him.

Quite a fussy civic and social life effervesced around the Harlem Y.M.C.A. where Howden lived, but he took no part in it. He did make the acquaintance of a law student from Fordham and of another student from Cooper Union and of one or two other people who lived at the Y, but these contacts never developed beyond the casual stage. Once he did go to a movie with the law student, who afterwards invited him to the apartment of some friends, but Howden was disappointed by the whole thing. The apartment was a dingy walk-up in 132nd Street, and the law student's friends talked with bated enthusiasm about communism and with astringent bitterness about the race question. Later a mixed company, including a pretty, Jewish-looking white girl, came in, and Marxist dialectic (though Howden did not really recognize it as such) crackled like an electric storm. The pretty girl tried to draw Howden out, really played up to him, but her conversation and her jaunty self-possession were frightening. And anyway, only white people who were communists—and Jewish, or at least foreign, at that—would go to a nobody Negro's apartment. Communism, it seemed to Howden, was merely a league of the dispossessed, and he did not want to think of himself as belonging to it. He put it in the familiar nutshell: the only communists were people who had no shirts to share. He himself had a dozen shirts. He had money in the bank.

On the race question his thinking—if it could be called that— was more complex, more deeply and intricately involved with his emotions. All he wanted to do, he told himself, was let the race problem take care of itself and live his own life as best he could. He really seemed to have a psychic block, at once cynical, self-assuring, and romantic. People who whined about the race question were simply rationalizing their own failures. He felt confirmed in this notion when he learned that the law student's friends were Wall Street messengers and porters, redcaps, and investigators for the Home Relief Bureau. He never went out with the law student again.

There were quite a few girls in and out of the Y, but Howden made no attempt to meet any. Indeed, he had a strange lack of conceit when it came to girls. He would see them in the lobby when he came down from the Heights late of an evening, and on Sundays he would see them in the Y restaurant—girls alone and with fellows and in pairs, some brown, some yellow, and some who might have been white. Sometimes he grew sick with desire for a woman, and then in shamed secret he would love himself. At the Y he always tried to pretend that the women were not there.

And when he walked the streets of Harlem, no one was there.

Head up, gaze fixed on any distant object straight ahead, crippled arm held a little stiffly, slightly inward bent at his side, he strode with an arrogant thrust and purposefulness quite different from the way he moved on the Heights. While he saw the kaleidoscopic shuffle of Harlem's multitudinous life, he ignored it. He knew vaguely that there must be people somewhere there who were secure, comfortable, stable, but he had no access to them. The Harlem that he saw was a crowded nigger slum with which he refused to be identified, which he could emotionally reject.

Thus he lived on two planes, each with a different level of awareness, and for each of which he had a separate and distinct personality.

He fully recognized this one day toward the close of his final semester when one of his professors at the University issued an invitation to the class. He was going to entertain the class at the Faculty Club, he told them, and he wanted them all there to eat sandwiches and drink coffee and exchange ideas in an atmosphere less formal than that of the classroom. He was a youngish, eager man, still an assistant professor, but all sorts of people flocked to his lectures.

After class that day, instead of going immediately to his office, the door of which opened behind the lecture platform, Professor Bradford left his books and notes right where they were and sauntered into the hall. He was standing there when Howden, always the last to leave, came out. He was waiting for Howden it seemed.

"Eh," Professor Bradford said, "eh—do you have a minute?" He looked embarrassed, but he looked determined too. "Step back in here a minute, will you?"

Howden felt himself go tighter and more wary. He followed Professor Bradford back through the classroom into the cluttered office. The professor sat down in the swivel chair before the desk and swung it around at an angle not quite facing Howden. It was obvious that, having got this far, he was now thinking how to proceed. He made a sudden gesture of impatience.

"Eh—I don't know quite how to say this," Professor Bradford said. His angular face took on a lively color from his embarrassment. He ran his fingers through his thinning hair.

Howden waited, tense, in-drawn. He could feel the perspiration start in his armpits.

"Eh, this informal sort of seminar I'm asking the class to participate in—" He paused and swung his head suddenly to look at Howden. "Do you think we try to be democratic here at the University?"

The question took Howden by surprise. He had not thought about it, but he said, "Oh, yes, sir," and managed a weak, uncertain smile. He saw Professor Bradford's lank, strong-lined face take on a different expression.

"Well, damn it, man, we don't!" Professor Bradford said incisively. "And you ought to know it as well as I. Do you mean to say—?" Then he checked himself. "Sorry."

Howden felt an odd sense of hurt, of unnecessary injury. He waited because he did not know what else to do. He did not know what Professor Bradford was thinking. He could not tell what was in his mind. He heard the burred, Western voice go on reflectively.

"I thought of this informal discussion group before. I thought of having it meet once a month as a matter of fact—and that's what I should have done." He grunted, pausing pensively. "I should just have gone ahead and done it. But no, I wanted to make it all regular. You don't know what sticklers we are for regularity around here," he said, his eyes glinting satirically behind the steel-rimmed glasses. "I brought it up in departmental meeting. And do you know what? Some of my precious colleagues, some of my best-known and most important colleagues, some of my democracy-loving, ism-hating colleagues advised against it, objected to it. And do you know why?" he demanded rhetorically, suddenly rising from his chair. His voice dropped a pitch but tautened. One hand beat a rapid tattoo on the desk. "Because they said there were Jews and a Negro in the class and some of the students might object to socializing with them. But that wasn't all. I know that. It was only an excuse. They themselves objected to it."

Staring at Howden, Professor Bradford sat slowly down again. There was a long silence. Howden could hear the professor breathing. Without looking fully at him, Howden was aware of the bleak and baffled expression on the professor's face, of the shape of the knuckly hands as he lifted them both and slowly massaged his chin with the tips of his fingers. Howden felt very alert, very careful, very cold. He was not sure what it all meant, but he did not want it to have anything to do with him.

"For four months now I've let that stop me," Professor Bradford said, his voice weary and then getting strong again. "No one told me not to do it, but for four months I've been a moral coward, fearing the criticism of my colleagues for doing what I know to be right, thinking of everything but the one real point. Howden, it's a matter of principle for me—and for you, isn't it?" He paused and flung his head up and looked at Howden again. "I want you to come to that party."

Howden dropped his eyes. He felt that Professor Bradford was being unfair to him, putting him on a spot, trying to get him unnecessarily involved. Somehow he knew that his major professor, the one who either would or would not recommend him for a degree, was one of those in the department who had objected. Howden felt trapped, defenseless. It was no matter of principle, he thought. It was a matter of practical common sense, of self-interest, and of reality for him. If he failed Professor Bradford's course, that would be bad enough, though he didn't need the credit. But if he went against the wishes of his major professor, he would not get his degree. All at once Howden knew what he would do.

Then it happened. He was totally conscious of another self taking possession of him and yet leaving a part of him free to watch and weigh.

"I was going to tell you, sir," he said, covertly studying Pro-

fessor Bradford's long, eager face. "It's like this, sir. I have an
engagement for that night. I—I might be able to get there late.
But it's about—you see, sir, it's about something very important
to me." He fumbled with the lie.

"Oh, I see," Professor Bradford said, obviously let down.
"Well—" He stood, smiling wearily. "But you understand, don't
you, about the principle of the thing?"

"Yes, sir. And I would do it if I could," Howden said with deceptive earnestness.

[2]

When, at the end of the summer semester, Shelton Howden was
granted his degree, and—thanks to the intercession of his major
professor—was shortly thereafter offered a job at Arcadia State
College for Negroes, he was glad to be through with the University and the North. He had put many things behind him, he
thought—the orphanage, for instance, and the railroad, and the
status he had known at New Hope. In two and a half years he
had written the Clarksons twice, and they were behind him too.

He had never recovered the ruddy undercast to his skin, and
now he was merely nondescriptly yellow, with yellow hair which
he wore in pressed-down tiny waves straight back from his forehead. All in all, he had a bleached-out look about him.

PART THREE

ARCADIAN COMEDY

IN THE first few days, while the simple machinery of Arcadia State College ground like a rusty motor through staff meetings and registration, nearly everyone on the faculty told Howden how lucky he was. Dean Bledsoe was the first to say it. A big rumpled bed of a man, with a surprising thin falsetto voice and a nervous tic that jerked his face into periodic spasms, he told Howden that "in terms of the times" he, Howden, was lucky and "in terms of the position" he was lucky too. The dean could not always get his grammar straight. "There was over fifty applicants for this one job. Fifty!" he squealed, "from pee aitch dees on down. Plenty of pee aitch dees walking the streets today. No two ways about it, you're just plain lucky," the fat brown dean said, shaking his head at the grim wonder of it all.

Howden expected to hear the same thing from President Wimbush, but that official, having left fully detailed instructions covering every possible contingency, was away at the time. Posted on the bulletin board in the faculty dining room, the instructions (three single-spaced typed sheets) were the subject of much guarded buzzing and many meaningful glances. During every meal at least one whispered argument would come up at one of the tables, and three or four faculty members would go, like worried Greeks to Delphi, to consult the posted instructions. In spite of this, it did not seem mere extraneous supervention for the faculty to remind Howden how fortunate he was, how fortunate they all were. It was as if they had a kind of mass contagion and a mass resemblance, as if they were all at the same stage of a baffling disease. They were nearly all men and women in their middle years, all of the same muddy shade of brown, and they all wore the same look of vague anxiety and fear.

But the president's secretary, Miss Laura Lark, was different.

She was a plump, jaunty woman of thirty-two who dressed like a girl of sixteen and whose light-skinned face was practically hidden behind a pinkish mask of powder and rouge. It was with her that Howden shared the only table for two in the faculty dining room. But Miss Lark was especially busy during the president's absence, and it was more than a week before she sat through a full meal with Howden. Bouncing in just as dessert was laid, she would eye him with sharp inquisitiveness, nod crisply, and fall to eating without a word. Miss Lark did not seem to talk with any of the faculty.

One evening some ten days after the opening of college, she surprised Howden.

"Well," she said, suddenly pushing her plate away and crossing her arms on the table edge, "are you all straight and everything?" It was a friendly question, and she smiled in a friendly way, but her eyes were searching.

"I think so," Howden said.

Miss Lark pushed her plate a little farther. The other tables were nearly deserted. Through the beaverboard partition they could hear the clatter of dishes being stacked in the students' dining hall.

"How do you like your schedule? How do you like your room, hunh? How do you like being over there in the old practice cottage all by yourself?" Her voice went higher with each question; it was as if she were singing an aria. "Do you like it?"

"It's all right," Howden answered a little guardedly.

"But do you like it? Do you like being alone, hunh?"

"Well—yes."

"But you'd rather be there, wouldn't you, than in the dormitory?" Miss Lark kept watching him narrowly. Beneath the smear of orange-colored rouge, she had a pleasant and knowing face. "Now just tell me. Do you like it here?"

Howden felt suddenly suspicious and careful and smiled carefully to hide it.

"Well—" he said slowly.

"You don't like it?"

"I haven't said that," Howden put in quickly. "After all, I haven't been here but a few days. Everybody—"

"Everybody what?" Miss Lark put in quickly.

"Tells me how lucky I am to be here."

"And you are," Miss Lark said, nodding. Then her voice changed. "But they don't know it."

They stared at each other for a moment.

"They're all zombies. Pay them no mind," Miss Lark said, dismissing them with a gesture of her plump hand. "But you are lucky. You know what? The Old Man's back."

"The old man?"

"The president," Miss Lark said.

"Oh," Howden said. He had heard President Wimbush referred to as "President" and "Doctor," but this was the first time he had heard him called the "Old Man."

"And you know what?" She looked at him with knowing brightness. There was no one else in the room now, but she lowered her voice confidentially. "He got a glimpse of you today. He likes you. That's the way he is. He can tell right off whether he likes you. He likes the things your major professor at the University said about you too."

Howden wondered what his major professor had said, and for a moment his mind went off on all sorts of tangents.

"I thought the dean—"

"What? You thought the dean what?"

"Passed on the applications," Howden said.

"Old Bledsoe?" She laughed on a high note of disdain and followed it up with a coarse popping of her lips. "Shoot! Him pass on applications!"

"But I thought—"

"When you're here longer, you'll know better," Miss Lark said.

It was all beyond Howden, and he said nothing. He was learning to wait, to conceal. He was acquiring a casual air to cover his thoughts and his feelings. Sometimes the very air of casualness helped him not to feel at all. But he began to like Miss Lark. Her sage and confident manner suggested that she was in with the president and that she knew a lot of things unknown to others.

"Listen. From Bledsoe down, don't let them fool you," Miss Lark said. "Don't pay them any mind. The Old Man hires, the Old Man fires, and he does everything else in between. Did you believe Bledsoe? Did you, hunh?"

"After all, I didn't know."

"From now on, you know," the president's secretary said, flouncing up.

[2]

They left the deserted dining room together. Three or four faculty people, whispering on the wide concrete stoop, looked at them suspiciously as they went out, but Miss Lark frisked by without a glance.

There was still some light in the sky over the river, but the study hour bell had rung and the campus paths were empty. The college buildings, some of brick and some of clapboard, were laid out roughly in the shape of an inverted U. Alone in the curve of the U on the high bluff above the river stood the president's house. It was a large, frame structure, gleaming whitely in the gloam, with many windows and a high front porch. Through the glass panels on each side of the double doors, they could see a light burning in the hall, and just as they passed another light went on in one of the downstairs front rooms, and someone drew the curtains across the windows. The house seemed withdrawn, aloof.

"What's he like?" Howden asked, nodding toward the house. Miss Lark's high heels stopped clicking as she slowed her walk.

Above the buildings on the opposite stroke of the U, Howden could see the shadowy black mass of the curving, encompassing, tree-covered bluff. Miss Lark turned to him.

"He's like white," she said, seeming to hold her breath, as if her words were a climactic summing up. "He's the whitest-acting colored man I've ever seen. You know what I mean, hunh?"

Howden knew what she meant, but he said, "I think so."

"Well, you won't have to think about it much longer."

As they walked along, she gave him a lot of historical details about Arcadia State College for Negroes. Sometimes her voice took on an almost fierce, defensive ring, as when she said that although Negroes didn't want to give him credit, the Old Man had really made the institution what it was. He had built it up, and the white people knew it, Miss Lark told Howden, no matter what the Negroes said. Just thirty years ago it had started with only the old plantation mansion, now the president's home, for classrooms, dining room, and dormitory, and now there were eight buildings exclusive of those on the college farm and the cottages for married faculty members down the road beyond the fill. And the Old Man had done it all.

"You know what? I believe his father was old Governor Perkins," Miss Lark said, again a little breathlessly. "No one's ever told me that, but I think it."

"Why do you think that?" Howden asked, pretending indifference. He was really impressed.

It was a matter of adding things up, Miss Lark said. First, there were the names. It wasn't just a coincidence, Miss Lark said, giving Howden a sharp, half-angry look, that the Old Man had the same name as the old Governor, even if it was turned around. Perkins Thomas Wimbush was not the kind of hind-part-before name that you'd be likely to give anyone unless it meant something special. The next thing was his education. The Old Man hadn't gone to New Hope or to Howard or to Fisk. He had gone to a boarding school in New England and then to Harvard. And forty or forty-five years ago, how many colored people from the South—or from the North either, Miss Lark asked—could do that? Her eyes, bright as glowing coals, came at Howden in the dark, and he had to admit that she was right: not many colored people could do that forty years ago.

They walked to the little bridge over the fill at the open end of the U. From the bridge the road ran down past the faculty cottages and through the college farm to the village a half a mile away. A mist was rising from the swampy fill and floating across the road.

Another thing, Miss Lark said, was the campus site. Stretching from the river to the railroad, it had been a plantation that belonged to the old Governor's family. Then, back in 1897, the old Governor had deeded it to the state on the condition that it be used for Negro education. That was right in the records for anybody to see, Miss Lark told Howden, and it was in a pamphlet which was gotten up to celebrate the college's twenty-fifth anniversary too. Just about the last thing the Governor did before he died in office in 1899 was appoint the Old Man first president of a college that wasn't even in existence then.

Miss Lark said it sounded like something out of a novel by Charles Chesnutt, didn't it, hunh? And Howden agreed with her, although he had never read a Chesnutt novel. He was thinking how lucky the Old Man was to have been born the son of someone who could do things for him. He was wishing that he could have been that lucky. He felt a little envious of the Old Man.

"The very year I came here twelve years ago, his wife died," Miss Lark said. "And do you know what?"

"What?" For of course he didn't know.

"There were only two mourners, the Old Man and the daughter. Wasn't that peculiar?"

"The daughter? He has a daughter?"

"Yes. She went away to school afterwards," Miss Lark said. "But wasn't that peculiar, only two mourners?"

It struck Howden that if he himself died tomorrow, he wouldn't have two mourners. The thought filled him with a kind of unreal sadness. They were approaching the dormitory annex where Miss Lark lived. Lights shone blurrily through the curtained windows; an indistinct soft murmur rose.

"It was the most forlorn, loneliest kind of looking funeral I've ever seen. Just to see the two of them walking out behind the coffin and getting in the car—the Old Man and this right young girl, all by themselves. There was the hearse and the car, and that was all." She heaved a sigh. "And he's lonely now. I just know he is."

Howden was thinking that the Old Man was fortunate just the same. Miss Lark couldn't know how fortunate. They were silent for a moment.

"If he's so lonely, why doesn't his daughter come home and live with him?" Howden asked. He was a little impatient with Miss Lark because she did not seem to realize the luck the Old Man had had.

Miss Lark slowly shook her head, and Howden saw her smiling sadly in the night. "That's not what I mean. Besides, his daughter's married up there in Boston now."

They stopped by the path that led up to the annex. Miss Lark's face brightened.

"He's going to send for you. I know it. He's going to send for you real soon."

"And until he does, what am I supposed to do?" Howden asked. But the sarcasm was lost on Laura Lark.

"Don't let Bledsoe or any of them fool you," Miss Lark said. "Don't pay them any mind." Then, her bounce completely recovered, "Nighty-night," she said cheerily, and her heels clicked like castanets as she skipped up the walk.

CHAPTER ELEVEN

FROM the first, Shelton Howden had been aware of the atmosphere of worry and harassment that clung to his thirty-five colleagues, and as the weeks passed, he came to recognize it as the stable condition of their existence. They were like creatures poorly prepared to face an unhappy inevitability, momently expected. They scampered from corner to corner but found no hiding place. Feeling no sense of pity, Howden could think of them as frightened mice in a room with a cat. The cat was President Wimbush.

Indeed, though he had not so much as met the president, on the rare occasions when he saw him—now and then in a faculty meeting, now and then in chapel—Howden thought that there was something feline in the Old Man's appearance. Perhaps it was the shape of the white, delicately structured face. Or it might have been the slate-gray eyes, alert and insolently amused. The small-knit body too, crisp and economic in its movements, was cat-like. Shelton Howden did not phrase it so, did not pick out the items thus; but he did think of the Old Man as a cat.

There was querulous talk about the president, and Howden couldn't help but hear. Whenever two or three faculty members met, the air hissed sibilantly with eager, outraged, and frightened whisperings. Somehow it annoyed Howden. He grew tired of his colleagues' complaints and unconsciously began to take the side of the president. If they felt so abused, why didn't they resign?

It was a question he asked Miss Lark one day, and she looked at him with prosaic indulgence.

"He doesn't want them to do that," she said matter-of-factly.

"He just wants to keep them in line." Then, as a new thought struck her, she leaned nearer across the table. "And suppose you were a married man with three children, like Purnell. Would you resign, hunh? Suppose you didn't have another job to go to?" She was just asking a question out of a vast and guileless curiosity; it had no ominous implications for her whatever.

"Well, he never bothers me," Howden said.

"But that's because he likes you," Miss Lark said.

"Oh, bushwa!" Howden said and laughed abruptly.

Just the same, he grew increasingly impatient with his colleagues. He avoided them. Sometimes after a faculty meeting or Wednesday evening chapel he would be caught in the midst of a faculty group and unable to sneak away; but whatever they discussed he had heard before. He had heard all about old Professor Tatum, who taught household chemistry, having his salary arbitrarily docked, and about Mrs. Noe, of Home Ec, being unjustly called on the carpet, and about Professor McKee being forced to pay for a crate of eggs some student broke in the poultry house. There were dozens of such stories current, but Howden could never quite believe in the faculty's entire innocence.

He had heard all about race too. No topic, Howden discovered, was ever more than one remove from that. All topics led to it. Howden found that his colleagues were all members of one progressive race group or another and that they held regular meetings in each other's homes and rooms, but he never went. The faculty were all conversant with the old, acidulous opinions of Dr. W. E. B. DuBois and with the new, bitter ones of Mr. Walter White and Mr. Curtis Flack, and their conversations crackled with these men's thoughts, their striking phrases. When his colleagues talked about race, it was like being surrounded by squawking parrots pretending to be screaming eagles. And Howden told himself besides that it was as futile as it was passionate. He did not want to become a party to their futility. What he wanted was peace. He did not want to think about the race problem nor live on two levels nor make life more difficult by trying to analyze everything. All he wanted was to get what he could out of life. He didn't want to spatter his brains against stone walls.

So what the newspapers, either white or colored, said did not interest him very much. Nothing that happened outside—he liked to think of it as "outside"—impressed him particularly. The bread lines grew longer all through 1932, and many of the banks that closed in 1933 never reopened, and later Mr. Roosevelt tightened the screws on capital, but none of it seemed to have anything to do with Shelton Howden. The number of lynchings increased, and Mr. Curtis Flack wrote a piece in the *American Fortnightly*, and Mr. "Cotton Ed" Smith arose in the Senate and said it was all a nigger lie, and there was quite a lot of controversy, but Howden wasn't interested. What he wanted was a victory in his private battle against life. There was trouble a-plenty outside, but it was a passing show which he could watch through a window of thick plate glass.

[2]

Early one evening in the beginning of spring, the president sent for Howden. The first bell for supper was just ringing, and students were marching in sloppy formation toward the dining hall as Howden hurried into the administration building. He paused to pull himself together. The bursar's office was empty and closed. Down the hall he could hear the faint clack-clacking of a typewriter and see the rectangular patch of light falling through the open door of the Old Man's outer office. He went quietly, walking nervously on the balls of his feet, toward that patch of light. Miss Lark did not see him until he spoke.

"He sent for me," Howden said softly.

"I know it," Miss Lark said. Then she smiled and pushed herself back from the desk.

"What—? Do you know what he wants?" Howden whispered.

"Don't look so worried," Miss Lark said.

He didn't know he was looking worried, and there wasn't much time to think about it, for Miss Lark was already entering the president's door. A moment later Howden found himself standing on the soft, deep-piled, coffee-brown rug in front of an enormous desk.

The president did not look up at once. Studying something on a sheaf of papers before him, he seemed to be entirely unaware that someone had entered the room. One elbow rested on the glassed-over top of the desk, and his hand, tapered, slender, and soft-looking as a woman's, supported his forehead. Howden could feel himself, for a reason he could not define, breathing quickly, shallowly.

Still not looking up, the president said in a quick, grating voice, "Can you make a speech?" And then his hand came down and his gray eyes accosted Howden's face.

"Why I—I don't know, sir," Howden stammered, and he flushed.

"Step back there," the president said, waving his hand at Howden. "Step back there where I can see you." His gaze swept Howden, head to foot; swept again, foot to head, without reticence, nakedly.

"Of course you can. Of course you can make a speech. You make speeches every day to your classes," the president said abruptly, decisively. "What's the matter with your arm?"

The question startled Howden more than the other. It was the first time anyone had ever asked him about his arm. He had thought that it was unnoticeable; but the president had noticed it. Howden moved his arm self-consciously, eased it a little behind him.

"I injured it, sir," he said.

"It's lame, isn't it?" the president asked, brazenly staring.

Howden had never been so self-conscious, so aware of his own appearance.

"Yes, sir," he said in a low voice. "They had to take some bone out at the elbow."

"Well, no one would ever know it," the president said. Then

he seemed to relax. The thing or quality that was so unreserved and naked in his eyes withdrew. The pale, thin-looking flesh crinkled, folding in the lines of harsh severity, and he was smiling. It seemed strangely out of character; and then it did not seem out of character. It was a sardonic little smile. But his voice was less grating when he spoke.

"You know," he said musingly, "a long time ago the doctors cut me open and took something out of me too." It sounded cryptic, and yet it did not sound that way. It seemed to be a kind of tie, and yet it did not seem to be.

Then the president must have thought of something else.

"Now—" he said with feline suddenness, but as if something indefinable had been settled, as if an objective had been achieved, as if an assumption had been proved. He picked up the sheaf of papers from his desk. "All right. I want you to take this and stand over there and read it."

"You mean aloud?"

President Wimbush nodded.

"Exactly as if you were speaking to an audience. Here. See that light switch against the wall? That's it. Now stand over there."

The light from the cluster in the ceiling flooded over Howden as he stood there looking blankly down at the first typed page. His mouth was dry. He could feel the president's clinical gaze upon him. Wetting his lips with his tongue, he started reading.

"Come now," President Wimbush said crisply. "Give yourself time. Are you in a hurry?"

"No, sir."

"All right, then take your time."

"Ladies and Gentlemen," Howden began again, "members of the Colored Progressive Clubs, I bring you—"

"Wait a minute," the president said, throwing up his hand. "Got to change that. Got to make a lot of changes." For a moment he gave Howden an empty stare. "Better say, 'Colored Citizens and Brethren.'"

"Colored citi—"

"Or do you think we ought to put 'Brethren' first?" President Wimbush broke in. He got up and walked to the window and back again. His small figure, expensively clothed, looked as dry and austere as a spinster's until, with his coat open, one noticed the protuberant little belly.

"Got to make them think you're one of them," the president said, sitting down again. "Now once more."

" 'Brethren' first?" Howden asked. He was feeling more at ease.

"Try it that way. Got to rub it in. Got to rub it—" He laughed with a sound that was half dyspeptic belch, half snort, and shot a glance at Howden. "You get the idea, don't you?"

Howden was not sure that he did get the idea, and he smiled in a dubious way, but he tried once more. When he had read through the first two pages, the president interrupted him again. One liver-spotted hand gently plucking at his lips, the Old Man thought for a moment. Then he said that the sense of the opening paragraphs could stand. They had just what they ought to have, those first paragraphs—plenty of gravy. A smile of sardonic amusement flitted across his face. He said it didn't matter much what the occasion was when you made a speech to Negroes, just so you gave them plenty of gravy. But there was one thing: there would have to be something in there to explain why he had sent a substitute.

"Sir, you mean—" and Howden hesitated. "Do you mean you're going to have somebody make this speech for you?"

The president looked at him. It was very quiet.

"Yes."

"You mean—"

The president waved his hand impatiently. "I don't have time," he said. "Have you got a blue suit?"

"I?" It took a moment for the import of it to hit him. His mouth hung open. He felt weak and inadequate. Then he heard the president's voice again.

"You know, son—" The epithet must have sounded strange to

him because he made a barely perceptible pause, and then he repeated it. "You know, son, I think I've sized you up pretty well.
You're a lot like me."

Howden didn't say anything. He felt that he was under a kind
of spell. He wondered what President Wimbush was thinking.
He wondered what picture of him the president had in his mind.
He could hear Miss Lark's typewriter going in the room behind
him, but otherwise it was very quiet. Through the window he
could see the lights spaced out on one stroke of the U. All around
him there was life, there were other personalities—Miss Lark in
the other room, people in the dormitories, people at supper—but
he felt strangely alone with the Old Man.

"Now, have you got a blue suit?"

"Yes, sir, I've got one," Howden answered.

"A blue suit dresses a speech up better than anything. A col-
lection of darkies will listen quicker to a blue suit and big words
than to a common meter hymn," the president said, snorting with
laughter. "Let's see now. We'll have to convey my apologies,
won't we?" Brow clouded, he made a tuneless humming sound
while he thought. "You can say you would not have under-
taken— Wait a minute. That'll about get it." He reached under
the edge of his desk, and Howden heard a buzzer whir in the
outer office.

Miss Lark skittered in, her eyes a-glitter with curiosity.

"Get this, Miss Lark," the Old Man said. "I bring you President Wimbush's sincere regrets that he cannot—"

"You want me to take that in shorthand?"

"What else?" the president snapped harshly. "Now you've
broken my train of thought. Where was I?"

"Sincere regrets that he cannot," Miss Lark said.

". . . regrets that he cannot be with you on this great occasion. He has asked me to say that only a thing of great importance— Wait a minute. Yes.—of great importance to his fellow
colored citizens of the state could prevent his being here." He

shot a mocking glance at Howden, and then he looked at Miss
Lark. "Now read it back. It's got to sound convincing."

Miss Lark read it back and said it sounded convincing. Closing
his eyes and tilting his head, the president went on dictating
without hesitation. Now and then a sardonic grimace of a smile
flicked across his face. He snorted once or twice. Otherwise he
went on like a scratched record on a talking machine. When he
had revised the whole introduction, he asked Miss Lark to read
it back again.

"Now, Howden," the president said, "start all over. You wait,
Miss Lark. See how it sounds. All right."

Howden cleared his throat. Miss Lark's eyes narrowed critically as she resettled herself in her chair. The Old Man cocked
his head.

" 'Colored Brethren, Citizens—' "

Howden read the paper through without a blunder. Though
he had never expected to use them, the tricks of voice that he
had learned in that public speaking course at New Hope came
back to him. He found himself anticipating passages that needed
emphasis, the places that called for an appreciative pause. In the
end his voice rolled sonorously to a full stop.

There was a moment's silence. The president was staring at
him with a thoughtful frown. Miss Lark was the first to speak.

"That's perfect!" she gasped on a long exhalation. "Simply
perfect!"

"There's something wrong with it," the president said.

"Mr. President," Miss Lark said, "it's a splendid speech."

"About halfway down, isn't there something wrong with it?"
He was still looking at Howden, but it was Miss Lark who
answered.

"Not a thing, Mr. President. Not a single thing," Miss Lark
declared, vigorously wagging her head. "I wouldn't change a
word of it. 'Colored Brethren, Citizens—' Why, it rings. Doesn't
it, Mr. Howden, hunh?"

Howden nodded in agreement, although he could not remember the ideas in the speech.

"All right," President Wimbush said and stood up. But he must have thought of something else, for he sat down again. "What if there're white people in the audience?" A snort of cynical impatience escaped him. "I wouldn't want to embarrass a darky audience by saying things I oughtn't to say in front of white people."

The silence was thoughtful while Miss Lark and Howden stared off into space. After a time Miss Lark said slowly that she didn't think there was a thing in the speech like that. The speech was inspiring and very sane. It said exactly the things Negroes needed to hear, no matter who was in the audience. Didn't they need to hear that nothing stood in their way but their own sloth and ignorance? They needed to be told that they themselves, and not white people, were their own worst enemies. They needed to be reminded that patience was a virtue. And Miss Lark wanted to know if the speech didn't make all these points ring.

There was another silence.

"All right," President Wimbush said, satisfied at last. "You get out a fair copy, Miss Lark. That fool from the colored paper in Carthage will be bound to ask for it, though he'll quote out of context. And, Howden, son, you come in tomorrow and we'll go through it again."

They all looked at each other for a moment, and then the president pulled out his watch. "My God, it's almost eight o'clock," he said.

Miss Lark bounced to the closet and got the president's gray topcoat and his gray felt hat. She handed the coat to Howden.

"Just around my shoulders," the Old Man directed, turning his narrow back to receive the coat. "And switch my desk light off." He did not pause in the outer office. "Good night."

With short, crisp strides, the president went out the door, and his firm, quick footsteps receded down the hall. He did not move like a man in his sixties.

"What did I tell you, hunh?" Miss Lark said, turning a knowing smile on Howden.

"Tell me about what?"

"He's never sent anybody to substitute for him before," Miss Lark said. Dabbing her face with a powder puff, Miss Lark looked at him over the top of her open compact.

"It doesn't mean a thing," Howden said.

"Didn't I tell you he likes you, hunh?"

"It's just bushwa," Howden said. He couldn't objectify any part of the evening's experience.

"Come on," Miss Lark said. "We've got to catch somebody in the kitchen if we want to eat. I'm hungry. Aren't you hungry, hunh?"

Howden did not see how anyone, looking at herself in a mirror, could possibly make up so badly.

CHAPTER TWELVE

ALL THAT summer, while broken-down country school teachers filled the campus with their nervous anxieties over courses for degrees, President Wimbush found extracurricular things for Shelton Howden to do. It was a casual but inveigling business. "Shel, son," the Old Man would say (Howden could not remember when being called Shel had started), "I want you to work on the alumni quarterly bulletin." Or, "Son, check these ag department requisitions against what they've got down there. Can't trust a darky's judgment." Or it would be the accounts of the boarding department, which, Howden discovered, was the president's private concession—a perquisite, like the house and housekeeper and student help, which went with the presidential position. Howden didn't know much about these things at first, but he liked detail, and he soon learned. His interests and his ambitions became involved.

When he was relieved of some of his classroom work in the fall, it became obvious to everyone that he "stood in" with the president. There was no official change in his status—nothing in the catalogue, nothing in black and white: he didn't even have an office of his own—but what was happening was reflected in the attitudes of his colleagues. They began to react to him in various ways, according to their natures: with timidity, with formal stiffness, with sullen suspicion, with presumptuous, aggressive cordiality, and with sycophantic flattery. There was no end to the variations, and Howden felt disdainful of them all.

It was very strange. It was like being possessed by another personality when he worked on things for the president. Though he sometimes experienced a slight sense of reservation, he could see the Old Man's point of view and assume his attitudes. Delivering speeches, which he did with increasing frequency, to Negro audiences up and down the state, Howden would remember the places in which, during the composition, the Old Man had laughed sardonically or had made some slanderous comment, or where—though the words of the speech marched on with seeming sincerity—his voice had dripped irony and his eyes narrowed with something that might have been hate. Standing before an audience, Howden would remember the president's private look and intonation, which had nothing to do with the public words; and once, he remembered, that in the middle of editing a speech the Old Man had broken off and looked across at him with that peculiar assumptive stare. "Son," he had said, "when you make these speeches, don't be loyal to me. Be loyal to the speech. You got to be a stage-actor. I've been stage-acting for more than forty years." Then he had croaked with laughter and gone on with his work.

But at first it was not exactly easy. At first sometimes that mental and emotional reservation would pop up from the depths of Howden's conscience and sit there frowning like a censor who expects to be ignored. Then, the censor gradually dissolving, Howden would become totally preoccupied with just his corporeal self, with breathing, with the color of his hand gripping the rostrum, with the ring of his voice sounding out the words the Old Man had composed with such amused, ironic, and triumphant tongue-clucking, with harsh, contemptuous bitterness and a sort of gleeful hate.

When the Old Man himself delivered them, the speeches were phenomena of the oratorical art. They were as devious and misleading as a chased fox's trail or as deliberately obscure as the bottom of a well; or they grandiloquently said nothing. There was no way to describe them.

Once Howden went to hear the Old Man deliver the main address to the State Negro Teachers Association of which he was the president. That speech was many things, did many things. It damned and praised, was arrogant and fawning, abusive and conciliatory, liberal and reactionary, slanted for black and slanted for white. It lashed and soothed, scratched and purred, laughed and wept. The white daily paper in Carthage made it the subject of a laudatory editorial. The Carthage colored weekly damned it with scurvy praise.

Coming back in the car, Howden confessed that he had never heard anything like it. The Old Man's eyes flashed a gloating look of triumph. "It's just the gravy, Shel," he said. "It's just the gravy and play-acting." Nodding at the back of the student-chauffeur and waggling one dainty, gray-gloved hand in warning, he closed his eyes and said no more.

[2]

The president's house disconcerted Howden. It was much bigger than any single dwelling he had ever been in. The long, high-ceilinged living room, the furnishings, which were old and good, the drapes, the rugs, the atmosphere of muted order were all outside Howden's experience. If it seemed to him that there was a faint, chill breath of sterility in the dining room, with the curtains drawn and the electric candles shining yellowly above the darkly polished surface of the sideboard and the silver and napery gleaming and the white-coated servant moving noiselessly about and the housekeeper occasionally peering in from the pantry—if it seemed to Howden a little forbidding and unlived in and that he himself had wandered there by mistake, he knew it was because of his own inexperience.

And later it was all right. He grew used to it quickly. He came to look forward to the after-supper period in the downstairs study. He felt very close to the Old Man then, and he knew that the Old Man felt close to him too. The study was a small and intimate room, and on the chill, damp nights of winter and early spring, a fire burned in the grate. There were pictures on the walls and books in shelves and on tables. The books, Howden noted without much interest, were on psychology, sociology, and history. Two of the chairs were of soft brown leather, and there was a matching lounge where the Old Man liked to sit with his back against one deep arm and his legs straight out on the cushions. At night after supper he drank quantities of a wine called angelica. There was always a glass of it in one hand and a cigar in the other. But his tongue never thickened; his eyes never glazed or dulled. He grew a little more garrulous perhaps, but he talked much anyway, and Howden did not think it was because of the wine.

The Old Man's mind skipped from one subject to another and back again, like a bee in a flower garden. But what his mind produced was not honey. With malicious glee he made most things seem ridiculous. He knew all of the important white people in the state and most of the important Negroes in the country, and when he talked about them he made them seem very commonplace, even a little silly. When he talked about race, which he often did, his voice would rasp and hiss and whine with malignant contempt for all those who let the issues of race affect them. In this way he made the race problem seem silly too, as if it were a trick he was born with the secret of.

The only subject he treated with gravity and without cynicism was his daughter, Gerry. When he spoke of her, he was a fond and fretful parent, going soft, sentimental, and somewhat querulous. It was another of those changes in him that at first seemed out of character and then did not seem so.

He didn't understand Gerry, he said. He did not see why she wanted to stay up there in Boston with that man she married since it was obvious that she was unhappy and since also she had a better home right there in Arcadia than Raymond Rudd would ever give her. Rudd was no good, the Old Man declared with peevish conviction, even if he did have a law degree from Harvard. "If he were any good," President Wimbush wanted to know, "would I have to send Gerry money every month? I can tell from what she doesn't say in her letters what kind of life he's leading her. He's just no damn good."

The Old Man sipped his wine in a long, morose silence and then moved on to something else.

Night after night it was the same thing (for soon Shelton Howden was having supper with the president three and four times a week): the Old Man would skip from one subject to another, to Gerry, to something else again. It was a kind of monologue. The voice would go on and on, its mocking, sarcastic rise and fall like a magic incantation, while Howden sat and listened like one bound in a spell. Occasionally the Old Man would come out with some whimsy or, his voice as abrasive as a file, with something so unexpected and perverse that Howden's mind was teased to working and his tongue to reluctant speech; but more often the endless, disjointed, and anecdotal talk created a hypnosis in which Howden did not hear words at all but only felt their content, as if the intonations, inflections, and rhythms alone had meaning and significance. His own thoughts and his own personality seemed purely derivative when he was with the Old Man.

He did not pretend to understand President Wimbush. Because he accepted and admired him, he did not try. He did not question what there was to admire. He could not tick off and catalogue the specific items of the Old Man's character. It was almost, Howden thought in hushed, inert, trance-like wonder, like being in love.

The idea gave him a distinct shock. And then it did more than that: it invoked a hot feeling of guilt and shame. For several days after the night the idea drifted up into his consciousness, he avoided the Old Man. When he did see him again, he experienced a tiny, irritating emotional block. It took several weeks—indeed, through the spring and part of the summer—for this to wear away.

The president was frequently absent from the campus for a shorter or a longer time. By virtue of his position, he was the Negro's representative on various boards and committees, state and national. He found amusing irony in the fact. "I am," he told Howden with a short, harsh laugh, "the *colored* member on the Tri-County Board of Child Health and Development, the *colored* member of the Southern Mammy Memorial Committee, and the *colored* third vice-president of the Benton Philanthropy Fund for Aid to Southern Students." He attended meetings of the Land-Grant college presidents in Chicago. He was gone for a week to the Conference of Interracial Affiliates in Atlanta. Twice in the month of July he was called to Washington, at the government's expense, to confer with somebody in the Department of the Interior.

In private the Old Man looked upon these activities with sardonic derogation and detachment. Returned from some meeting, which the colored papers had naïvely hailed as marking a milestone of Negro advancement, he would regale Howden with maliciously amusing stories about all sorts of well-known people and contribute slanderous sidelights that never got into the colored papers. He always, it seemed, ran into Dr. J. C. J. Twiddy, erstwhile chiropractor, who now decided what Negro should get the Federal post of Recorder of Deeds, and Alice Alene Applewhite, who, by the sheer specific gravity of her personality, had risen from country school teacher to college president, to special adviser to Madame Secretary of Labor. Or perhaps he had chanced to see Smiley Shifflette, known to the colored press as the "mystery man of Negro politics," who was, the Old Man snickered, as ubiquitous as the wind, always turning up somewhere.

The Old Man would tell Howden what had happened—or rather, what hadn't happened, for nothing important ever seemed to—and what had been said off-the-record, and what an organization like the Interracial Affiliates proposed to do when the time was ripe, if it ever was ripe. He ridiculed the N.A.A.C.P. and the League for Interracial Comity and the Negro press. These pressure groups made a lot of noise, the Old Man said, and took a lot of credit, but actually less than a handful of people controlled the forces that shaped the darky's fate. "Why, son, they don't know what anything's about and neither do their sounding boards, the nigger papers." The papers never knew what went on behind the scenes where the Old Man had been with a famous Southern Congressman and old J. C. J. and Alice Alene, and a half a dozen more.

"But you ought to read the darky papers," the Old Man said. "You do, don't you, Shel?"

"Yes, sir," Howden answered, "once in a while." Reading the colored papers gave him the same feeling that he sometimes got when he listened to the Old Man. It was a feeling of being totally ignorant of things going on in another world. There were really two worlds outside his own when he read the colored papers. There was the social world of Carthage, Memphis, Washington, and New York, which he could think of as exclusive and desirable; and then there was the brassy, belligerent, raucous world of extremely race-conscious people.

"Well, you ought to read them all the time."

"How come, sir?"

"To strengthen your disbelief," the Old Man said, chortling softly.

"My disbelief?"

"In the ability of all those people and organizations whose names you read in the papers to change things. You don't believe they can change things, do you, Shel?"

"To tell you the truth, sir, I hadn't thought about it."

"Well, don't think about it, because they can't. They can ride herd on gradualism and write open letters and hold mass meetings every other day in the week, but they can't change things. They've created a crackpot world for themselves, and in it they're as utterly confused and crazy as a bunch of blind dogs in a meat house. Their world doesn't have much relation to reality."

Howden could well believe it. When he read the colored papers, he reacted to the idea of that world with a bored and vexed annoyance, although he could not think of it as real. He could not get it through his head that it existed anywhere except in the colored papers and that it would go on existing whether he turned the page or not.

The Old Man went on casually to other matters that seemed to have no connection with what had gone before. He talked about the college and about Dr. Doraman, who was state superintendent of education, and then his voice suddenly changing with contemptuous humor, he was talking about his faculty. He said that he had to keep behind them all the time so that they wouldn't knock things apart. He said that the men among them represented a pretty common type—the type that considers itself to be almost the apotheosis of something called race man. They all wanted to be a Monroe Trotter or a Walter White or a Curtis Flack, who were race men too—except that they made a living out of it. And the men who made a living out of it had to be smart enough to intellectualize it all and to make a pretense of having their racial programs conform to principles of reason.

The ordinary type of race man—the men on the faculty and

the darkies who edited the papers and the local big shots who were always getting up delegations to wait on mayors—weren't that smart, the Old Man said. They had never learned, or would never acknowledge that there was nothing to be solved 'but the problems of their own frustration. They were all victims of a disease called racial absolutism, the Old Man said, which blinds them to the fact that there are no absolutes: there are only continuing extremes which none but fools try to reach. There is no absolute equality, no absolute justice, no absolute freedom, no absolute truth or morality, the Old Man said. And the damnedest, funniest irony of all, the Old Man declared, is that there is no absolute race—although the race men hadn't learned it yet.

Howden sat there listening, not trying to follow, knowing that he was no good at abstract thought. Insects worried the night. He could hear them pop against the screen of the side porch, trying to get to the dim light that glowed in the living room. He could see that light brokenly reflected in the decanter of wine on the porch table at the Old Man's elbow, and he could smell the fragrant smoke of the Old Man's cigar.

"Fortunately, son," President Wimbush went on reflectively, "people like us aren't answerable to the race men. If we were, there'd be no balance in the thing, and the race men's madness would destroy us all. People like us are the equilibrators of the unequal balance. It's not our fault that it's unequal. We didn't set it up, and we can't turn time back to the year One. It's only common sense to accept the world as we find it. What else are we going to do but that?" He snorted cynically and impatiently in the pause. "That's what I do, and after nearly three years of watching you, I'd say that's what you do too. But then, people like us are born with a sense of reality."

Howden stirred, his mind at last, though reluctantly, framing a question which his lips reluctantly spoke. "People like us, sir?"

But the Old Man went on as if he had not heard.

"That sense of reality is important, Shel. It's what establishes values. It's what makes one man a success and another a failure.

Even a saint without it is just a damn fool miscalled an idealist. But people like us have got it."

Howden stirred and asked his question again, and this time the Old Man heard.

"We're a caste, son," he said lightly and casually.

Howden could not see the Old Man's eyes, but he knew their look of unwithholding, cynical detachment, of sportive malice.

"In the truest sense, my boy, we're the white man's niggers."

Howden did not know why he felt no shock, why all that happened was that a pulse seemed to come alive and flutter in his throat through the long silence. He did experience a faint desire to reject and deny the definition; and this is what he would have done had anyone else said it. Now he felt drugged, even while his mind sorted out the despicable images that the phrase "white man's nigger" invoked.

When the Old Man spoke again, it was as if he had read Howden's thoughts.

"It's only because of the concept that it seems contemptible," the Old Man said derisively, "and the concept's not important." His voice quickened as in relished anger. "There's nothing wrong with being the white man's nigger. We can't help it, can we? And we're conditioned to it, aren't we?"

"Conditioned?"

"To being the white man's nigger." It was a jeer uttered in high gaiety. "Of course we're conditioned to it. Our instincts were corrupted at our birth, by the very circumstances of our conception, and the conditioning has been going on ever since. That exonerates us, my boy. And contempt doesn't really attach to us. It's another matter altogether." He drained his glass of wine. "Yes, sir, that's another matter altogether."

"How come, sir?" Howden asked at last.

"The thing is," the Old Man said, "that our fathers begot us in scorn and loathing, and we'll go on avenging ourselves on our mothers until we die." Abruptly he laughed with sarcastic glee. Then, picking up the decanter, he held his stemmed glass toward the weak rays of light from the living room and poured. Howden could detect just a faint trace of revulsion in himself. Except for that, he had never felt so detached, so cynical, and so mature.

When the Old Man spoke, his voice was low, mild, and indulgent.

"You know, Shel, boy, the truth's a curious thing. It either sets you right or kills you altogether."

CHAPTER THIRTEEN

WHEN old Professor Ramsey, who had taught general social studies at Arcadia for a quarter of a century, died in the middle of Shelton Howden's fourth year, there were at least fifty applications of qualified people on file. The president had Howden go through these applications first, eliminating the least desirable, and among the nine that were left, the president said that it was simply a matter of eenie-meenie-minie-moe, since by and large all darky teachers were alike and there was not much time. The choice thus fell on an applicant named Spurgeon Kelly, who came, unobtrusively enough, at the end of February bringing a straw suitcase and some books in an orange crate tied with rope.

Kelly's application contained the information that he was thirty-two, called Memphis his home, and had graduated from college in 1930. All arms and legs and neck, he looked like something whittled out in an odd moment by an amateur with a dull jackknife. His nose stuck out of his umber-colored face like a conical hillock in a plain, his chin was a rough square protuberance, and his ears, set low against the jaw, flanked his face at right angles. Standing or sitting, Kelly looked as if he were waiting for someone to come along, fold him up, and stick him away in a closet.

Although Kelly lived in the next room in the practice cottage, Howden might never have spoken a word with him except under necessity. Indeed, practically all of the contacts Howden had with his colleagues were strictly professional. He had both little inclination and little time. Getting out a monthly alumni bulletin, supervising the new NYA unit on the campus, and handling all sorts of details kept him pretty busy. But he did have to go to Kelly's room to collect the dollar that every faculty member was asked to contribute for the quarterly staff social.

"Whose idea is this anyway?" Kelly wanted to know.

"You mean the social?" Howden asked.

"Yes, and the money."

"The socials are a kind of tradition," Howden said, "and the money has to come from somewhere."

"Does the president want to entertain us? If he wants to entertain us, why doesn't he pay for it?"

Howden didn't say anything. He felt defensive and hostile. He had not expected the questions nor the bland, composed, quizzical stare. Standing in the center of the untidy room, he felt chagrined, embarrassed. Kelly had not risen from the table against the wall. His steel-rimmed glasses sat far out on his nose. Open in front of him was a book, and several other books lay on the unmade bed, the other chair, and the dresser.

"What happens at these socials anyway?"

It was the complete lack of ceremony, the singular forthrightness, that bothered Howden.

"Talk?" Kelly asked. "I have no talent for small talk." Taking off his glasses, he held them up to the light and squinted at them. His uncovered eyes made him appear even milder. "I've just got no talent for the niceties of social conversation," he said soberly.

"Well—" Howden began ambiguously.

"I'm not saying that maybe it isn't a useful talent for some people to have," Kelly said, "but I haven't got it."

Howden said nothing to this either. He could think of nothing to say. He wanted to master the situation, to keep Kelly in line.

"This social sounds like a waste of time to me," Kelly said.

"It's all a matter of your point of view," Howden said, bristling.

"Everything's a matter of your point of view," Kelly said. "But I'm not going, and I'm not going to pay for something I don't get."

"But everybody pays it," Howden said sharply. "It's just one of those things you do without giving it a thought."

Kelly's wooden face broke into a smile that was not at all wooden. It was a smile of grave discovery rather than pleasure.

"People here do a lot of things without giving them a thought, don't they?" It was not so much a question as a documentary statement confirming something in his mind. He sighed. "Well, old Kelly tries to think about things." He stood up, unfolding like a collapsible chair. "I'm not going to the social. I'm not going to contribute a dollar either. You see my point of view?"

"It doesn't matter whether I see your point of view or not," Howden said.

"No," Kelly said slowly, "I guess it doesn't."

Going to his own room, Howden found himself filled with a kind of self-indignation. Without quite knowing why, he experienced a feeling of having been made to seem ridiculous, as if he had been discovered with one of those signs saying "I'm a Fool" pinned to his coattail. He did not like Spurgeon Kelly. He resented the man's easy air of equality. He'd have to show Kelly, Howden thought.

As time went on, though Kelly seemed to be genial enough in a placid sort of way, none of his colleagues was sure that he really liked him. Everyone said that Kelly was, well—a peculiar man. When he talked, which was not often, they listened, but the things he said and the forthright way he said them seemed to

create unease. Miss Lark said that Spurgeon Kelly gave her a
feeling that she was made of glass.

Howden could understand it. He remembered the day when,
leaving his room in the practice cottage, he had been unable to
avoid running into Kelly. It was a week or so after the faculty
get-together, which Howden had no wish to mention; but meeting Kelly there in the hall of their common quarters made for an
embarrassing social situation in which something had to be said,
and there was no point of contact except the get-together.

"We missed you the other night," Howden said.

"You mean at the social?"

"Yes."

"Why should you tell me that?"

Howden flushed at the flatness of the question.

"Because it happens to be true," he said. "The president asked
where you were."

The bland quizzical expression on Kelly's face did not change.
"Did you tell him I didn't pay the dollar?"

"No," Howden said.

"You should have told him," Kelly said. "Were you afraid to
let him know you couldn't get me to pay it?"

Howden eyed Kelly with sudden sharp distrust. It was as if
Kelly had looked straight through him.

"Afraid?"

"You know, it's sometimes better to admit a failure than to have
a success," Kelly said. "Well, see you later."

That was all there had been to it, but Howden thought of it
as he walked across the campus with Miss Lark and she told him
that Kelly gave her the feeling that she was made of glass. To hell
with him, Howden thought. But he heard Miss Lark's voice going on.

"Let's forget Kelly," Howden said.

Women students in blue Hoover aprons and men students in
long, gray shopcoats were marching to their afternoon classes in

applied arts. The "Hep, hup, hep" of the leaders sang out on the
April air, but there was no verve or zip.

"Suppose Mrs. Noe is right, hunh?" Miss Lark asked.

"Right about what?"

"About what Kelly's teaching. Suppose he really is teaching his
classes that there is no God?"

"Oh, bushwa," Howden said. "How did it come up anyway?"

"In faculty meeting, that time when you and the Old Man
were away. Mrs. Noe said one of her students told her he was
teaching them that. He had them reading a book that said it too."

"There're lots of books that say there's no God," Howden said.

"I know, but Kelly—"

"Good Lord, do we have to talk about Kelly?" He opened the
door and followed Miss Lark in past the bursar's office and the
stairway that led to the classrooms on the second floor.

"You should just have been there," Miss Lark said.

"I'm glad I wasn't there," Howden said.

"And you know what?" Miss Lark went on, lowering her voice
now that they were in the outer office. "While they were talking
about it, Kelly got up and just walked out. It was—"

Suddenly the door to the inner office opened, and there stood
the Old Man, crisp as cold lettuce. His quick gaze shifted from
Howden to Miss Lark as he stood there in the doorway.

"I've been waiting for you, Shel," he said.

"I was just telling him about that faculty meeting," Miss Lark
said.

"What faculty meeting?"

"I was telling him—"

"Never mind about that now," President Wimbush said. He
had a look of grim preoccupation. "The Governor's coming."

Miss Lark, in the act of sitting down, stood up straight again.

"You mean— Mr. President, you mean—"

"Somebody just called me long-distance from the State House,"
the Old Man said. "Come on, Shel. Come on in here." He pushed
the door open wider.

"Oh, my Lord!" Miss Lark said.

"Don't let anybody interrupt us," President Wimbush said to
Miss Lark. Then he closed the door.

[2]

The Old Man had no real precedent to follow, although white
visitors at the college were not unusual. On a special day of the
year they came from the surrounding rural communities and
gawked in white-eyed silence at the handicraft exhibits, listened
in cold imperturbability to a program of Negro spirituals, and
later, in watchful isolation, ate box lunches of fried chicken and
potato salad on the lawns.

But the Governor's visit would be different, and President
Wimbush was worried.

"I can't ask the Governor to eat a box lunch," the President
said pettishly.

"No, sir. I guess you can't," Howden said.

"And another thing. Everybody's got to be there to welcome
him," President Wimbush said. "We've got to plan it all out to
the last detail."

They worked on plans all that afternoon and far into the night.
For three days it was like being on a two-man board of military
strategy. There was a plan for a clear day and a plan for a rainy
one. Classes were suspended and the college population was mo-
bilized like an army, each squad of students commanded by a
faculty member. Buildings were scrubbed inside and out. Cement
walks were washed down in a solution of picric acid. Every scrap
of paper that might be blown into the shrubbery was the object
of search. In the grove on the bluff the underbrush was cleared
away, and the bricklaying department built a huge barbecue pit.
The carpentry department was busy; the painting department
was busy. The home-making department shed nervous tears. And
President Wimbush was everywhere, clapping his hands imperiously, grating out harsh commands.

"Hey, you boy there—you in the red sweater! Go back and rake again. I don't want a dead leaf left!"

Feverish, intense activity, the whirring of muscle-powered mowers, the scrape of rakes, the clat-clat of hammers.

"Mobley! Where the devil's Mobley? Bledsoe, go find Mobley."

Young men busily whitened the stones on the edge of the fill, busily slapped lime on the bridge railing.

The president himself selected the pigs to be barbecued, and after the terrified squeal, the plunge of the knife, the wobbly, buckle-legged stagger while the blood ran, stayed to see them properly scraped and butchered.

Young women washed windows, washed paints, waxed floors, polished the benches and the lectern in chapel.

"Go back there. There's a spot you missed. Do the whole thing over! Do it twice over! Shel, boy, you have to keep behind the darkies all the time."

When it was all done at last, the campus was like the Circus Maximus awaiting in mock gaiety the emperor and the gladiators. Pennons flew over the doorways of the college buildings and wickered from poles set up around the circumference of the college lawn. Not a cigarette butt, a scrap of trash, or a crumb of dirt marred the naked neatness of the walks. Below the bridge, where the road ran to the village, the temporary arch of welcome was decorated with fresh boughs of blossoming dogwood and streamers of crepe paper. The road itself, freshly oiled, shimmered in the sun. The ditches were clear of weeds. Windows gleaming, shades all in line, the faculty houses beyond the fill passed the president's last rigid inspection at nine o'clock on the morning of the day.

At ten o'clock students and faculty, led by the college band, marched out through the arch and formed a line on each side of the road. The young men were dressed in dark suits; the young women wore starched white. Dark faces shone; highlights played like crown fires in thick, greased hair. When President Wimbush appeared, hatless and scowling, everyone stiffened to attention. The president walked slowly between the lines, swinging his head sharply from side to side, missing no detail. His eyes squinted in the sun. Reaching the end, he turned, took a few steps backward, and ordered the lines to straighten up—heels together, toes out, shoulders back.

"Is everybody here?" His voice rose with a thin and brittle quality. "Bledsoe, you stand on the other side, there next to Miss Stanky." His voice rose higher, thinner. "Give these lines some balance. Is everybody here? If any of you people are chewing gum, spit it out. And give these lines some balance! Where's Kelly? Tatum, you should have polished your shoes. Why didn't you polish your shoes? Where's Kelly?"

"Professor Kelly's not here, Mr. President," someone said.

"Why isn't he here?" the president demanded, looking around. "Shel, go get him. He's supposed to be here. Everybody's supposed to be here. Tell him I say to come at once. Go find him."

[3]

It was easy to find Spurgeon Kelly. He was right in his room, and when Howden knocked on the door, Kelly told him to come in. He was lying on the bed with his head propped against the footboard and the sunlight through the window falling across his knobby shoulders. He was fully clothed except for shoes. A book was spread open on his drawn-up knees, and a newspaper lay rumpled on the floor by the bed. Bland, wooden, and intractable, he looked at Howden.

"They're waiting on you," Howden said, trying to say it casually, trying to pretend to believe that Kelly's making them wait was just an oversight.

"Who? Who's waiting on me?"

"They're all out there," Howden said, "waiting for the Governor."

"I see," Kelly said. He moved the book a little and looked at his bony hands. "I'm not coming. Did you think I was coming?"

"They're waiting," Howden said again, and his voice took a slightly different key. "The president sent me."

"He's always sending you somewhere, isn't he?"

It was an entirely simple and sober question asked out of sober curiosity, but somehow it brought Howden a feeling of embarrassment. He stared at Kelly blankly for a moment.

"Well, anyway, I'm not coming," Kelly said, again studying his hands.

"You'd better come."

Kelly looked at him, and then he moved. He swung his feet to the floor and felt around with them for his shoes, still looking at Howden; and then he squeezed his feet into his shoes, but he did not get up. He sat there on the side of the bed.

"I suppose you won't understand it," he said tranquilly, "but I've got certain notions which I'm not changing just to hold a job or to get ahead in a job. One of those notions puts me dead against playing monkey for white folks."

Howden felt angry and frustrated, although he tried to look sardonic. Somewhere in the background were all the arguments he had accepted or rejected, but none of them seemed to have anything to do with the case. It had no business coming up, but there it was. You could never get away from the business of black and white; you could never get away from race. The neutral ground you wanted to stand on was always raked with a whining crossfire.

"No one's playing monkey," Howden said carefully, defensively.

"Oh, yes," Kelly said in his mild but intractable way. "That's all the white folks want. In exchange for the rights they permit us as men, they want us to deny our manhood."

"That's too metaphysical," Howden said sarcastically.

"Is it? I wonder," Kelly said. Like a hobbledehoy slowly toppling over, he bent down and picked up the newspaper and threw it on the bed. Then, sighing resignedly, he stood up. "Just tell Itchy-Britchy that I'm not coming."

"You don't want me to call your bluff like that," Howden sneered.

"Just go back and tell him I'm not coming, that's all," Kelly said. "Just tell him that."

But when Shelton Howden got back, it looked as if he would not have to tell the president anything. The band had struck up a lively march and was playing it very badly, although no one seemed to notice because all eyes were down the road. They were all watching the student who had been sent as a lookout to the little rise of the railroad embankment nearly a quarter of a mile away. Standing a little forward of the lines, looking taut and grim like a champion awaiting the crisis of battle, the president squinted into the sun. But he saw Howden before he could slip unnoticed into his place.

"Did you get him?"

"He's si— He's sick, sir," Howden said.

"Sick? What the devil's the—?" He did not finish, for at that instant something made a flashing tatter of brilliance in the sun on the railroad embankment. The president raised his voice.

"All right now, remember. The lines fall in behind the cars and march, *march* to the lawn in front of the administration building. I want perfect order. No talking. Shut up, Professor Tunnell! I said no talking, and that means you too. Not—" He broke off. "Here they come!"

Above the music, which played bravely on, came the piercing scream of sirens on the escorting motorcycles topping the embankment and roaring down the road between the canefields and the faculty houses. Howden counted eight motorcycles in a wide-spaced double column. They were there in a flash and a banshee wail of sirens. Ridden by insolent-looking, lithic-faced men in gray-green uniforms and polished black boots, the cycles wheeled just short of the lines and faced back down the road as the first two cars swooped to a stop. The Governor's car, long and sleekly black as a hearse, pulled up. Behind it were four other cars, each driven by a man in uniform.

The Governor stood up. He was a youngish man, with a meaty, swarthy face and a loose, thick mouth. As he looked at the tensely rigid lines that walled the road, his face broke into a smile and then into the freer lines of laughter under the brim of his linen cap. The president stepped smartly to the side of the car, and the Governor glanced down at him.

"Professor, it makes a real pretty sight," the Governor said in a strong, easy-laughing voice. "Why, I be dogged if I don't believe y'all got some soldier blood in you. Yes, sir, y'all got soldier blood sure as you born."

"Your Excellency—" the president began and stopped. He drew himself up a little straighter, cleared his throat, and started again. "Your Excellency—"

He went on speaking in fast, jerky, high-pitched snatches. It was the speech of welcome he had read to Howden the night before, but it was different now. Although he stood but a few feet away, Howden could catch only scattered phrases of it: ". . . the honor of your presence . . . the small resources of a grateful people . . . which you were instrumental . . ." The Governor stood there looking down on him with an indulgent smile. Once also the Governor looked at the newspaper men, who had got out of the last car, and gave them a slow, sustained wink.

"And so," Howden heard the president say, "you are welcome to this seat of a humble people's endeavors. Welcome because you have ever been the friend of the poor and humble; welcome because without your support this institution would wither and die; and welcome because you are the honored head of this fair and generous state."

The president bowed and stepped back while the newspaper men looked at him and then up at the Governor. There was a moment's silence.

"Now that was a mighty pretty speech, Professor," the Governor said in his strong, easy-laughing voice. He seemed to gather

himself together, and the full, powerful tide of his voice rolled
out as it did when he made campaign speeches in city audito-
riums, in one-street villages, and from ditch banks, luridly lit by
gasoline flares, at country crossroads.

"I want to tell you people now, I'm right proud to be here. And
I want to tell you something else. I came here irregardless to
what effect it'll have on next month's primary and on the drivel-
ing, lying, thieving game of politics." Thrusting his massive head
forward, he shook it. "I ain't no politician. I don't figure out
everything beforehand. All I do is follow the dictates of my heart,
and the heart that God put in this clumsy body of mine and told
to beat ain't led me wrong yet. It's a man's head that always
makes trouble, and when it comes to politics, I don't use my
head for nothing but to put my hat on." He paused for a moment
and blinked angrily all around. "But I got enemies, and this great
state's got enemies, and the whole country's got enemies—big-
headed men with teensie-weensie, chinchy, dried-up hearts.
They're the politicians. That's the kind you got to be to be a
politician. And they done sat so long in the velvet seats of power
and swilled so much in the fleshpots of graft that they got plumb
corrupted. They're the big city fellers up in Carthage and cross
north in Havenport, and I'm just a little ol' red-neck cracker
feller, poor as any darky that ever squatted behind two shoes,
with corns on his hands and the hope of God in his heart. But
you mind my words and hear me good now," the Governor ad-
monished. He struck his chest and shot his fist up, yanking his
rumpled coat awry. "I, Sam Lee Glass, the little old red-neck
who ain't got nothing but a heart, will drive the politicians out,
up-dump the fleshpots, and return the privileges of government to
the poor and humble where they belong!"

The president, looking quickly and meaningly around at the
line behind him, started the applause. As the sound of clapping
gathered solidity, the Governor licked his lips and stared about
him in a dull kind of way, as if, just waking from sleep, he wondered where he was. He blinked stupidly at the men in the cars

in front of him, at the reporters standing below him, and at the cavalcade of cars behind him. At last, heavy and clouded and mesmerized, his eyes came to rest on the columns that lined the road up to the arch. Then he shook himself, and his eyes seemed to clear momentarily.

"Understand me good now, and let the newspaper-writin' fellers get this straight," the Governor warned. "When I talk about the poor, I ain't talking about one class of the poor. In the brotherhood of poverty, there ain't no class distinctions. Yonder in Carthage, a laid-off dock worker without no money ain't no better and he ain't no worse than a quarterin' farmer back here in these flats. In the tyranny of labor and toil, cornbread and sorghum, moss bedding and shotgun rent shacks, there ain't no heir-apparents to privilege." Again his voice fell to a sort of powerful, dreamy whisper, and he looked far away over the heads of his listeners. "In the day I see coming, coming in God's own sweet time, there won't be no silks for one class and sackcloth for another. There won't be no begging for bread and getting a stone. There won't be no deserts of ignorance where folks perish from thirst for knowledge. Under God, before God, and around God, I'm going to make shining temples in the wilderness, build havens for the storm-tossed, and make a paradise for the weary."

Once more the applause, spontaneous this time, seemed to recall the Governor to himself, and once more he looked around blinking. Howden found himself clapping like everyone else. He looked at Professor Tatum, who was standing next to him, and the professor was slapping his hands together, and his soft-looking, earth-brown face wore a look of childish, immaculate gratification. All up and down the opposite line Howden could see this same expression on the faces of faculty and students. It was absolutely inexpressible.

Now the Governor was smiling, and his spirit seemed to lighten. He pushed his cap back off his square forehead so that his shaggy dark hair was visible. Beaming now, he threw out his arms in an expansive gesture. His voice came easy, soft and strong. "But I don't have to make that kind of speech to y'all," he said, laughing. "I just come down here 'cause the notion struck me to see y'all and my good friend the professor here, and to see what an' all y'all was doing, and to have me a good old relaxing time. I just wanted to get away from my responsibilities for a while. I'm mighty glad to be here, and I want y'all to show me you're glad to have me. Come on now, let's make some jubilee."

At a barely perceptible signal from the president, the band struck up "Happy Days Are Here Again," which made the Governor and his party laugh with unrepressed delight because it was the tune of the old campaign song. The Governor's car swept forward. Then the sputtering motorcycles dashed ahead, and the whole line of cars began to move under the welcoming arch between the still applauding columns.

[4]

There were a great many things at Arcadia College for Negroes that the Governor and his party had no idea were there. (The newspaper reporters had a field day, and the Sunday edition of the Carthage *Argus*, the Governor's own paper, carried a half page, written in a captivating, humorous vein, on the home-making department, the course in household chemistry, the mattress shop, and the C rating from the State Educational Rating Board.) At lunch, which the party ate in the decorated exclusiveness of the faculty dining room, the president stood like a major-domo behind the Governor's chair and answered all sorts of questions. The Governor declared it a right fine lunch.

When the party continued its tour of the campus, there seemed to be a good many things that were amusing too. Once as they trailed at a respectful distance, the president and Howden were invited to share the fun. The Governor, laughing, turned and beckoned them.

"You know what I was just telling them," the Governor said to the president. Five or six men of the party crowded around. The president's face twisted itself into a grin.

"No, sir, Your Excellency," he said.

"When I see what an' all you got here, makes me think you ought to have old Uncle Abe Posten down here. He's one of the smartest and best-educated darkies going," the Governor said, laughter beginning to gurgle out of him anew. The president's grin livened up, and he nodded his head appreciatively. But there was a measurable pause before the Governor went on again.

"Yes, sir. Old Abe knows more about what to do with balky mules an' Niggra gals than any darky I ever seen."

The laughter held off for a moment while the Governor looked down at the president, and then, in a sort of furious spurt, it broke from all the throats at once—the president's and Howden's with the rest.

The party was delighted with everything. They laughed happily at the exhibition of folk-dancing on the lawn in front of Domestic Science Hall and at the tricky formations of the college band and marching club. They roared with convulsed amusement when, during the exhibition of farm stock, a blooded bull had a sudden attack of diarrhea and spattered the white cotton stockings of the young woman leading a heifer directly behind him. The Governor said it was better than a circus. Yes, sir, it was more fun than Barnum-Bailey.

When the sun turned the river to molten, reddish gold, and the pines cast long shadows, and the sky in the east was cool with lavender and pink and green, the party's laughter rang through the grove on the bluff above the river while students scurried about serving paper plates of barbecued pig, and the rich voices of the choir floated through the woods, and the president, with Howden at his side, stood at a distance and kept his eye on everything,

And in the end, standing in the back of his car, collar upturned against the evening chill, and the lights of the escorting cars and motorcycles focused on him, the Governor made an easy-laughing final speech. He said he hadn't had so much real downright pleasure since he was a bug-eyed boy laughing and cutting the fool with the Niggras on his pappy's sorghum cane plantation. It kind of put him in mind, he said, of the old darky who was always slipping off from work and bedding down in a pile of lint cotton. One day the boss man caught this trifling old darky and told him he'd have to take drastic measures if he ever caught him sleeping on his time again. "Which kinda measures was them, Cap'n?" this old Niggra wanted to know. "Drastic. Drastic measures," the boss man told him. This old darky scratched his head a time or two, and then he looked up at the boss man and said, "Cap'n, since I don't know nothing 'bout measuring drastic, does y'all mind if I just sleep while you doing that?" The Governor said that this was one day he hadn't thought a thing about drastic measures, and the very first time he got another chance, he was going to slip off down to Arcadia again and get him some more of that good ol' barbecue and listen to some more real ol'-time Niggra singing. Yes, sir, the Governor said in his farewell speech, this was one day when he hadn't had no more respect for the dignity and honor of his high office than a skunk had for a dressed-up darky preacher.

When he had finished, everybody sang the state anthem and "The Star-Spangled Banner." Then, with a roar and a swoosh, their red warning lights flashing like monstrous angry eyes and the beams of their headlights plunging insolently into the dark, the vanguard of motorcycles careened away and the cars swept swiftly out behind them.

Howden looked at President Wimbush, who was standing beside him. The Old Man's face was a ghostly, insubstantial blur. Students were marching past them in the dark, making a massy, ambient shadow. Howden could see them as they passed under a light further on, appearing, dissolving, vanishing as if by magic. Soon they were gone, but the Old Man stood there, and Howden stood there too.

"Let's forget it! Let's don't say anything about it!" the voice said in fierce anger, suddenly. The Old Man was so directly in front of him and so close that Howden could smell the sourish but not unpleasant odor of his breath. "Goddamn it, I never said it was easy! I never said it was easy for people like us."

He stepped back a little and turned his head away from Howden and stared into the darkness for a long time.

"Well, Shel, son, it's been quite a day," he said at last, almost plaintively. And then he laughed abruptly. Taking Howden's arm and leaning somewhat heavily upon it, he turned in the direction of the big house in the bend of the U.

CHAPTER FOURTEEN

SHELTON HOWDEN was dreaming. In the dream there was a stream that widened and grew turbulent the moment he started to step across to join someone on the other side. Who this someone was he did not know. Suddenly a ship materialized. It strained and pitched against singing hawsers that stretched out of sight into eternity. He saw the Old Man aboard, and the Old Man was the captain; and Inky Spillman, and Spillman was the entire crew. Above the roar of the waters, which were now ocean-wide and in terrific motion, the captain screamed out something that must have been an invitation, for he kept making violent come-on gestures. When Howden tried to get aboard, climbing up some rigging over the side, Inky Spillman leaned far out over the deck rail and struck him a hard blow on the head. The blow made a distinct, sharp sound, and Shelton Howden awoke.

Now, lying awake, he remembered that it was Sunday. He

could always tell Sunday by the stillness, by the limpid, liquid-seeming quality of the sunlight. Twisting to find a fresh place on the pillow, eyes already closing again, he heard a knock. Then it came a second time. Muttering to himself, Howden slipped into his robe and went to the door. It was Spurgeon Kelly, dressed even to his finger-bitten hat, and carrying an armload of books.

"Sorry to disturb you," Kelly said.

"All right, all right," Howden said grumpily.

"Will you turn these books in for me?" Kelly asked, indicating the load in his arm.

"Why can't you turn them in yourself?"

"I won't be here when the library opens tomorrow," Kelly said. "I'm leaving here this morning."

"Leaving?" Howden asked, surprised in spite of himself. Then he felt triumphant, and a mocking smile curled on his lips. "So Itchy-Britchy gave you your walking papers?"

"No," Kelly answered calmly.

"You're just leaving?"

"That's right," Kelly said with no change of expression. "I'm just leaving."

"What brought this on?" Howden asked jeeringly.

Kelly looked at him, not quickly, but with a sharpening of his quizzical stare.

"Don't you know?" he countered quietly, shifting the books a little.

"If I knew, I wouldn't ask," Howden said. But he knew, and he hated all the implications of it, the assumption of moral right-eousness upon which it was based. He felt an unreasonable kind of anger. He wanted to sting Kelly, to wipe that wooden imperturb-ability off Kelly's face. "I'm no mind reader."

"I don't suppose you'll understand it—"

"You said that yesterday," Howden cut in rudely.

"Did I?"

"But you've got certain notions," Howden mocked. "Crap!"

The word came with ugly, drawn-out scorn. "I don't want to hear about your notions."

"No, I don't suppose you do," Kelly said, his eyes going over Howden with calm inscrutability. "I don't suppose you do," he repeated. He hitched the books closer against his side and made as if to back from the doorway.

But Howden did not want him to go yet. The resentment he had always felt—not so much against Kelly as against something nameless, amorphous, and ineradicable that Kelly or any one of a hundred men he knew might represent—swelled in him. But here was Kelly standing before him wearing the very look of that thing that would not let him be. This was not conscious thought in Howden. He was conscious only that he had not aroused Kelly at all, and his anger demanded that token. He felt thwarted, defeated.

"You're a race man," he said derisively, noting with satisfaction that Kelly stopped. "You've got no notions. All you've got is a clutter of accumulated passions over what you call the race question. That's it, isn't it? All you want to do is sit back on your black behind and tell the world how bad you're treated," he said with great sarcasm. "All you want to do is call attention to your terrible suffering. All you want—"

"Suffering? Oh, good God, no," Kelly said. It was not an exclamation, just a denial, the more effectively ironic because it was so bland. And he went on in that same mild, unemphatic way.

"Why, we're a happy breed, we Negroes. We've got hides as tough as pig iron, and as impervious. We've got mithridatic stomachs. We feed on poison every day, but we do not die. We don't even have pains from stomach cramps. We're wonders, we are; God's chosen people. Oh, no, we're not sufferers by any means. God wouldn't let us suffer."

Suddenly he stooped and dropped the books just outside the door. "I'll leave them there, if you don't mind, and you can tell the library where they are." He paused the barest fraction of a minute. "Well, so long," he said and turned like something made of wood.

"I won't be responsible for those goddamn books," Howden shouted, but Kelly didn't answer.

Howden stood there, hearing Kelly go up the hall and into his own room, hearing him come out again, walking heavily now but swiftly. Pivoting toward the window, he saw Spurgeon Kelly, a straw suitcase jerking stiffly on one side, a cardboard carton on the other, swing down the path and across the lawn until the shrubbery hid him. Then Howden went to the door and picked up the books and carried them to Kelly's empty and deserted room. In a childish, futile rage, he took the books one by one and destroyed them, tearing cover from binding and leaf from leaf and littering the floor with paper.

CHAPTER FIFTEEN

SHELTON HOWDEN of course heard the various versions of how and why Kelly had left Arcadia College so suddenly. The first story was that the president had fired Kelly for inefficiency, incompetency, and unco-operativeness. Later it was whispered that Kelly had played fast and loose with one of the women students and had run away to escape the consequences. Finally the faculty told each other in sniggering confidence that the true story was that Kelly was sexually perverted and that one of the students whom he approached had exposed him.

It did not bother Howden's conscience to let these fancies go unchecked. Indeed, the Old Man, who knew as much of the truth as did not reflect on Howden, thought corrections would be bad for faculty morale. Snorting, he said telling the truth to the faculty would be as cruel as disillusioning children about Santa Claus. The faculty, he said with amused contempt, were children.

They had to believe that anyone who went out of their group life was forced out. Sitting there in the twilight darkness of the side porch, the Old Man talked about it for some time. He said it was a stupid but stubborn herd-pride and a sort of instinctive desire to preserve the herd-life from criticism and attack. Anyone who left the herd voluntarily was a traitor. No matter how unbearable the group life was, the Old Man said, none of the ins wanted it known to the outs; and so those who got out were always driven out by some groundless folly or desperate accident or graceless sin. Group ethics or morality demanded no less than this.

"But we're above all that, Shel, son, and way, way beyond it."

"How do you mean, sir?"

The light on the end of his cigar made an arc in the darkness. "My God, son, group or race ethics, race morality—it's got nothing to do with us, and it's got nothing to do with reality either. And as for Kelly," he went on without a break, although his laughter died, "I'm going to put him on the black list. He'll never teach in college anywhere again, the damned fool."

[2]

From early May, when most of the rural schools had their closing exercises, Howden was busy. He substituted for the president at half a dozen graduations, at a district alumni meeting in Havenport, and at the State Negro Teachers Association in Carthage. For this latter speech, the Negro weekly paper in Carthage was forced to take note of him, though in a captious kind of way. But the Old Man said it was all right: it didn't make any difference what the nigger papers said.

Then the day after commencement at the college, President Wimbush quietly created a new position and put Howden in it. Howden was as surprised as anyone else, but it looked good when he saw it for the first time on the summer school brochure— Shelton Howden, Director of Summer School. It meant having an office and a secretary of his own. It meant having an administrative budget. It meant mastering a lot of new details. He engaged in his new responsibilities with a feeling of sober importance, even of apprehension, although on the day he had his organizational plan ready, Miss Lark told him there was nothing to worry about because certainly he knew that the Old Man liked him.

"I know," Howden said absently, thinking of other things. "Where is he?"

"He's not here," Miss Lark said. "He hasn't been here all afternoon."

Howden felt disappointed. He had wanted the Old Man's assurance.

"You look worried," Miss Lark said. "You still look worried. Isn't everything all right?"

"Everything's fine," Howden said.

"Well, you don't look it."

"Don't I?"

"You look far away," Miss Lark said.

"Do I?" It was a perfectly senseless conversation, but somehow it fitted his mood.

"What's the matter, hunh?"

"I wish you wouldn't keep asking me that," Howden said. He could discover no reason for the way he felt, unless it was that he was tired and lonely—although Miss Lark was right there. He went through the open door of the president's office to the window and stood there looking out. He was in effect the second officer of the college now. The Old Man had told him once that success was just a matter of mastering one's environment. Well, was he not mastering his? As Miss Lark said, the Old Man liked him; and he had money in the bank. The security and the sense of place he had always wanted were materializing at last.

But these thoughts lightened his mood only a little, for at this moment he felt that he had never been so lonely and so desirous of something he could not name. He sighed deeply, and Miss

Lark must have heard him, for from the outer office she asked again what the matter was.

"Nothing," Howden said.

"Well, you sound like something's the matter. Tell Laura Lark, hunh?"

It sounded silly and coy for a woman past her middle thirties, but Howden somehow liked it. It was Miss Lark's way of mixing genuine solicitude with curiosity.

"Nothing's the matter," Howden said. "Oh, I don't know, it's—" His voice trailed off.

The purple shadow of the bluff was creeping across the campus, and the early summer evening was beginning to sing its melancholy song. On the near stroke of the U, the buildings were folding back into the blueness. The students were all gone for the summer; the campus looked lonely. A last frantic shimmer of sun danced on the top of the trees in the fill.

"Laura," he called, "let's take a walk after supper." It was the first time he had ever made such a suggestion. It was the first time he had ever called her Laura.

"What—? What did you say?" It came with a sort of breathless fluttering, although Howden did not realize it.

He walked back to the door. "Let's take a walk after supper," he said again.

Compact in one hand and powder puff held motionless against her chin by the other, Miss Lark studied him for several seconds.

"I mean—that's strange," she said. "I mean, do you want to, hunh?"

"It's just that— Well, we could—" Howden said, and then he stopped because the telephone was ringing, louder than usual in the empty evening quiet. Miss Lark lifted the receiver quickly.

"Hello," she said into the telephone, but she smiled brightly at Howden just the same. "Arcad— Oh, yes, sir—" Her expression changed.

Howden could hear very faintly the voice on the other end.

"He's right here," Miss Lark said dully. "Do you want to talk to him? Well, he's— Yes, sir." She put the phone back into its cradle.

"You might as well forget a walk this evening," she said to Howden. "The Old Man wants to see you."

"Is he coming over here?" Howden asked her.

"Who goes to who around here?" Miss Lark snapped. She picked up her compact, turned her face toward the best light, and swabbed on powder with a fast and angry motion.

The door to the house was open and the screen unlatched, and Howden went in without ringing. There was a light on in the hall, and the Old Man himself, head slightly twisted and tilted upward, was standing in the curve of the staircase.

"Well, don't be long," Howden heard him say to someone upstairs. Then as he started down and saw Howden, "Oh—my daughter's here."

Months later Howden told Gerry that something seemed to leap in him when the Old Man announced it.

"She's—?"

"Surprised me," the Old Man said, frowning, but he sounded pleased. "Called me from Carthage around one o'clock, when her train got in, and I had the boy drive me up there to get her."

"You didn't know she was coming?" Howden asked. He had to say something.

"I never know whether she's coming or going," the Old Man said, croaking a little ruefully. "Come on, we'll start."

Everything was as it always was when he had supper there. He was sitting, as always, with his back to the folded doors from the hall. There was the same silver flatware on the dark sideboard, and the decorative border of hand-painted plates resting on their edges in the grooved molding around the wall, and the white linen cloth on the table. There was an extra place laid opposite him, but the food had the same bland nourishmentless taste of the food that was generally served for supper. The Old Man talked to Howden as he always talked to him—sardonically, with intimate, careless looseness of locutions—and Howden tried to follow what was said, but something kept pulling him away. Something kept making him swallow his food without chewing and tasting it. When the bread was served, he took two slices instead of one. Still he must have made responses because the Old Man went right on talking.

"Of course that's the way to look at it," the Old Man said. He was taking his weight on his elbows, which were supported on the arms of his high-backed master chair. He had laid his knife and fork aside. When the Old Man got wound up for talk, it always took them an hour to eat.

Howden did not know what was to be looked at that way, but he replied, "Yes, sir."

"You got to look at it that way. You got to take it with a handful of salt. You got to see the irony in it. If you don't—"

Then Howden heard a voice behind him. It was exactly as if he had thought himself alone in a dark room and a hand had suddenly reached out and snatched him around. His breathing stopped. He held his fork poised above his plate.

"You've got to see the irony in what, Poppa?" It was a vibrant, febrile-sounding voice, intense, even a little strident, quick.

Howden scrambled up, and there she was looking at him. Her light taffy-colored hair was cut short and curled all over her head. Beneath her pale ivory skin, the fragile bony structure of her face was plainly visible. She had both a consumed and a consuming look. She was like a jet of flame. Her bold eyes, a trifle darker than her father's, seemed to grab like sheathed talons and then let go as they moved quickly from Howden to her father.

"Oh," the Old Man said, without getting up. "Gerry, this is Shelton Howden. Shel, my daughter."

Her eyes came back to Howden like swooping hawks, and she smiled and said, "Oh, yes. Hello, Shel," before she moved from the doorway. She walked with a kind of tensive aggression, as if moving through a medium heavier than air, but easily, quickly. Howden stepped around to the other side of the table and pulled her chair.

"Now, Poppa, you've got to see the irony in what?" Even with her arms folded on the edge of the table, she gave the impression of being almost hysterically alive.

"I was talking about life in general," the Old Man said.

"What a subject," she said. "Everybody talks about it." She tasted her soup and pushed it aside.

"What's the matter?" her father asked with a kind of harsh concern.

"I'm all right, Poppa."

"Then why don't you eat? You've got to eat."

"Now, take it easy, Poppa," Gerry said. "Don't get upset."

"I'm not getting upset, but I mean for you to eat. What do you want?"

"I'm all right, Poppa. I'm fine."

"You want some milk?" her father asked her. "I think you ought to drink milk."

"You're going to look out for me, aren't you, Poppa? You're not going to let me down, are you?" Suddenly she looked across at Howden and smiled. Her lips, red as blood in her pale, famished-looking face, parted, and her even teeth showed. Tiny, very white lines radiated from the outer corners of her eyes.

"Isn't he too, too wonderful," she said. "Do I look like a child to you?"

Howden was glad that he did not really have to try to answer that. She was quite outside the ordinary terms of his experience. He wanted to place himself in the proper role, but he just stared at her blankly, as if she were a sign in a language he couldn't read.

"She won't take care of herself," the Old Man said peevishly, "and that no-'count darky up there in Boston won't take care of her."

"Isn't he precious?" Gerry said, looking at Howden again. "Isn't he too, too precious?"

"Don't worry. I've been telling him about you," the Old Man said.

"Has he? Has he been telling you about me?" Her eyes widened and grew brighter. It was like stepping up the power in lighted bulbs.

"Of course I have—and about that worthless darky too," her father said.

"What did you tell him, Poppa?" Gerry asked with metallic gaiety.

"Everything," her father answered. It must have struck him as a kind of mirthless joke, for he laughed tartly. "Everything."

"Not everything, Poppa," Gerry said, smiling down at her cup of warm milk in a private kind of way. "You don't know everything, Poppa," she said quietly. "You only know what I told you, and I don't tell everything."

The Old Man's fork clattered to his plate. "I know enough!" he said explosively. "I know—"

"Take it easy, Poppa, and don't be so neurotic," Gerry said. She was still smiling in that subdued and secret way. "You mustn't put my business in the street. Take it easy."

"He'd put you in the street if he dared—and your business too."

"Not Ray," Gerry said. "You don't know Ray."

"I know you ought to divorce him!" the Old Man replied harshly.

"But I can't divorce him, Poppa," Gerry said, looking up, her eyes widening. "It's not like that."

There was an incredible sharpness of reality over the whole scene. Howden could see the Old Man sitting there, one liver-spotted hand grasping his napkin beside his plate. He could see Gerry, her lips frozen in their secret smile, holding her cup of warm milk by both handles. Father and daughter stared at each other, and for a moment it was as if they had been turned to stone. Then the Old Man spread his napkin across his knees again and dropped his eyes.

"Now, Poppa—" Gerry began, as if something had been definitely settled between them. But her father cut in.

"Don't tell me to take it easy!" He lifted his fork and jabbed at his baked potato. "Rudd! Rudd!" he sneered. "What kind of a name is that? You ought to have your own name back."

"And leave me rudderless, Poppa?" Gerry said, her brows lifting, a very bright smile electrifying her eyes. She looked across at Howden, and Howden knew it was all ending exactly when and as Gerry wanted it to end.

"He wants to leave me rudderless," Gerry said. "Isn't he too, too damned neurotic!"

CHAPTER SIXTEEN

WHEN Shelton Howden looked back upon it later, that summer of 1937, when he was thirty-five, and the year that followed made up the most irrational, unaccountable period he ever lived through. Things happened of course by laws of sequential logic of their own, but it seemed to Howden that events themselves had no logic in them. Everything came about capriciously, as in a dream or a motion picture that skips whole frames, and neither in time nor continuity did one event depend upon another.

For instance, he could see no reason why the Carthage *Negro Advocate* should write up his appointment as director of the Arcadia College Summer School six months after the circumstance—when summer school itself was over—and use it as a springboard for a scurrilous attack upon the president. The terms of the attack distressed Howden. The editorial was especially unkind, implying that Howden was just a lightweight whom the president could maneuver to some dark and selfish end. The college, in fact, the whole state system of Negro education, the editorial said, should be thoroughly investigated, for, among other things, "it was still offering a horse and buggy education in the age of flight."

When the Old Man himself read the editorial, he snorted scornfully and told Howden to take it easy (he was picking up his daughter's slang) and not to worry, because he could handle anything that came up.

It seemed to Howden that everyone was always telling him not to worry. Indeed, he did begin to experience a sense of exemption from responsibility, a feeling of being borne along on a strong and willful tide. It seemed to him that everything was happening loose-endedly. Circumstances and events fell crazily into life, like gangling boys stumbling into a swimming hole.

There was no logic in his falling in love with Gerry, and no reason for her to fall in love with him, except that they were thrown into a good deal of contact late that summer. She took him places. She had friends in Carthage, and everywhere—people of the sort Howden read about in the society columns of the national colored weeklies—and she took him among them. Although, as Gerry said, she was not a child any longer (she was twenty-eight), it warmed and flattered Howden to feel that her father trusted them together. Once, it is true, he was shocked and abashed by the Old Man's telling him that he ought to start to think of getting married. But Gerry was right there when he made this remark, and she said later that it had nothing to do with *them:* Poppa was just thinking of Howden's career. "He lives in a moral vacuum," Gerry said, although Howden could not see the relevancy. "Don't you know that yet? He's submoral, sugar baby. He's neurotic." She was always uttering opinions about people, including her father, which were questionable.

Twice on steamy week ends after summer school had closed, Gerry took Howden down to Bay Nemeesha, to that Carthage doctor's summer place, where there were at least a half a dozen other guests all thrown together in a camping-out, immodest sort of way. It was a strain on Howden the first time, but the second trip was pleasant. It was quite jolly sleeping on canvas cots on the screened porch overlooking a reedy backwater of the Gulf and yet to know—as one of the married men jokingly put it—that the women were right there in the house if they wanted them. Had he had any previous reason to consider it, Howden would never have thought it could be fun to eat breakfast in robe and pajamas with eight or ten other robed and pajamaed people, most of whom had been total strangers to him the night before. He would never have thought it fun to loll around all day watching the endless poker game (he did not play poker) and the steady drinking (he did not drink either until Gerry insisted that he have just one, and he discovered drinking's value as a social equalizer) and listening to the hard, bright gossip about other people he didn't know.

But that was the way it was that summer and fall: a lot of things he had never done, or even thought of, he enjoyed doing with Gerry in the highly mobile world she knew.

Still, no matter where Gerry took him and how gay a time he had, figuratively Howden kept throwing anxious glances back at the Old Man. He would wonder aloud where he was, what he was doing, and what he was thinking they were doing. Gerry upbraided him. She upbraided him one night in the late fall.

"He's not thinking anything," Gerry said, "except that we're going to Carthage to a party, which we are."

Howden said that he did not want to lose her father's confidence, and that his falling in love with her, if her father knew, would certainly seem unrealistic and lacking in logic.

Gerry told him, To hell with logic.

And that was the way it seemed to Howden with every phase of their relationship, and with everything else—to hell with logic.

"Love isn't supposed to be logical," Gerry said. "It's the most illogical thing I know."

"I wish you wouldn't drive so fast," Howden said. And then: "You're not in love with me." It was now an old, sad reproach. He had never seen how she could be. He had never really believed it. He had a strange, total lack of conceit about women.

"You're simply crazy," Gerry said. "Why don't you take it easy?"

"I am." Sometimes he could take it easy and sometimes he couldn't. There were moments when no concession, no solicitude, no generosity of hers completely satisfied him. There were times when something she possessed, some unnamable something she seemed to represent, could never be transferred to him. The road, running straight and implacable as an arrow through the drab countryside, rushed at the headlights. There was considerable Saturday traffic at village crossroads where the gas station-general store-cafés were. Passing through a narrow town, around the unvarying memorial square, Howden got snatched glimpses of cars and mule carts slanted head-on into the curb like monstrous flies on the rim of a saucer, and of people, mostly men, standing in lax but somehow violent habitude under the stark lights of stores.

"You're not," Gerry said. "You weren't taking it easy the first time I ever saw you either."

Howden did not see why she wanted to go all the way back there, and he laughed. "No?"

"That first time, you were like a weapon drawn against me," Gerry said.

"How do you mean?" he asked her. He wanted to know the picture of him that was in her mind.

"You were like you expected to be insulted or stepped on any minute, sugar. Even though you were sitting down, you looked like you were tiptoeing."

Howden did not say anything. He was trying to link together all the circumstances that led to this time and place. He could not remember the start, unless it was that night back in the summer. The Old Man, just in from a trip to Atlanta, had gone to bed early, and Howden and Gerry sat on the side porch long after Howden thought he should be leaving. But Gerry was talking in her bright, exaggerated, and uninterruptible way. Then suddenly she had stopped talking and left her place on the porch glider, and before Howden knew it, she was standing in front of him, looking down at him. It startled him so that he stood up, pushing his chair back a little. In the dim light he could see her taut face, her hungry-looking eyes. But when she spoke her voice was only taunting.

"Don't you want to kiss me?" she had asked. Surprised, he said nothing. Indeed, he drew back.

"It's simply damned crazy, but I want to kiss you. I want you to kiss me. It's been a long time since a man has kissed me," she had said.

Feeling suspicious and afraid, feeling a fool, and feeling cheapened and humiliated too, he had stood still and stiff. She lifted to her toes and leaned toward him, but he drew back, half turned. With a metallic sound that was not quite a laugh, she flung her head back, grasped the lapels of his coat, and snatched him down to her with tensive strength.

"Put your arms around me," she ordered. "Now kiss me. Kiss me, you fool!" she commanded with bright and savage anger, jerking at his lapels.

He had made no motion of kissing, but her moist, soft, and then softly parted lips found his for longer than a moment, for long enough for him to taste and feel a bittersweetness, a reckless sharpness of desire, the oncoming of a heady, nervous surge of passion. And he was kissing her, almost against his will, kissing hungrily, as she kissed him.

When she loosened her grasp of him, he had nearly tottered forward, and she had laughed, swung around behind him, and sat down again. He had stood there, feeling drained and empty, trembling with something like fatigue and, all at once, with the certain knowledge that she could command him anything.

"What's the matter?" she had taunted brightly. When he did not answer, she went on. "Forget it," she had said. "It was just a harmless little accident that might have happened to any man just then."

At the moment he had felt that he hated her.

But that had been the definite start, he thought. Now, speeding through the wickering night with her, remembering, seeing the glow of the dashboard light on her face and the arched, nervous line of her throat, it occurred to him that there had been a lot of little accidents—and here they were.

"You're driving pretty fast," Howden said.

"We have to get there. It's going to be a good party. I feel like a good party," Gerry said.

"You always do."

"Of course," Gerry said. "You just relax and have a good time. You always have a good time when you relax, sugar baby."

That was true, he thought. After a couple of drinks, when he relaxed, he always had a good time.

"Well, you take it easy," he said.

The remark reminded him again that he was picking up a lot of her expressions. It brought back a feeling that had been growing on him for some time and that he had been trying to find words to make explicit—the feeling that he was just a satellite revolving in Gerry's social orbit.

Gerry started talking about the people who were going to be at the party and about a lot of people who weren't—people she knew way up in Philadelphia and New York and Boston. Geography didn't seem to mean much. When Gerry talked, the world of her friends contracted to the size of a tent, and Howden liked the feeling of being in it. It was a world on a level of habits and attitudes and adjustments subtly different from the one in which, but for the Old Man, he would still be a poke. The social world, Gerry's world, complemented and afforded escape from the other. It was the place where men of his own heart went to join their women after the long day of living a dual existence was over. Howden could think of the men whom he would see to-night as intelligent, successful, even charming, and he could think of them and himself as deserving the haven their women made for them.

And yet there were vague misgivings as Gerry went on talking.

He had had no experiences to match hers and those of her friends. He had not been born in comfortable circumstances nor had a home and parents. He had not gone to house parties when he was in college and there and then met the men who were now prosperous physicians, dentists, federal employees, and insurance managers. He had not known their wives when they were girls. It was a small world, but he was not really in it. Thinking this, there came back the old feeling of being on the fringe, of not belonging. He was not listening to Gerry's cheery, fast, malicious chatter any longer. All at once he was experiencing a painful urgency that had nothing to do with what she was saying, although it must have grown out of his sense of exclusion.

"Gerry," he said, turning impulsively toward her. "Listen, Gerry."

"I'm listening, sugar," she said.

"Gerry, will you marry me?" He had asked it before, and he hoped she wouldn't say what she always said. He hoped she wouldn't laugh and say that he didn't want to marry her really and that love was fun without marriage. He hoped she wouldn't tell him what her father had been telling him—that he ought to think about finding a nice girl somewhere. He looked at her, leaning forward so as to see her whole face. He saw her lift her head a little higher and toss it in that now familiar gesture; and he saw that, when she had done this, her expression was different —waiting, attentive, and perhaps too bright.

"Gerry, I want to marry you," he said. "I want that more than anything right now."

"Right now? Only right now, honey?" she twitted.

"I didn't mean it like that," he said, feeling angry and frustrated. "Why do you want to twist it?"

"That's what you said. Isn't that what you said, sugar honey?"

He did not want her to put it on the plane of a joke. He did not want it to trail off into inconsequential, evasive argument. He had seen her control her father by willful misunderstanding and distortion. He had seen her take a moment of seriousness and rip

it into tatters of almost hysterical frivolity. He did not want that
to happen now.

"Gerry, I love you."

"Do you, honey?" She was smiling brightly.

"Gerry—"

"You're number one in my book too," Gerry said, reaching
out one gloved hand and patting him on the knee.

"Listen—" He paused to control the tension in his voice, to
control the irritation he felt against her. He looked away from
her into the steady luminous funnel made by the headlights.
Fringing the ditches filled with water that the late fall rains had
left, tall grass gyrated like spotlighted dancers in the draft of the
car. He could see the slanted, canted shadow of the car racing
beside them. He could smell the moist, raw-beefsteak odor of the
marshy land.

"I'm still listening," Gerry said, her voice lilting gaily.

"Are you going to divorce him—or let him divorce you, I
don't care which—and marry me?"

"Damn it, Shel! Oh, damn it!"

He did not know what she meant by that. It did not sound
amused, though it had a quality of high, false glee.

"It's natural for me to want to marry you, isn't it, since I love
you?" he asked with strained patience.

"Oh, goddamn it, Shel!" she said, putting her hands up higher
on the wheel.

"Listen—"

"I'm bitchy, honey baby," Gerry said. "Don't you know I am?
Didn't I throw myself at you?"

"I didn't ask you that!"

"I'm trying to be fair with you," Gerry said mockingly.

"Just answer my question," Howden said through clenched
teeth. "Are you going to give me a chance to marry you?"

"You don't need to be generous, sugar."

"Just answer my question, will you!"

"We'd never get along, sugar," Gerry said with bright gaiety.

"Wouldn't it be damned awful if I took advantage of your generosity, and then we didn't get along?"

He loved her so much that he could have slapped her. He loved her so much that he wanted to hurt her and make her cry and take her gently in his arms while she cried. He loved her so much that he could not, in his loving-anger, speak for a moment.

"You find a nice girl, honey," Gerry said. "Maybe there'll be one there tonight. That would be wonderful."

"Good Lord, Gerry, cut it!" It was an anguished, angry cry.

"I'm only trying to be fair with you. You haven't seduced me. You haven't forced me into anything. You haven't even been to bed with me, and I've been to bed with a hundred men. Don't you know I have, honey baby?"

"Gerry!"

He did not believe her, of course. But he could not help recalling how it had all started. He locked his hands together to keep from striking her. He had never felt so tormented, so frustrated, so helpless and uncertain, and so much in love.

"If you say anything like that again—"

"Baby," Gerry said, "you wouldn't hit me, would you?"

"I'll— I'll—" He lapsed into miserable silence.

"Of course, it's not literally true about the hundred men. Don't you know it isn't, sweet? But I don't want you to feel that you have to marry me. Don't you see? And I can't marry you anyway, can I?"

"You could if you wanted to," Howden answered wretchedly.

"But I do, sugar honey," Gerry said, and Howden knew without seeing that her eyes widened. "But I can't. You know I can't."

Now there were a good many cars, and neon-lighted roadhouses with cars parked around them, and big service stations where trucks making the haul from Memphis to Carthage to New Orleans to Dallas pulled in. When they rolled onto the high bridge, there was the city spilling light over the opposite shore of the river, and down below them on right and left the black docks and wharves and warehouses jutted out over the blacker, oily water, which shimmered with zigzag paths of reflected light.

A stale fishy smell coming from the river mingled with the baked-ham odor from the cotton oil mills. Waiting for a freight train to pass, a line of cars was stopped at the city end of the bridge. Gerry pulled up behind them.

"What makes you like that, Gerry?" Howden asked in a pained and weary voice.

"You're sweet, Shel," Gerry said, the hysterical brightness toned down. "You're too, too sweet. Please kiss me. Wait a minute—this goddamned wheel." She turned under the wheel and put her arms around his neck. "Now." And then she went hard and tense, murmuring against his mouth. There were cars in front of them, and the lights of cars were approaching from the rear, but she did not free him.

"Gerry—"

"I love you," Gerry murmured. "Don't I love you, Shel, honey?"

"Then, why—?"

She loosed her arms. "Don't be so solemn," she said and pulled playfully at his chin. "We're going to a party, and we're going to have a good time. Aren't we going to have a good time? Don't be neurotic tonight, honey baby." The double term of endearment came soft, tender and voluptuous, like the very act of love.

CHAPTER SEVENTEEN

WHEN the maid, especially hired for the occasion, opened the door, the noise of the party met them, and Gerry said that Marge Groomes' parties were always different. Gerry's eyes shone, and her face had a smoothed-out minted look, except at the outer corners of her eyes where the tiny lines

were very white. While they stood there in the hall waiting for
the sullen-looking maid to find Marge Groomes, Gerry said that
it was going to be quite, quite a party.

"Listen," she said, "don't I hear Mary Beaubean?" and she
tossed her head back and listened.

Howden did not know whether she heard Mary Beaubean or
not, especially since he did not know Mary Beaubean. Coming
from the living room around the bend of the hall was a confused
gibble-gabble of mixed voices.

"Gerry, do you suppose there'll be many strangers?" Howden
whispered, although there was no need to keep his voice down.

"Relax, darling," Gerry said, touching his arm. "You'll know
everybody in a little while."

Howden wanted to tell her that all he wished was for her not
to leave him stranded because he was never at ease with strangers.
He could hear ice clinking in glasses and laughter coming in
waves.

"Gerry—" Howden began. But he was interrupted by a delighted little scream coming from the foot of the stairs in the
bend of the hall, and he saw two women approaching.

"Ger-rie!" Marge cried, running down the hall. She threw her
arms around Gerry and laid her cheek against Gerry's cheek and
rocked happily from side to side.

"Honey," Gerry said.

"Precious," Marge said ecstatically. Her petite figure was
rounded, her complexion a deeply tanned brunette's. "I've been
looking and looking for you!" She stared at Gerry for several
smiling seconds.

"Well, here we are," Gerry said.

"And Shel!" Marge said happily, although she had seen him
only once before. She held out her hand and took his and grasped
it in a warm, friendly way. Still holding his hand, she turned
to the woman who had come downstairs with her.

"Gerry, you remember Flash Hoggard—from Chicago," Marge
said. "And, Flash, this is Shelton Howden."

"How do you do," Howden said, trying not to stare at Miss Hoggard.

"Goddamn it, Marge, I've told you not to introduce me as Flash," Miss Hoggard said languidly. Though it had nothing to do with her manner, which seemed torpid and concentratedly indolent, nor with her voice, which was soft and liquid and indolent too, the name fitted. She had a great mass of red hair, and with her blue-white, unrouged, unpowdered skin, she looked like a lit match.

"Darling, it's all right," Marge soothed. "We're all good friends."

"It's not all right," Flash Hoggard drawled, "and I don't care if we are all good friends."

"Darling—" Marge breathed.

Then Gerry cut in abruptly, tartly, it seemed to Howden.

"What did that maid do with my bag?" Gerry wanted to know.

"Come on," Marge said. "And, Shel, give me your things. And, Flash, you and Shel go in the living room with the others. You know nearly everybody."

But Flash Hoggard merely watched languidly while Marge mounted the stairs with Gerry. Sighing deeply, she dropped into the ladderback chair by the hall table.

Howden said nothing because there was nothing to say. He tried desperately to think of something. He wished he had a drink. He could hear the voices, which seemed to be getting louder in the living room, and music from the radio. If he had had a drink, he told himself, he would have found something to say to Miss Hoggard. There were all sorts of clever things he could think of to say once he'd had a drink.

Miss Hoggard lit a cigarette from the lighter on the hall table, and then her gaze drifted toward Howden. The smoke curled from her pursed lips. She looked at Howden placidly for a long time.

"What's the matter?" she asked after a while. "Are you supposed to be the strong, silent type?"

Howden gave a start and looked at her. She just sat there, her
legs crossed at the knee so that her long full skirt, swooped away
like a theater curtain, framed her long legs. One green-sandaled
foot swung slowly. Taking a slow, deep drag on her cigarette, she
stared back at Howden.

"Why don't you say something?" she asked. "I hate the silent
type."

"I—I—" Howden stammered. He put his hands in his pockets
and took them out again. He was conscious of his flush.

"Well, you can answer my question," Miss Hoggard said. "Are
you?"

Howden flushed deeper, affronted but helpless. He did not
know what to do. He just stared.

"Why don't you tell me to go to hell? That's what I'd have
told you," Miss Hoggard said. "Then we could have had a nice
little scene."

"What do you want a scene for?"

Miss Hoggard shrugged lazily and then slowly, quietly smiled.
"To attract attention to myself, of course," she said. "What else?"

It was easier for Howden now that she had smiled. His next
remark was a happy inspiration.

"Oh, you don't have to do that," Howden said. "You naturally
attract attention."

"I haven't got a penny, but here's a cigarette," Miss Hoggard
said, laughing. "Do you always stroke the cat?"

Now again he was lost. He did not know what she meant.
He felt stupid and clumsy again.

"The cat?"

Miss Hoggard's laughter was soft. "Or other clawed animals,"
she said. Then her voice, though still languid, changed meaningly.
"And I know you know some."

It was the kind of talk that he had heard at other parties, especially among the women, and thought that he would never get

the hang of. But he was beginning to get a lot of things he had not had before. He heard Marge and Gerry coming back. Gerry had put on a sleeveless black party dress with a red velvet rose blooming in the skirt. Her arms were slender, unfleshed, unrounded.

"You two—" Marge said. "Why didn't you go in?"

"We were talking," Howden said. He saw Gerry's shining eyes swoop first at Flash Hoggard and then at him.

"Was it interesting?" Gerry asked coolly.

"Sweetie-pie," Flash drawled, getting up, "wouldn't you like to know?"

There was no pause at all, really, before Marge was saying soothingly, "Well, come on. They're way ahead of you in there. Come on, Gerry. Flash."

"Goddamn it, Marge, don't—"

They were moving past the off-set that led from the hall to the rooms that were Ben Groomes' waiting room and dental office. The noise from the living room was quite loud. The radio was going and voices were going and ice was clinking. Howden felt Gerry tug on his arm.

"Shel, what do you think of Flash?" It was a strident whisper.

"Shush," Howden warned. "How do you mean?"

"You know what I mean," Gerry said shortly. "Did you fall for her too?"

"Oh, Gerry," Howden said reproachfully.

"Well, I just want to tell you," Gerry said, "her last abortion shows."

Now they were shoving into the living room, and everybody was calling Gerry's name and Flash's name. The women were rather shrill, and they put their cheeks against Gerry's cheek and against Flash's cheek, as Marge had done, and one or two of the men slapped Howden on the back, although there were quite a few people whom he didn't know. While they were standing there, a black boy in a white coat came up with some drinks and Howden took one gratefully. There were more people there than he had ever seen at one of these parties. Marge started introducing Miss Hoggard to some people, and Gerry got lost somewhere in the crowd, and Howden was left standing pretty much alone. Everyone was talking, the women's voices predominating because there were so many more of them. The air was blue with smoke. Swallowing his drink quickly, Howden looked around for the boy again.

He wandered around the edges of various groups, trying to get to Gerry, and then he saw another black boy with drinks. The boy was serving a total stranger when Howden came up, but the stranger grinned amiably and showed a row of massive teeth. He was a slick-haired, sandpaper yellow man with a crooked nose and a tight, rounded stomach. He looked like he might belong to the Elks for other than purely professional reasons.

"This is just what the doctor ordered," the man said in a deep, Southern-slurred voice. He held his glass up. "Here's how." Downing his drink, he looked at Howden with expansive approval. "It's a good party, and I like it. Good party. I'm all relaxed. Good bunch of folks. But, look—" and he lowered his voice—"who's that redhead?"

Howden did not need to look in the direction the stranger indicated.

"You haven't met Flash yet?" Howden asked. "She's the Groomes' house guest."

"I was out in the kitchen sneaking a couple of straight ones," the stranger said, "and then Ben came out and started talking about Haile Selassie and a lot of other crap. That redhead—what's her name—Flash?"

"Flash Hoggard," Howden said. He was drinking his third highball slowly. He was beginning to feel relaxed himself.

"Well, I want to meet her. Redheads do something to me. They get under my skin," the stranger said. "Flash—that's cute. That's damned cute." He laughed with pleasure.

Now that Howden thought of it, it did seem cute, and Miss

Hoggard herself seemed that way too. She did not seem surprising or disconcerting to him any more.

"She's from Chicago," Howden volunteered.

"I was out there building up a head of steam on the old elixir when Ben comes out and traps me in the breakfast nook, talking about Haile Selassie," the stranger said. "Hell, Selassie's no kin to me. But Ben—you know Ben."

"Everybody knows Ben."

"What do I care about the wages-and-hour law? That don't have no effect on the funeral supply business," the stranger declared just a bit thickly. "That house guest—"

"Are you in the funeral supply business?" Howden asked him.

"Benswich and Seeny, biggest colored suppliers of funeral items and equipment in the damn country. I'm Seeny, junior," the stranger said, thrusting out a big, soft-looking hand. "Sam Seeny, junior."

"Please to meet you," Howden said. "Shel Howden." It was the first time he had ever called himself Shel to anyone.

"You say she's from Chicago?"

"Yes."

"Well, when're you're putting on a head of steam and somebody comes up to you and starts slinging some bull about how the hour-and-wages bill is making it hard for Negro labor, and all about the Lion of Judah—" He stopped to catch the drinks as they went by. He gave one to Howden.

"That's Ben," Howden said, nodding sagely, although he didn't really know Ben Groomes very well.

"He's all tied up in knots," Sam Seeny said. "Always discussing the question. Hell, the question don't do nothing to the funeral supply business except to make it better. And it sure don't hurt Ben's teeth-pulling. If it wasn't for the question, Ben couldn't make a living pulling teeth, now could he? If it wasn't for the question, where would any of us be? If everything was brotherly love between colored and white, there wouldn't be no Benswich and Seeny. But that redhead—"

"Come on," Howden said. "There she is over there."

They pushed through a crowd to find Miss Hoggard sitting cross-kneed on the arm of a sofa talking to William Leathers. Somebody was singing to the accompaniment of the radio, and over in a corner a man was saying something that made the women around him squeal with shocked delight. As Howden approached with Sam Seeny, he saw Miss Hoggard's languid gaze drifting around the room, but she seemed to perk up when she saw him.

"Here's someone who wants to meet you," Howden said.

"What, another one?" Miss Hoggard said. "Does he stroke the cat too?"

"If it's the right cat," Howden said, "and you seem to be the right one." The drinks made him feel clever, even brilliant. After he'd had a couple of drinks, it was very easy to talk.

"Miss Hoggard," Howden said, "this is—"

"Seeny," the stranger broke in heartily. "Sam Seeny. Hello—" He hesitated for an instant, grinning completely. "Hello, Flash."

Slowly Miss Hoggard sat more erect on the arm of the lounge. "Goddamn it," she drawled insultingly above the noise immediately around, "who told you—who gave you permission to call me that?"

A sudden hush fell and spread outward, like a storm-laden cloud, a little way. Beyond it Howden could still hear voices chattering, voices laughing, the radio going; but within a space of a dozen feet all was still. Sam Seeny's face went sick, and with eyes that were all at once as expressionless as two gobs of phlegm he looked at Howden and then at Leathers and finally at Flash Hoggard. He backed away, as if he would escape. His lips moved, but he did not speak. For a moment no one spoke. Within the circle of twenty people, all eyes were fixed on Sam Seeny and Flash Hoggard. It was like a pantomime. Miss Hoggard's insulting gaze did not leave Seeny's face.

"Whoever told him he could call me that?"

"I told him that's what they call you," Howden muttered, hoping she would smile, hoping she would somehow indicate that she was only fooling.

"Look, lady—" Sam Seeny began.

"And don't 'look, lady' me either," Flash Hoggard said. Rising regally from her seat on the sofa arm, she moved slowly through the silent circle to another part of the room.

Like a boy shocked and angered by an unjust whipping, Seeny looked dumbly around. But no one looked at him. Howden did not know what to say. He knew only that he didn't want to be in that spot any longer. The noise from the rest of the room filtered in again, filling the vacuous silence. The radio sounded as loud as ever, glasses clinked, and the man over in the corner was still entertaining a bevy of giggling women.

"Jesus!" Howden heard Sam Seeny say at last. "I want a drink. I need a drink."

It was exactly the way Howden felt, and he started looking for the boy again. He had had no idea that Flash Hoggard would really do a thing like that. When he stopped to think about it, he had no idea what anybody would do. He wanted a drink, and he wanted to see Gerry too.

When he had had his drink, he felt all right again. He put in a word here and there among several clusters of people. Once he found himself talking to someone about New Orleans. For quite a while he talked about the good times he used to have in New Orleans when he was a student at New Hope. Then he saw Gerry.

[2]

"Hello, honey sugar," Gerry said.

"I've been looking for you," he said. He felt a little drunk. He felt good.

"Come on," Gerry said. "I want to look at my face." She led him through the crowd toward the dining room.

"Your face is all right. Your face is beautiful," he said, and then he laughed because he remembered that it was what Flash Hoggard would call stroking the cat.

"What's the matter? What's funny?" Gerry asked.

"I was just thinking about Flash."

"What about her?" Gerry asked, her eyes narrowing suspiciously.

"Nothing. She's just funny." And he laughed again.

Gerry looked at him for a moment longer, and then she turned to the mirror over the buffet and reddened her lips.

"Good Lord, Gerry—that Flash!" It was not so much a question as an exclamation that gave expression to everything. It expressed his wonder and delight. It expressed his kinship with all these people, no matter where they came from. In this crowd, geography meant nothing.

"You seem to have her on your mind," Gerry said icily.

Her tone of voice sobered him, and he looked at her. She was watching him in the mirror. He shook his head.

"No, not Flash. It's just everybody. Everybody's on my mind," he said quietly.

"And where am I?" She turned angrily from the mirror and faced him.

"Oh, Gerry," he said, hurt. He loved her very much. His eyes grew moist.

"All right," Gerry said, and then she kissed him and smiled. "Come on, let's go back where the crowd is." She was suddenly gay again. "Isn't it a lovely, lovely party? Aren't you having a good time?"

He was having a good time too, although Gerry went off somewhere again, leaving him alone under the archway that led to the hall. Two or three couples were dancing in the hall, and Howden stood there watching them.

"How goes it?" he heard a voice say. "How's every little thing?" It was a voice he had heard before, but he could not place it. When he turned around, there was the little man who was Marge's husband. Ben Groomes gave him a weary smile.

"How goes it with you?" Howden asked.

"I was just talking to Gerry," Ben Groomes said. "She said you were over here."

"Is that so?"

They stood looking at each other for a moment because the conversation seemed to be ended. Howden could look down on the top of Ben's bald head.

"Having a good time?"

"Yes," Howden said.

Ben Groomes looked at him, and there was another silence while Howden finished his drink.

"If you take many of those, you won't be able to drive back," Ben Groomes said.

"This is my first," Howden said.

"Well, there's plenty of it here," Ben Groomes said, looking at him with weary incredulity, "and I guess everyone's having a good time."

"Don't you want everyone to have a good time?"

"If you've got internal resources, you don't have to get pie-eyed," Ben said.

"Nobody's pie-eyed," Howden said.

Ben looked around the crowded, noisy room, and then, smiling with weary triumph, he looked at Howden again. Somebody was pie-eyed all right. Marge had Sam Seeny in the middle of the floor showing him a new dance step, and Sam was jigging and weaving awkwardly with the frantic concentration of the drunk. Several people, including Marge, were laughing encouragement. Marge too was a little tight.

"There's nothing to worry about," Howden said.

"They end up drunk. Marge always ends up drunk. They get that way and then they all swear they're having a good time," Ben Groomes said dourly.

"There's nothing to worry about," said Howden again. He was wondering what chain of circumstances had brought Ben Groomes and Marge together, and what curious affinity held them. He was wondering if they had stumbled blindly into each other, or if the fate that controlled such things cared what it was doing at the time.

"Isn't there?" Ben asked sententiously.

"It's just a jolly crowd," Howden said. He could think of them as his crowd—and Ben's crowd too, even if Ben did criticize them. Everyone there belonged, and Ben was simply exercising one of the privileges of belonging. "They're just relaxing," Howden said.

"From what?" Ben asked, turning on a sad little smile. "From the strain of being colored or from the strain of acting white?"

Howden was annoyed. Sooner or later, even when you relaxed in your own crowd, someone brought up race. Always there was some seek-sorrow who spoiled things. The fatuous, indulgent grin with which he had been covering Ben frozen on his face, Howden looked steadily across the room at nothing. He saw the blue smoke like a tattered canopy hanging loosely from the ceiling, and then he saw the faces of *his* crowd. They were of all ages between twenty-one and sixty, and they all knew each other, and they were all having a good time.

"What are you griping about?" Howden asked Ben Groomes.

"I'm not griping. It's just an interesting question," Ben said.

"Why don't you go and have a good time like everybody else?"

Ben smiled wearily and shrugged, but before he could answer, Gerry came up.

"I want to dance," she said. "Come on, Shel, dance with me."

"Ben's sour tonight," Howden said.

"Ben's sour every night," Gerry said. "Aren't you sour every night? Ben's just neurotic. Come on, Shel, let's dance."

They went out into the hall and danced. The music was just loud enough for them to hear it.

"Shel sugar, are you having a good time?"

"Yes."

"That's good," Gerry said.

They danced down the hall. He could feel the hard, thin, nervous length of Gerry pressing vibrantly against him.

"Shel," she said, "I love you. Don't you know I love you, sugar? You feel so good to me."

Because he did not know exactly what she meant, the remark made him self-conscious. He stood a little back from her and looked down into her face. She smiled and put her head against his shoulder. They danced up the hall.

"I called Poppa," Gerry said.

"What for?" he asked.

"Because I knew you'd be scared if I didn't. Wouldn't you be scared?"

He did not see why she should think there was any more for him to be afraid of now than there ever was when they went out together. He did not see why she had called her father.

"I have to do everything," Gerry said. "I have to keep it going. If it were left to you, we'd be nowhere, honey baby, wouldn't we? I have to take all the responsibility. Don't you make me take all the responsibility?"

"For what?" he asked her.

"For us."

He held her a little closer, liking the thought that she took all the responsibility—whatever she meant by that; liking the thought of her feeling that he was dependent upon her—because in a way he was.

"I told Poppa that something had happened to the car," Gerry said with a deceptive lightness of tone. "Now don't get upset, sugar."

"Has something happened to the car?" he asked her, again standing away so that he could look into her face.

Gerry smiled. "What's the matter, honey? Don't you want to go to bed with me?"

"Gerry!" He was hurt. He wished she hadn't put it on such a frank, low level.

"Don't worry," Gerry said, pressing her hand against his back,

making him move close to her again. "I know what I'm doing.
I've got Poppa fixed. Don't be scared and neurotic, sugar honey."
They danced.

"Gerry, I wish you'd marry me," Howden said sadly.

"I want to, darling. Don't you know I want to? But this will
have to do for now. Don't you see it'll have to do?"

"I guess it will," Howden said.

They could scarcely hear the music, but they danced.

CHAPTER EIGHTEEN

IT SEEMED to Shelton Howden that everything moved very
fast that year. At mid-term his teaching load was reduced
to a single course in world history which, the president said,
there was scarcely any point in teaching to darkies. But the course
was a new state requirement, and the president said that he didn't
have time to argue with the curriculum people up in the state
department just then. When he got around to it, he said, he
would convince them, up there in Carthage, that world history
and a year of French and the survey of western civilization were
a waste of time for his students. Darkies didn't need to know
such things.

Howden saw a good deal of the president in executive action
and, although he did not realize it at the time, because things
were moving pretty fast, he learned valuable lessons in administration. Ever so often, the president would summon some
member of the faculty and lay down the law. The people who
taught extension classes all over the state would come in once
every two weeks, and Howden would have to be there because

he checked their reports. When they faced the Old Man, they
never seemed to be sure of anything. They stumbled over their
words and got mixed up in their figures, and the Old Man would
sit there behind his big desk, which was as orderly as a desk in a
show window, and stare coldly from under his hand. When he
got tired of listening, he'd wipe out all they'd said with an impatient gesture of his hand, and then he'd say what he had to say.
Extension enrollments were not up to what they should be, he'd
say, and he wasn't going to spend public money just to keep
some teachers on the payroll. He wasn't going to connive against
the government like that. He wasn't there to aid and abet laziness.
So he wanted them to get out of there and get those extension
enrollments up, and if they couldn't do that in the next quarter
of the term, then they could just draw what salaries were owed
them because he'd find somebody who could.

Sometimes an official from the state department of education
would pay a call. The president seemed to become a little distracted and more than usually waspish when he expected it. He
complained that people had been neglecting things and that he
had everything to do himself, and he generally kept Howden
shuffling through papers until the last possible moment. Then
when Dr. Doraman, who had charge of all education in the state,
or Mr. Means, the chief of vocational training, or Mr. Chisholm,
whose status was powerful but indefinite, actually got there, the
president would be all right again but different somehow. It was
as if, between the expectation and the arrival, he had gone
through some natural, organic change.

The moment he heard one of them in the outer office, he would
get up briskly and step to the door, and there would be a careful,
receptive sort of smile on his face. Quickly gathering up papers,
Howden would slip out the side door just in time to hear Dr.
Doraman or Mr. Means or Mr. Chisholm greet the Old Man.
"Hello, Pee Tee," Howden would hear the visitor say; and once
just before he slipped out, Howden heard Dr. Doraman call the

president a sly old rascal. "Hello, Pee Tee," Dr. Doraman said, "you old sly rascal you."

Howden often wondered what went on behind those closed doors when the state officials were there.

The Old Man took many trips in February of that year. He made quite a mystery of them. Once he was gone for three days, and another time, toward the end of the month, he was gone for a week. He sent for Howden the afternoon he returned from the last trip, and it was obvious that he was pleased with himself. He glowed with a sense of accomplishment. "Shel, boy," he said, "I beat 'em out of bed." His tart laughter crackled. "I beat 'em!"

Though Howden heard it directly, in the detailed way the Old Man liked to talk, it was not until he read the Carthage *Negro Advocate* that he fully understood the significance of the Old Man's victory. The paper did not mention President Wimbush at all. The paper did not know that it was he who had caused five school principals to be fired in the middle of the year. The paper didn't have any of the meaningful facts, and all it could do was use such words as "arbitrary" and "dictatorial" and demand an investigation, which, of course, was never held.

"Son," the Old Man told Howden gleefully, "they don't know I was behind it. They don't know what happened. They don't know that you keep your power hidden if you want to keep it strong."

The Old Man said that he had been hearing rumors all the fall that there was a certain element of Negro teachers trying to organize opposition to his control of the Negro State Teachers Association. It was not so much that he wanted to be president of the Association, the Old Man said; it was just that the presidency was a strategic position from which to exercise power. Besides, the supposition was that being president gave you a following, made it look as though you spoke and acted with a general mandate. As a matter of fact, the Old Man said, he knew he had more enemies than friends in the Association. Still, it was stupid for this dissident element to try to get rid of him, or even to want to get rid of him, because he was the only person in the state who could intercede for them with the white people. But darkies were not people for seeing their advantages, especially when they got under the influence of the N.A.A.C.P. and the League for Interracial Comity and other trouble-making groups.

He kept getting these rumors, which didn't bother him at first, the Old Man said disdainfully. There were always rumors, and there were always fawning or vicious or merely disgruntled darkies to peddle them. But what happened was that Dr. Doraman heard the rumors too. They reached him in a very circuitous way. The Havenport white high school had a colored janitor whose daughter taught somewhere in the rurals, and this daughter had got a mimeographed letter soliciting her support of Professor Solomon Baxter, the principal of the colored school in Carthage, for the presidency of the Negro State Teachers Association. The daughter told her father, and the father, ignorant and worried, told the white principal, and the white principal, no doubt enjoying it as another niggershine, told Dr. Doraman.

But Doraman did not look upon it lightly as another niggershine. He was disturbed. The thing about it was, the Old Man explained, that in the four years he'd been principal at Carthage, Baxter had demanded this and demanded that of the state department, and he was troublesome. No white man wanted to deal with a pressure group of darkies, and under Baxter that's exactly what the Association would become. So Dr. Doraman was in the middle, and he couldn't do anything about it. The Association was a private professional organization and colored at that, the Old Man said, and its members could elect whom they pleased, set up whatever rules they pleased, and do whatever they damned well pleased. And even though it accepted the blessings and even some financial aid from the state, some of the Association's members would yell that it was an infringement of their democratic rights if the state department so much as criticized a course of action.

Thus, the Old Man said, Dr. Doraman's hands were tied, and

yet he wanted something done. He wanted enough done so that he could act. And the Old Man did it. It was quite simple, the Old Man said. All he did was get ahold of a few of those letters, copies of the one the janitor's daughter got and that the five principals had been sending out, and call to the attention of Dr. Doraman the fact that hundreds of such letters had been written on paper supplied by the state, mimeographed from stencils probably cut on time that belonged to the state and on machines supplied by the state, and more than likely mailed with postage that belonged to the state. Dr. Doraman then fired the five principals for the misuse of state funds and state supplies.

"Son," the Old Man said, "I'll bet those fool darkies are still trying to figure it out. I'll bet they're still wondering what hit them and why, since none of them can possibly believe that Dr. Doraman really cared that much about a few dollars' worth of paper and ink, and none of them want to believe that he was so inconsequential in his job and his community that he could be fired for a little ink and paper. Son," the Old Man said with derisive glee, "I'll bet their trying to make heads and tails of it is like trying to read a book with many scattered pages missing."

[2]

And that's the way so many things were that year—like a book with scattered pages missing. Events moved in sudden jerks, without transition or motivation. Even the seasons came and went abruptly.

Shelton Howden had not realized that it was spring until one night when Gerry mentioned it. They were in the study, and there was a fire in the grate because a chilly rain was falling outside. All evening the Old Man had been talking, but now he stood up and drained his glass.

"Well, tomorrow's another day," he said, "and I'm going up."

It was the kind of remark that embarrassed Howden. He got up also.

"I think I'd better be going too," he said.

"In this rain?" Gerry asked, her eyes widening. "What makes you so restless?"

"I'm not restless," Howden said.

"Yes, you are," Gerry said. "And, Poppa, you're restless too." It was just her exaggerated way of talking, because the Old Man was never restless.

"Now, Gerry, you can sit up all night if you want to," her father said, "but it's almost eleven, and I'm going to pile in."

"All right, Poppa. I'm going to find an umbrella for Shel," Gerry said, and she stood up and threw a conspiratorial glance at Howden. "Where would one be, Poppa?" she called, following her father out into the hall.

Howden could hear the Old Man already mounting the stairs, and in a moment Gerry came back. Her eyes shone. Her mouth was a bright, bright red.

"I knew you were going to say you had to go the moment Poppa stood up," she said. "Did you think I was going to let you go, sugar baby? Men are dumb." And then she laughed.

Sometimes it worried and saddened him that she should be so clever. All manner of disturbing, shadowy doubts possessed him when he thought of it.

"Don't you know it's spring, honey?" Gerry asked.

It had nothing to do with anything she had been saying or anything he had been thinking. He could hear the rain against the windows and the wind muttering in the chimney, and there was the fire glowing in the grate.

"Spring? It's not spring yet."

"What's the matter, honey? Have the months slipped by you?" Her voice dropped to a gently mocking murmur. "Have they gone fast because we've had good times?"

They had had good times, Howden thought. They had had them right there in the study, listening to the Old Man's endless talk. They had had good times there because there was no strain, no effort. All together in the study, they were like a family.

There was warmth and security and peace. But he knew these were not the good times Gerry was thinking of.

"What's the matter?" Gerry asked again.

"It's just hard to believe that winter's gone already," Howden said.

"It's past the middle of March. Time and tide and more to the same effect," Gerry said. "Tempus certainly fugits, doesn't it, honey?"

Howden looked at her, annoyed because her silly question put everything on the level of a ridiculous wisecrack. She was always reducing mountains to molehills or building molehills into mountains. He looked at her ringleted hair, her pale, carved, alabaster face, and the nervous line of her slender throat. She was smiling at him with quiet, assured possessiveness, and he loved her very much.

"Come on. Come on and sit by me," Gerry said, drawing her legs up under her and patting the lounge. "Come on. I always get restless in the spring too."

"I'm not restless," Howden said.

"I'm not either yet, but I think I will be soon. I always get restless in the spring," Gerry said. She patted the lounge again. "Come on, sit here by me. Poppa's in bed."

The weather cleared toward the end of March and there was a stretch of beautiful, lambent, spring-green days. Dogwood bloomed among the dark pines on the bluff, and the river below thickened and turned red-gold in the sun, and the Old Man set a squad of students to weeding out the dandelions on the campus lawn, and Gerry did get restless. In the middle of April she announced that she was going away. She said that she had a smothered feeling and that she was going away where she could breathe. It didn't make sense to Howden, and he told her so.

"It wouldn't make sense to you, would it, honey? You wouldn't know how I feel, would you?" She spoke with bright insouciance. "I'll bet you wouldn't know that I want a kiss either."

They were in Howden's office at eleven o'clock in the morning, and Howden's secretary was somewhere close by. Howden had never got used to Gerry's utter disregard of time and place.

"What will your father say about your going?" Howden asked.

"Poppa?" Her eyes widened with bright incredulity. "Do you think he can stop me? Do you think I care about Poppa?"

He wouldn't go on with that because he didn't want to think that she really didn't care. He didn't want to think that she was ungrateful and mean-minded and— He didn't know what to think. He could will not to think anything. He could reject past circumstances as having never prevailed. Sometimes he could cling to an illusion with psychotic fixity.

"I wish you wouldn't go," he said.

"You wouldn't fool me, would you, baby?"

"You're always joking about us," Howden said reproachfully.

She grew very still then and looked at him. And then she tossed back her head.

"If it's a joke, darling," she said dryly, "then I've carried it pretty far."

In the course of the next few days it began to be plain that Gerry was going away and that there was nothing anyone could do about it. Her father offered counter-suggestions, but Gerry said she didn't want to wait until July and go to Chicago and Detroit and across into Canada with him; she wanted to go away right now. Her father said he wouldn't give her any money, he'd cut off her allowance. But Gerry only laughed in a glassy, disdainful way. She became more brittle and whitely drawn, as if tensions that no one knew or could know about were tearing her apart in silence. Then her father took an attitude he never took with anyone else. He tried to impose on her the tyranny of his injured feelings. At supper, and in the study afterwards, he looked doomed and baffled. The bafflement perhaps was real. He said he hoped she wouldn't go to Boston. He said he hoped she wouldn't let that no-'count husband get her involved again.

"Poppa, damn it, please!" Gerry screamed and ran from the room.

But the day she was leaving, the Old Man made one more try—although he must have known that it was too late for anything and that it was just his perversity and hers. Gerry's bags were already in the hall. They were waiting for the boy to bring the car around. Until her father started speaking, Gerry seemed quite gay.

"Poppa, I'm not going to argue with you here at the last minute," Gerry said.

"I'm not arguing," her father said placatingly. "I'm just thinking of your own good."

"Oh, God!" Gerry said. "Don't be so damned neurotic. If you were thinking of my own good, you'd keep your mouth closed. But you just don't understand." She looked at Howden angrily too. "And neither does Shel."

For the past two weeks he had stood helplessly by through the bickering, and he did not see why she had to bring him into it now. All his doubts had re-assailed him since her announcement. If she loved him, he thought, she wouldn't want to go away. But in the past two weeks a somewhat cynical sense of inevitability and impotence had hardened around his love for her.

The Old Man said, "No, I don't understand."

"And I'm not asking you to," Gerry snapped. She went on less harshly but still in an angry mood. She said he needn't think that she was going to Boston, if that was what he was making so much fuss about. What she'd left in Boston could stay there. Her father said that that was better, that was something like it. Gerry said she didn't know whether it was something like it or not, she was just saying how it was. But she didn't want anyone to ask her when she'd be back because she'd be back when her restlessness was over. Laughing glassily, she said it was all very simple and for no one to say anything else about it because there was the boy with the car now, and if Poppa was going to see her off, he'd better hurry because she didn't want to miss the midnight out of Carthage.

"I'll write you, Poppa. You know I will. I'll have to write you, won't I, Poppa?" She was gay again, but still a little guarded. "And I'll write you too, Shel."

"Here," Howden said to the boy, "I'll take one of the bags." When he and the boy finished putting the bags in the trunk, Gerry and her father were already in the car. Gerry sat forward on the back seat. For a moment she looked as though she might lean forward over the door glass and kiss him, and all at once Howden hoped she would. All at once he had an inexpressible desire to drop pretense, a wild, crazy wish for the Old Man to know, a mad hope that the Old Man would understand. He knew that it was partly a matter of conscience and partly the simple wish to walk frankly through the world. No one, he thought with an inner sneer, walks frankly through the world.

"I'll write you, Shel, real soon," Gerry said.

"Well, don't stay too long," Howden said.

Gerry sat back, fumbling in her bag. "Poppa, please tell him to step on it. And, Poppa, what did you do with my reservations?"

"Don't get excited," her father said. "There's plenty of time."

"Good-by, Shel," Gerry said as the boy shifted gears.

CHAPTER NINETEEN

HE MISSED her very much: missing her as soon as the car sped around the curve and down the stroke of the U and disappeared through the fill; missing her many times when he went to the house for supper and afterwards sat listening to the Old Man; missing her achingly at night there in the study and on the porch; missing the staccato brightness of her voice, the glitter of her eyes, the holocausts of her unpredictable, strange passions. Because he missed her very much, he admitted with reluctance the sense of relief he felt.

But things would be simpler for a while, he thought, and nothing had been really simple with Gerry. There had always been the fear of an exposure endangering his future. There had always been the Old Man to think about. Since Gerry had been gone, her father had mentioned again that Howden should find a girl to marry.

"Didn't Gerry introduce you to any girls?" the Old Man asked Howden out of the blue one day.

It startled Howden, and he stuttered an affirmative reply.

"Well, son, it's time you were thinking about marrying. There must be a girl somewhere," the Old Man said.

Howden had no wish to be defiant. He had everything to lose, including Gerry. But now that she was gone, he had a breathing spell from her constant demands for some kind of expression, for her often savage possessiveness.

As the summer matured, he again began to feel that he was building up to something permanent and secure. He had not consciously thought about it for almost a year, but now that nothing distracted him and he could concentrate, he realized that the Old Man was bringing him right along. The spiteful faculty talk of his being "groomed," whisperings of which came to him from Miss Lark, gave him secret, gloating pleasure. And the Old Man, who must have heard the talk also, did nothing to put an end to it. As a matter of fact, his actions would have increased it had the faculty but known.

Howden went with the president on frequent trips to the State Department of Education and to the State House, and although the president, wise in the way of propriety, never formally introduced him to any white man and he was often left to loiter unobtrusively in anterooms, Howden was surprised to find how many of the education officials and state legislators came to know him and to call him by name.

"Son," the Old Man told him, "I want all those people to get to know you. They're part of the environment you've got to control. It's a different kind of control, but it's control just the same. They run things, but in a way you run them," he said, snorting. "You'd be surprised at the people you've got to handle in this state. And they've got to get used to you. White folks have got to get used to you before they'll let you do anything with them."

The Old Man no longer watched Howden carefully and clinically when he made such remarks. It was as if a doctor had gradually come to know a patient so well that without diagnosis or a pulse check he could tell what the patient was feeling and what dosage to prescribe. It was as if doctor and patient were one. Howden knew that he need not tell the Old Man that he could never get used to white folks, no matter how used they got to him. Howden knew that he didn't need to say that he seemed to have two personalities when he was around white folks.

The Old Man was in a garrulous mood that night, and his voice kept going in a discordant singsong.

"Darkies who go around saying they don't give a roaring hoot what white people think, and who pretend they're independent of every and any white man ever born, just show their ignorance. They don't take a bit of skin off the white man's tail, though the damn fools seem to think they do. Why, son, if every darky in this country, including you and me, up and died this minute, it would no more affect tomorrow morning's ham and eggs and grits on white folks' tables than a single unknown darky's dying would. White folks don't have to give a damn. But we do. We have to give more than a damn about them because no matter whether you love or hate 'em, the country's theirs by a kind of right of eminent domain, and, in a way, people like you and me are theirs too."

He paused and knocked the ash from his cigar and threw his hand out in the semi-darkness of the porch and picked up his glass of wine.

"I'm talking about reality, Shel. Idealism and ethics and justice's got no more to do with it than a hog's got to do with Christmas. It's just common sense to admit it. So—"

He drank from the glass, and then he laughed. When he spoke again, his mind seemed to have gone onto an entirely different track.

"If Henry Ford said it, he was wrong, because history's not altogether bunk. It's just that the strongest people don't give a damn about it. Take F.D.R. He don't care about historical precedent or the Supreme Court or the Federal budget either. But he's a strong man, and in the South there are no strong men any more. Down here men are the dupes and slaves of history, and history itself is cheapened."

He paused again, drew on his cigar.

"It's the fault of the radio and the newspapers. Those damned announcers make even the advertisements sound like world-shaking events. M-O-U-N-D-S," the Old Man mocked. He sounded funny trying to be sonorous, and he laughed. "My God, Shel, I been hearing it every morning for months, and every morning it sounds like the world's on fire. But it's just a nickel candy bar. A lot of so-called history is like that—wrapped up in thunder and heralded with lightning, and it just turns out to be five-cent candy bars.

"The radio brings every event closer, and radio announcers make big ones out of little ones, and people don't have any sense of historical judgment any more. They try to make history out of horse races and prize fights and moving pictures and the style of Miss Frances Perkins' hats, and that destroys historical perspective, and when that is gone, social perspective goes too."

He stopped again and drew his hand down over his face, and then abruptly he was back where he had started from, as Howden knew he would be back. His voice went harsh.

"I keep my perspective, Shel. When I deal with white folks, I know damn well all history and all patterns of thought, all logic and precedent are against me, and I know there's not a single, solitary, goddamn thing I can do about it. And that's what the white folks you deal with have got to know you know. That's the thing in you you've got to make them sure of. History ain't all the bunk."

They held a communion of perfect silence for some time. The noises of the summer night came to them. Through a break in the foliage that screened the porch, Howden could see the lights of the women's dormitory going out one by one. Howden did not know that he was thinking anything, feeling anything. He stirred.

"When you're with them," he said, "do you seem to have two personalities?"

The Old Man's harsh laughter spurted out. "Son, I feel like I got two personalities all the time," he said.

[2]

Howden did not feel that way all the time. But the day he and the Old Man met Judge Reed just outside the latter's office in the capitol annex building, he felt it.

"Pee Tee, you here?" the judge asked. "Doggone your time, I just saw you in Bluffport less'n a week ago."

"Yes, sir, Judge, that's certainly right," the Old Man said, taking off his hat.

Howden took his off too. Though of course he knew of Judge Reed, knew that he controlled and all but owned the biggest county in the state, knew that he was a state commissioner of education, and knew what everyone knew—that the judge made Negroes his particular concern, his hobby and, some said, his hate—it was the first time Howden had ever seen him.

"You ain't hounding me again already?" The judge's flat, grainy voice carried an intimate note of friendly condescension. He was a flabby hulk of a man, a slowly liquefying mountain of a man, with brownish tobacco stains at the corners of his mouth and down the front of his seersucker suit. Above the black string tie, his face looked gray and sodden, like dirty dough; but his china-blue eyes were hard under the rimy eyebrows.

"Judge," the Old Man said, "I had to come up here on a lot of little things." Then he made a reference to Howden. It was entirely complimentary, but it was like referring to a child or to someone who was not there. "He's my right hand, Judge. I've told you about him."

"You're always telling me something, Pee Tee," Judge Reed said, with mixed amusement and annoyance. The head, with its limp, discolored panama, rolled slowly around in Howden's direction. Howden could feel the blue eyes upon him, and as he smiled in response to the white man's relentlessly impersonal and lenient stare, he could feel his other personality emerge.

"He a good boy?" the judge asked, looking away from Howden now and along the floor. He pursed his lips and sucked, and then he let go a jet of tobacco juice that spattered against the marble wall.

"Is, hunh? Tell me though—" the judge said.

Howden was certain that it was the Old Man who did it, deftly, as if by magic, without seeming to do it, without touching the judge, with no sign of anything like motion. The judge just turned ponderously and waddled away a few steps with the Old Man.

As Howden stood there hearing their voices without catching their words, he had an uneasy sense of an elaborate, secret ceremony going on beneath the surface of speech. He had the same feeling that came to him when he heard certain kinds of music: he could not get it through his head that it was as casually played as it sounded. He could not get it through his head that it was not carefully rehearsed. There were all sorts of complexities beneath the surface, and he was sure that this was not just an illusion—like geography.

[3]

Gerry had written that in her first letter. "Geography," she had written, "is all an illusion, because I'm still right there with you."

It was a nice thing to say, but she was not right there with him. She wrote first from Philadelphia and then from some place in New Jersey (the postmark was blurred), and then a letter came from New York. There was a three weeks' silence after the third letter, and then they started coming once a week. The letters did not quite satisfy Howden. They were full of gossip about people he didn't know, but they said almost nothing about Gerry.

When he was going through his mail on a morning toward the end of June, Howden recognized one of Gerry's envelopes. There was mail from prospective students and from book companies and from the magazine *Success* (which warned him that his subscription was about to expire), and he read it all before he picked up Gerry's letter. Slitting the envelope very carefully, he pulled out the crinkly, washed-green sheets. The letter was all one paragraph, full of dashes, like all her letters.

> Shel, honey— [he read] Well here I am in Boston and I didn't mean to be at all—don't you know I didn't?—and it happened this way. I was in N.Y. with the Bruens and Mary decided she had to drive up to the Cape to see about the cottage after the winter and from the Cape we came to Boston—though I didn't want to. I haven't seen Ray—and if I do it'll be an accident and it'll have to be soon because we're leaving to go back to N.Y. not later than day after tomorrow or the next. I hear from some friends that Ray is in love with a terribly neurotic girl who will have marriage or nothing— And you see where that puts me, don't you, sugar?—It puts me right in the middle, because the point is that if Ray does something about the divorce—which he'll have to do if he's to have his neurotic virgin—then things will break that everybody's been speculating and guessing about for five or six years and of course the papers will have it too— and you know the nig papers. And if he doesn't do something about it, then I can't. . . .

Here Howden stopped reading and stared at the wall. That phrase kept running through his mind—"And if he doesn't do something about it, I can't"—and he was wondering again why she couldn't. His mind went over its speculations dispassionately. Then he was thinking how little he actually knew about Gerry, or about Raymond Rudd either, and a feeling of impotence possessed him because a certain part of his fate was in their hands. He could view it all with a kind of contemptuous sophistry. People really knew very little about each other, he thought. Everyone was reticent, even with his best friends; even when one was in love, there was that fear of telling too much and giving away too much because no one wanted to be entirely defenseless.

> It's just too mad [he read], but that's the way it is. But nothing may happen at all—I know Ray like a book, sugar—and then things will be none the worse. When you hear from me again I'll be back in N.Y. and facing south after a few more days there. Don't mention to Poppa that I've been to Boston—and keep sweet, honey— Love— G.

Howden found himself reading certain lines again, hunting for them almost furtively, as if they were in a message addressed to someone else. But his mind was not so much on the letter as it was on his memories, and these brought him a vague sense of something that he had wanted and had never got. He could not name it, he did not know exactly what it was; and there was no use trying to analyze it.

As he picked up a sheaf of summer school data from his desk, a sense of frustration took hold of him. He started to call into the other room for the clerk, and then he remembered that Miss Bridgeforth was on vacation and that her substitute had a name he could not recall. He went to the door and spoke to her.

"I want you to take a letter," he said.

He sat thumbing through the sheaf of material, sorting out that on which he needed the president's advice. The substitute secretary waited with a kind of distant patience. She was dark brown and young, and she sat looking out of the window where some work students in dirty gray shop clothes were emptying trash disposal cans into a mule-drawn cart.

"You wait here," Howden said, looking at her for the first time. He scowled. "You don't chew gum in this office," he snapped. The young woman's face went stiff.

"You don't chew gum here," he said, eyeing her coldly. "The wastebasket's on the other side of the desk. I'll be right back."

CHAPTER TWENTY

I F YOU didn't keep right behind them, things piled up, and it was worse when President Wimbush was away. Somebody always wanted to know about his credits, or Miss Wilkins, the summer school teacher of Leisure-Time Activities for the Classroom, wanted her Friday schedule rearranged, or the boarding department needed a reorder of salad greens. The flyers and illustrated bulletin, which showed unrecognizable, retouched views of the campus and which had been sent to every colored teacher in three states, stressed the slogan "Learning with Pleasure," so Howden found himself busy with the details of the weekly lyceum and talent night, the Saturday-night dances in the gym, the sightseeing tour to Hangman's Point, and picnics in the grove on the bluff. The president was away a good deal during the summer session that year.

He was away when Gerry came back entirely unexpectedly in mid-July. Howden had just had a letter from her from New York two days before, and (as he told her later) when she walked into his room that night, a feather could have knocked him over. Because it made it cooler, his bedroom door was open, and he was sitting in bathrobe and pajamas proofreading the president's edi-

torial for the summer quarter of the *Alumni Bulletin*. He did not
hear Gerry come in and close the door quietly behind her.

"Hello, Shel sugar," Gerry said.

As he started up, the sight of her made him feel suddenly
weak. She had done something to her hair; she looked a little
thinner and more finely drawn. But her return was not as he
had pictured it. He was not prepared to see her leaning back
against the door smiling at him.

"Gerry!" he said.

"Don't look so startled," she said. "And turn the light out."

He groped blindly for the light cord and pulled it.

"Surprised?" he heard her ask, and then he felt her against him,
her arms about his neck. "Honey baby," she said.

"But, Gerry—"

"Just kiss me," she said.

It was as if a screen suddenly rolled up, or a cloud blew away.
He had not known how much he wanted to see her. He had not
known how much he missed her.

"Honey," Gerry said, laughing, and stepped back.

"Your father's not home," Howden said dubiously.

"I know it, and so what? I called him long-distance night before
last. He'll be gone four days." She sat on the edge of the bed. He
could just make her figure out. "What's the matter? Don't you
want me here?"

"Oh, Gerry." The feeling of being in her hands, the passion of
dependency—it was all back again. It had never been away. Lurking
somewhere in his consciousness, it had waited for this moment
to creep out and overwhelm him.

"Well, then you might act like it," Gerry said. "Come over
here."

He went over to the bed, seeing her distinctly now, and leaned
down and kissed her. Then he sat down beside her.

"You don't know how to treat me, do you, Shel?" Gerry asked
almost sadly. Then her tone lightened. "But I know how to treat
you. I know you like a book. Don't I know you like a book?"

He did not know whether she knew him like a book or not, but she was always saying it. He was not sure that it was possible to know anyone like a book.

"I came around behind all the buildings, through all that wet grass," Gerry said. "Feel my feet," she said, lifting her legs to his knee. Her legs were bare, and they were wet and cold from walking through the uncut grass. Howden could feel blades of grass clinging to her ankles.

"I'll get a towel," he said.

Taking off her sandals, he wiped her legs, which looked so clean and white in the faintly luminous dark, and her feet, which, for all the warmth of the night, were cold. An inexplicable impulse took hold of him, and he kissed the arched instep, and then he laid his cheek against the firm calf of her leg for a moment, and then he kissed her instep again.

"Darling, do you love me very much?" she asked. "Do you love me all there is in the book?" She leaned over and kissed him on the mouth, and the next moment, with a sudden movement, she turned lengthwise on the bed and held out her arms to him. "Come on up here. Come on, baby sugar." Pressing softly, with her whole flexed length, her arms tensed around him.

"It's been a long time. Hasn't it been a long time?"

"Yes," he said.

"You missed me, didn't you?"

"Yes," he said again.

"And you're glad I'm back, aren't you, honey?"

"Yes."

"Is that all you can say?"

"No," he said. She made him feel like a child, and that was the way he wanted to feel. He wanted to feel that he belonged to her. Though he could not have expressed it, he had a desire for a complete nullification of himself.

She squeezed him suddenly, fiercely. "Then say something else," she said.

"I love you," he said.

"I know you do, honey. I know. I know," Gerry said, laughing quietly, with a strange pleasure. "I know all about you."

"Do you know I need you?"

"I know that too," she said.

"Why did you stay away so long?" he asked her.

She moved higher on the bed, until his cheek rested in the hollow of her shoulder. Then she lay still except for one hand that played idly at his throat and chest. She lay still for a long time.

Suddenly, matter-of-factly, she said, "I was sick and in a lot of pain. It was too awful, sugar."

He raised himself to one elbow and looked down at her. "What was the matter?" he asked.

"Don't you know, honey? Don't you know why I had to go away, really?"

His throat felt suddenly parched. "No," he said with difficulty.

"I was pregnant, honey," Gerry said insouciantly.

"Oh, Gerry!" he said, and his dry throat seemed to flood with something warm and phlegmy. "Why didn't you tell me?"

"But now it's all right, sugar baby," Gerry said, laughing softly, putting her arms around him again and pulling him down to her. "Would you have wanted me to have a baby for you?"

"You're the only woman I'd ever want to have one for me," he said.

She laughed quietly again at that and pressed him to her.

"But now I can't. I'm all fixed, honey. I can't have a baby now."

He was sorry and he was glad. He could not analyze it. He didn't want a child, and yet if he had wanted one, she was the only woman who could bear it.

They lay for some time without speaking. Her arms tautened and loosened around him, the whole hard length of them caressing him, close but not close enough, possessively but not possessively enough. He wanted to be inside of her and to have her know him absolutely, without his making an effort for her to know.

"Sugar, do you want me to take off my dress and things? You do, don't you, honey?"

He had not thought about it, but she was already sitting up, and he could feel her lifting, straining a little. He saw her firm fluid, flexed white body emerge from her clothes. She leaned across him and threw her clothes onto the chair near the bed, and then she lay down and put her arms around him again.

"Baby, baby," she said, "it's been a long, long time."

CHAPTER TWENTY-ONE

W HEN it's over, are you going somewhere for a vacation too? Hunh?"

"When summer session's over?" Howden asked her.

"Yes," Miss Lark said, "when all these fossils go back to their country schools and start spreading ignorance again."

"I don't know," Howden said. It had never occurred to him. The truth was that time was moving so fast that he had not realized that the summer session was almost over and that it was a month since Gerry had returned. But now as he walked toward the Administration Building with Laura Lark after lunch and saw scattered groups of middle-aged summer students, he thought they all gave off an aura of happy anticipation now that the summer grind was nearly done.

"Well, I'm going away," Miss Lark said decisively. "As soon as the Old Man pulls out for his vacation, I'm pulling out for mine."

"He's not taking a vacation," Howden said.

The president had changed his mind about the automobile trip to Detroit and Canada. Instead he was going to an interracial meeting in Chicago, and Gerry was going with him. Gerry had told Howden that she didn't want to go—she wanted to stay right there with him; but she had finally agreed that perhaps it was better for her to go.

"At least he's getting away from routine, and I'm going to get away too," Miss Lark said. "I'm going up to Georgia to see my people."

Howden could not think of a single place where he could go. He had no people to visit, and there was no place to go where he would feel at home. All the home he had was right there at Arcadia.

Miss Lark sighed. "I wish this time week after next would hurry up and come."

"It's no use wishing that," Howden said. No matter how fast time went, people were always wanting it to go faster. "When you wish that, you're just wishing yourself closer to death."

"Don't you ever wish time would pass? Hunh? When you were a kid, didn't you ever wish Christmas would hurry up and come?"

"I'm not a kid now," Howden said, "and neither are you."

Miss Lark did not answer because Miss Wilkins, one of the summer school teachers, stopped her at the door, and Howden went in alone. There were several people standing in the hall outside his office, and he noted the respectful silence as he approached. He could see some of them smiling ingratiatingly in his direction, and this gave him a feeling of annoyance. He had no charity whatever for the stupidity he thought he saw in those dark faces. Beneath those smiles, the Old Man always said, lay nigger bluff two inches thick. Without looking at any of them, he entered his office and closed the door behind him. His clerk, Miss Bridgeforth, was there.

"Find out who's first, and find out what they want," Howden

told her, although Miss Bridgeforth knew the routine very well. "That Miss Tarver's first. She was there when I came from lunch," Miss Bridgeforth said. "It's about her credits. She says there're three semester hours and one quality point due her." "She's got everything that's due her," Howden said. He was tired of them all. "All right. Tell her to come in. But I'm not going to let her have anything she hasn't earned."

"And Mr. Crawley," Miss Bridgeforth said stoically. "What do you want me to do about his transcript?"

"Ask me about it later," Howden said. "Just send the Tarver woman in."

"Mr. Crawley just wants—"

"Miss Bridgeforth—" Howden began sharply, and then the door opened. It was the president. Howden scrambled up.

"Shel," the president said, "the heat's got me, and I'm going home. Can you come over to the house?"

"Right away, sir? There're a lot of summer school people waiting to see me."

"No hurry, son," the Old Man said. "Two or three hours won't make any difference."

Howden always remembered afterwards how casual it seemed. In the light of what it meant to him later, that afternoon seemed singularly free of premonitory excitement. It was as commonplace as any afternoon when he held conferences with summer students and dictated memos to staff members and signed orders for blackboard crayon and canceled book orders that someone had sent in without consulting him. It was just an afternoon of routine work, a little heavier than usual perhaps, but he got through it.

When he crossed the porch of the house and opened the double screen door, the Old Man's voice greeted him from the downstairs study.

"Is that you, Shel?"

He was lying on the lounge over against the wall under the framed photographs of the ruins of Pompeii and the Parthenon.

When Howden came in, his grimace of a smile broke. His coat was off and he was wearing white suspenders and a white belt on his white linen trousers. He looked as neat and crisp lying down in his shirtsleeves as he did sitting at his desk.

"Take your coat off, son," he said, "and turn that fan so you'll get some of it."

The room was pleasantly dim and cool. The windows were closed and the closed Venetian blinds kept the sun out. Howden could feel the breeze fluttering on his ankles.

"I could come back, if you were getting ready to take a nap," Howden suggested.

"A nap? Not in the daytime," the Old Man said, shaking his head against the cushion. "I can't sleep in the daytime. Once I wake up in the morning, that's it."

"I can't sleep in the daytime either," Howden said.

"It's all right for women, but it never does men any good. Look at Mexico. Everybody down there takes a siesta, and look at the damn country. And darkies—that's what's the matter with the vast majority of them too. They sleep too much."

They both laughed a little, and then the Old Man turned his head sharply and looked at Howden.

"Son, as the first full-time supervisor of Niggra schools in the state, you want to remember that," he said.

The words did not mean anything to Howden at first. Like the siesta in Mexico, they had nothing to do with him. Then they struck him all at once. But, even so, he reacted slowly. He drew his legs up and in and sat up straighter in his chair. When he spoke, his voice was weakly strained.

"What did you say, sir?"

A shadow passed over the Old Man's face, and he lay still for a moment, still looking at Howden with that naked but somehow unrevealing completeness that Howden knew so well. He hiked himself up until his head rested against the arm of the lounge.

"Shel, you're going to be the supervisor of Niggra schools in this state," he said simply, mildly.

There was a complete pause, a suspension of everything, while they stared at each other. Howden felt as if his insides had been sucked out; and then he felt wronged, and his mind went off wildly on all sorts of tangents. He flushed, conscious of the Old Man's intent gaze.

"Mr. President," he said, his voice dried almost to a whisper, "are you asking me to sever my connection with the college?" He did not know why he put it so formally.

Grasping the back of the lounge, the Old Man raised himself higher. "My God, no," he said harshly, and Howden knew that the Old Man was disappointed in him, in his reaction.

"If I wanted to get rid of you," he went on in a vexed, petulant tone, "I wouldn't shilly-shally like that. Why should I go to all that trouble, pulling wires and doing what it took when all I'd have to do would be to fire you if I didn't want you?"

That was true. If the president wanted to get rid of him, all he'd have to do would be to fire him. Still, this other was a shock to Howden, even when he remembered all those trips to Carthage and all the white people who had come to call him by name. He must have known in a general way that there was something in the back of the Old Man's head, but he would never have guessed it to be this.

"I thought maybe you were letting me down easy," Howden said with a sickly smile.

Aggrieved, the Old Man said, "Now, Shel, that's pretty stupid. If I want to fire somebody, that's it. My God, why should I want to kick somebody I fired upstairs?" He eased himself slowly down on the lounge again. There was a silence.

"No, son," President Wimbush said after a while. "There're two or three things, and the first is that I want you to ripen. And then I want you to have something on the record that no dog-gone darky who thinks he knows it all can say is favoritism. When I step down here and you step up—course, it's going to be a while yet," he added with a sly note of caution—"but when that happens, I want the Niggras to know the white people are behind you. We got to do it step by step, and this is the first one."

Howden did not want to leave Arcadia. For the moment, he was not sure that he wanted to be president at the price of leaving now. He was trying to comprehend what it would mean to leave. He did not want to face an entirely new set of problems. He did not want to be supervisor of Niggra schools.

"See, son?" the Old Man asked, looking at him now in mild expectancy.

Howden nodded slowly. "Yes, sir. I see."

Again a shadow passed over the president's face, and Howden, knowing that he was still disappointing him, perked up. He even smiled.

"It's so you can ripen," the Old Man said.

"It took me off my feet at first, that's all."

"I didn't want to say anything about it until it was all arranged," the president said, "and it took a lot of arranging."

"You mean the whole thing's been—?"

"Just the first step, son," the Old Man broke in quietly. "The other will follow."

Howden was thinking of having to leave Gerry. He was thinking of the evenings he had spent right here in this room. A poignant sense of loss took hold of him.

The Old Man sat up. "It may sound complicated to you— Move that fan a little, son. I feel it on my knees— And it is complicated." Then, leaning back crisply and lifting one silk-clad ankle to his knee, he went on talking.

Though he could not have phrased it, there always seemed to Howden to be something indestructible, even unassailable, about the Old Man. It was a quality that, had it been less subtle and less modified by others, might have bordered on the vulgar. As he listened to the rise and fall of the president's voice, Howden could think of this quality as a self-confidence and mastery, entirely different from the brassy self-assertiveness common to the little Negro leaders and race men who pushed themselves up like obnoxious weeds. President Wimbush was different from them.

Into him had gone long years of cultivation in a fixed back-ground. He had a sense of security and an inextinguishable knowledge of what was mutable and what was not.

There were a lot of little compromises, the Old Man said, and a lot of little angles that had to be explored. A lot of wires had to be pulled and a lot of people seen and a lot of different kinds of pressure brought to bear. For instance, Mr. Douthit, the budget director, didn't want the state to supply a car and be responsible for its upkeep too, and that had to be compromised. Then, when that was settled, Mr. Douthit thought that four dollars per diem, which was what white supervisors got, was more than a Niggra would need on the road, and they had to make a compromise on that. Then, nobody up there in the department in Carthage thought the salary should be the same as white supervisors', so they cut down on that.

But long before things got to the point where the people in the state office could argue over such details, the Old Man said, Dr. Doraman had to be brought around. Dr. Doraman wasn't against the idea. As a matter of fact, he was all for it; but Dr. Doraman was dead sure that the three state commissioners of education, who probably didn't know what he and the Old Man knew, and who, excepting Judge Reed, Dr. Doraman said, probably wouldn't give a damn if they did know—those three commis-sioners, the Old Man said Dr. Doraman figured, would have thought the state superintendent crazy if he had asked them to okay a Niggra supervisor for the actual reason that one was needed. And even if they were convinced of the reason, they would have wanted to know how come the state superintendent hadn't done a better job of picking Niggra teachers. So Dr. Dora-man wouldn't approach the commissioners. He told the Old Man that he wasn't going to put himself in the position where the commissioners would think him either a damn fool or a damn poor superintendent or both.

The Old Man took a cigar from the humidor on the table, studied it critically, put it back, took another, and bit the end off very carefully. He did not light it right away, although he struck a match. His mind made one of those excursions common to it, for he came out with something that seemed at first to have nothing to do with what went before.

"Son, there's one thing I learned long ago, and that is that a white man will admit of a professional or strictly business relationship only between himself and another white man. Between a white man and a colored, so far as the white man sees it, there just ain't no such thing. Between a white man and a colored, the white man wants it on a personal basis, and if he can't have it there, he won't have it at all." Then, quickly lighting his cigar, he blew the match out.

When he went to see Judge Reed, the Old Man said, he didn't have to do any card tricks. He never had to do card tricks with the judge. The judge knew what was going on, and he was all for the idea of having someone give full time to supervising Niggra schools because, the judge said, the Niggra schools were getting some pretty uppish teachers, and some radicals were getting in among them and trying to stir things up about equal salaries and all, especially in the towns. But the judge wasn't convinced that the supervisor should be a Niggra, not by a doggone heap. The judge said that practically every educated Niggra these days was a ruined Niggra, and there was only one he'd trust in a job like that.

Here the Old Man stopped and waited for Howden to rise to the bait.

"Meaning you, sir?" Howden asked, although he knew the answer.

Snorting, the Old Man nodded. " 'Pee Tee,' the judge told me, 'you'd make a good one, but I don't know nowadays another educated Niggra I'd trust further than I can sling a bull.' "

Howden could hear Judge Reed saying it. He could see the massive head rolling on the shoulders, the rimy eyebrows bristling over the cold blue eyes—although he had seen the judge only once.

"I told him not to worry because I had just the Niggra for it," the Old Man said, waving his hand through a cloud of smoke.

"And that meant me," Howden said.

"Now, son, who else would it mean?"

Howden could see his life at Arcadia moving before him like pictures on a screen. Getting up suddenly, he went to the front window and pulled the cord of the Venetian blinds. It was that time between late afternoon and evening when the atmosphere is so infused with limpid sunlight that sunlight seems all there is. He could see the end of the campus where the old practice cottage was and next to it, but separated from it by a stretch of lawn, the men's dormitory. He had always thought both buildings unsightly, but now everything was softly glorified in the limpid light. Bordering the campus road, the ragged live oaks were lovely. The lawn was as smooth and bluish green as any lawn in the world. He had had a good life here at Arcadia, he thought. Then, with an acute ache, he was thinking of Gerry. "Sugar darling," she had told him once, making it as always, two distinct terms of endearment, "the way things are is the way they'll have to be." He could hear those words again, as if the vibrations her voice had set up in speaking them had never petered out. He must have sighed now because the Old Man spoke to him.

"What's the matter, son?"

"I sort of hate to give Arcadia up," Howden said.

"That's not my idea. You won't be giving it up. You won't be giving anything up."

"But I think that I will," Howden said dourly. "It's kind of complicated."

"How?"

"I don't know," Howden said. He was thinking of Gerry, but of course he couldn't tell her father that.

"Look," the Old Man said, a trifle impatiently. "Your headquarters are going to be in Bluffport because that's more central, and it's in that part of the state where most of the Niggra schools

are. Your records and reports and things will go to Dr. Doraman and the commissioners, and Judge Reed's right there in
Bluffport. There're seventy-four darky schools, and you'll visit
them all, all over the state. They're going to furnish you with
a car. You're—"

"I can't drive a car," Howden said.

The Old Man was exasperated. "That's all right. You can
learn!"

It was a small point, but it seemed to drive it all home. It
seemed to make it irrevocable. Howden turned from the window
and came back to his chair.

"Yes, sir, I guess I can learn," he said, sighing again.

He was thinking that everything he wanted was right there at
Arcadia—security and position and the woman he loved. Everything was right there, and he was getting ready to leave it. No
one spoke for some time.

"Shel, who are your friends?" the Old Man asked suddenly.

Howden looked blank because he had never thought of it.
Names out of the past rose up in his mind, but he rejected them
all. He thought of all the people he had met through Gerry, but
he had to reject them too. The Old Man was watching him again,
a half-smile on his face.

"Well, you are—" Howden began.

The Old Man laughed with grim self-deprecation, but Howden
could see that he was pleased.

"Leaving out you, I've got no friends either. My God, it's the
goddamnedest thing," he said sardonically. "We're right in the
middle. We're the white man's nigger and the nigger's white
man. We've got to make white folks think we ain't when we
are, and we've got to make niggers think we are when we ain't."

Howden did not have to respond to this, for someone was coming down the stairs and then along the hall. It was Gerry. Her hair
was caught up in a curly, ribbon-tied fluff on top of her head. She
looked virginal. She looked like a very young girl just out of a
bath.

"Gerry," her father said, "I want you to teach Shel to drive."
Gerry's eyes widened. "Why, Poppa," she said, "I'd love it."
Then she looked at Howden. "Are you going to stay for supper?"
"Of course he is," her father said.
"Then I'll give him his first lesson right after."
"That's a good idea," her father said.
"I always have good ideas, Poppa," Gerry said. "You just don't
know. Don't I always have good ideas, Shel?"

PART FOUR

THE TIME ON THE
CLOCK OF THE WORLD

IN THE late spring of 1940, when he was thirty-eight, Shelton Howden married a young woman named Nan Mariott. He did it cynically, in cold blood as it were, because, as the Old Man had told him, he would have to marry sometime—and Nan Mariott was right there. She was twenty-six, and she loved Howden very much, although he told himself that she did not. This delusion was possible to him partly because Nan was not too expressive about her feelings. When he was with her, her very inarticulateness tended to make him facile in thought and word.

Howden had met her the year before, when she had given up teaching at a private school for the handicapped in South Carolina and returned to Bluffport to be with her father during the last weeks of his life. She was a honey-colored, yielding-looking girl, a little taller than most, with smoky, blue-black hair, dark grave eyes, and a way of dressing that best suited the low heels she wore. When Howden met her, she had been in Bluffport several weeks, her father was dead, and she was straightening out his jumbled, carelessly kept, small-town affairs.

If Howden had not come back to Bluffport unexpectedly one mid-week, he might never have met Nan. It was as accidental as that. She was not the kind of person you would be bound to run into flitting through the mobile social world to which, by birth and position, she might easily have belonged. She was not, so far as that goes, the kind of person you would be bound to meet socially even in a town as small as Bluffport.

Following their marriage, Howden was always reviewing the circumstances that led to their meeting. If, for instance, on the preceding Saturday Judge Reed had not brought up the subject of race friction again, disturbing Howden so that he forgot to have the judge sign his mileage voucher; if Walter Ringgold, in whose house Howden had a room, had had more patients in his Wednesday free clinic; and if the private entrance to Walter's office had not been open when Howden came in from the street, Walter would not have seen Howden and called him to come and meet an old friend.

Walter Ringgold, as ebullient as a Seidlitz powder, had a lot of old friends he was always wanting Howden to meet. Although Howden liked Walter in a casual sort of way and appreciated having the freedom of Walter's house, he was frequently embarrassed by some of Walter's friends. They included all sorts of local characters—a variety of jackleg preachers, country school teachers, proprietors of pool halls, juke joints, and beer gardens, sagging domestics, laborers in the box factory and the paper mill —in whom it was hard to see any attractive qualities. Howden supposed that all small-town physicians made friends of their patients. He was occasionally annoyed when someone called his name up on the town square and he looked around to see some brash, overfamiliar, down-at-heels darky to whom Walter had introduced him on a plane of equality. On the other hand, he had met some nice people at Walter's, people of position and consequence who happened to be in the area and stopped for a day or two. But, taken all in all, Howden thought that, for a person of his position, Walter certainly had some unaccountable tastes.

When Howden entered the house that evening in mid-week, Walter called to him through the open door of his office.

"Hey, fella, what you doing back on a Wednesday night?" Walter called with loud geniality. "Come in here. I want you to meet an old friend of mine."

Howden hesitated in the hall. He shifted his brief case. Walter, a cinnamon brown bear of a man, came to the office door.

"Come on," Walter said, beckoning to Howden in a way that could not be denied. "What brought you back anyway? Look. I want you to meet Miss Mariott—Nan Mariott. Her daddy was responsible for my coming here."

She was sitting very straight in the chair by Walter's cluttered desk. Rather wide through the eyes and high in the cheek and tapering to a squarish point of chin, her face was not pretty. But she had a lovely, honey yellow complexion, slightly flushed with tan, and lovely hair, and when she spoke in a low, throaty voice, her wide, mobile mouth brought him a sharp memory of someone he had known. She did not look at all like Valrie Tillet, he knew later, but somehow she reminded him of her.

"How do you do," she said, glancing up at him quickly and quickly lowering her eyes again.

"Did you ever meet her father?" Walter asked. "But no, no, I guess you didn't." He was taking off his soiled white office jacket and rolling down the sleeves of his shirt. The office smelled of disinfectant because the door to the clinic was still open.

"But I've heard you speak of him and of Miss Mariott too," Howden said.

He expected her to respond to that, to give a smile of acknowledgment at least, but she did not. She gave Walter an uncertain glance, and then suddenly she stood up and buttoned her mannishly cut topcoat. It struck Howden that she was very self-conscious.

"Come on, let's go across to the living room," Walter said. He was always inviting people in.

"Oh, no—no, thanks, Walter," Nan Mariott said quickly, with a low, nervous laugh. "I've got to go. I just came in about the things. Really, Walter—" It was not so much a refusal as a plea.

"All right. I'll drive you home," Walter said. He grinned at her suddenly, affectionately, his moon of a face cracking into a dozen lines. "And don't say no, cause I'm goin'a do it if it kills you."

"Please—I wouldn't want you to go to that trouble," Nan said.

Howden thought they were putting on an act, and it amused him.

"Don't be like that. It's no trouble," Walter said, hauling on his coat. "Come on and go, Shel."

Howden shook his head. "I'd better not."

Howden could never understand why he remembered it so exactly. Once much later, when he and Nan were talking about it, he found all the details there in his mind. He told himself that it had not seemed possible then that that meeting would lead to anything, or even that it *could* lead to anything. He recalled that she had walked out into the hall with a long, hurried, almost frightened stride, and that with Walter lumbering out behind her, he had got no clear impression of her total appearance. As if it were an afterthought which struck her as she reached the front door, she turned and murmured an indistinct good night to him.

The whole thing was there in his mind, like a scene from a play he had committed to memory.

He was in the living room when Walter came back a few minutes later and wanted to know what had brought Howden to town in the middle of the week.

"I forgot my mileage voucher," Howden told him. "I forgot to have Judge Reed sign it."

The corners of Walter's mouth drew down. "That bastard. That boil on the ass of progress." He was full of strong talk and volatile emotions, often vulgarly expressed. "Does he have to sign the goddamn thing?"

"After all, he's a commissioner of education," Howden said.

"That cracker," Walter said. "How do you stand him?"

"I don't have to stand him," Howden said indulgently because he was still amused. But sometimes Walter annoyed him by putting him on the defensive, although Howden tried not to show it. Walter could go on and on about crackers and the race question. He always made too much of it, always exaggerated it, Howden thought. There were times when Walter's insistence upon it aggravated Howden very much.

"Well, how did the clinic go tonight?" Howden asked.

"The same. Always the same," Walter said. "Then Nan came in."

"What was the matter with her?" Howden asked. He thought Walter looked at him skeptically. He knew that he sometimes annoyed Walter too. Two years now they had spent alternately kidding and annoying each other, but they managed to get along.

"What do you mean, what was the matter with her?"

"Did you fix her up?"

"Look, Shel," Walter said, "if you're talking about what I think you're talking about, then I don't like it worth a goddamn."

"You're putting the wrong construction on it," Howden said lightly.

"If you think Nan's like that, brother, you're wrong."

It was not convincing, Howden thought. "I didn't say she was like that or like anything else."

"Nan's all right," Walter said. The phrase "all right" was an intensive the way he used it. "She's a fine girl. I'm not a complete dog," Walter said.

It still didn't sound convincing, but Howden listened as Walter went on. Walter said that Nan's father, who for years had been the only Negro doctor in Cahoosha County, had brought him there. He had practically seen Nan grow up, Walter said, and he felt like an uncle or something to her because after all he was nearly twice her age. As a matter of fact, Nan had called him uncle until she had got through college at Fisk. In a way too, her father had put her in his hands when he died, and he was going to protect her—especially now. Dr. Mariott had left a sizable amount of real estate and insurance, and Walter said he wasn't going to let some cracker lawyer get into it, as one had been trying to do already, and cheat and fast-talk Nan out of it.

"It looks like a good setup," Howden said, glancing around the living room. "You need a wife." He was still kidding, but it was true about the wife. The woman who worked for Walter— who had been working for him ever since Mrs. Ringgold, bored

to hysteria, Howden suspected, had left him—didn't half do.
Bearing traces of former elegance but now full of man-things
and medical books, the room was shabby, its furniture dull and
scarred, its Turkey-red carpet encrusted with dust. "And apparently Nan needs a husband," Howden said. "Why don't you
marry her?"

The tone of derision was lost on Walter.

"I wish I could," he said earnestly. "I wish to God Nan felt
that way about me. Nan's about the finest girl I know. Nan's
all right."

[2]

Sometimes when he reviewed the whole business, Howden did
not see how any of it really had time to happen, or why it should
have happened, except that some inexorable fate was pushing
him on. Certainly he had had no conscious thought of going as
far as marriage with Nan Mariott. He told himself that he had
not even had time to think about it—and then, all at once, marriage to her seemed inevitable.

That fall and winter of 1940, which was the beginning of his
second full year as supervisor of Negro schools, Howden was
much troubled by talk of an equal salary suit some unnamed
teachers in the east of the state were threatening. There were even
disturbing rumors that a representative of the N.A.A.C.P. or the
L.I.C. had been right there in Bluffport, trying to persuade one of
the teachers in the Cahoosha County Training School to be a
litigant in such a suit. There was a good deal of sub-rosa talk
among school people, and the Carthage *Negro Advocate*, gloating, hinted at some kind of secret activity. But Howden could
trace nothing to its source. Judge Reed, who heard the talk too,
said something should be done; but there was nothing to do.

"Can't have some irresponsible element of Niggras trying to
stir things up," Judge Reed told Howden. "By Jesus, can't have
that. Don't know what's happening to the Niggras."

That was exactly the way Howden felt—he didn't know what was happening to the Niggras either.

It took President Wimbush to convince the judge that Howden shouldn't go around trying to beat the guilty parties out of the bushes. The Old Man pointed out that Howden had to have the confidence of school people and that he couldn't have it if he started bushwacking. The judge said that he didn't give a damn whether Howden started bushwacking or not: all he wanted was that the radicals be brought to light, and he didn't care how it was done. But the judge cooled down after a while and listened when the Old Man said it would all probably die out in a month or two. And the Old Man seemed to be right.

President Wimbush was very helpful when other things came up that year too. He kept smoothing Howden's way and telling him to take it easy, and Howden did not worry about much of anything when he talked to the Old Man. Sometimes when he visited Arcadia on week ends, Gerry would take bold chances on stealing to his room at night, and he was inclined to worry then. Once in half-grim jest he told her that she was like some of those school people out in the east—she was trying to put him on a spot. Her answer to that was that she knew what she was doing, and anyway it was a wonderful spot, and they were on it together. There were times when she made him want to live out his life like a flame, their lives mingling together in one high, consuming blaze of passion.

But it was true about the school people. They were always giving him something to cope with when he least expected it. Some too aggressive school principal, like Howard Pretlow of Cahoosha, or some brassy head teacher was forever wanting him to arouse sleeping dogs. What annoyed him most at first was the unquestioning assumption that he would *wish* to arouse them. Later it was not so much this as that everyone seemed to challenge him. As he told the Old Man, he did not know where these brash, pushy people came from or what they thought he could do about complaints that had lain dormant for years.

In Halifax County there were some ugly difficulties about school buses. The *Negro Advocate* had written an exposé of the diversion of federally provided free lunch supplies from the colored to the white schools in Kanawha County. And in Cahoosha County itself, someone (Howden suspected it was Professor Pretlow) wrote articles about the general school situation in the state to one of the national colored weeklies. But all of these matters were patched up by compromises or squelched by methods which the Old Man had been using effectively, in one situation or another, for thirty years.

Howden had some ideas of his own too that fall and winter. He liked details, and he felt it incumbent upon himself to learn as much as he could, so he gathered all sorts of statistics on the Negro schools of the state. He knew what the average daily attendance was at each school and how many pupils dropped out each year and how many teachers each school had and exactly what was being taught in any school at any hour of the day. Although it was not generally known, it was Howden who created the phrase "One Teacher-One Goal" when Dr. Doraman found it necessary to defend against attack by a radical Negro element the continuance of one-room Negro schools in the face of the extensive consolidation of white schools. It was Howden also who first thought of organizing colored principals and teachers into county-wide Schoolmasters' Clubs, in order (as he wrote in his report to the state superintendent) "to facilitate the exchange of professional ideas and experience." Dr. Doraman was enthusiastic about the plan. He instructed the white supervisors to organize white teachers along the same line.

It was President Wimbush, however, who provided the germ of the idea upon which Howden worked hardest and on which he received the warmest official congratulations. This was the idea of grading teachers according to the condition of the physical plant in which they taught, the facilities they had, the average daily attendance, and other such criteria, and of paying them by grades. Although Howden could not have foreseen it, the report which he thrashed out and the conclusions he reached contained the principles that, when a little extended, formed the basis of the state's defense against the charge of maintaining a discriminatory salary level for Negro teachers. (Some years later, the state was able to show that there was only one salary scale for all teachers and that the grades within the scale represented a just and equitable evaluation of teacher-effectiveness. The state won a smashing legal victory, but it was Howden and the Old Man who had worked out the curious principle that the poorer the buildings in which teachers worked, and the scarcer the facilities provided for them by the state, the less they should be paid.)

Howden began to understand that although his job was no sinecure, it was less difficult than he had imagined. A commonsensical facing of reality was what was chiefly required. There were a lot of errors of thought and feeling which he did not see how anyone could fall into once he had faced reality. The trouble was, as the Old Man said, few darkies ever did face it.

Aside from matters that had to do with his specific job, a good many other things helped occupy Howden's time, especially through '40, when there seemed to be a growing general restiveness and ferment. No matter how he felt privately, things were expected of him as a public figure. He had to be, at least nominally, a member of the N.A.A.C.P. and the L.I.C. and other uplift groups, and he had to make a show of attending meetings when he could. He filled a lot of speaking engagements over the state. He took part in forum discussions. He attended civic-social meetings which he did not want to attend. His presence was almost mandatory at these affairs now that he was in a key position.

People expected him to share responsibility in many matters. Some fraternal or social or religious group was always sponsoring an oratorical contest or a children's day or a parents' day or Negro History Week, and Howden could expect to be called upon for a speech or a few remarks or at least to sit in a place of honor on the rostrum with the local dignitaries. So far as he could see, these meetings never accomplished anything except a temporary bond of warm racial fellowship, which he did not share, and a vague feeling of hope for the future. The people who attended them never faced reality. But they must have found some inexplicable satisfaction in meeting together, for they met again and again—in Dixwell, in Miapolis, in Carthage and Havenport.

[3]

It was at one such meeting right there in Bluffport that Howden saw Nan Mariott for the second time. She was sitting in the audience, about halfway back, and he picked her face out at once. In that sea of dull brown and black faces, hers stood out in sharp contrast. All through his speech on "Where the Negro Stands Today" (it was a Negro History Week meeting), and even after he sat down, his gaze kept going back to her. When the meeting was over and he was receiving congratulations, he saw Nan slip from her seat and start for the door at the back of the church auditorium. Her passage was blocked by the crowd for a moment, and then he lost sight of her.

Although it seemed an interminable time before he got away, Nan Mariott was outside talking to two frowzy old women when Howden left the church. One of the old women was patting one of Nan's gloved hands between both of her own, and Howden could see that Nan was listening gravely, looking quietly down into the old woman's black and wrinkled face. Nan seemed quite at home. Even if she did have an income, Howden thought, she was just a small-town girl with such a girl's naïve manner and address. She suffered by comparison to Gerry, he thought. Nan was wearing a black felt hat and a plain gray cloth coat of no particular style. Howden saw her take her hat off and run her hand over her hair as she turned away. Then he spoke to her.

"Miss Mariott," he said. His voice seemed to startle her a little, for she stopped in her tracks. Her smoky hair drifted against her cheek as she turned back again. Howden approached her.

"Oh," she said, "good afternoon."

"I'm going your way. I'll be glad to take you," Howden said.

He could tell that she was giving thought to his offer, although he did not see what there was to think about. A few people were still coming out of the mouse-gray weathered church, and others stood about on the narrow, unpaved sidewalk. Along both sides of the street, the unpainted houses, flimsily reared on high pillars, looked like the deserted shelters of some monstrous insect tribe. It was a drab, ugly little street, pitching down to the swamp and the river.

"Thank you, but I wouldn't put you to that trouble," Nan said quietly.

It was one of her standard small-town answers, Howden thought. He had heard her say the thing before. He felt irritated.

"It's no trouble," he said.

Her eyes darted at him uncertainly, but she said, "Thank you, then," and walked across the cinder pavement with him to the car.

She sat very straight, with the backs of her legs pressed against the front edge of the seat and her feet close together. They went up the hill to the town and around the town square, with the Confederate monument in the center, and then down and across the bridge over the marshy fill. In The Chute, as the main Negro street—and, in fact, the whole section—was called, quite a few dressed-up-for-Sunday darkies loitered. Howden saw them standing on corners and going in and out of the poky little joints where they sold beer and pickled pigs' feet and juke box music and where the sports hung out to ogle any women passing by.

"Do you go to meetings of that sort often?" Howden asked. He felt constrained to make conversation.

"Yes," she replied.

"Why?"

"Because I'm interested in—well, in my people," she said.

The phrase jarred on him. A small-town race woman, he thought, or a woman starved for anything that promised excitement. Then, remembering their first meeting, he wanted to laugh. She wasn't fooling him. He felt patronizing and indulgent.

"Did you like my speech?" he asked her.

She hesitated, and he glanced at her. He did not quite believe in the beauty of her skin nor in the luxurious blackness of her silky hair.

"Some of it," Nan Mariott said quietly.

"Why just some of it?"

"Because—" she said and stopped and half turned her head toward him and then away again at once. Her hands played with the brim of her hat. "I'd rather not say—I'm not sure."

"Why aren't you sure?"

"Please—I'd rather not try to say," she said.

He felt superior, and yet he felt annoyed too. For a moment he could think of nothing to say, and she sat there not offering anything at all. There was no way of explaining how he felt. He wanted to tear away whatever cloak this was in which she wrapped herself. He wanted to get beneath her stupid small-town resistance and what he thought to be her false modesty and reserve.

"I suppose you have a lot of friends here?" he asked.

"A few—old friends of my father's," she said. "I've been away quite a while."

"What, no boy friend?"

For a bewildered second she looked at him. "No," she answered simply.

They were passing Walter's house, which always seemed out of place in the shabby, gray-toned street. Cupolaed and bay-windowed and freshly painted white, it looked as if it had wandered down from the north side of the square. Howden always experienced a twinge of jealousy when he saw it. Walter might consort with some very queer people, and he might have crazy ideas, and he might be overemotional and unrealistic about the race question and social justice, but he was doing all right for himself.

"What about Walter?" Howden asked.

Again she hesitated. "I don't understand," she said. In her lap her hands were very still.

"You like him, don't you?"

"Why, yes," she said slowly, "I like Walter quite a lot."

"What do you mean by quite a lot?" he asked, his voice edged with malice.

"Walter is my oldest friend," she said.

Among his jumbled feelings he recognized frustration.

They rode on in silence for a moment more, and then she said, "I turn at the corner. Really—you needn't take me, Mr. Howden."

But he had already turned off The Chute into a curving street that suddenly became a country road. The nigger shacks thinned out, were left behind. They passed the graveyard, as ragged and untended as a swamp, and then crossed a culvert. Some distance beyond this, all alone, stood Nan's house. It was a two-story porched house, painted tan and green, and surrounded by a large hedge-bordered yard. It was quite as nice a house as Walter's.

Nan Mariott got out of the car carefully and stepped back. Howden could see that she was making some kind of effort, and again he felt superior and amused. He looked at her boldly.

"Would you—would you care to come in?" she asked at last.

"Not now," he said, "but sometime—soon."

"Well, thank you," she said in a low voice and turned at once.

He watched her walking stiffly across the yard, and he could tell that she was conscious of his gaze. She was tall and straight, with long, shapely legs. As she mounted to the porch, he turned, backed, and drove away.

CHAPTER TWENTY-THREE

ONCE when they were reviewing some circumstance that went back to the autumn of 1940, that whole scene came into Howden's mind, and he asked Nan if she had really expected him to come in that day. They had been married for more than a year, but he could see that the question disturbed her. They had got on together. Through trial and error, and in spite of discordant moments, he had worked out formulas for getting on with her.

"That first time I drove you home, did you expect me to come in?" he asked her.

"No," Nan answered thoughtfully in her low voice, "I don't think I really expected it."

"Did you want me to?"

"I don't know," she said, pausing in the act of brushing her hair. Her brow puckered. "But in some way I must have wanted you to, Shelton."

He preferred to keep it on a level of badinage, but he could see that she was taking it seriously. Yet he asked her another question.

"Why do you say that?"

"Because—well, I invited you in, and if I really hadn't wanted you to—" She paused for a moment. "I try to be honest."

"You're not being honest now," Howden told her. "You looked as if you didn't care whether I came or went."

She was sitting on the little bench in front of the dressing table, and now she turned more fully toward him. The light streamed over her, suffusing her flesh with a warm radiance, etching out the rounded lift of her breast under her flannel robe.

"I'm sure I must have meant it," she said.

"But why are you so sure?"

He did not know why he pressed it, unless it was because he wanted to get an admission from her that would relieve his conscience. He did not want to feel that all the unspoken things that were wrong were his fault. Some of them were her fault too, he thought. Some were the fault of the fate that had pushed him inexorably on. He did not like to feel that Nan had given up any more than he had, or that he owed her any more than she owed him, or that she was making any greater contribution to the stability of their marriage than he. Yet it must have been this feeling that made him pursue the topic. He could see her looking at him in that perplexed and troubled way she had.

"You can't say you were in love with me," Howden said. "We'd only seen each other once before."

"Oh, no," Nan protested quickly, softly. "I couldn't say that," she said more slowly. "I don't think I was then."

"Of course you weren't."

"Don't say it like that, Shelton."

"Like what?"

"As if—" She stopped and threw out her hand helplessly. "Oh, I don't know. As if it had something to do with later—and with now."

"Nan," he said, "when did you fall in love with me?" He supposed that under one circumstance or another every married person had asked this question of his mate. He could see that Nan was making an effort to think back.

"I'm not sure," she said with a nervous little laugh. "It just seemed to happen."

"You were just lonely. You were lonely and I happened along at the right time."

"Don't say that, Shelton. Please don't. It's not true. You make it sound— I wasn't lonely like that."

He knew she was distressed. "It was just fate," he said.

"Oh, Shelton, I wish you'd—" She stopped again and ran her hand absently over the bristles of the brush.

It was not on the plane he wanted it on at all.

"All right," he said. "Get your hair done."

He picked up the magazine *Success* and readjusted the bed lamp, although the hour was later than usual. The week ends he was to come home Nan always waited up for him, no matter how late it was. He could recall instances when he had got home past one o'clock and found her waiting, still keeping supper hot for him. It was the kind of solicitude he wished she would get over showing because it disturbed him. Raising himself a little higher on the pillow, he turned to that section of the magazine called "People and Things," and then he heard Nan's voice again.

"Shelton, it was a queer courtship, wasn't it? I mean, when you think about it, it wasn't really a courtship, was it?"

Howden felt himself go hostile in the way he always did when he was put on the defensive. He might have known that she had been thinking about it all the time instead of doing her hair. She never seemed to know when a discussion was over.

"Why wasn't it a courtship?"

"I never thought I'd—" Catching her lower lip between her teeth, she looked at him.

He could see that it still troubled her. Virginity, he had told her once, was only an unimportant physical condition; but it was what, in some inexplicable way, she seemed to hold over him. He did not want to talk about it now, and the only thing to do was to treat it lightly. He felt what he had first felt all those months ago—what she still made him feel: he was master. Yet he was uncomfortably aware that there was a hard core of privacy in her that he had never penetrated and could never violate.

"There wasn't anything the matter with it," he said. "It didn't hurt anybody. Grow up, Nan."

"You didn't—I mean, you didn't ever—"

"I didn't ever what? Now look, Nan," he went on, trying to

sound reasonable, "if it wasn't a good courtship, you can't say it was my fault."

She had moved to the side of the bed and had started to take off her robe. Now she paused and looked down at him with troubled eyes. Howden thought that she was making too much of it, since it was all over long ago.

"Oh, no, I didn't mean that. Only—" she sat down on the side of the bed and took her robe off slowly and held it. "Only I was afraid you weren't going to ask me to marry you. I was surprised when you did."

"Good Lord!" Howden said, and then he laughed. It was better to treat it lightly. "You weren't too surprised to say yes."

"It's not quite a joke," Nan said.

"All right. Now let's forget it, and tell me what's been going on this week. Did the man come to fix the radio?"

Nan told him yes, and then, as if she were glad of the distraction, she went into considerable detail about what happened while he was gone between Monday morning and Friday night. Howden could keep half his mind on his reading while she talked. She said that whatever was the matter with the radio couldn't have been much because the man repaired it in five minutes, although he charged five dollars. Nan said she had made up part of that because Miss Rebecca didn't come in to clean either on Tuesday or Thursday, and she had done all the cleaning herself. Howden roused to say that that was the trouble with darkies— you couldn't depend on them; and Nan said quietly that when Miss Rebecca wasn't ill, she was quite dependable.

"I wish you wouldn't call her Miss Rebecca," Howden said. "Why do you want to make an equal of her? And the man who takes away the trash once a week is named Butch, just plain Butch."

"But, Shelton—"

"Don't try to show them more respect than they can appreciate."

"But I couldn't call him Butch."

"Well, don't call him anything."

He did not listen again for five minutes, and then he heard
Nan saying that she would have forgotten all about promising to
help sponsor some of the Cahoosha County Training School girls
who wanted to organize a health club if Walter hadn't reminded
her of it. So on Thursday she had gone across town to the school,
and she and Walter and Professor Pretlow had met with some of
the older girls.

"They want to have something like a Four-Aitch Club eventually," Nan said.

"What they need is a personal hygiene club," Howden said.
"Whose idea is it anyway—Walter's?"

"No," Nan said. "They asked him to be a sponsor, and they
asked me to be one. It's Professor Pretlow's idea."

Howden grunted disdainfully. He didn't care for Pretlow or
for some of Pretlow's ideas either.

"Pretlow's got teachers for things like that. That's part of their
job," Howden said.

"But they wanted sponsors from the community too," Nan said.

"Let Pretlow find somebody else," Howden said, closing the
magazine and putting it on the night table. He reached up and
switched off the bed lamp. He stretched out and sighed. No
matter where he'd been or what he'd been doing through the
week, he always seemed to sleep best on Friday nights.

"Oh, yes," Nan said, "and Walter asked me to remind you of
the meeting next Tuesday night."

"Walter knows I'm never here on Tuesday night."

"He said to remind you anyway, just in case you were," Nan
said. "He said the local chapter of L.I.C.—"

"Good Lord, that again!" Howden said. "Walter's always trying to get you tied up in something." Irritated, he lay there thinking about Walter. He knew that he could never acquire Walter's
point of view. He could not afford to be as unrealistic as Walter.
In a sense, it was a result of Walter's living in a small town. If
Walter had gone to practice in a city like Carthage, where he

would have had social outlets, he wouldn't be the way he was. "Walter's a fool," Howden said.

"But you do like him, don't you, Shelton?"

He did not see why she asked that, except that she wanted him to share her affection for Walter. He had a casual, indulgent kind of friendliness for Walter, but he wished Walter were not the way he was because in a sense it made Walter one of his enemies. It made Walter an enemy of the kind you could not openly declare against or openly fight, but an enemy nevertheless. Someday he might have to do something about Walter.

"Go to sleep," he said. "It's getting late."

"He gave me away," Nan said softly, and then she sighed.

It was pure sentimentality, Howden thought, and there was no need to answer her because it was not so much a declaration as the expression of a wish to relive a moment in the past, to do it all over again perhaps in a different way, to go back to a positive beginning before everything became blurred. Perhaps Nan felt about it as he sometimes did—incredulous.

[2]

It was the same feeling he had had while he stood waiting in the room that had once been Dr. Mariott's office. It was a rather frilly and feminine room now, for Nan had had the whole house done over in preparation for her wedding. Nan's old college roommate, a social worker from Toledo, came in to tell him that the bride had just come downstairs, but that he mustn't try to see her before the ceremony because it was bad luck. The bride looked very lovely, Nan's old college roommate said, and Howden wished that she would not refer to "the bride" in just that gushing, sentimental way. Then he heard Gerry's voice, very strident and quick and gay, out in the hall, and then someone brought the Old Man into the room.

"Now take it easy," the Old Man said. "I've got the ring right here."

There were not more than thirty guests, but the living room and the dining room beyond seemed crowded, and, in spite of the flowers, there was an odor of new wallpaper. The old people— Nan's father's friends—seemed out of place among the group from Carthage, whose unabated chatter gave the rooms a tone of gaiety. But everybody fell silent when the hired pianist softly struck the opening chords of "O Promise Me." Howden was wondering how he had got there in this inescapable position between the minister and the Old Man. He could see Gerry, who suddenly lifted her head and smiled whitely at him from under the floppy brim of her hat.

When the music changed, everyone stood up, pushing back the rented collapsible chairs, and looked toward the door from the hall. Howden's attention was centered there too. He saw Nan coming. She was wearing a soft blue hat and a gray suit, and there was a spray of rosemary pinned at her breast. She walked firmly erect, looking straight ahead, and there was no expression in her face. Her hand was clutched on Walter's arm. At a nudge from the Old Man, Howden turned and faced the minister, and Nan was right there beside him, although he did not know how she had got there. He saw her hands, clasping her gloves and a white leather Testament, trembling, and he heard the prayerful voice of the minister saying:

"What God hath joined, let no man . . ."

Turning to kiss Nan, as the minister instructed him to do, he saw that she was crying. He could never quite believe in the clear beauty of her complexion. For a moment she clung to him. Then the guests were all crowding around, and the whole atmosphere changed at once. Suddenly everyone seemed to be very gay and relieved. He saw Gerry, and Gerry winked and smiled at him. But while everyone was grouped around Nan a moment later, and he was standing alone and lost, Gerry came up to him. Her eyes were hard and burning.

"She may be the bride," she whispered tensely, "but I'm still the woman you need!"

[3]

Howden thought of it as he lay there in the dark, and the whole emotional content of his wedding day poured over him like a cold deluge. He never thought that the mere memory of it could make him feel that way again—as if all freedom of choice were denied him, as if his marriage to Nan had robbed him of some vague hope or dream. It did not seem possible that it had happened, and there was no reason why it should have happened except that he and Nan had both been right there. He stirred uneasily and tugged at the covers, which were never folded back quite high enough for him. He was surprised when Nan spoke.

"Shelton," Nan whispered, as if she were afraid of waking him. "Shelton, are you asleep?"

"No."

"I haven't been asleep either," she said.

"Well, go on to sleep," he said. "It's past midnight."

"Shelton—"

A change in her voice made him turn his head quickly, though he could not see her in the dark. He felt impatient with her for still wanting to talk at this time of night.

"Good Lord, Nan, why don't you go on to sleep!"

"Shelton, Walter—" She hesitated, then went on with breathless slowness. "He can't be sure yet, but Walter—Walter thinks I'm going to have a baby."

"What? My God!" He jerked up and fumbled for the bed lamp and stared down into her wide, uncertain, and waiting eyes. A braid of her hair, black as a raven's wing against the pillow, was already unraveling tendrilously. Drawing her breath in sharply, she caught her lower lip between her teeth. Her face filled with anguish, and she covered it with both her hands and turned away.

"Don't—please, don't." Her voice cracked. "Don't look at me that way. Please turn the light out."

He turned out the light and lay down again, and lay there for a long time without moving. He didn't want a child. He didn't want to have to bring up a darky child— But there was no use trying to put it into words. He wondered what had happened, after all the care he took. Had Nan—? Perhaps it was as much his fault as hers. He could feel Nan's body trembling with sobs.

"All right," he said, more roughly than he meant. "Stop crying now, and go on to sleep."

"I thought—I hoped—" Nan gasped brokenly.

"Go on to sleep," he said again, more gently. He lay there staring up into the dark.

CHAPTER TWENTY-FOUR

ON HIS way to have Judge Reed sign the final mileage voucher of the school year, Shelton Howden felt conspicuous. It was always an ordeal to walk around the square. As he emerged into it, having parked his car a block away, he was conscious of making an effort of will. He pressed his brief case flat against his body and lowered his head.

It was too soon after the noonday dinner hour for many people to be about. The benches around the Confederate monument in the ragged little park were deserted, but there were a few old Fords and Chevrolets and Plymouths nosed at an angle into the curb. As he passed the Metro Sugar Bowl, Howden could see the shirtsleeved clerks from the bank and the county offices and the girls from Penney's Dry Goods store and the Ou-La-La Beautie Shoppe sitting on the little stools before the counter eating greasy hamburgers and drinking Coca-Cola out of paper cups. Howden never understood where all the salesgirls and clerks came from or how business supported them, except on Saturdays. He pressed his brief case flatter because he did not want to seem conspicuous. He felt better when he had passed the low frame structure that housed the post office. Between it and the county annex there was only the vacant lot where, every now and then in the spring and fall, some traveling evangelist or a road show pitched a tent. Howden relaxed. He took a longer firmer stride—almost as long and as firm as if he were in The Chute—noting with satisfaction that there was no one between him and his objective.

But he found himself half hoping that the judge would not be in. He still had some gasoline coupons left, and he really didn't need a signed voucher yet. It was not that he feared Judge Reed as he might have feared a white man he didn't know. The judge liked him. Howden had heard it from President Wimbush, and then Dr. Doraman had confirmed it. "Boy," Dr. Doraman had laughingly told him a long time ago, "you sure stand in with the judge." But his relations with the judge could not be explained in such simple and offhand terms. The Old Man understood this. The Old Man knew it was not so simple to stand in with Judge Reed, or with any other white man.

Howden thought of this as he mounted the dark enclosed stairs at the rear of the building. The stairs smelled of oil and dust and staleness, but it was the only way he could go since the sign on the elevator plainly said "Negroes Use Back Stairs." As he went up, he could hear men's voices from one of the rooms on the second floor, and he could feel the vibrations that the old weighted-type elevator sent through the half-empty building. Howden paused to catch his breath in the gloom of the third-floor landing. Then he went up the narrow hall, past the office of the County Co-operative Growers Association and several doors whose frosted glass upper halves were dark with the shadows of things stacked against them, and knocked at Judge Reed's door.

Miss McCaslin, who was sitting at the desk behind the railing, glanced up and went on typing for a moment longer. Miss Mc-Caslin always struck Howden as an anomaly in that shabby office.

"I thought that was you," she said in her reedy voice. "Every time somebody knocks on that door, I know it's you."

In spite of the number of times he had been there, he could not get it through his head that it was at least a semi-public office where knocking was wholly unnecessary. No matter how important it was for him to go there, he could not rid himself of the feeling of being an intruder, although Miss McCaslin always smiled at him.

"Is Judge Reed in? I brought my mileage voucher for him to sign," Howden said. He wanted her to know that he was not bothering the judge needlessly. He always stated his specific business to Miss McCaslin, and he never mumbled indistinctly. It embarrassed him when a white person had to ask him to repeat something.

"He went to dinner, but he ought to be back any minute now," Miss McCaslin said, glancing down at her wristwatch. "He wants to see you."

Howden looked at her blankly. He could see her corn-silk hair and her shallow eyes and the creases that betrayed her age in her slender neck. Then he realized that he was staring at her and that she could take offense.

"The judge wants to see me?"

"He'll likely be back any minute," Miss McCaslin said. "You better wait."

There were two chairs against the wall opposite the railing, but Howden stood there in the middle of the floor. He and Miss McCaslin were old acquaintances, and sometimes she talked to him about all sorts of things he wished she wouldn't, but he never wanted her to feel that he took social liberties such as sitting down in her presence. She had talked to him about her family and her friends and President Roosevelt. Recently she had been talking to him about Washington, D.C., asking him if he thought she should go up there and take one of those government jobs they were advertising on those flyers stuck up in the post office.

She said she was just plain sick and tired of Bluffport where there wasn't a thing to do.

Sometimes she kidded him in a way that was too intimate for his comfort. Right after his marriage, she had jokingly cautioned him to be extra careful and not let any of those brown-skin mammas, whose hearts he had broken, get after him with a razor. There was no use telling Miss McCaslin that none of the people he associated with carried razors because she went on to tell him what trouble the girl who worked for her sister had with her man. Then she wanted to know if Howden knew Mattie, the girl who worked for her sister, or Mattie's man either. When Howden smiled diffidently and told her no, Miss McCaslin said that was funny because Mattie was quite a society girl down in The Chute. Miss McCaslin had made it seem almost mandatory for him to offer some logical explanation why he did not know the girl who worked for her sister. Howden had said that there were a lot of people in The Chute, nearly two thousand of them, in fact almost as many as there were uptown, now that the box factory was turning out ammunition cases for England. And he didn't live exactly in The Chute any more; he lived a little way out, where they have R.F.D. Besides, he was away a good deal, as Miss McCaslin knew, and when he got back on week ends, he didn't have time to socialize.

But apparently Miss McCaslin had forgotten the details of this conversation because now she was asking him about someone else down in The Chute.

"Rowbottom?" Howden repeated. He vaguely remembered the name in some connection, but there were a lot of names he vaguely remembered. "I've heard the name, ma'am, but I can't place it."

"He's some kind of preacher," Miss McCaslin said.

"Oh," Howden said, "he must be the one at the Baptist church on Starr Street."

"How long you reckon he's been here?" Miss McCaslin asked.

"I don't know, ma'am," Howden said.

"Judge Reed thought— Oh, here he is now."

The door opened, and Judge Reed came in. The bow of his black string tie had come undone, and his doughy face, which no amount of sun ever tanned, looked soft and pasty.

"You here, are you?" the judge said. "Thought it's about time. What you been running that car on—water?"

It was a joking tribute to Howden's economy (which the judge was always commending him for), but Howden could see that the judge was saying one thing and thinking about another.

"Well, come on in," Judge Reed said, trundling heavily through the little gate in the railing toward the door of his private office. "Come on."

The private office smelled like the inside of an old trunk, although it must once have been rather sumptuous. Now its roll-top desk and high-backed leather desk chair were merely antiquated. For years the bookcases against the wall had not been opened, and the carpet on the floor was raveled and showed a threadbare path from the door to the desk and to the window overlooking the square. Howden often wondered why the judge did not get some new furniture and change things around a little. It did not occur to Howden that the only objective answer was that the judge did not want to change.

"Getting my kind of weather now," Judge Reed said, sitting down in front of the desk. He swiveled the chair around and propped one Congress-gaitered foot against the baseboard below the window. Behind him, Howden stood by the desk. "Weather like this, I feel's good as new. How you feel?"

"I feel fine, Judge," Howden said.

Looking out of the window where he could see straight across the square, the judge was silent for a while. Then his massive head turned slowly around and his eyeballs rolled up until only the dull whites showed.

"Professor, what's going on down there in The Chute?" he asked.

The formal term of address warned Howden. He felt like a pail three quarters full of water into which the judge had dropped a stone. The level of his emotions rose. He swallowed hard.

"Going on, Judge?"

"What's this I been hearing?"

It was a simple question, but Howden couldn't answer. He wondered exactly what it was the judge had heard. He could feel that other personality of his emerging, guarded and alert.

"I don't know, sir," he said with effort. "About what, Judge?"

Judge Reed turned his head back to the window again. From where he stood, Howden could see cars slanted into the inside curbing around the park, and he could see two women standing in front of Cartwright's drug store, and he could see the sun making a brilliant, undulating shine on the tin roof of Jester's Ford Sales and Service. But his mind was not out there in the square.

"What 'bout that preacher down there—Rowbottom?" the judge asked, still looking out of the window. "Know him?"

It was the same question Miss McCaslin had asked, and he answered it in the same way.

"What's he think he's doing?"

"I don't know how you mean, sir," Howden answered. There was no way to tell the judge's expression from the back of his head.

"Doing some funny kind of preaching, tell me. Hear it ain't 'xactly the word'a God he's preaching."

Howden hesitated. "I don't know, Judge, because I don't ever go there. I think he's a jackleg, Judge."

"Tell me he's likely up to something though. Tell me he's kind'a set on stirring up trouble."

"Is that so, sir?" Howden asked. "I hadn't heard about it, Judge." Then, realizing that this was a kind of contradiction of the judge, Howden laughed weakly and started again. "I mean—"

Judge Reed had turned his head to look at him once more.

"Tell me him and some more—that Niggra doctor—what'sis-name?" Judge Reed asked mildly.

"Ringgold?"

"Tell me him and some more, Rowbottom and the Niggra doctor and some others, are up to something sure as you're born."

Howden stood a little straighter. He put his hands in his pockets and took them out again. He was regretting that he knew Walter Ringgold, that he had lived in Ringgold's house for two years. He resented the fact that he was in this embarrassing, defenseless position because of Walter and his damn-fool activities.

"Judge," Howden said, "Walter Ringgold's just hot air."

"Is?" It was less a question than an expression of mild surprise.

"He just talks a lot."

"Does?"

"Ringgold's just—" He wanted to repudiate him in strong terms, but he could not find the proper words.

"Know him pretty good, don't you? Lived there with him a while back, didn't you?" Only the whites of Judge Reed's eyes showed, and his grainy voice was mild enough.

The tightness in Howden increased a notch, and he felt sharp hatred for Walter, but he managed a weak laugh.

"I didn't see him much, Judge, and then he just did a lot of crazy talk. It didn't mean anything. Judge, I think somebody's been exaggerating it."

Turning his head toward the window again, the judge did not speak for several minutes. In a way, Howden thought, the judge's silence was an exaggeration too, and he was afraid of exaggeration. There was already too much of it. Almost no one was reasonable about anything now that there was a war on. He was thinking of a conversation he had had with the Old Man some weeks ago. The Old Man had said that the trouble was that everyone was trying to prove something. The "hot" music and the outlandish cut of "zoot suits" and the jitterbugging and the religious sects that went in for snake-handling were all part of it. There was a great deal of intemperance that seemed to express itself in racial terms and in racial struggle. There was a lot of talk about the "Aryan race" and the "Japanese race" and the "Jewish people"—all in connection with the war. No one seemed to realize, the Old Man had said, that the only struggle worth anything was the personal struggle, and that whatever fulfillment there was in life was a personal fulfillment.

All Howden could see of the judge's face was the puff of flaccid jaw where the judge habitually carried a quid of tobacco.

"Tell me, though, they've started some kind'a organization down there in The Chute, some kind'a league or something. That so?"

Howden had joined the League of Interracial Comity because joining was the kind of gesture anyone in his position would be expected to make. Now he wondered if he could explain to the judge. He wondered if he had to.

"It's the League for Interracial Comity," Howden said uneasily, trying to gauge how far he should go, trying to decide whether he should confess and explain his membership. "There's been a local chapter for a long time, Judge, but they're just holding meetings again."

"Goddamn it, boy, what have they got to meet about?" The intense blue eyes were back on Howden, but the voice was still mild.

Howden could not answer because, in truth, what did they have to meet about? They were fools. They were riding for a fall. Howden tried to arrange his face in the kind of a smile that would indicate to the judge how foolish it was of them to meet.

"That one of them organizations with headquarters up North? Tell me it is. Tell me it's a troublemaker," the judge said.

"I don't think it amounts to much, Judge," Howden said.

But it was obvious that the judge thought it amounted to something.

"Ain't goin'a stand for nothing like that, specially with a war on," the judge said, shaking his head. "Ain't goin'a stand for that League for whatever-you-call-it or for any other radical bunch to come in here and try to mislead our Niggras. Ain't no white man in Bluffport—ain't no white man in the whole of Cahoosha County goin'a stand for nothing like that. That Niggra doctor down there, he knows better'n that. And that preacher, Row-bottom—where'd he come from anyway?"

"I don't know, sir," Howden answered lamely. He felt used up, as limp as a wet dishrag.

"Was a time when Niggras knew their best friends, but between the New Deal and the war, tell you, it's different. And now, goddamn it, why tell me some agitators been stirring up Niggra cooks and maids up in Carthage, and white women ain't safe from their own Niggras. And down here there's this what-you-call-it League."

All at once an incontrollable impulse seized Howden. He did not know where it came from, unless it was from some wild sense of guilt and a desire to confess and be absolved. As he stood there looking at the back of Judge Reed's head, he felt absolutely certain that his whole future lay within the judge's keeping. He felt certain that the judge was the representative of all those powers one must propitiate in order to survive. All Howden wanted, he thought, was to live his life in reasonable security. All he wanted was sufficient mastery of his surroundings to permit this.

"Judge," he said, "I pay dues in the League." He saw the judge's head turn slowly, like one of those heads on a mechanical effigy in the Mardi Gras.

"Do?"

"But I don't go to meetings."

"Don't?"

"No, sir."

"Why you join then?"

Howden hesitated, slowly licking his lips. He had already gone too far, he thought, and now he was trapped. He wished the Old Man was there. The Old Man could have handled it. The Old Man could have got him out of it.

"You see, sir, there's a kind of code that a person like me—a person in my position—is expected to follow. It's a racial ethic, Judge, sir," he said. "President Wimbush could tell you how it is."

"You mean Pee Tee?"

"Yes, sir," Howden said. "It's an ethic, and no matter what a person in our position—I mean mine and Pee Tee's—no matter what we think, we're caught in it." Because he was conscious of not saying it clearly, he stopped. He was trying to see it all objectively and to offer some logical explanation, and he could see that the judge was listening carefully. He looked past the judge's head and out of the window where there were some women and now also a few blue-jeaned men on the shady west side of the square. He could not explain to the judge about the code in the terms that the Old Man had used, and yet he tried again.

"You want to live your own life, but the code forces all this other upon you. You have to pay lip service to it, Judge. You don't owe it anything, and you don't believe in it, but—" He stopped again, for all at once he realized that he was saying much more than he intended, perhaps much more than was necessary, and none of it was any better. "Do you see what I mean, sir?"

The head came around; the mouth pursed in thought. There was a stain of tobacco juice on the lips, and the tongue came out in one corner and went slowly, absently to the other, licking the stain.

"Think you ought to go to some of them meetin's, boy," Judge Reed said flatly. "Think you ought to know what's goin' on down there."

Howden's mind caught on with difficulty. A whole lifetime of unorganized thought and impacted experience had flowed from him since he had spoken, but nothing was changed in his relation to the judge. He felt relieved. The judge was not blaming him; the judge understood.

"Don't want nobody down there trying to inflame things," the judge said. "Don't want some irresponsible rapscallion Niggra making trouble, do we, boy?"

"No, sir," Howden said.

"No use them getting all riled and unreasonable. South's still the South," the judge said.

Howden could feel the judge waiting, but he did not know

what to say or whether to say anything. It was only two-thirty in the afternoon, but he felt utterly weary.

"That kind'a stuff, meetin' and speechifyin'—why, it ain't goin'a get them nowhere. Looks like they'd know it. Looks like if they don't know it, time they learnt."

"Yes, sir," Howden said.

"Can't change things. Ought to know it," the judge said. "If they don't know it, looks like somebody's got to learn them."

Howden said nothing, but he drew a deep breath in the silence, and the tightness he felt began to relax. Staring out of the window in complete cessation of both speech and thought, the judge seemed to be through. Howden pulled out the folded mileage voucher and, fearful of interrupting the judge's silence, worked at the creases with his fingers. Then Howden heard a strangling sound which he could not believe was laughter. He realized with amazement that this was the first time he had ever heard Judge Reed laugh. It was like some violent organic change occurring unexpectedly. The judge choked and sputtered and heaved massively in his chair.

"Old Sher'uf Milner," the judge choked. "Mind me of him. Sure knew how to keep them in their place. Old Sher'uf would send him a message down there in The Chute every once in a while. Use to say to tell them black bastards we got some mighty fine trees up here on the square." His head rolled around, and he looked at Howden with laughter-wet eyes.

Howden laughed.

"Old Sher'uf Milner—" the judge said, and a faraway, reminiscent look came into his eyes.

Howden respected this too, until the judge, swinging his chair around, held out his hand for the mileage voucher.

"It beats me, boy," the judge said, "what you make that automobile do on the gas you get."

"I try not to waste it, sir," Howden said.

"You must be weaning the goddamn thing," the judge said, and Howden laughed again.

"Be going to Arcadia pretty soon now, won't you?" Judge Reed asked.

"Yes, sir," Howden said.

"Well, when you see Pee Tee, you tell him I say to go goose himself," the judge said.

CHAPTER TWENTY-FIVE

THE SUMMER at Arcadia was like any other, except that Shelton Howden went down to Bluffport to see Nan on three of the twelve week ends. At first Nan had taken it for granted that she was going to Arcadia with him, and Howden had thought that he would have to disillusion her. He rehearsed all sorts of plausible-sounding reasons for not taking her, but in the end Walter made it unnecessary for him to use any of them. Walter said that Nan might have a difficult time, especially as she approached her fourth month, and he was not going to let her go up to Arcadia where he couldn't keep a regular check on her. Walter said that he didn't want to sound like an alarmist because there was nothing to be alarmed about, but he just thought it best for Nan to stay right where she was. In that case, Howden said, he didn't think Nan should stay in the house alone, and what about hiring a practical nurse to stay with her? But Nan said that if Shelton would just come home some week ends, she wouldn't need anyone to stay with her. Howden told her that of course he would come home the week ends he could get away.

Then, when it seemed all settled, and Howden had convinced himself of his own rectitude in the matter, Nan said softly: "Shelton, I wish I could go."

There was no use her wishing that. Howden thought it was

unfair of her to assume a wounded tone. It was not his fault.

"Walter's the doctor," he said, "and if he says you ought to stay, then you ought to stay. Everything's going to be all right."

"I hope so," Nan replied. "I hope everything's going to be all right."

He was certain that she had put a special emphasis on "everything," and he lifted his head sharply and looked at her.

"What do you mean by that?" he asked. But he knew what she meant. She meant all the unspoken big and little things. "Good Lord, Nan, of course it is."

"Is it, Shelton?"

"Good Lord, Nan," he said again.

They were both silent while Nan broke a piece of toast and laid it uneaten on her plate. Howden wished that she would stop acting as if it were his fault. He wished that circumstances did not make it appear that she was the one who made all the sacrifices.

"Shelton, you—you don't want me to have a baby, do you?" Nan asked quietly, looking down into her plate. "And if I drove up there with you, perhaps—"

He lowered his cup at that, his hand trembling so that the coffee slopped over, and pushed his chair back. She had no business playing the role of martyr, he told himself. But Nan went right on speaking.

"I know," she said with unhappy conviction. "I could tell that night, Shelton. I think—" She had been speaking quietly, with control, but now, as she looked at him, her voice quavered and she bit her lips. "It isn't my fault, Shelton. It isn't my whole fault."

"Now look here, Nan," he began with defensive anger, and then everything seemed to go out of him except a feeling of guilt and a sense of her wretchedness. He got up and went around the table to her and put an arm around her shoulder.

"All right. All right," he said. "For the Lord's sake, don't cry! Everything's going to be all right."

[2]

At Arcadia that summer, the war agencies were a little bother-
some. The Red Cross, for instance, sponsored a course in first aid
which everyone had to take. Twice someone came from the
Office of Civilian Defense and lectured on fire bombs and demonstrated how to smother a fire with sand and indicated where sand
buckets should be placed, although, as the president pointed out
tartly, the war was five thousand miles away. Howden had to organize the faculty into a local civilian defense corps, and there
were air-raid drills and first-aid demonstrations and lessons on
what to do in case of a gas attack.

But these activities did not bring the war any closer to Howden
or make it any more real to him than the newspaper correspond-
ents and the radio commentators did. It was not even brought
any closer when he was called up to Carthage for an examination
for the draft. "With that arm," one of the doctors told him, "you
couldn't fight your way out of a paper bag." That was all right
with Howden. He had no wish to fight. It was not his war. All
he wanted was to secure a separate peace.

Indeed, barring little inconveniences and minor disturbances of
routine, the war did not seem to have much to do with Arcadia
State College. The atmosphere the president created smothered
it out. Once a team of traveling morale-builders came on the
campus and tacked a big picture poster of Joe Louis saying "We'll
win because we're on God's side" to the display board outside the
student dining hall, but the Old Man ordered it taken down.

It was the same old sixes and sevens so far as Howden's work
was concerned. It was like easing into a pair of well-worn slippers
and dropping into the comfort of a familiar chair. No longer did
he have to think through the old problems of quality points and
grades and credit hours. The answers were all on the tip of his
tongue. When there were not conferences with summer school
students, Howden attended to a good many other details. The

Old Man did not come in of afternoons because his doctor had told him to take it easy, especially in the heat of the day; and Howden checked all requisitions, dictated routine letters, and interviewed salesmen. There were not so many salesmen since the war. It was a crying shame, Miss Lark said, the way you couldn't buy things any more. She said the war was just a pain.

The remark was addressed to Howden, but he didn't answer because he was tired of hearing about the war. Everybody talked about it, and sometimes it led to arguments that were far afield. Howden recalled that the last week end he was home, he and Nan and Walter had somehow got into a conversation about the war and it had ended with Walter bringing in the Detroit race riot and the race question in general and Nan nodding in sympathy with everything Walter said.

"I wish it was over," Miss Lark said. "Don't you, hunh?"

"I don't see what difference it makes to you. You're not fighting it," Howden told her.

"I wonder what it is like in the WACs? One of the students here joined the WACs the day she graduated," Miss Lark volunteered.

"And now she's a Waccoon," Howden said, repeating one of the Old Man's derisive jokes.

"And now she's in the South Pacific," Miss Lark said, "doing whatever women soldiers do."

"It's not her war," Howden said.

"Well, at least she has plenty of sugar for her coffee, and she doesn't have to bother with ration stamps when she needs a pair of shoes. Isn't rationing a pain?"

"Listen, Laura," Howden said, "I hear enough about the war when I'm outside, and I want to think about something else. Don't talk about the war."

But when the Old Man brought it up that evening, Howden could not very well tell him not to talk about the war. And anyway, the Old Man did not talk about it at first nor for very long. At supper he had started a conversation of considerable scope. He had begun by talking about food, and then he had touched upon history, and then—no doubt having it brought to mind by the dress Gerry was wearing—he had gone on speaking about the midriff halter dresses the women were beginning to wear that summer. Now he was off on something entirely different, although Howden was the only one there to listen since Gerry had gone to the village to put some letters on the evening train.

The Old Man said that if there was one thing that got his goat more than anything else, it was the conviction that so many stupid people had that expediency was opposed to morality. Of all the asinine beliefs, that one was the trump. When you came right down to it, the Old Man said, expediency and morality had a great deal in common. Since history was Howden's field, could he think, the president wanted to know, of a successful expedient in history that had ever been called immoral? Howden could not think of one, and the Old Man said that of course he couldn't, and did he know why? It was because success carried with it the privilege of establishing its own morality, that was why. Success was a law unto itself. And not only that, success was just another and perhaps a higher morality, the Old Man declared. The end of his cigar glowed in the dimness of the side porch.

"Take the war. Whoever wins is going to be right, son. If Hitler wins, he's going to be right, and history will say so a hundred years from now. On the other hand, if we win, we'll be right."

"It's the might-makes-right philosophy," Howden said.

"I know it," the Old Man said, a trifle impatiently. His speech dropped into the intimate idiom. "I ain't trying to say anything new, but you might's well be realistic about it. How does it work out? Nobody has to tell you. All you got to do is look around you. Might does make right. Morality's always an afterthought."

Howden did not say anything because it was entirely unnecessary. No silence he kept with the Old Man was ever embarrassing.

"Success in war is always moral, son, and everything is war in a kind of way," the Old Man went on. "But the struggle for success is completely amoral. It's not until the struggle fails that everybody starts pointing out the immorality of it."

Howden could see the pale blur of the Old Man's face. He could see a faint glimmer of ruby light reflected from the glass the Old Man held up. He did not know what it was—some quality in the night perhaps, some sequence of vague ideas—but suddenly he felt a weak kind of arousement, an ill-defined sense of resistance that dissolved even as he felt it. Sighing, he said, "There's always struggle."

"Everything is war in a kind of way," the Old Man repeated with half-grim smugness, and then the tone of Howden's voice must have registered, for he asked what the matter was.

"I don't know. I was just thinking," Howden replied. "Is success for the individual always moral too?"

The cigar glowed and cast a reddish light on the Old Man's face. As he shifted his position, the wicker rocker cried. He drained his glass before he answered.

"Shel, if there's one thing that's right, it's respect for reality. That's the only item in our moral code. There're things you have to take and things you have to do, and even if they don't square with what some people think is right, they square with the way the things are that nobody can change. They square with what's real." His voice harshened perceptibly, grated. "It's not always easy—I've never said it was—and it's never as simple as some goddamned fools think; but it's what you're bound to if your personal living's not to be plain hell."

Howden had always hoped that life would get simpler, easier, as time went by. He had always hoped that it would reduce itself to a single plane of thought, a consistent pattern of action. Eventually, he had believed, a time would arrive when all questions would be answered.

"Reduced to its simplest terms," the Old Man said, his voice resuming its tone of ironic philosophizing, "morality is the recognition of what will work, and the visionaries who think otherwise are just plain damn fools."

Howden could recall a great many things the Old Man had said from time to time, and now those phrases were running sluggishly through his mind again. Like formulas, like incantatory charms, the Old Man had used them often, stabilizing life on a fixed plane for a time. But only for a time—a few moments of a day, a few days of a year, a few scattered years of a lifetime. "Beat them out of bed," the Old Man was always saying. "Master your environment . . ." "What works is right . . ." "People like us . . ." Howden could remember them all, and he could hear again the exact tone of the Old Man's voice when he said them.

Now, feebly roused by some juxtaposition of thoughts, Howden asked a question almost idly.

"Prexy," he said, "what ails us?"

"Why, son," the Old Man said, turning his head toward Howden, "what ails who?"

"Prexy—" Howden began again, and then he heard the telephone and felt relieved. He didn't want to know the real answer. A long time ago the Old Man had said something that would serve. Perhaps there wasn't any other answer, and if there were, perhaps it was the one real thing that the Old Man had never learned to recognize.

The telephone rang sharply, peremptorily again.

"I'll get it," Howden said.

CHAPTER TWENTY-SIX

HOWDEN walked through the living room to the hall and then to the study. Just as he lifted the phone from its cradle, he heard the front screen door fall to.

"Hello," he said into the telephone.

"Bluffport calling Mr. Shelton Howden. This is a party-to-party," he heard the flat voice of the operator say, and then he experienced a sudden pang of conscience. He had not seen Nan for a month now. Though he had heard from her twice a week, he had written her only three perfunctory letters. He told himself that he had been busy. And it had not seemed really necessary to write her more often since the time when he would go back to Bluffport was so close. Now, if anything had happened—

"Go ahead, please, here's your party," he heard the operator say to someone on the other end.

Gerry, her eyebrows raised, her eyes bright with inquiry, was standing in the study door. Howden wished she would not stand there watching him at a time like this.

"Shelton?" It was Nan's voice coming as unmistakably clear and low as if she were at his shoulder.

"What's the matter?" he asked, more sharply than he intended. "What's the matter?"

"Nothing's the matter, Shelton," he heard Nan say.

He felt a strange mixture of relief and annoyance. "Then, why—?"

"I just wanted to talk to you," Nan said. "I just wanted—"

"Good Lord!" Howden laughed shortly, without mirth.

"I just felt— Shelton, it was all right, wasn't it, for me to call the president's house?"

He did not see why she had to ask that, and he answered defensively, "Of course it was all right. Of course. Certainly."

"I thought you'd be there," Nan said.

It made him wonder, but he did not ask her why she thought he'd be there. She sounded all right. Her voice was low and clear, and he could picture her in her flannel robe sitting on the side of the bed by the night table.

"Well, how is everything?" Howden asked her.

"Everything's all right," Nan said. "I just felt lonesome."

The fact that there really wasn't much to say brought him a feeling of guilt again. "Well, what have you been doing?"

Gerry came slowly into the room and went over and sat on

the arm of a chair and watched him. There was a question in her eyes and a pucker of curiosity on her forehead.

"Shelton, it won't be long now, will it?"

The slang phrase came strangely through Nan's voice, but Howden knew she wasn't using it in that way.

"What won't be long?"

"You know—before you're through up there."

"No," Howden answered. "Another week and it'll be over for the summer."

There was a silence.

"I just wanted to talk to you," Nan said.

He wished she wouldn't keep saying that. As much as he was away ordinarily, she hadn't been saying it. He had always heard that pregnancy made a woman do strange, unpredictable things, and perhaps that was Nan's case. He was glad that Gerry could not hear Nan's end of the conversation.

"Well, what have you been doing?" he repeated.

"I went to an L.I.C. meeting with Walter," Nan said. "They wanted to put me on a committee, but Walter—"

"What committee?" Howden demanded sharply. If he had hoped for any good from her pregnancy, it was that it would prevent her going to meetings and programs. "I don't want you on any L.I.C. committee or any other committee," he said.

"But I'm not really on it, Shelton. Walter wouldn't let me be, because—well—" she laughed uncertainly—"you know. Then they wanted to put you on one, but I told them—"

"Good Lord, what committee? I can't be on it, and you can't either," Howden said.

"The Ways and Means Committee. And you're not on it, Shelton," Nan said. "Walter and Professor Pretlow and some others are on it."

"Rowbottom, is he on it?"

"I believe so, but I've forgotten," Nan replied. "Shelton, is it cool up there? It's nice and cool here now. I think we're going to have an early fall."

"Well, September's just around the corner," Howden said. He could not believe time had gone so fast.

Gerry was still watching him, and now there was a faint, knowing, and yet enigmatic smile on her face. She was sitting with one foot on the floor and the other caught up on her bare knee. Howden could see the pale inside of one of her thighs. Nan's voice came again.

"Well, I just wanted to talk to you for a little while," she said hesitantly. "I guess I ought to hang up now."

"All right," Howden said.

"Shelton—you're not sorry I called, are you?"

"Good Lord!" He did not see why she had to ask him that.

"Good night," Nan's voice said softly. "Good night, Shelton."

He put the phone down carefully. Gerry was watching him with that faint smile on her mouth. Then, as she tossed her head, a single note of strident laughter broke from her. She got up suddenly, quickly, and came to him and kissed him.

"Is Poppa still out there, sugar?" she asked. "He knows he ought to be upstairs." With her swift, tensive stride, she went down the hall and across the living room to the porch. "Poppa," she called, "it's almost ten o'clock, and you know what the doctor ordered."

[2]

After the Old Man had gone up, it was a long time before either Gerry or Howden said anything. Gerry was sitting in one corner of the wicker lounge, and Howden was in the Old Man's chair. As she lit a cigarette, Gerry's face jumped out whitely in the flare of the match, and then she asked Howden to bring her the smoking stand.

"What are you sitting over there for anyway?" Gerry asked him.

"I don't know," Howden said. "There's no reason."

"Then come sit over here," Gerry said. "But get me my bolero first. It's on the stand in the hall. I'm chilly."

Howden did not see that the bolero made any difference because it was sleeveless like the dress, and it did not cover her bare midriff either. As she made room for him on the lounge, Gerry took his arm and drew it around her waist and held his hand against her stomach. He could smell the faint perfume of her hair.

"Did you get your letter on the train?" he asked her.

"Un-hunh," she said.

"Would you like me to get the portable radio?" he asked her.

"I just want you to stay right where you are. I don't want you to leave me. All summer you've been leaving me," Gerry said. "Haven't you been leaving me?"

It was another of her exaggerations, but he liked her not wanting him to leave her. Though he did not always believe in it, he liked the feeling she made him have of being important to her happiness.

"No," he said.

"Yes, you have. And those week ends you've gone to Bluffport—"

"Now, Gerry," he said, pressing his hand against her stomach.

"All right," she said, "I won't talk about it."

By turning his head a little, he could see through the foliage the lights in one of the dormitories, and he began thinking of something that had no connection with the week ends he'd gone to Bluffport. He was thinking of that song that all the radio entertainers were playing and singing: "When the Lights Come On Again." Then he found himself thinking about the war, and then the plaintive words of that song were running through his head again. What he could never figure out was the chain of associations that led from one thought to another.

"But don't think I've liked it," Gerry said, reaching out and crushing her cigarette in the smoking stand. "Don't you know I haven't liked it, honey?"

Howden pressed her stomach and said nothing, but he felt newly warmed by the fact that she hadn't liked it.

"You don't want to leave me now, do you?" Gerry asked. It was as if she were forgiving an injury. The thing about her was that he could never fathom her, could never anticipate her moods, could never tell what she was thinking.

"No," Howden said.

"Are you happy now?" She turned her head against his shoulder and looked at him.

"Of course."

"I could keep you happy all the time. You're neurotic, but I understand you, honey baby. You have to understand a man to love him."

What she said had a pathetic ring, like an unrealizable ideal. It was sentimental, he thought, and Gerry was not usually sentimental.

"No one ever understands anyone else very well," he said.

"I understand you," Gerry said, rubbing her hand slowly up and down his thigh.

They did not talk for a while. The top of Gerry's head was against the angle of his jaw and her shoulder was against his chest, and he could feel her stomach rising and falling with her breathing. But he was not thinking so much of her as he was of the past and the future. And that popular song was somewhere in the back of his mind too. Gerry turned her head. She was suddenly alert in some strange way.

"What did she call up here for tonight?" Alertness was in her voice, which had gone just a bit expectant, and her hand lay alertly waiting on his thigh. He could not see her face, but he could tell the look it wore.

"She just wanted to talk," Howden said.

"What did she want to talk about?"

"I don't know. She didn't want anything in particular."

"Then what was her idea?"

"I don't know," Howden said.

"She must have said something," Gerry said, and her voice went a half pitch higher. "What did she say? You can tell me what she said, can't you?"

"She didn't say much of anything," Howden said. "Something about an L.I.C. meeting. And she said it was cool down there." Gerry seemed to relax. Again her hand began absently to stroke his thigh. She leaned back against him again.

"Well, I don't get her idea. Do you, sugar? Is she pretending that she loves you or something?"

"She just—" Howden began and stopped. "Gerry," he said, "let's don't talk about her. You see, she's going to have a baby."

Gerry went very still and stiff for an instant, and then she bolted up and faced him. He could see that her eyes blazed with fury. Her hand came up and struck him hard across the face, blinding him momentarily.

"Goddamn you!" she said with tense, savage quiet, striking again. "Goddamn you!"

He grabbed her wrist and tried to hold it, but she clawed at him with her other hand.

"Gerry!" he cautioned. He reached toward her, trying to take her hand, but she backed away.

"What did you let her do it for? What do you want a baby by her for?" But the anger must have fled, for she started to cry.

"No, Gerry," Howden said, reaching out again and taking her hand. Then he put his arm around her, feeling now for the first time that he was her man and her master, feeling good, made somehow triumphant. She stood passively in the circle of his arm, and she was still crying. "No, Gerry," he said again.

She pushed away, and her eyes blazed up once more. "I hope she dies having it," Gerry said fiercely. "You belong to me as much as you belong to her."

CHAPTER TWENTY-SEVEN

SHELTON HOWDEN did not know what had awakened him, but for a moment, as he lay there in the shock of returning consciousness, he thought he heard a babble of confused voices. For a moment he thought he heard someone calling him quite clearly above the babble and that there was a hand shaking his shoulder.

When he came fully awake, he was sitting on the side of the bed. A stiff breeze whipped the curtains at the windows and blew damp upon his back. He was chilly. It was the cold wind that had awakened him. He did not see how Nan could sleep with that wind blowing in upon her and nothing covering her but a thin summer blanket.

But he had had a dream too, although he could not remember what it was about. Whenever he ate those dried salt fish and spiced meat and the other semi-digestibles that Walter served with highballs, he was sure to dream. Howden felt around for his slippers and stood up. Then he heard Nan's low, startled voice.

"Shelton, what's the matter?"

"Where're the blankets?" he asked her irritably.

"In the closet in my room," Nan said. She still called the middle room "my room" and the room where they slept "father's room." It always reminded him that this was her house. It always reminded him that he had not put a thing in it except the radio in the living room and the rug on the floor of their bedroom and more books in the room that had once been Dr. Mariott's office.

"Are you chilly, Shelton?"

It was a foolish question under the circumstances, and his frown grew deeper.

"Turn on the light," he said, "so I can find my way out of here."

Nan switched on the light, and he saw that it was three o'clock. It did not seem possible that they had been in bed nearly two hours. He had just closed his eyes, it seemed, when he was wide awake again. Into his mind out of nowhere came a phrase that he had heard earlier in the evening: "Do you know what time it is on the clock of the world?" As he fumbled in the closet in the middle room, that sense of annoyance which he had experienced when he first heard it—that feeling of derision which he had tried to hold onto during the whole meeting, when Rowbottom spoke, and when Curtis Flack spoke—was back with him. It was not what was said so much as it was the fact that everyone listened. No one seemed to understand that that phrase of Curtis Flack's, which, doubtless, he had thought up in the isolated security of the national office of L.I.C., was just meaningless rhetoric. "Do you know what time it is on the clock of the world?" Howden reflected sourly that it was the kind of rhetorical trick that Curtis Flack was good at because he made his living being good at it.

And yet the curious thing was that he envied Curtis Flack. There was something about his platform presence and something in his speech that impressed the public. He had also an easy assurance in his social bearing that must have come from years of attending just such little get-togethers as Walter had had after the meeting. Howden told himself scornfully that Flack was just a smoothie, that's what he was, and his wife Alice was a smoothie too. He could think of them as characters out of the novel *Nigger Heaven*, which he had read a long time ago. If you knew them socially, you couldn't believe in the sincerity of their public utterances because people like the Flacks, Howden told himself, had nothing in common with the Pretlows and the Rowbottoms. And neither did Walter Ringgold.

But no matter how much Howden told himself this, he did not quite believe it. He was not quite convinced that Flack was just a smoothie.

When he came back with the blanket, Nan sat up to help him straighten it on the bed. He could see the bulge of her pregnancy under the covers, and her movements were beginning to be a little awkward, but she still retained a virginal, untouched look. Her honey-colored skin was smooth and firm and glowing under the light. Her arms were slenderly rounded. As always when she had been asleep awhile, her hair had come undone and smoked over her shoulders.

"What's the matter, Shelton?" she asked him, a worried pucker between her eyes.

"I was just thinking about tonight," he said.

"You mean the meeting?"

"No," Howden said shortly. "It was just another meeting. Why should I think about that?" All race meetings were alike, and Nan ought to know it. People got up and made high-sounding speeches about race solidarity and brotherhood and democratic rights, and then everybody went home and forgot them.

"I was thinking about Walter's afterwards," Howden said. Something else came into his mind as he turned off the light. "I wish you wouldn't sit up like a clam when people try to talk to you at little get-togethers like that."

"But I talked, Shelton," Nan said quietly. "Alice Flack and those two ladies and I talked for a long time before you men came in from the meeting."

"Well, you certainly didn't talk afterwards," Howden said. "You sat over there in that corner like a stick of wood."

They were both wide awake, and he had to get up in the morning. There was enough light in the darkness for him to see the bulky outline of the old-fashioned chiffonier against the wall at the foot of the bed and the chest of drawers and the platform rocker onto which he always flung his robe at night.

"Shelton, you haven't said what you thought of Curtis Flack's speech," Nan said.

"I didn't think anything about it," Howden said. "It was just hot air."

"You mean—"

"It was all put on," Howden said.

"Put on?" Nan repeated, a low note of surprise in her voice.

It annoyed him because Nan was thinking the same thing that everyone in that ignorant darky audience had probably thought— that Curtis Flack was sincere. In a way it showed him how dangerous a smoothie like Flack could be.

"You didn't hear his speech," Howden said. "You asked me for my opinion and I told you. It was all put on."

"But I heard Walter say—"

"They're old friends, and I don't care what Walter said. Walter wouldn't know. Anybody can sell Walter a bill of goods." Then he laughed unpleasantly. "Walter's soft in the head."

"But later, when Curtis Flack was talking to us at Walter's," Nan said. "I mean, if it was put on—" Her voice was inflected to the pitch of a question, and she waited.

Howden stirred irritably. He could see that audience again, leaning forward, breathless for every word, and he could hear their murmurs of approval as Curtis Flack talked. He could see Flack's banana-just-turning-ripe colored face with that look of intense awareness upon it which no one seemed to realize was just a theatrical trick. Howden felt very alone, and suddenly he felt tired too. He and Nan were always talking in bed at night when they should have been asleep.

"Look, don't you understand that Flack makes his living at it?" he said patiently, reasonably. "He works at it all the time."

A chill breeze from the window crawled up Howden's pajama sleeve, and he put both arms under the covers. October had come very quickly. There had been September and all the schools opening and all the school statistics reflecting the effects of the war, with a good many older, retarded boys and many young teachers quitting to work in war plants or going into the army. Now it was October already. October, 1943. He could not believe that all the years had gone so quickly. He could not believe that he was in his forty-first year.

He grunted and then laughed mirthlessly. "Do you know what time it is on the clock of the world? Good Lord!"

Nan's head turned on the pillow, and he knew that that puzzled pucker was there in the wide space between her eyes.

"What do you mean, Shelton?" she asked.

"Flack said that in his speech tonight: 'Do you know what time it is on the clock of the world?'" Howden repeated scornfully. "And that's exactly the point: what does it mean? It doesn't mean anything. It's just clever rhetoric."

"Shelton, you sound prejudiced against him," Nan said gently.

He had tried to be objective and realistic, and now Nan was saying he sounded prejudiced.

"I'm not prejudiced! Why should I be prejudiced? But—" He stopped. He did not want to go on with it. He made a great stir turning over on his side of the bed. "Forget it, and let's go to sleep."

But he did not go to sleep, and neither did Nan, for after a moment she said thoughtfully: "I think I know what he meant. Tonight at Walter's he said this was a new day. He said that human relations were changing—"

"What's changing about them?" Howden cut in. "And this isn't day, it's night, and I want to go to sleep!"

He lay there on his side, wondering why he was always so irritated by her and so impatient of her opinions, and he told himself what he had told himself a dozen times recently—he must be more careful with Nan. Then he was thinking what it had been like with them. He was thinking that they really hadn't seen much of each other. With his coming home only on week ends and being away in the summer, they hadn't had a chance to know each other. Suppose he told her frankly that this or that in her displeased him? But what? He could not put his finger on what annoyed him in her. Her simplicity? Her reticence? Her race-mindedness? And if he told her, what would happen then? She would probably listen gravely, but— "Do you know what time . . . ?"

He did not know what time it was on the clock of the world, but on the clock of their lives it was time for something.

[2]

Howden usually awoke promptly at six o'clock. At home it was his habit to lie abed and arrange the day's program in his mind. He called this "straightening out the day," and he felt that he was one of a select brotherhood that followed this practice. Most people just went through their waking hours haphazardly, without giving them much thought, but he had read in the magazine *Success* that progressive men got each day straight before them and then marched through it directly to their objectives.

On his official trips, he would get up promptly on waking, build a fire in the woodstove or grate, whichever the particular room afforded, and heat water for shaving in the collapsible saucepan he always carried among his things. Though he was always guest in one of the best homes—usually the principal's at whose school he had business—few of them had modern conveniences, and his early rising had at first caused consternation among his various hosts. They would come knocking timidly at his bedroom door at seven-thirty or a quarter to eight to bring him a kettle of warm water and to inform him that breakfast would be ready soon, and there he'd be, washed, shaved, dressed, and quietly getting the day straight before him. His hosts would laugh sheepishly and say that he certainly was an early riser, and Howden would answer that he couldn't afford to stay in bed —he had a full, hard day before him.

The magazine *Success* gave him many helpful hints on ways to achieve a good life. It had a section called "Culture for the Successful Man" which, month after month, showed the same distinguished-looking gentleman of early middle years absorbing or about to absorb some kind of culture. Sometimes it showed him in a velvet smoking jacket, reclining in a leather chair, his slippered feet at ease on an ottoman, reading a book. Sometimes it showed him in top hat and Inverness cape, stepping out of a chauffeured car under a glittering theater marquee. Once it showed the man of culture in a tweed suit and cap, leaning at the rail of a luxurious ocean liner and gazing with calm anticipation at the spectacular beauty of the foreign harbor toward which the liner steamed.

There was also a section on clothes for the successful man and one on health for the successful man. Once a year the magazine carried photographs of the twenty-five best-dressed men of the year, and sometimes there were interviews with highly successful mining engineers, industrialists, bankers, politicians, and Hollywood actors. It seemed that they all lived very disciplined lives, according to strict rules, the observance of which brought grace, intelligence, and wealth.

Of course Shelton Howden realized that there were many things he could not follow through completely. He could not follow through on clothes for the successful man because, even with the addition of Nan's modest income, a hundred-and-fifty-dollar suits, twenty-five-dollar hats, and five-dollar neckties were clearly beyond his means. Then there was that stern injunction, delivered by a heavily muscled man with a V-shaped torso who pointed a warning finger straight out of the page: "Stay in the Pink! Join a Good Gym Under an Expert Physical Culturist!" Howden could not follow through on this because even the nearest Y.M.C.A. was in Carthage. But the mornings he was home, he took the setting-up exercises prescribed for the successful man.

The morning after the get-together at Walter's, Howden must have fallen asleep again between six-thirty and seven, for when he next knew anything, Nan was shaking him gently. "Shelton. Shelton," she called.

He came instantly awake, kicked the covers off, and swung his feet to the floor. "Good Lord!" he said. "What time is it?" He looked at the clock on the night table and saw that it was after eight. "Why didn't you call me?" he asked Nan. He did not like to sleep so late.

"I thought you needed to sleep," Nan said.

"But you're up."

"I know," Nan said, smiling faintly.

Howden was thinking that he was losing his resiliency. There was a time when he could sit up until all hours and still awaken refreshed at six o'clock in the morning.

"You should have called me when you got up," he complained.

Nan was wearing one of those maternity dresses, which really did somewhat disguise her condition, but her face had the pale, drawn look it sometimes had now early in the morning.

"It was pretty late last night," she said.

"I know, but you should have called me. I never like to sleep late on weekdays." She never seemed to realize that he tried to live by a fixed schedule. Darkies liked to sleep late. Darkies were lazy. Successful men lived on a schedule; they did not lie abed.

"It's already Thursday," Nan said. "Shelton, why don't you make this a long week end?"

He was irritated. "Now look, Nan, I shouldn't be here at all. I should be at the other end of the state today. I just came for that dumb mass meeting because Walter and them expected me."

"Well, the water's hot," Nan said. "I'll finish getting breakfast."

Howden stood up, stretched, and skinned out of the tops of his pajamas. He hated the sailor-blouse pajama tops, but since the war they were all he could get. The war was getting to be a lot of little bothers. He walked to the window over the tawny-carpeted floor between the pink rose-papered walls. He knew now that the wallpaper was a mistake of the kind that Nan would make more often if he didn't watch her. It did not go with the heavy walnut bed, the marble-topped walnut chest, and the solid platform rocker. He looked out through the tied-back white dotted curtains. Glancing off the tin roof of the porch, the sun made him close his eyes against the instant shock. Then he looked down into the street. There was not much to see. Indeed, it was not properly a street but a dirt road running between a steep-falling field and the scattered, inward-curving short row of houses of which this house was not quite one. Howden had often wondered why old Dr. Mariott had chosen this site for his house and office.

The house trembled as he exercised. When he had brought out the perspiration, he looked at himself in the mirror over Nan's dressing table. His reddish yellow body was practically free of hair. His belly bulged, although he told himself no more than it should for a man in his forties. He touched himself with rueful appraisal—his fleshy jowls, the loaves of fat on his ribs. He told himself that he had to keep his weight down. He looked fairly trim in his clothes, he thought, but it was when you stood half naked before a mirror that you could tell about yourself. The last two years or so had added weight to him.

As he started toward the bathroom, he sniffed the aroma of coffee, and the thought of food struck him with momentary repugnance. The trouble with most darkies was that they ate too much. They grew fatter and lazier and unhealthier. They dug their graves with their teeth. Successful men did not do this—men like General MacArthur and Justice Douglas and the president of Harvard.

Howden stopped on the hall landing. "Nan," he called, "come here a minute." He waited until he heard her coming through the dining room. "Do you think I'm taking on weight?"

"Why, Shelton," Nan answered, "you're all right."

"Look." Naked to the waist, he lifted his arms and turned slowly around. Nan smiled up at him, and then she began to laugh quietly.

"What's the matter?" he asked her, stopping. "What's funny?"

"Don't be angry, Shelton," Nan said.

"I'm not angry," he told her sharply. "You're always saying I'm angry. I just want to know what's funny."

"Shelton—" she said, and then she began to laugh again, but he could see that she had not meant to.

"You shouldn't have given your father's scales to that health club," Howden said. "All right. Am I taking on weight?"

"I don't know," Nan said carefully. "But it doesn't matter, does it, if you take on a little weight. You can't help the physiology—"

"It does matter." But there was no use going into it. There was no use telling her that it could probably be proved that there was some correlation between body weight and success, just as there was between brain weight and success.

"Don't fix me any grits for breakfast," Howden said, "and no cream for my coffee."

Before the mirror in the medicine cabinet, he peeled off the tight-fitting woven cap he wore to keep his hair unmussed at night. Almost at once his scalp began to itch, and he dug into it gingerly with the tip of a forefinger. He did not want to disturb a single strand of hair, which lay frozen in tiny, glossy corrugations, like a stamped sheet of metal fitted to his skull. When he looked at himself in the mirror, he always felt that with a little something more, or a little something less, his hair would have been straight and fine-grained, his lips thinner, his yellow skin more white. Given a slightly different tilt to the scales of genetic chance and he might have been a white man. He often speculated on what his life would have been like then.

CHAPTER TWENTY-EIGHT

ON CLEAR mornings, if they sat late enough at breakfast, the sun would top the row of bushes that marked the property line outside and shine through the window and slant geometrically through the door from the kitchen. It glinted

through the glass front of the closet, which was filled with the
gaudy china that must have been gifts to Dr. Mariott. There were
stacks of unmatched plates and little flute-edged ice cream sau-
cers and dishes in the shapes of boats and pagodas. The drawers
and closets in the back bedroom were full of things too: pewter
pitchers and cruets and crockery vases and camphor-smelling
quilts and old illustrated books about "illustrious Negroes" and
about Negroes in all the wars the United States had fought. Howden had told Nan that he did not see the good of keeping all
her father's junk, but once when he had to prepare a speech for
Negro History Week, Nan had brought out all the books about
Negroes and had helped him put the speech together. He did
not believe in Negro History Week; he did not believe that the
men who wrote the books knew what they were talking about—
but that had been a good speech.

There was no reason why he should be thinking of it now,
but he was. The room looked as it always did when the sun came
in—bright but a little worn and sad. There was the ivory molding, which had been set too far below the ceiling. There was the
dull picture of a dish of fruit on one wall and the mirror in a
gilt frame decorated with a spread-eagle hanging over the buffet
on the other. He could see that faded spot on the wallpaper
where it had been washed after someone's head had left a grease
spot there. It was like any morning when he was home except
that it was not Saturday or Sunday. It was like any morning
when they had run out of conversation and he did not know
what Nan was thinking. He watched her pour another cup of
coffee, and she must have felt his gaze because she looked up and
gave him a wavering smile.

"I didn't say anything," he said.

"But didn't you start to say something?"

He did not know whether he had started to say anything or
not, but he may have, for all at once he did not want to give his
thoughts silence to go on in.

"I was just wondering what you were thinking," he said.

A look of hesitation came into her eyes, and her smile fluttered. "I'm sorry you have to go to the other end of the state today," she said. "Shelton, couldn't you stay here just one extra day?"

He had had several changes of mood that morning, and now here was another. It was a little unfair of her to seem the one who always put forth the effort. Though she never seemed to realize it, he made efforts too. The trouble with her was—well, what was the trouble? He was always graphing teaching contact hours and pupil mortality rates and intelligence scores, but there was this he could not graph.

"No," he said, "I have to go this evening."

She did not look disappointed; she simply looked resigned. He felt a stab of compunction. She put her hand on her cup but did not lift it, and turned her head toward the window where the sun came in. He could see the pulse fluttering beneath the clear skin of her throat.

"Nan," he said, "come go with me."

"Oh, Shelton!" Nan said, turning to him with quiet eagerness. He felt a sharper twinge of conscience. "Do you really want me to go?"

It would have been better if she had just accepted it. It would have been better if she did not always want answers. He was thinking what he had thought earlier.

"Yes," he said. "We don't see enough of each other. We need to get together more."

They stared at each other across the table, but he could not tell what her smile meant.

"It's queer, Shelton, but I was just thinking the same thing." Her smile wavered and went out altogether, and she bit her lower lip. "What's the matter with us, Shelton?"

"Matter? There's nothing the matter," Howden said defensively.

"If there's something the matter, be honest with me, please, Shelton," she said in her low voice.

It was all coming at the wrong time. Whatever was the matter could not be set right with words. He could not sort out in his mind all the things that made the wrong and that had contributed to this moment.

"I wish you'd tell me," Nan said with quiet urgency. "I thought that— But I don't know now, the way things are and a baby. I'm—"

"If I've said or done anything to make you think that—" Howden started.

"To make me feel, Shelton," Nan put in softly. "I've tried not to think. I've gone on from day to day trying not to think. It's just been getting through each day without letting myself think."

"But there's nothing the matter," he said again, although he could see that he was not convincing her. She sat silent, with one elbow on each side of her plate, her hands joined and her fingers interlocked. She was waiting. The waiting was in her grave and troubled eyes, in her face.

"Good Lord, Nan, I tell you there's nothing the matter," Howden said. "If you don't want to go with me, you don't have to bring up—"

"I didn't say I didn't want to go, Shelton," Nan said.

"We could have made a week end of it. Saturday and Sunday, we could have—" The telephone rang, and he got up, still talking, and went to the stand under the arch between the two rooms. "You haven't seen the spillway. We could have—" And then he picked up the phone.

"Hello," he said.

"Shel?" He did not recognize the voice at first.

"Oh, hello, Walter."

"Shel," he heard Walter say, "what about you and Nan driving up to Carthage with me to see the Flacks off? We ought to leave around eleven."

Howden could feel his mood changing again, and he hesitated, looking at Nan.

"I can't make it, Walt," he said. "Now that I'm in town, I

ought to see Pretlow, and then I've got to go to Douthin County."

"How come? You can do that later," Walter said. "You can do that next week."

No one seemed to realize that he had a schedule, even if it was temporarily deranged. But he felt better. He felt almost gay.

"You doctors are the only guys who can take any old time off. I work for a salary," Howden said.

"Crap!" Walter said. Then he must have said something to someone else in the room because Howden could hear voices. Then Walter was speaking to him again.

"Well, what about letting Nan go?"

"What am I supposed to be, her jailer or something?" He looked at Nan, who was sitting motionless at the table. "Wait a minute. You ask her. She's right here."

"Ask me what, Shelton?" Nan inquired, but she made no move to get up.

Another voice was speaking to him over the phone.

"Shel, this is Alice."

He was glad that she had not called herself Mrs. Flack and him Mr. Howden. You could never be sure how people would think of you the next morning, even if they had called you by your first name the night before.

"You can't come?" he heard Alice ask. Her voice was warm and light over the phone. She sounded as if she had known him for years.

"No, Alice, I can't."

"Why, what's the matter?"

"I wish I could," Howden said, "but you know—"

"Well, why can't Nan come?"

"I didn't say she couldn't," Howden said.

"All right," Alice said. "What does she say?"

"She's right here," Howden said, and he pulled at the base of the phone to unravel the cord, but Nan did not get up. He could hear confused voices on the other end, and then Walter was back.

"Let's work it this way, Shel," Walter said. "You call me back. If it's all right, we'll come by and pick Nan up."

"Never mind, Walt. I've got to drive in that way. I'll bring her," Howden said.

"Okay," Walter said. "It'll do her good to get away for a few hours."

Howden hung up. Nan was looking at him with a puzzled frown. He did not think she would enter into the spirit of it.

"They want you to drive over to Carthage to the airport," Howden said.

Her frown grew deeper. "Is that what you want me to do, Shelton?" she asked.

"You might as well. It'll do you good," Howden said lightly. "When they're not preaching race, the Flacks are all right. They're good to know socially."

"Shelton, I thought—" But she stopped abruptly and bit her lip. Reaching out slowly, she began gathering the soiled breakfast dishes.

"Here, I'll help you," Howden said. "There's lots of time."

[2]

Howden did not know what made him think of the "Jazz Age" as he sat at the table in Walter's dining room. It may have been because Curtis Flack was talking about his lost illusions. Flack said that his last cherished illusion had been stripped from him by the experience of an interracial couple he knew, and then he went on to tell about it. But Howden did not listen to the experience of the interracial couple because he was back in the Twenties, and he was thinking of the "lost generation."

When he was a graduate student at the University in New York, he had heard a professor say sneeringly that the phrase "lost generation" was just a poetic rationalization of failure—

and Howden could well believe it. Now, as he looked at Curtis Flack—at the nervous, weary face and the dramatic eyes restlessly absorbing whatever they looked upon—Howden relished remembering the professor's sneer. Curtis Flack, he thought, had rationalized his own failure, and was now—the professor's exact words came back to his mind—"in a kind of perverted seriousness and desperation, pursuing a chimera."

Howden had listened to the story of the Negro soldier who had been sentenced to die for a crime he did not commit and to the one about the young Negro girl who had written to the papers suggesting that Hitler would understand the sufferings of the Jews if he could be brought to America and put in a black skin. ("Imagine," Curtis Flack had said, "a girl of thirteen thinking such a thing! Imagine her being forced to know enough to think it!") And now Flack was still talking about the interracial couple. He did not look like a man who, on the floor of the Senate only recently, had been accused of impeding the war effort, of putting race above nation, of being a traitor to his country. He did not look like the fire-eating champion who, some Southern papers screamed, "commanded the Congressional votes of half the Representatives in the North." In Walter Ringgold's dining room, he did not seem at all out of place. He was sprawled half turned from the messy breakfast table, with his thin legs stuck out into the room, like any other man at home among friends. Nan was sitting where Walter had made room for her, between himself and Alice, listening intently while Flack talked. The atmosphere seemed one of almost casual ease, and yet somehow it was charged with excitement too, perhaps because of the stories.

"So I've got no illusions about any of it. God, no!" Curtis Flack said, and he laughed quietly but bitterly. "I know what the score is on the race question. They've got us at least ten to one, and all I do is plug along and try to even up the odds a little. I've got no illusions."

"Nobody has any illusions any more," Walter said.

The fact was, it seemed to Howden, that illusions were just what they did have. He did not speak.

"Curt," Alice said, "you ought to use that story in a speech. It's a wonderful commentary. Don't you think so, Walter?" She was an incredibly polished-looking woman. Her prematurely gray hair shone like silver; her olive-brown skin looked newly buffed; her teeth were bright. She had just finished touching up her fingernails with red lacquer, and she was holding her slender fingers spread to dry.

"Well, what happened to Sybil and Jeff tore away my last illusions," Curtis Flack said. "But it is better not to have them. God, yes!"

"But you go on fighting, Curt," Alice said, "and that's the important thing."

Howden told himself that it was all rehearsed for just this kind of private conversation. He felt irritated with Nan—and Walter too—for being taken in. The Flacks had no kind of background at all against which to make their race-chauvinism plausible.

"Yes," Flack said, with a sudden tightening of the tired lines around his mouth, "I go on fighting. You can do that when you've got no illusions. You can give back to the white folks some of the hell they give you every day."

"You said that in your speech last night," Walter said. "It was a damned good speech."

Howden knew that Walter would think that too.

Curtis Flack looked at his watch, and then he stood up. His clothes were good and he wore them carelessly, because he had always worn good clothes. He was a slender pole of a man, slant-shouldered, vibrant. He pulled back his coat sleeve and looked at his watch once more. The action reminded Howden of something else that had been said in that speech last night. He could think of Curtis Flack as looking at the time on the clock of the world.

"Isn't it getting late?" Flack asked. "It's something after eleven."

"I know," Walter said, "but everything's all set."

"Everything's all set if they don't bump us off the plane in Memphis or some place," Flack said dryly.

"They won't bump you off," Walter said. "They wouldn't put you off the last flight out of Memphis at night. What the hell would they do with you? They'd have to find a place for you to stay."

"Boy, you'd be surprised," Flack said.

"Curt was bumped once, and they found a place for him to stay all right, and it wasn't in the South either," Alice said. She had started to get up, but now she sat down again. "Curt, tell them about it."

There was a disillusioned smile on Flack's face, but he shook his head.

"Curt," Alice said, "you know it's a wonderful story, and you ought to tell it."

"It's already after eleven," Curt said.

"What happened?" Walter asked.

"I just had to give up my seat in Harrisburg, that's all," Flack said. "It was when they first started air-travel priorities."

"But there's a story there," Alice said, getting up and smoothing her skirt behind her and sitting down again. "Harrisburg holds a story, a very special story. Tell it, darling."

They were all waiting. Howden looked at Nan, for he wanted to give her a glance of annoyance. But under the brim of her soft felt hat, Nan was watching Flack. Walter was watching too, and his look of credulous commitment made Howden want to laugh with irritation. Even Alice, who must have heard a dozen times all the stories that Flack had to tell, was giving him an absorbed look.

"But, God, it was funny," Curtis Flack said, and he laughed again with quiet bitterness.

"Tell it, Curt," Walter said. "We want to hear it."

It was the last thing in the world that Howden wished to hear, but he was caught. What he wanted was to get away. He saw

Flack glance around at all of them, and Flack must have forgotten that it was already after eleven because his words were not hurried when he spoke.

He had to give up his plane seat in Harrisburg, he said, at five o'clock one afternoon last year. He was on his way to Chicago. They were getting ready to set up a sort of city bureau of interracial affairs in Chicago, and he was going out there to act as policy consultant. It was a particularly ironic touch, he said, because of what happened to him when he had to give up his plane seat.

When he was bumped, he thought nothing of it, because he had no travel priority, and another man was bumped too. The other man was just going to Pittsburgh and decided to take a train, but the people at the airport in Harrisburg assured Flack that they would find a seat for him on a later flight. Meantime he just sat around the airport lounge. Six o'clock came and a couple of planes came in, but there was still no seat for him. There was no restaurant at the airport, but a girl in uniform brought him a supper of sandwiches and milk, and by the time he had finished eating, it was pretty close to seven o'clock. He knew that the last Trans-Western flight took off for Chicago and the West at seven-fifteen, but still no one had said anything to him about a seat on it, and so he went to the passenger agent's desk.

This official was very nice, Flack said. He was sorry for Mr. Flack's inconvenience, but Mr. Flack knew how things were in wartime. The passenger agent was pretty sure that there wouldn't be space on the incoming flight because it was really a sleeper going through to Denver. But of course the airline would be happy to provide Mr. Flack with accommodations for the night— that is, if Mr. Flack had not already taken care of his own accommodations. Had Mr. Flack done so? Certainly he hadn't done so, Curtis Flack told the passenger agent, because he had expected to be in Chicago by eight-thirty, and since he wasn't going to be there, and since he wasn't going to get a seat on a flight before morning, then the Trans-Western Airlines had to provide him with accommodations for the night.

The passenger agent was very nice and said of course, of course, and would Mr. Flack please wait—which was the only thing Curtis Flack could do. Then the passenger agent went scooting off up some stairs and out of sight.

By this time the seven-fifteen flight had come in, and people, many of them army and navy brass, were scurrying back and forth through the lounge under the mechanical-sounding voice of the public address system announcing the plane to Denver and Omaha. The whole place was in disciplined, exciting movement. Curtis Flack could hear the little electric trucks that went to meet the plane coming back. It was dark outside, but in one direction he could see the lights bordering the runways and he could see the light from the control tower reflected on the gleaming sides of the plane. In another direction he could see the airline's limousine taking on passengers for the city. Every time the doors to the concourse swung open, he could hear the patient, controlled, and even clat-clat-clat of slowly turning propellers. A colored porter was stowing away bags on top of the limousine. Behind the little glass cages along one wall of the lounge, clerks in slate-gray uniforms were busy at telephones. Then Curtis Flack heard the public address system make a different, premonitory sound, like a man smothering a cough. It went off, but a moment later it was back again.

"Hold the limousine for the city," the public address system said. "Another passenger for the city. Check. Sam. Sam. You're wanted in Mr. Bang's office right away. Repeat. Right away in Mr. Bang's office."

Curtis Flack gave this a second thought only when he saw the passenger agent coming back, a porter at his heels. The porter looked at Curtis very suspiciously and forbiddingly, as waiters sometimes looked at you when you went into a dining car traveling south or as the colored bellhops looked at you when you registered at one of those resort hotels up in Maine.

"Mr. Flack," the agent said, "if you'll just follow the porter, the car will take you to the city, and we'll pick you up for the first flight in the morning."

Flack asked him what time that would be, and before the agent could answer, the porter growled eight o'clock.

(Curtis Flack began to laugh quietly because it really was amusing, he said, although it was sad too, for the whole thing represented something fundamental, something stubborn and evil that would have to be eradicated before the legions of progress could advance. But it was funny too.)

"Come on, brother," Sam the porter said, "follow me." Sam had a mean-looking scar curling from one corner of his thick mouth, and he talked with a hoarse, phlegmy vibration. He started off without Flack's bag, although it stood in plain sight at his feet.

"Don't forget Mr. Flack's bag, Sam," the agent reminded him, and Sam gave Flack a baleful look.

The wide seats in the airline's limousine were built to hold three people, and there were two of them entirely empty, but Flack got into one with another passenger because he did not want to appear to segregate himself. Sam flung the bag on top of the car and got up front with the driver. There were seven or eight other passengers, some of whom had had to give up their plane seats also, and they all talked about the war as the car took them into the city. They had quite a pleasant trip—so pleasant, in fact, that Curtis Flack was surprised when the big, bus-like, richly appointed car stopped and everybody started getting out.

(Curtis Flack began to laugh again. He put his hands in his coat pockets and looked down at the floor, laughing quietly. The rest of the story, he said, was fundamental and illuminating. God, yes.)

He got out, like everyone else, when the car stopped. They were parked in front of a hotel that had a brightly lighted marquee—Harrisburg was inland and wasn't dimmed out—and all the looks of a first-class hotel on a first-class street. The hotel structure towered up into the darkness, and Flack could see lights in many of the windows up there. He could also feel that sort of still sense of composure which really good hotels give off. There was a uniformed doorman in white gloves, and three middle-aged men, who might have been jockeys in their youth but who were bellboys now, came out and started taking the bags as Sam the porter handed them down from the rack atop the car. Flack's bag was not among those handed down, and when Sam himself climbed down, Flack asked him about it.

"This ain't your stop," Sam said, giving him another baleful look. "Get on back in." Then he again climbed into the seat with the driver.

But Curtis Flack stood uncertainly on the pavement. All the other passengers had gone into the hotel by this time. The doorman stood eying him curiously.

"What's the point?" Curtis asked both Sam and the driver, who sat placidly chewing a matchstick and staring straight ahead. "What is this?"

"This just ain't your stop," Sam said.

Sam did all the talking, and the white driver just sat there as if he weren't there at all. Curtis knew that Sam was lying because the airline probably kept rooms reserved in the hotel for just such a contingency. Flack was of half a mind to balk, but he did not want to make a spectacle of himself there on the street with people passing in and out of the hotel and the doorman and the driver listening. Besides, he was curious. He climbed back into the car; Sam lowered the glass that separated the passengers from the driver's seat, and the car started off. They left the wide, well-lighted street after a while, and Flack could hear Sam giving the chauffeur directions.

"Doesn't he know where he's going?" Curtis Flack asked. "Hasn't he ever been there before?"

Sam turned on the seat. "Brother," he said, "I got everything under control."

It was impossible to describe Flack's reactions when the car stopped again, this time in a dark street of houses making a solid

mass of forbidding shadow. The whole thing struck Flack with
the force of a blow, and he just sat there in the car until Sam
opened the door and told him that this was it. Sam's ridiculous
brusqueness and officiousness were maddening, but all at once
Flack realized that the porter had no conception of how evil a
thing he was doing. On the contrary, Sam doubtless thought that
he was doing a good thing. He got the bag down, and the car
poured off into the darkness.

"What place is this?" Flack asked.

"This is it," Sam said. "This is where you going to stay at
tonight."

There was nothing that looked like a hotel. It was a street of
shabby brick houses all with the same frontage and all joined together. Dim lights showed here and there, but most of the houses
were shuttered or curtained, and they looked very sinister and
still in the darkness.

"I don't see any hotel," Flack said.

But Sam did not answer him as they crossed the pavement.
Then Sam was opening the door in one of the houses and calling,
"Becky!" The moment he stepped into the hall, where a sickly
yellow bulb was burning, Curtis Flack could tell that the house
was full of people. It was not that he heard them, though of
course he must have, but the house just had that crowded, packed,
and sour smell. Then he got a glimpse of men in shirtsleeves sitting around a newspaper-littered table in the front room off the
hall and of other men standing around another table in a corner.
The men were trying to talk above the sound of a blaring radio
that showed all its insides on the mantel. Someone came down the
stairs at the back of the hall.

"What kind of a place is this?" Flack asked Sam.

"What you mean?" Sam asked. Then he said with laconic
emphasis, "It's a colored place, ain't it?"

"Who are all these men?"

"Them's traveling men, railroaders," Sam said. "This here's the
place for colored travelers."

Sam's whole attitude had changed. He grinned affably. The scar curled from his mouth like a living thing.

"Fix him up a place to sleep, Becky," he said to the woman who had come down the stairs.

"Now wait a minute," Curtis Flack said. "I want to know whose idea this is—yours or the airline's?"

Sam looked at him. He pushed his stiff-brimmed porter's cap back from his forehead, and his grin turned to a leer.

"Listen, brother," Sam said. "This is my house, see? Get this straight. I'm doing you a favor. And, brother, let me tell you this," he said, thrusting a finger toward Flack's chest, "I don't have to do it. But you know something? I'm a funny kind o' nigger. I hate like hell to see my color make a fool of theirselves. Brother, you colored just like me, and let me tell you something— this is still the white man's world."

Flack didn't argue because he was too convulsed with laughter. It came out of him, he said, in gasps of pain. The irony grew sharper all the time. He didn't sleep all night. It wasn't the fact that there were three double-deck bunks in the room where they put him to sleep or the fact that the air was foul with the odor of a stopped drain in the toilet at the end of the hall or the fact that some card players argued and thumped cards on a table all night long. It was the fact—

Well, Curtis Flack said, looking around the dining room, did he have to say? Did he have to tell them what it was? And as for the laughter, unless one had experienced it, he cannot imagine how it rips and tears you with pain.

[3]

Curtis Flack stopped, a small, blighted smile on his face. No one spoke for a moment. Howden looked down at his fingertips. He knew that no one else felt as he felt—that the whole thing was exaggerated, that its meaning was forced, that too much was made of too little. Everyone had listened, just as all those people had listened to the speech last night. And then a phrase came into Howden's mind. "Still the white man's world . . ." It had a familiar ring, and all at once he could not shut out the knowledge of where he had heard it before. He could feel himself flush, although he did not know why, and to hide it, he looked at his watch. It surprised him to see that it was still not noon. He seemed to be hearing the speech again. He seemed to be hearing the story. He had been with Curtis Flack in Harrisburg and waited with him at the airport and ridden with him in the limousine and stood with him in the hall of Sam's house, and then it had lost all value because it had no value in the first place. It didn't mean anything. He hated Flack for pretending that it did mean something, and Walter for believing it.

He could see Nan, who was sitting with her hands locked over her gloves, looking down at the table. He saw Alice stir a little. Walter was diddling pensively with a fork. They were all pretending, Howden thought. Then he was surprised to hear Nan's low voice.

"But—" Nan said, and she stopped and looked up at Flack gravely. "It was a kind of betrayal. I mean—it's not quite funny."

The smile freshened on Curtis Flack's tired face.

"God, no," he said. "There weren't any supernatural visitations, and the earth didn't groan, but it was a kind of betrayal. That's exactly the point, Nan." Then he began to laugh with melancholy disillusionment. Then Walter laughed, and Alice laughed in the same way. Howden, getting up abruptly, made more noise than he needed to going through to the living room.

[4]

No matter how difficult meetings and introductions were, Howden knew that, when the time came, saying good-by was always more so. The hard thing was not to show relief. As he stood on Walter's front porch with Curtis Flack, he tried to think of something to say. Alice and Nan had gone upstairs at the last minute.

Walter was down at the curb putting the Flacks' bag in the trunk of the car.

"Well?" Curtis Flack said expectantly, turning and smiling at Howden.

But there was nothing to answer to this. Howden found it embarrassing to be standing there with Curtis Flack.

"You'd better step on it," he called down to Walter.

"Of all the places we've been since we left New York six weeks ago," Curtis Flack said to Howden, "this has been the most pleasant."

"Well," Howden said, "that's good."

"Those people at the meeting last night, they did things for me. That fellow Pretlow and that minister—they're corkers." He came a step closer and looked at Howden, and his voice dropped. "And you know, Howden," he said impressively, "it may work. God, yes."

Howden hesitated a moment.

"What may work?"

"The committee's plan," Flack said.

"Oh," Howden said. But this was the first he had heard of it. He had not attended a meeting of the local L.I.C. since spring.

"There may be just enough of the element of surprise in it when they go to see the registration official that he'll let them register to vote."

"Oh," Howden said again, involuntarily this time. He felt himself stiffen a little, and he waited, trying not to show anything.

"Those three hundred and more poll tax receipts will walk up there like natural men and demand to know how come," Flack said with almost childish happiness. "That Ways and Means Committee's done a job. God!"

"You mean—" Howden began slowly.

"Rowbottom and Pretlow and Walter," Flack said. "Thanks to them, some three hundred and more Negroes have paid poll taxes in this county. Paid by mail and got receipts by mail. This county's— What's its name—Cahoosha? God, what a name!—This county's got all those Negroes qualified to vote."

Howden could see it all now, and all at once he knew what he must do. He knew it without shock of any kind. Rowbottom and Pretlow and— He looked down at Walter and said nothing, felt nothing. He was thinking how unrealistic it was of Walter to suppose that such a plan would work. You couldn't surprise white people; they were jumps ahead of you. Howden wanted to laugh at the utter naïve stupidity of anyone's believing that a thing like that might work. He put his hands in his pockets and took them out again. Curtis Flack had taken several steps along the porch.

"Walter," Howden called, "it's getting late."

"Tell the women," Walter called back. "They're holding it up."

"You know how women are. That last swipe of the powder puff, that last peep in the mirror," Flack said, laughing. "Howden, you've got a lovely wife."

Had anyone else said it, it would have sounded like cheap flattery.

"Thanks," Howden mumbled.

Eyes aglow, the brim of his soft hat slanted cockily over his brow, his topcoat flopping on his arm, Curtis Flack took several turns on the porch.

"Do you know what?" he said, stopping suddenly and swinging around to Howden. "This morning—right now—this minute—I could almost accept the universe."

Howden looked across the street and down the street. "Flack," he said and paused to control his irritation, "what else are you going to do with it but accept it?"

"Try to change it," Flack said without hesitation. "Get together with other men of good will and try to change it. God!"

It was not so simple as that, but there was no use telling Curtis Flack that you could not change the universe. There was no use telling him that the best one could do was try to control his individual relation to it.

"Almost nobody likes it the way it is," Flack said, "and yet almost everybody is content to live in it the way it is. Even a lot of Negroes. Can you imagine Negroes—?"

"Aren't you working overtime?" Howden asked, managing a smile. Flack laughed quietly but seriously too. Howden did not want him to go on with it, but Flack went on.

"But can you imagine Negroes anywhere being satisfied with the way things are? Just look around you. Look at those huts down the street there. Look at the street itself."

Howden had never tried so hard to control himself. "It's the personal equation too," he said.

"What do you mean, 'It's the personal equation'?"

"You don't live in a hut; Walter doesn't live in one; I don't live in one. It's the personal equation."

There was a silence, and Flack came closer.

"Do you think that because a few of us are lucky—?" He paused, flung his topcoat from one arm to the other, and held up his hand. "Look, Howden, maybe I don't follow you. Do you mean to say—?"

Howden interrupted him with a laugh which sounded rather hollow, as if the whole thing were a joke inadvertently carried too far. "You don't have to go to work on me," he said.

Flack looked at him for a moment longer, and then he too laughed.

"But there are people who think just like that," he said. "There are some s.o.b.'s who think—"

"Here come the women," Howden said. He could hear them coming down the stairs into the hall. He heard Alice laughing, and he wondered what Nan had said to make Alice laugh like that. Alice had put on one of those off-the-face hats, and she had draped the knee-length coat of her three-piece suit around her shoulders. She looked very smart.

They went down to the car.

"Well," Curtis Flack said and held out his hand.

"While we've got Nan with us," Alice said, "we're going to make her promise that you'll both come to New York sometime."

Howden was visualizing them at the airport in Carthage. He saw the big, arrogant, silver-colored plane coming in, and he saw people hurrying as Curtis Flack had made them hurry at the airport in Harrisburg. He supposed all airports had public address systems, and he could hear that barking too. He could imagine the white people wondering what special Negroes these were for whom the trains weren't good enough or fast enough.

"Sorry you couldn't stay longer," Howden said.

"We've been away too long now," Alice said. "I'm anxious to get back to the kids."

"Kids?" He did not know why he should have assumed that they had no children. It made him go back and try to figure them out again, fit them into a new context.

"That's what Nan and I have been talking about all this time," Alice said.

Howden remembered to stick his head in at the door and kiss Nan. Then everybody was saying good-by, and the car shot into the middle of the road.

CHAPTER TWENTY-NINE

HOWDEN must have heard the singing before he finished parking his car on the edge of the ragged schoolyard, but he was not really aware of it until he stepped into the bare front hall. A class somewhere in the building was singing a hymn, and he could hear the childish voices ringing with a thin, hard plangency. He could not say that the sound filled the hall, for there were those other noises which he always associated with

schools. He could walk into a school building and close his eyes
and know what was going on by the sounds he heard.

> *Be not dismay' what'er beti'e*
> *God will take keer of you.* . . .

They were singing with those elisions and slurpy mouthings
of syllables that always seemed to him so sloppy and gross.
Though he knew approximately what time it was, he pulled out
his watch and looked at it. This was no time for hymn-singing.
It was no time for any kind of singing.

> . . . *take keer of you.* . . .

It was very hard for Howden to remember that he had no
direct supervision over classrooms. He was supposed to take up
classroom matters with the principal. But now, walking down the
hall where great sections of the ceiling were naked to lathing
and joists and where children's coats and grimy, rat-gnawed
sweaters and greasy paper bags of lunches hung from nails in the
wall on both sides, he found himself shifting his hat to the hand
that held the brief case, and the next moment he was opening the
raw pineboard door to the room from which the singing came.

The teacher's back was toward the door, but the children stared
at him, their singing faltering. Howden could feel the teacher
sense his presence. Lowering her arms, she looked around. She
was a dark young woman with spikes of stiff hair, as short as a
man's, slanting back from her knotty forehead. Plainly abashed,
she tried to smile, and Howden noticed that the edges of her
teeth were dark and uneven. He could never understand where
the notion that all darkies had white and lustrous teeth came
from. Scowling, he pulled out his watch again and stood rubbing
his thumb over the crystal.

"Is this the time you ordinarily give to devotions?" Howden
asked her.

"Why, no, sir," the teacher answered. She glanced quickly at

the roomful of children, who were watching in absolute quiet.
"Do you know what time it is?"

"Yes, sir," the teacher said, "I know about what time it is." She
was what Howden called flub-tongued. There was a thickness
in her speech.

All at once Howden hated her, although he had never seen her
before. An unreasonable rage gripped him. It had nothing to do
with the singing, nothing really to do with her. It was only that
she was a Negro and he was a Negro too. It was entirely impersonal. There was no way of explaining it.

"You disturb the whole school when you have a class singing
at this time of day. Don't you know that?" he asked icily.

"I didn't think of it," the teacher said. She glanced at her pupils
again and then back at Howden. "I sure wouldn't want to disturb— I— No, sir. I didn't think of it."

"Don't you have a lesson plan? If you have a lesson plan, then
what are you doing singing at—" he glanced down at his watch
again—"at eleven-fifty in the morning?"

He could see the children staring. Pasted on the unshaded windows through which the sun poured were pictures of pumpkins
and of shocks of corn and of witches on brooms and of impos-
sibly luscious fruits. They had been cut from magazines in cele-
bration of Halloween.

"Yes, sir, I have a lesson plan," the teacher said, "but you see—"

"You were following a lesson plan?"

Obviously confused and embarrassed, the young woman turned
gray around the mouth, and her nostrils quivered pitifully. She
licked her lips slowly.

"Why, you see, John Henry—" She turned to the class, and
her voice went higher. "Stand up, John Henry." She turned back
to Howden again. "Well, this morning—"

Something clattered to the floor, a pair of feet scraped, and
near the back of the room John Henry stood up. Howden did
not look at him. In these schools there was always a child named
John Henry, or one named King Edward or Prince William or

Governor, and he had seen too many of them. He did not have to look at John Henry because John Henry looked like all the other filthy nigger boys.

Howden heard the teacher trying to explain how John Henry had disrupted her lesson plan, but he did not listen.

"Hereafter, you follow your lesson plan," he said abruptly.

"Yes, sir, but this morning—"

"I don't care a thing about this morning! Follow your lesson plan and stop this business of singing at all hours."

He was standing just within the doorway. Now he backed out of it and closed the door behind him and stood there staring at it. His heart was racing, his blood pounding thickly. After a moment, he turned and started down the hall to the principal's office.

[2]

It was of no use for Howden to tell himself that dealing with Professor Pretlow on a professional basis was all that was required. In the relationships he had with principals, there was only a tenuous and crooked line between the professional and the personal, and Pretlow was always overstepping it. That was the kind of darky Pretlow was, a species of that pushy, brassy, presumptuous type, Howden told himself, that was trying to get a foothold everywhere. A whole new substrata of socio-political economy, which Howden blamed equally on the New Deal, the communists, and the war, had formed in the last ten years, and the new, brashy people were trying to find places in it. Setting themselves up in opposition to the old workable pattern, they were trying to destroy it. Whenever they wrote open letters to Senator Bilbo or attended a race meeting or had their appendices out, they sent their pictures to the colored weeklies. Howden could deal fairly with them whenever he had to meet them professionally, but nothing could make him like them.

And he had dealt fairly with Professor Pretlow, Howden told himself. Each spring when Pretlow's name came up for rating,

Howden had rated him of average efficiency. Still, Howden felt at a disadvantage whenever he went to see the principal. He had that careful, embarrassed feeling of trying to observe the amenities with someone who did not know any of the rules. Pretlow always acted as if there were a great deal between them in common. It was a thing which Howden often met nowadays. The pushy people assumed all sorts of relationships that were farthest from his wishes. When they did not have the quality of social camaraderie, then they had that other equally odious quality of leagued conspiracy.

Howden tapped lightly on the office door and entered. Pretlow, who was sitting at a plain pineboard table, got up at once. A dark and fibrous man in odd coat and trousers, he held out enormous bony hands for Howden's brief case and hat.

"Well, well," he said, smiling easily. "How you doing this time?"

"Good morning," Howden said, with cold formality.

"Get held up?" Pretlow asked, still smiling. Even his head, as bald and brown as a weathered rock, seemed to smile.

"No," Howden said.

It was not much of an office, even with the old Oliver typewriter on a homemade tabaret and the wastebasket under the table, and the pictures of Marian Anderson, W. E. B. DuBois, and someone unidentifiable on the walls. Books in various stages of decomposition stood in ragged piles under the window and on the narrow window sill.

"Have a seat, such as it is, which sure isn't much," Pretlow said, laughing ruefully. He swung toward Howden a chair with a wired-up writing arm. "Say, what's this I hear about Johnson over in Dade County? Did the draft get him sure enough?"

Howden nodded absently. He was looking at the pile of books.

"What are the books? Are you getting ready for harvest closing already?" Howden asked. All of the colored schools in the rural eastern part of the state closed for cotton harvest, but October was too early for it.

"Oh, no. Those they sent over from the white school in town," Pretlow answered soberly. Going casually to one of the piles, he lifted three or four books off the top. He took one of the books by its cover and flipped it over, and all of its leaves fell out and fluttered around his feet. He took another book and the same thing happened. Looking at Howden meaningly, he put the grimy covers back onto the pile.

"Mr. Howden," he said simply, "I refuse to give them out to my pupils."

They stared at each other in silence for a moment.

"You won't get anywhere by not giving them out," Howden said at last. "Nowhere at all. How school books are apportioned and distributed is decided by the county supervisors and Dr. Doraman."

"The colored pay for new books, just the same as the white," Professor Pretlow said. "Why can't they have new books, just the same as the white? Why the colored always have to take the white's leavings?"

Except for the pitch of it, it might have been a rhetorical question, and Howden ignored it, although it increased his defensiveness. He looked at the pages of books scattered on the floor where Pretlow had left them. Fumbling in his brief case, he pulled out the papers he was after.

"I've been thinking about those books ever since they sent them," Pretlow said. "I've been thinking about them, and I've been thinking about this closing colored schools down for cotton picking. I've been doing some figuring on that."

Howden said nothing.

"No sense in closing for cotton picking, especially in this county," Pretlow said.

Howden still said nothing.

Going to the drawer of the table, Pretlow pulled out a sheet of paper. He had the figures for the past five years, he said, and they showed that not four per cent of the children in the Cahoosha County Training School came from sharecropping families. When you thought about it, he said, it was obvious that the number would be small, because sharecroppers couldn't afford to send to school their children who were big enough to work—and they got big enough mighty soon. And what was the sense of closing school down for three per cent of three hundred and seventy-nine pupils?

"The thing about it," Pretlow said, "it means extra money for the white. We're suppose' to get paid eight months to the year, but what happens when school closes down? We lose a month, month and a half salary. It's not so much for this one little old school, but when you take all of them, it comes to considerable. And that money goes to the white." He paused briefly. "Mr. Howden, had you ever thought about that?"

Howden looked at him, but before he spoke he looked somewhere else. "No," he said tartly, a touch of superciliousness in his voice, "I can't say I ever have."

In the hall outside, the lunch recess bell clanged stridently, and suddenly the building was filled with the sound of raised voices and running feet. Pretlow's voice rose above the noise.

"It's just a notion, but I believe the figures for the rest of the counties won't show much different from these for Cahoosha. If they are pretty much all alike, and if the higher-ups in Carthage had all the mathematics, don't you reckon they might cut out this closing down the colored for cotton picking?"

Howden flushed slowly, newly angered by Pretlow's presumptuousness. He had not come here to have Pretlow make suggestions. He could hear children scampering along the hall and yelling in the yard outside. He did not look at the principal.

"Professor," he said, giving the title an edge of scorn, "I want to tell you something. Your job is running this school." He saw the principal's feet shift and then move past him. There was a sudden increase in the volume of sound as the office door opened, and then he heard the principal clapping his hands for order in the hall.

[3]

It would be a matter of starting all over again when Pretlow came back, a matter of putting it on a professional basis and keeping it there. He had some forms for Pretlow to fill out, and he put these on the table. One of the older students came in with a bowl of soup and two slices of bread and a cupcake on a tray. " 'Fessor said to bring it," she said. "He be back torectly." She was gone before Howden could tell her that he didn't want it, to take it away.

He had always avoided visiting the Cahoosha County Training School near lunchtime because he had doubts about the cafeteria. He looked at the bowl of soup and considered the delicacy of the situation. Not to eat might cause all sorts of questions, none of which he would want to answer. Dipping the tin spoon into the watery mess, Howden took a sip. It tasted like a good many other things had been tasting the last few months—synthetic. There were certainly a lot of things that were no longer themselves. He was thinking of synthetic rubber and synthetic silk, and there was, he had read somewhere, synthetic coffee too. Once, also, there had been synthetic gin—but that was after the last war, back in the Twenties.

Back then there was jazz music and the Black Bottom and the Charleston and something called the Boston. Now there was swing music and hot music, and people jitterbugged and jumped the boogie and rug-cut. The names were different, but it occurred to him that they were the same things, the identical emotional expressions. He could remember how jazz and the crazy dances of the time following the last war seemed to make many people somewhat mad. And now people were somewhat mad too. Everybody was *flying hot*, the new slang had it. There was a different idiom now, but it was all the same business as before.

The present war was not over yet, although it might as well be because it was easy to see how everything was going. The darkies were fuming and fretting, and their papers and organization journals were already carrying so-called "inside," now-it-can-be-told stories of how colored boys were faring in camps and at the battlefronts, and of how, in spite of their treatment, they were serving nobly, heroically. Later there would be stories of job lay-offs, and all the nigger papers would blossom with the symbolic drawing of a dejected darky in the tattered remnants of a uniform: "You Gave Him a Gun—Now Give Him a Job!" There would be pictures of colored veterans who, still in uniform, had been assaulted without provocation by white hoodlums or white policemen in Charleston or Savannah or Memphis or Carthage. All these stories and pictures in the nigger press would be distorted or altogether faked, but they would build up and build up until the riots broke, as after the last war. As always, the whites would be the victorious rioters, and after a while life would settle down again in much the same old way. There would be—he remembered the phrase from somewhere—a return to normalcy. The old relationships, the old patterns, the old attitudes would reassert themselves, giving renewed validity to the one indisputable fact that white people were on top of the heap. And when the war was over, they would still be on top, in spite of the Flacks and the Rowbottoms and the Pretlows and the L.I.C. and the N.A.A.C.P. and the March-on-Washington and everything else.

Shelton Howden found it surprisingly easy to make a fresh start when Professor Pretlow came back. "Pretlow," he said, "I've put some forms there for you to fill out." Then he went on his routine tour of classroom observation. It was one detail of his job that meant very little, but he gave it all it was worth. He went to each classroom. He demanded to see lesson plans; he demanded to see schedules of home-room activities. He made some teachers nervous by taking notes in a little black book. But he was back in the office in an hour. He felt controlled, masterful. The principal was just finishing the forms, and he stood up and rested his hands on the back of his chair.

"Mr. Howden," Pretlow said, "will you tell me something?

What do the higher-ups in Carthage do with all these forms?"

"All you've got to do is fill them in," Howden snapped. He laughed unpleasantly. "This school business gets more complicated every year, Professor."

"It sure does," Pretlow said.

"It's a full-time job, Professor," Howden said.

"Looks like, then, they'd pay colored full-time salary, same as the white," Pretlow said without hesitation.

Howden was thinking that it was a kind of duel. The usual sounds came into the room. When a school was working, you knew it by the sounds you heard. This school was working now, Howden told himself, because he had been to all the classrooms and all the teachers knew he was in the building.

"They sure play all the angles," Professor Pretlow said.

"Professor, you worry about it too much," Howden said.

"Don't you worry about it?" Pretlow asked.

Howden was on the defensive again. Personal questions could put him there every time. He picked up the forms, riffled through them, and looked around for his brief case, although it was right there on the table where he had left it.

"Professor, I'm going to tell you something," Howden said.

"Wish you would," the principal said. "I sure wish you'd do that."

The tone of Pretlow's voice made Howden glance at him sharply, with a new surge of anger. But the way the principal's big hands lay quiet on the back of the chair, the way his dark face remained impassive made Howden change his mind about telling him anything. There was no use trying to tell Pretlow anything.

"Never mind now— Someday when I've got more time," Howden said. He walked across the room and took his hat off the rusty cabinet.

"The way I feel is that more people ought to worry about it," Pretlow said. "It's like Mr. Curtis Flack said last night. This is a new time now, a new day."

Something in Howden tightened. All those phrases of Curtis Flack's were back in his mind. He wanted to sigh, but instead of sighing, he spoke. All at once he felt a peculiar disregard for the consequences of whatever he might say.

"If I were you, Professor, I'd let it go," Howden began.

" 'Scuse me, but—"

"The times may be changed, but in school business we're still working on the old time." He could hear his voice growing more emphatic, although he did not seem to will it. "In school business, you have a job to do, and it's not a part-time job. It's my observation, Professor, that even running a little two- or three-teacher school takes all of a principal's time. You can't devote your time to other things and still stay in school business. You can't go flying hot and running all over the county, like a chicken with its head cut off, just because there's a war on." He was sweating in all the secret places of his body, and his clothes felt sticky, but he pressed his offensive. "Get realistic! You're old enough to know what it was like after the last war. It's not going to be any different this time. It always comes back to the old balance, and school people ought to realize it sooner than anybody else."

He felt tired, but the organs of his body—heart and lungs—kept going at an exaggerated tempo. Breathing in quick, shallow draughts, he tried to compose himself. He wondered why he had bothered to say so much since nothing now could change what he had to do.

Pretlow had been holding onto the back of the chair, rearing it off its hind legs. Now Howden saw him let the chair slowly down. He heard Pretlow's voice coming as if from a great distance. He could not tell whether it was touched with bravado, whether he heard the merest riff of laughter.

"I just want to ask one little question, and then I'll have it straight," Pretlow said. "Mr. Howden, are you trying to give me warning about working with L.I.C.?"

"Professor—" Howden said, and then he paused to go on more carefully. "I haven't said a word about L.I.C. All I'm saying is that being principal of this school is a full-time job."

"Well, thank you, Mr. Howden," Pretlow said. "I sure thank you for that piece of advice."

There was no mistaking the smothered riff of laughter in his voice.

CHAPTER THIRTY

D o you know what time it is on the clock of the world?" As he parked his car in The Chute and started walking toward town, Howden was thinking of that phrase again. It had already been a long day, but it was still only two o'clock in the afternoon. The sun was warm. The Chute had that kind of sluggish demi-life which Howden associated with squalid darky neighborhoods. A few dirty children played in the dust of the street; a few burr-headed women leaned hunch-shouldered out of the windows of shacks and watched them. Seeing them there made Howden think of Harlem. But here there was no avenue. There was only the red dust and the smelly cafés and beer joints and a few nigger men of all ages lolling as relaxed as bundles of old clothes on the backless benches in front of them.

Crossing the bridge over the green-scummed slough at the end of The Chute, Howden could see the clock tower on the county courthouse. The clock had not run for years, but that phrase was back in his mind, though he was only half thinking of it. Then he fell to wondering whether the county courthouse clock had stopped in the daytime or at night; but such speculation was short-lived. He could see the geometric slant the sun had, like a

theatrical lighting effect, in the street leading to the square. A
man in a big leather apron was tossing stiff bundles of dried pelts
into a hand cart drawn up in front of the little place that dealt
in raw hides. A truck was loading empty barrels at the box factory warehouse. A car came down from the direction of the
square, braked suddenly, backed up, turned, and bounced away
again. All around—from Blazer's Auto Repairs, from the whole-
sale butcher's, from the back of the Ou-La-La Beautie Shoppe—
rose sounds of activity. About this street there was nothing torpid
and inert. It was a small-town street just off the square, but it
made Howden think of one of those side streets in lower Man-
hattan because New York kept running through his mind. Then
he was thinking of the Flacks. It was something after two, and
the Flacks would soon be taking off.

When he came to it, the square was not like Washington
Square or Union Square either. It was just as it had always been
and always would be, he thought, with its permanent wooden
awnings around the first stories of some of the buildings on two
sides of the park. There were porched and cupolaed frame houses,
which were now tourists' homes, on the third side, and the yellow
brick county courthouse, and the old brick annex, and the Tivoli
motion picture house, and Porthouse Hotel on the fourth side. It
all seemed very old and familiar and everlasting. There were the
same women with paper shopping bags going in and out of Fish-
back's and Penney's and examining the fruit and vegetables in the
open bins on the curbing at Twiddy's Fancy Grocery. The same
Fords and Chevrolets and Plymouths, with rusted fenders and
opaque windshields, slanted into the curbing around the park.
From his whitewashed cement pedestal, the Confederate soldier
in his crushed cap and sleeve-ripped coat, his musket at the ready,
watched over the tieless, faded blue-shirted, rosette sleeve-gar-
tered, drooping old men who sat in quiet indestructibility on the
green wooden benches. Every part of the picture was there and
in focus, timeless, changeless.

No matter how hard he tried to avoid it, Howden always saw the sign telling Negroes to use the back stairs. He went quietly on the balls of his feet. He could hear typewriters going, and then masculine voices, flat as the sound of bare hands slapping raw beef. On the third-floor landing he stopped because the climb had winded him. He told himself that he must do something about his weight more energetic than setting-up exercises. This and a variety of other things passed through his mind as he stepped into the hall.

The sign on the frosted glass of Judge Reed's office door was dim with dirt and years, but Howden could read it. "Jefferson A. Reed" was all it said. Howden ran his tongue over his lips. He suddenly felt very much alone and tremulous and empty. He found himself taking off his hat before he knocked. The knob rattled, and he had to turn it several times before the latch responded, and of course Miss McCaslin would be sitting there at her desk behind the railing, looking with knowing amusement at the door when he opened it.

But Miss McCaslin was not there. Sitting in her place was a strange young woman with dry, strawy hair. She had hard, light eyes and a straight, thin mouth.

"Well, what do you want?" she asked.

"Judge Reed, ma'am, please."

"What do you want with him?"

"If he's not busy, that is. It's something about The Chute. The Niggras down there—" He stopped. Betrayal couldn't be this simple and easy. It should be accompanied by strange visitations, he thought cynically, remembering Curtis Flack, lightning and thunder, shakings of the earth. But he felt nothing except a desire not to annoy further this strange young white woman.

"What's your name?" the young woman said, pushing herself angrily back from the desk on the little wheeled stool.

"Howden, ma'am. Shelton Howden."

The young woman went to the door of the inner office, tapped lightly, and went in. When she came out again, she let her eyes slide over Howden as if he were a familiar unused piece of office furniture.

"All right, Shelton," she said, "you can go on in."

"Thank you, ma'am," Howden said.